Terence Strong was br...
the Second World War...
journalism, publishing ...
bestselling novels (which ...
copies in the UK alone) include *President Down*, *The Tick
Tock Man*, *Wheels of Fire*, *Cold Monday* and *White Viper*. He
lives in the south-west of England.

Visit www.twbooks.co.uk/authors/tstrong.html

Acclaim for Terence Strong

'An expert miasma of treachery and suspicion building to
a thrilling climax' *Observer*

'Belongs to the action-man school of writing, backed up
by hands-on research' *The Times*

'Tension ratchets up wickedly – a strong sense of reality is
reinforced with powerful emotion and gritty characters'
Daily Telegraph

'An edge-of-the-chair thriller with the chilling grip of
authenticity' *Independent on Sunday*

'Well plotted and genuinely exciting' *Sunday Telegraph*

'An extremely good topical thriller' Jack Higgins

President Down

Terence Strong

POCKET
BOOKS

LONDON • SYDNEY • NEW YORK • TORONTO

First published in Great Britain by Simon & Schuster UK Ltd, 2008
This edition published by Pocket Books UK Ltd, 2009
An imprint of Simon & Schuster UK Ltd
A CBS COMPANY

3 5 7 9 10 8 6 4

Simon & Schuster UK Ltd
1st Floor
222 Gray's Inn Road
London WC1X 8HB

www.simonandschuster.co.uk

Simon & Schuster Australias
Sydney

A CIP catalogue record for this book
is available from the British Library

ISBN 978-1-4165-2206-5

Typeset in Bembo by M Rules
Printed by CPI Cox & Wyman, Reading, Berkshire RG1 8EX

Dedicated to

HELP *for* HEROES

*The new charity offering support for
Britain's recent war-wounded*

One

I didn't like it at all.

It was all too damn easy. A small voice in my head was nagging away, telling me this was wrong, and my instincts rarely were. Like a wary animal, I could almost smell the scent of danger in the chill summer night air.

Yet the large English suburban house and garden I was viewing through the small image-intensifying night-sight could not have appeared more tranquil. The optical device jacked up the ambient light to create a ghostly green and white image that was something akin to that of a strong full moon.

All the house lights had been off since eleven o'clock, and that had been nearly an hour earlier. Mullah Reda Rashid was a man of habit.

Every day for the past five that I had been watching him, the imam had retired at that time to pray in his bedroom, one final act of worship before sleeping. Every morning he rose at five. What looked like black tea was taken to him by one of the two young male theology students who shared the house with him. Then one of them would drive Mullah Reda to the nearby mosque in time to take morning prayers at six. Every night he would be driven home again at around seven-thirty, when he would eat the evening meal that had been prepared for him.

After supper, the cleric would potter around in his extensive garden, lovingly pruning roses and watering the potted plants. As the light faded, he would return indoors and work on his laptop until bedtime. Very occasionally he would watch a television soap or catch the news.

That was the routine. There was nothing suspicious about it all.

According to Lassiter, my liaison officer at MI5, the imam was known as a soft-spoken, mild-mannered, kindly moderate cleric with a generous sense of humour. It had even earned him the affectionate nickname of the 'Merry Mullah' amongst some of his congregation. But then I'd known Joe Lassiter for a long time, long enough to realize that he liked to hold his cards close to his chest and could be very possessive of his little pile of secrets.

So why, I had asked him, were government funds being allocated to a trusted private investigator and former soldier like me to keep such a man under costly surveillance? Lassiter had pulled one of those infuriating, enigmatic little smiles of his.

'Listen, Phil, if Mullah Reda is such an innocent and peace-loving cleric,' he replied, 'we have to ask ourselves why he surrounds himself with high-security fencing and has CCTV cameras installed? And why have two Dobermanns wandering around loose in the grounds of a grand house he can't possibly afford – given what we know about his financial circumstances?'

That was all I got from Lassiter. Of course, there was more to it than that, but it was clear that I wasn't going to be told what.

I was just a humble 'alongsider' as we are known in the intelligence trade, usually former military or police officers, with impeccable security credentials, who are hired as freelancers in low-priority cases to ease the Security Service's workload. And I knew that since the 9/11 disaster, when members of the al-Qaeda terrorist network flew two hijacked airliners into the Twin Towers in New York, MI5's resources had been stretched to breaking point and beyond.

Then, in July 2005, it all moved much closer to home with the deadly, co-ordinated London bombings.

The trouble was, there was no quick-fix available. All the British intelligence agencies had been run down since the collapse of the Soviet Union and the uneasy but ongoing peace in Northern Ireland. Of course, they all knew about the threat from the Islamic fundamentalist movement, which came to be called al-Qaeda by the Americans, but it hadn't been given quite the high priority it deserved. Then 9/11 changed all that, big time.

But MI5 and the Secret Intelligence Service, MI6, which operates overseas, were in a poor position to infiltrate the Arab and Asian communities at home and abroad to gain the vital information needed to protect

British interests. In desperation they tried to recruit staff from the ethnic minorities in the UK, but met with little success.

Gradually it became clear that many more young Muslims than had first been realized were being sucked into the terror networks in Britain. So the number of possible suspects needing investigation just grew and grew, and grew.

That, I guessed, was why Lassiter had given Mullah Reda to me to have a look at. I wasn't complaining. The money was good and, by God, didn't I need it just now!

I repositioned myself in the tree, trying to get a little more comfortable. It was going to be a long and no doubt fruitless night.

The tree, an oak, had probably been standing there for three hundred years – long before the 1930s house had been built and the garden fenced it in. I'd had to do my squirrel act, using a lightweight ladder to reach the branches of an adjacent chestnut tree on the outside of the garden. After hauling the ladder up after me and securing it amongst the leaves, I'd crawled out onto a bough, then swung myself precariously across onto a branch of the oak where they crossed over each other.

I hadn't done that sort of thing for years, even as a sniper in the Royal Marines, and there's no bloody way I'd have considered it had there been any other position that gave me both the view and cover I needed. Although I'd learned to cope with it in my military life, I didn't like heights and, at forty-three, I knew I was definitely too old for this sort of thing. It was a long way down and the ground was bone-hard.

I'd just raised the night-sight to my eye for a quick check on the darkened house when a movement on the lawn caught my attention. A shadow appeared to detach itself from one of the low evergreen shrubs and dart across the lawn and patio, past the closed French windows. It was so quick I barely had time to realize that it wasn't a cat but an urban fox.

Even as that registered, dazzling light exploded in my eyes and head like the Second Coming. The sudden blaze from the thermally triggered security lights was literally blinding as it was magnified through the night-sight, seemingly burning into my retinas. I'm sure I gasped aloud as I dropped the device into my lap, trying to steady myself on the branch.

Then the air was filled with the menacing yap of dogs, as the two huge Dobermanns rounded the corner of the house, neck-and-neck, each in a frenzy to find the intruder before the other. One pulled up short, salivating in his anticipation of prey, foam streaking from its powerful jaws. It halted at the shrub from which the fox had emerged. The second dog slowed and turned, watching its kennel mate as the creature rapidly began to follow the scent trail across the lawn towards the patio. The two of them vanished from my view, but then the barking began again.

That was when the light came on in the main living room and the French doors were suddenly thrown open.

Mullah Reda's two theology students emerged, looking decidedly anxious as they rapidly surveyed the floodlit garden.

I was surprised they were still fully dressed as all the house lights had been out for some time. But what was much more disconcerting was that they were both carrying automatic pistols and looked as though they knew how to use them.

Instinctively I drew back a little into the leafy cover of the oak. I was used to doing surveillance work as a sniper when I held all the cards and was armed to the teeth. Like this I felt as naked and vulnerable as a new-born babe. I thanked God I'd made the decision to dig out my old army 'ghillie', a special hooded camouflage overall draped with naturally coloured hessian strips. It was designed for snipers, with fitments that allowed them to attach additional natural foliage. Ghillie-suits were named after the Scottish estate gamekeepers who first came up with the idea in their fight against poachers at the turn of the twentieth century. And to think I'd almost considered it would be over the top for a low-priority civvy assignment.

And just how wrong had I been? Very, it seemed now, as Mullah Reda also emerged from the French windows, wearing his white tunic and lacy skullcap. So he hadn't gone to bed either. Seemed like I'd made one dangerous misjudgement after another.

'Probably just a cat,' I heard one of the students say.

The other one nodded. 'I think so, Imam, there was nothing on the cameras.'

But Mullah Reda didn't look so convinced and scratched at his beard. 'Don't be too certain, we cannot afford mistakes tonight,' he warned. 'And remember, if we are being watched, it will be by professionals.'

God, that was a joke! Me stuck up a tree with no self-protection, no back-up and my only form of communication was a mobile phone with the battery on the blink.

'Then we'd better do a thorough search,' the first student decided.

'I think that is best,' Mullah Reda agreed. 'And let the dogs have a good sniff around.'

The cleric returned inside the house while his two henchmen walked off cautiously in opposite directions to circle the house, their automatics at the ready.

It was a tense few minutes up in the tree as I hardly dared breathe, watching and waiting tensely, my leg muscles starting to cramp and a niggling tickle trying to develop at the back of my throat. The desire to cough just grew and grew until it almost took on the form of torture. I hardly knew what to do with myself.

At last the two students returned, the dogs now back on the leash. One of the hounds kept looking in my direction, I'm sure, but thank God it didn't bark or growl. Maybe its head was still filled with thoughts of the fox that got away.

They took the dogs inside, closed the French windows behind them, and drew the curtains. This time the lights stayed on.

I felt my shoulders relax and my lungs begin to work again. I cleared my throat at last, and considered what to do.

I had Lassiter's private mobile number, but didn't think he'd appreciate a call at this time of night. All I had to tell him was confirmation that Mullah Reda didn't seem as innocent as his reputation suggested, and his two theology students were tooled up and acting as minders. I figured that could wait until the morning.

It would probably mean he'd now get authorization to put MI5's own expert 'watchers' on the case. So I was probably just about to put myself out of a job.

In fact, knowing that there were actually armed men in the house, I thought it over and decided that probably discretion was the better part of valour. I'd give it another hour and, if everything remained quiet, I'd call it a night and withdraw from my leafy eyrie.

Of course, to do that I'd prefer that the house flood-lights be turned off but, irritatingly, they remained on. Perhaps the minders were still watching on the camera monitor for signs of an intruder.

As I waited my mind wandered; I was aware of my eyelids becoming heavy with fatigue. Forcing myself to concentrate, I glanced at my watch. I couldn't believe it; only half an hour had passed.

Just then I noticed the headlights of a car as it turned into the residential avenue below me. It was closely fol-lowed by another. The first car slowed as it approached Mullah Reda's house, before turning into the space in front of the electric gates. The second car stopped behind it.

Suddenly there was movement at the house. The double front doors opened and the two minders appeared under the ornate portico at the top of a short flight of ter-racotta steps. Then the electric gates slid silently back to admit the two vehicles while the two minders advanced to meet the new arrivals. But they were taking no chances, their automatic pistols kept at the ready.

I reached for my digital camera with the zoom lens.

Both cars were older Mercedes saloon models with darkened windows. All the doors were thrown open at virtually the same time and the gravel drive was suddenly filled with people. I quickly counted eight. All were male and most had swarthy, dark features that suggested either Middle East or Asian origins. Everyone wore Western-style clothes, two older men in sharp, expensive suits and the rest dressed in jeans, sports tops and baseball caps. Two of the younger men made no attempt to conceal the Ingram mini-machine guns they carried.

I tried to snap the older men first, then moved on to the bodyguards. The group paused for a moment, con-fronting Mullah Reda's two minders. Both parties seemed tense and uncertain, eyeing each other suspiciously. Then the brief stand-off ended as everyone seemed to decide that all was well. Reda's two minders turned and led the way back inside the house.

I thought I'd got good shots of the older Arabs, but I only managed to frame three of the bodyguards before they had their backs to me. Even so, my guess was that the peaks of the baseball caps would prevent positive identification.

The front door shut, one of Reda's minders and one of the newly arrived bodyguards remaining outside as sentries. Annoyingly, the garden floodlights remained on as the soft, summer night silence settled in again.

Clearly, something big was going down here. It was obviously some sort of secret meeting between armed Arab or Asian groups in the suburbs of Birmingham in the middle of the night. Maybe they were terror cells, maybe criminal gangs. Either way, Lassiter had to be informed. But if I made a move with the arc lights on, I'd certainly be spotted and would be a sitting target . . . or rather a falling one with a forty foot drop. If I used the mobile phone in the tree, there was a serious risk that the sentries would hear me as sound was carrying well in this still night air.

Dammit, a text message. I never used them, hated them. Texts were for kids who couldn't afford their phone bills. Now I wished I'd practised more after my secretary Kate had explained it to me, because I was still all fingers and thumbs. It would take forever for me to send a comprehensive message.

I'd just have to risk making the call. I took the mobile from my pocket . . . the screen lit up, which meant at least the battery was working, even if it was down to just one bar.

I scrolled to Lassiter's number and called.

But I wasn't hopeful as it began to ring. Lassiter would be asleep and might not even hear the ring tone, assuming he'd remembered to leave it on.

So it came as a welcome surprise when he seemed to snatch it up. 'Phil, you okay?' He sounded wide awake, and concerned.

'Yes,' I whispered. 'Something's going down here.'

'Sorry,' he replied. 'Can't hear you very well. Speak up.'

Bloody idiot, I thought. 'Can't, I'm in the OP and may be heard.'

'Oh yes, of course. What's going down?'

'Reda's two minders are tooled up and two cars have arrived for a late-night meeting of some sort. They are armed too.'

'Two Mercedes?'

That threw me. 'Er, yes. Do you want the reg numbers?'

'Won't be necessary. There are two visitors, yes?'

'Eight. Two older guys in suits, Arabs, I think. And six younger men.'

'Yes, their bodyguards.'

'What the hell's going on, Joe? You seem to know all about this.'

'I'll explain later. You just stay put.'

'Joe—!'

'Trust me.' And the line went dead.

Jesus, what was all this about? Stay put, he'd said, as if I had an option.

I'd been distracted and failed to notice that the two

young Arabs on the front door were moving down the steps and walking very slowly in my direction. They were frowning, heads cocked to one side as if trying to hear something. And I had a damned good idea what. Mostly their eyes were scanning the shadowy shrubs, but occasionally they glanced up at the trees. Suddenly one of them appeared to be staring straight at me. Then he turned his head away and I breathed again. Once more in my life I'd been saved by the ghillie suit, its rough patterning and added oak sprigs merging with the leaves of the tree to break up my recognizable human shape.

'You sure it was a voice?' one of them said. He was now standing right underneath me.

'Sounded like "Joe".'

'Or an owl?'

The other one shrugged. 'There was an owl around earlier.'

That devilish tickle in my throat returned dead on cue.

It was then that all three of us heard the racing V8 engines and the complaining squeal of tyres as the first of a line of vehicles swung into the residential avenue. Below me, the two men looked at each other uncertainly.

But they could not see what I could see from my perch. The leading white Range Rover, with its reinforced cow-fenders and mesh-covered windscreen, accelerated in a tight arc at the front of the garden. The driver pushed his right foot to the floor and the nose of the vehicle smashed into the electric gate with a deafening crash, ripping the steel bars from their mountings and driving them forward like two giant bat's wings.

Half a dozen more police vehicles, cars and people carriers, rushed in through the demolished gateway and fanned out on either side of the lead Range Rover. Suddenly the driveway was filled with armed police in blue body armour and NATO-style helmets, carrying Glock automatics or Heckler & Koch sub-machine guns. It was clearly a well-rehearsed manoeuvre as dozens of men broke out into prearranged groups. One headed for the front door, including two burly officers who carried a massive steel battering ram between them. Two other groups split right and left to encircle the house, whilst the fourth settled into support and sniper positions with Enfield Enforcer rifles, using their vehicles' engine blocks to provide hard cover. Immediately the onslaught began, windows shattering with well-aimed single rounds to allow the follow-up launch of gas and smoke grenades. The mayhem inside could be imagined, the sudden burst of disorientating fog and the acrid, choking fumes. All this gave the assault teams vital seconds to launch their main attack through the lower windows, which followed the ear-piercing screech and blinding flash of stun-grenades.

I'd been so taken aback by events that it took a few moments for it to dawn on me that this had all been set up. Lassiter must have had Special Branch and specialist armed-response teams sitting at the end of the road in anticipation of my call. I'd been set up and almost fed to the bloody lions.

Of course, the whole operation had only taken a few seconds. It was very professional and the speed of the operation had been awesome, but there was a developing hazard of which the police were totally unaware.

Immediately beneath me, the two startled gunmen were frozen in surprise, gawping with their mouths open at the sudden start of the police assault. But as soon as it became clear to them what was happening, their evident terrorist training kicked in. I'd little doubt they'd be happy to take the short cut to heaven if they could take half-a-dozen infidel coppers with them. They didn't even hesitate or seek cover before they raised their weapons in unison. They'd left me no choice.

'ARMED HOSTILES!' I bawled suddenly and as loudly as I could. 'OVER HERE!'

A couple of officers in the support group heard me, and turned their heads in my direction. At the same time the two gunmen below me looked up, startled.

Oh shit, I thought as I saw the automatic of Reda's minder aimed at me.

'ARMED POLICE!' someone yelled from the drive. 'HALT OR WE FIRE!'

The muzzle flash, discharge and whistling bullet from the minder's automatic were a simultaneous blur of sound and vision, along with a sharp razor-burn sensation in my left bicep. Half-a-dozen rounds of fire burst raggedly from the police support group and the two gunmen beneath me dropped instantly as if their legs had been chopped from under them.

I put my right hand to the left arm of the hessian ghillie, saw the ragged hole and the blood on my palm. It dripped solemnly down onto the two corpses below me.

Clenching my fist and working my fingers, I tried to determine how bad the damage was. Everything seemed to be functioning. It must be a flesh wound. My lucky day.

Six officers raced across the lawn towards the bodies beneath the tree. As they approached, two held back to cover the remaining four as they pounced on the corpses, not knowing for certain they were dead but taking no chances anyway. Slack arms were wrenched hard up behind their backs and their wrists snapped into PlastiCuff shackles. There was no resistance. Only then were the bodies carefully turned over and the injuries inspected. The police caution was well vindicated, as one officer detached something from the belt of one of the dead and stood up.

'What is it?' asked his colleague.

The officer held it up. It was a hand grenade. 'Would have taken us with 'em given half a chance.'

The other man nodded, glancing around the shrubbery. 'Who the hell shouted that warning?'

'God knows – but I'm fucking glad he did.'

This was tricky. Although there'd been no gunfire from the house, the noise and confusion continued as the room clearance began. The police team beneath me had just been shot at, their blood was up and they would be on a fearsome adrenalin rush. If I was suddenly spotted, there could be an immediate reflex reaction before anyone stopped to think or ask themselves a question.

I made a snap decision. 'DON'T SHOOT!' I yelled. 'SECURITY SERVICE! REPEAT DON'T SHOOT!'

The six men looked up, Heckler & Kochs pointed, a torchbeam flashing in my face. 'What the fuck . . .?'

I forced a smile. 'Covert OP,' I explained.

The guns stayed pointed. After a tense pause, the lead officer said, 'Throw down your weapon.'

That was a good one. 'Don't have any friggin' weapons, officer. This is a surveillance operation.'

Again the guns stayed pointed. There was another hesitation. 'You'd better get down, mate, we'll have to check you out.'

That was when I noticed Lassiter. He was trudging across the lawn, a dumpy hunched figure in a navy summer raincoat and dark fedora hat, like a man who carried the weight of the world's problems on his shoulders. But he also seemed oblivious to the fact he was in the middle of an armed police operation.

He came to a halt behind the semicircle of policemen and looked up at me. There was a deadpan expression on his face as he said in that slightly squeaky voice of his, 'It's all right, gentlemen, he's one of mine.'

The lead officer looked relieved. 'Right, sir. But we'll probably have to call him as a witness to the Coroner's Court.'

'I don't think so,' Lassiter replied quietly. 'But then you can always ask.'

Things seemed to have quietened down at the house and some members of the assault teams were starting to emerge. I recognized Mullah Reda and some of his visitors, who were now handcuffed and being bundled into the white police vans.

As the officers below me waited for the arrival of the scene-of-crime specialists, Joe Lassiter came closer and looked up again, with that oval face that always reminded me of a pumpkin. I could see his eyes squinting through his specs.

'Look like the Cheshire Cat perched up there,' he said, smiling for the first time.

I was angry enough without that. 'Do I look like I'm bloody grinning?'

'Who rattled your cage?'

'You, as usual,' I retorted.

He ignored that and proceeded to light a cigarette. 'Anyway, Phil, well done,' he said absently. 'Better come down from there.'

I said, 'We need to talk.'

'Sure, tomorrow.'

I knew Lassiter well enough to know that, if it suited him, tomorrow never came. He could be as elusive as a shadow. 'No, now. I've some questions that need answering.'

He gave a pained expression. 'I'm a little busy just now, Phil, as you can see.'

'Not good enough, Joe.'

He sighed. 'Tell you what, I'll come round and see you as soon as I've wrapped up here.'

'Don't feed me that bullshit, Joe,' I warned. 'I'm not in the mood.'

'No, I promise. Grandmother's grave and all that. You still staying at that travel lodge on the outskirts?' He didn't bother to hide his disdain. That didn't bother me, Joe Lassiter didn't have a wife divorcing him and milking him for every penny he had. I couldn't afford to be proud, I needed to save money wherever I could.

'I'll give you a couple of hours—' I began but the sentence was cut off by the sudden blast of an explosion.

It blew out a couple of upstairs windows, a crystal cloud of glass floating momentarily in the arc-light glare, and sent roof tiles spinning into orbit like demented Frisbees. Following the initial blinding fireflash, I could see the flames raging within the building and the acrid smoke start to tumble out into the night. My blood went cold.

'Holy Mother,' I heard Lassiter mutter below me, 'that's all we need, a bloody booby trap.'

I called down, 'That was Reda's study, just next to the bedroom.'

But I don't know if Lassiter heard, because he started walking away towards the house.

I called after him, 'Don't forget, Joe! Two hours!'

He didn't bother to turn back, just raised his hand in acknowledgement.

Somehow I didn't believe he'd show, not for a few days anyway when he'd hope some of the venom had gone out of my anger. He knew full well the answers I wanted and why. He'd just damn near got me killed.

Still seething, I packed away the optical surveillance equipment in my belt pouches and began wriggling back along the branch, ready to perform my ape-man swing over the fence to the adjacent tree. Although I'd some-what perfected it now, I wasn't at all unhappy to think that this would be the last time I'd have to do it. I grabbed the next tree branch with both hands and dropped my feet onto a lower limb before edging towards the trunk. From there I scaled down the uneven succession of branches until I reached the lightweight aluminium ladder I'd concealed some ten feet above the ground. After lowering it carefully, I climbed down until I had the blessed feel of solid earth beneath my feet once again.

In the shadows, I removed the ghillie oversuit and stuffed it into a small rucksack with the rest of my equip-ment. Then I began making my way to my sorry-looking old Ford Transit van, which I'd parked a couple of streets away. The bits of it that weren't rust were faded blue, a typical tradesman's vehicle that wouldn't get a second glance. It wasn't much, but it was ideal for surveillance work and it was home – well, it had been on a few occa-sions. Kip-mat, sleeping bag, camping stove and boxes of provisions, what more could a man ask for?

I turned on the interior light, took my tobacco tin from the glovebox and began rolling a cigarette. It was only then that I realized my hands were trembling slightly.

Hardly surprising, I reasoned, it had been some time since I'd been shot at. In fact ever since I had lost the taste for shooting back. That reminded me, and I inspected the wound on my bicep that was beginning to throb. As I suspected, I'd been 'winged' as they used to say in the old cowboy films for kids. A bloody gouge about a quarter of an inch deep and an inch and a half long. The friction heat of the bullet must have torn and semi-sealed the flesh as it zipped past, so that now it was only weeping slightly. There was no medical kit in the van – an oversight I would have to correct – but I wasn't concerned. It could wait until I got back to the motel. In the meantime I fished my hip flask from a pocket in the rucksack, and doused the deep graze with whisky before taking a welcome mouthful to finish it off.

By that time I was feeling better, the trembling had almost stopped and my anger at Lassiter had ebbed – well, a little anyway. I'd wait to see what he had to say for himself . . . if he showed.

I started the engine and began the journey back to the travel lodge on the outskirts of the city. The advent of these cheap, functional motels with all the basic amenities were excellent for families, small businessmen like me and corporations trying to keep down the soaring cost of salesmen on the road. In my line of work, they also offered the bonus of absolute anonymity. Of course, there are many chains of them nowadays, some good and some bad. This one was somewhere in the middle, the worst thing about it was that its meals were provided at the adjacent theme pub. A leather-sole steak and soggy chips in dirty grease was the most appetizing dish on the menu.

Since I'd been on this operation, I'd taken to eating salads on the basis that their chef couldn't get that wrong. A mayonnaise-covered slug crawling through the lettuce had rather hit that notion on the head.

At least the motel had a duty manager on the desk all night. The bored, sleepy twenty-year-old was clearly irritated at having her late-night listening to Radio BRMB disturbed and ungraciously began hunting around for the statutory medical kit. She produced it after five minutes of rooting around beneath the desk.

'You can't take it away,' she said sternly.

'I'm not going to steal it.'

'You'd be surprised what people nick, just about anything what's not nailed down. And that's my responsibility,' she replied as I opened the lid of the green plastic case and peered inside. 'You'll have to use it here. What you looking for?'

'Haemorrhoid cream,' I said mischievously. She gave me a very uncertain look until I added, 'Just joking.'

She looked relieved and almost managed a smile as I extracted some TCP, gauze and bandage. As I rolled up my sleeve, she wrinkled her nose. 'That looks nasty. You cut yourself?'

I couldn't resist it. 'Someone shot me.'

Her smile broke through for a second. 'Quite the wag, aren't you?'

I cleaned the wound in TCP, then added the gauze and bandage, which the girl offered to tie up for me when she saw me struggling one-handed.

I thanked her for her trouble and handed her a fiver. 'I'm expecting a friend along shortly—'

She interrupted, 'We don't allow no – er – you know, professional ladies . . . Company policy.'

'He's male and heterosexual,' I replied with a grin. 'It's business.'

She glanced at the lobby clock. 'At this time?' She giggled. 'You a drug-smuggler or something?'

'If I told you what I was, I'd—'

The giggle developed into a chuckle. 'Yeah, yeah, you'd have to kill me.'

I smiled. 'Just be sure to let him in, will you?'

'Sure, don't want to fall foul of you, Mister, do I?'

I played along. 'You'd better believe it, honey.'

Leaving her in a better mood than I'd found her, I went to my room. It was a good size and blandly decorated with a king-size bed and the obligatory electric kettle and multi-channel pay TV. I passed on the minibar, instead taking a bottle of my own Scotch from my suitcase and pouring a couple of slugs into a tumbler.

As I took a gulp, I caught sight of my face in the mirror. It was a bit of a shock, an unexpected glimpse like that in a certain light. God, I didn't look good. Apart from the day's growth of beard on my chin, my face looked lined and gaunt. Even my naturally dark Latino skin appeared pale and my greying black hair was in dire need of a cut. My eyes, which I always remembered being slate-blue and mischievously cheerful, were tired and sunken. I could see I'd lost weight – the 'stress diet', as I quipped if anyone commented on it, was getting beyond a joke.

I raised my tumbler to the haggard image in the mirror. 'Cheers, Nina, thanks a bunch!'

Then I turned away. I didn't want to dwell on her and what had happened to our marriage. I stretched out on the bed and waited, none too hopefully, for Lassiter to arrive. Instantly I was asleep.

The sharp knock on the door startled me awake. I was momentarily disorientated, still half in the world of a bizarre dream where I'd been swinging on jungle vines like Tarzan while being chased by angry nuns armed with Kalashnikov rifles. The dial on my wristwatch showed four o'clock.

I struggled to my feet and opened the door. Joe Lassiter stood there, a miserable expression on his face that was part shaded by the brim of his fedora. 'What a cock-up,' he announced. 'I need a drink.'

I stood back to let him in. As I closed the door, he was already examining the room, his eyes searching out the whisky bottle. 'Thought you'd have some hooch.'

'Is that the only reason you came, Joe?'

His thin lips upturned a fraction, but it was difficult to tell if his eyes were smiling behind the specs. 'Course not. My word is my Bond, James Bond.'

I ignored the bad joke he'd made more times than I cared to remember. 'Water or ice with it?'

'No, as it comes. A large one.'

'Help yourself,' I said, watching as he picked up the bottle and examined the label.

'Tesco's own?' He didn't bother keeping the sneer from his voice.

'It's all I've got,' I replied flatly.

Lassiter was as tight-fisted as they came; I reckoned he must somehow have Scots, Yorkshire and Jewish ancestral blood flowing through his veins. He was on an enviable salary and pension package from the Security Service and had a generous expense account for wining and dining his agents as part of the attraction of working for him. Yet he was always on the scrounge and was always the last one to put his hand in his pocket for a round in the pub. He hadn't changed in all the years I'd known him since that first time in Belfast.

When he'd filled his tumbler to the brim, he tossed his fedora onto the bed, exposing a head of thinning black hair carefully combed to hide his bald crown, and perched himself on an upright chair. Not for the first time I thought how shabby and sort of seedy he always managed to look. Crumpled raincoat with food stains on the lapels and a grubby white shirt underneath, with his tie askew. I'd never been sure if it was the image of a spy he'd culti-vated from reading too many trashy novels, or if it was just Lassiter being himself.

For the first time his eyes focused on me properly. He noticed the bandage that had seeped a little blood. 'You hurt yourself?'

'That's why I wanted to speak to you,' I replied sharply. 'You got me shot tonight.'

Momentarily his pale face went sheet white. 'Holy

Mother, you haven't been to A and E have you? Did they ask—'

'Relax, Joe, I know the form. It's just a flesh wound, luckily. Another few inches and I could have been killed.'

Colour returned to his face. 'Your lucky night then. More than I can say for us.'

I wanted to retort, but I recalled the explosion at Mullah Reda's house. 'Was anyone hurt back there?'

'None of ours . . . well not really,' Lassiter replied in an abstract manner that suggested he didn't really care that much one way or the other. 'Those two minders shot dead, of course. And the dogs. Oh, and one policeman suffered minor flash burns when that bomb went off, dammit. Destroyed all the evidence.'

I realized what he meant. 'It was in Reda's study, wasn't it, next to his bedroom?'

Lassiter nodded gloomily and took another swig of my whisky. 'An incendiary charge. Must have been set up under his desk for just such an event. Totally destroyed his computer, mobile phones and all his paperwork before our chaps could get to it.'

I began rolling a cigarette. 'So what's going to happen now?'

'Not a lot,' Lassiter replied with a shrug. 'We'll probably be able to get most of the youngsters – the minders – on firearms and/or attempted murder charges. But if their lawyers are any good, Reda and the other two will probably walk. The ones that matter.' He took another slurp of whisky. 'Probably get them on Control Orders, I suppose, which is some consolation. You know, curfew, daily reporting to the nearest nick, no use of mobile phones or the Internet, and no home visitors without our prior permission.'

'Guess that'll restrict their style,' I said. 'And who are the other two, by the way?'

Lassiter scratched at the stubble on his chin. 'One runs an Islamic bookshop. It's believed to be a front for recruitment to al-Qaeda in this area. You know the sort of thing. Inflammatory fundamentalist literature. Video speeches by bin Laden and footage taken in Iraq and Afghanistan depicting so-called atrocities by American and British forces. Stuff to get young recruits riled and fired up.'

'And the other one?' I asked.

Lassiter sounded weary, as though he'd answered these questions a hundred times before. 'Wealthy entrepreneur. Runs a chain of Indian restaurants, but he's actually Pakistani. So are most of his staff. We suspect he's involved in illegal immigration, or possibly a conduit for al-Qaeda "facilitators".'

I was out of touch with spooks' jargon. 'Facilitators?'

'Support from professionals,' Lassiter explained. 'Money men, bomb-makers, communications experts, fieldcraft trainers. Wherever al-Qaeda operates in the world, these foreign experts usually come in to set up operations with local recruits. Then they bugger off out of it before the balloon goes up. Don't mind young hotheads blowing themselves up, but they're not so keen on the idea themselves.'

I knew what he meant. 'But nothing much has happened in the UK since the July 7 bombings and the July 21 attempt, has it?'

His smile was thin. 'Only because we've got lucky – so far. We've disrupted some two hundred planned attacks.' He sighed. 'We'll be raiding the premises of the bookseller and restaurateur and all his outlets' – he glanced at his watch – 'even as we speak.'

'Then maybe you'll crack it.' I tried to sound optimistic.

'I doubt it, Phil, these are wily bastards. Probably professionally trained in the al-Qaeda camps. Not given to leaving trails of evidence.'

'And Mullah Reda himself?' I asked. 'The carefully-groomed moderate face of Islam?'

Lassiter nodded. 'Probably he's been a recruiting sergeant. Picking up disillusioned or dysfunctional youngsters passing through the classes at his mosque. He befriends them when maybe their families and others don't, tells them how Islam holds the answers to their woes and sends them off to study more.'

'To the bookshop?' I guessed.

'That seems to be the pattern. Hard to prove anything concrete.'

'But the bomb in his study?' I suggested.

Lassiter almost laughed in my face. 'He'll say it was a result of the police assault! Might not be much left after that explosion and fire to prove or disprove anything. As with the other two, we'll probably be left with wobbly or circumstantial evidence from us, MI6 and GCHQ, which Her Majesty's Government won't want to air in court.'

I tried to sound upbeat. 'At least it might torpedo any immediate plans –with them cooling their heels on remand.'

Lassiter drained his glass. 'I hope to God you're right, Phil. Trouble is we don't know how many other Redas are out there . . .'

I'd almost forgotten why I'd insisted on seeing him that night. 'So, Joe, knowing all this, you sent me in there on a surveillance operation, unarmed and without back-up.'

The dark eyes blinked behind the specs. 'Didn't turn your nose up at the money, I recall.'

Anger flashed in my head as I remembered the moment that the Arab's gun was pointed at me. 'Don't be cheap, Joe. I was deliberately kept in the dark. D'you seriously think I'd have taken it on if I knew we were talking about a known al-Qaeda cell guarded by armed terrorists?'

'We didn't – we still don't know that's what it is.'

'Don't give me that bullshit, Joe,' I retorted. 'I'm not the bloody judge and jury you have to convince. You bloody knew all right! Dammit, you had that police firearms unit on immediate standby. D'you think it would matter to me that you just couldn't prove it to the satisfaction of the courts? You screwed me, used me.' I paused for a second to gather my thoughts. 'Although I can't think why the hell you did. Why in God's name didn't you use MI5's own surveillance people for the job? I don't understand.'

For the first time Lassiter looked just a little embarrassed. 'Mind if I have another drink, Phil. My nerves are bad.'

God, his nerves were bad. He should have been sitting up that tree. 'Go on, help yourself,' I snarled.

I waited with growing impatience while Lassiter took his time pouring another tumblerful, settled down and prepared to talk himself out of trouble.

At last he said, 'Not my decision, you see, old son. It's down to my dreaded section chief. The Ice Queen.'

I shook my head in despair. 'What?'

'That's what we call her,' he explained, adding, 'behind her back, of course. Felicity Goodall. Late thirties, or early forties. Tall, blonde and a body to die for.'

'Yeah,' I said quickly. 'But I don't want to die for it.'

Lassiter chuckled at that. 'No, mate, you wouldn't. Because behind her cover-girl looks, she's one mean, hard and ambitious bitch with a black heart. That's the trouble with the Service nowadays. The women have all but taken over. At least we've now got a bloke back at the helm, but most of the Heads of Desk and a few Branch chiefs are female. And they all hate each other, all scoring points and backbiting. Life's not much fun any more. They don't think like us, Phil, they're a different species.'

I felt Lassiter was sidetracking me. 'What's this to do with me being stitched up?'

Lassiter contemplated me like I was a dumb schoolkid

who couldn't even understand elementary arithmetic. 'The Ice Queen's clawing her way to the top. She wanted a result on this and she wanted the result to be all hers. Our section stumbled on this cell . . . but it was, as I've explained, very circumstantial information from our section's field agents. If she'd made an issue and called in A4, then it would have to be referred to Head of Desk.'

'A4?' I queried.

'The "Watchers", our surveillance experts,' he explained irritably.

I nodded. 'So what's wrong with referring it to her Head of Desk.'

'To Melissa Thornton?' Lassiter thought the concept a huge joke. 'Medusa and the Ice Queen hate each other with a vengeance. As schoolgirls they were rival prefects at The Godolphin School in Salisbury. Melissa would probably have refused to sanction the operation on principle – or else taken it over and claimed all the glory. So Felicity kept the lid on it and put you on the case, but charmed and blagged the local chief constable into putting a firearms unit on standby.'

I shook my head in disbelief. 'A comedy of errors,' I murmured.

'Not unusual in our game,' Lassiter conceded.

'Once it all comes out, won't this Felicity Goodall be in trouble?' I asked.

Lassiter shrugged. 'Probably not. It's results that matter and Felicity's got a result, of sorts. Besides, Melissa's and Felicity's boss is the Head of G Branch – fundamentalist terrorism – and he's got the hots for Felicity. Need I say more.'

'Very Machiavellian,' I commented acidly.

An almost genuine smile settled on Lassiter's face. 'So you see, Phil, it was out of my hands.'

He wasn't wriggling out of it that easily. 'Not really, Joe. You could have created a stink, put your head above the parapet and told this Felicity Goodall woman she was wrong to do what she did, put her right.'

Lassiter leaned towards me. 'I told you, the place is run by women now. Doesn't matter how good you are, if your face doesn't fit or they don't like you, you're finished. And Felicity doesn't like me much, so I just keep my head down and do what I'm told. I've got a huge bloody mortgage and three kids at private school.'

'My heart bleeds,' I replied with all the sympathy I could muster.

Lassiter drained the last of his drink and stood up. 'Well, if it makes you feel better, I'll make damn sure nothing like this happens again, Phil, you can be sure of that. And I'm certain Felicity will be very pleased with your work. Maybe there'll be a bonus in it for you.'

I was very tired now, and didn't want to hear any more of this garbage. 'Just get out, Joe, will you? I've had enough.'

'Sure, mate, you look all in. Thanks for the drink.' He picked his fedora off the bed and moved towards the door. 'See you around.'

When he'd gone I stretched out on the bed and again

was asleep as soon as my head hit the pillow. This time there were no dreams, no mad nuns with Kalashnikovs.

I slept well, too well. As soon as I started to come to, I just sensed that it was late. The light was still on and I was fully clothed. When I glanced at my watch I could scarcely believe that it was nearly eleven o'clock. I'd planned to be back in London by that time.

Mentally rearranging the day's schedule, I put the kettle on for some coffee, drew the curtains, turned the TV on and ran the shower.

I was just unbuttoning my shirt when I saw the news broadcast. Two massive car bombs found in the early morning in London's West End. A deadly mixture of petrol, gas cylinders and nails, suspected to be the work of al-Qaeda. One outside the Tiger Tiger nightclub in Haymarket and a second, waiting to catch any survivors who escaped, in Cockspur Street.

If it hadn't been the good fortune of a paramedic spotting vapours in one of the two Mercedes and the subsequent bravery of bomb disposal officers, hundreds of innocent civilians would have been killed and horribly maimed.

Shocked, I sat down heavily on the edge of the bed and stared at the screen in disbelief. Christ, was this the work of Mullah Reda and his friend? We could so easily have been one day too late.

The kettle began boiling, but I suddenly needed something a lot stronger than black coffee.

I reached for the whisky bottle. It was empty.

'Lassiter,' I muttered, 'you selfish bastard.'

Two

'D'you like my new shoes, Phil?'

Kate wandered into my study-cum-office of the basement flat I rented in Brixton. I looked up from the handwritten report I was struggling to type on my laptop with two fingers. It was for my best regular client, Messrs Tapsells, a firm of top City solicitors, and it was a week overdue.

I regarded the nineteen-year-old sternly. 'What time d'you call this?'

The wall clock was certain it was ten-thirty.

'Oh, Phil, I know, I'm so sorry! I forgot to set my alarm,' she explained, her beautiful sleepy blue eyes glistening with genuine remorse. 'And I was so tired after eventing all weekend . . . I'm never very good on Mondays . . . Then the tube trains were running late because of another bomb scare . . .'

'I tried to ring your mobile.'

She looked even more shamefaced. 'My battery was down, sorry. Not very good, is it?'

'You can say that again.'

But it was impossible to be angry with Kate. She was

the sweetest, prettiest, most charming and useless secretary a man could hope to have. Apart from being a delight to have around, seeming to light up a room when she entered, she also came cheap. Known as 'Dizzy' to her friends, she was the daughter of an old army friend of mine who worked at British Land Forces HQ at Wilton in Wiltshire. The real love of her life was horses and, by all accounts, she was a talented eventer with good prospects of one day making the Olympic team. Not having been academically minded, her father thought some real work experience would knock some sense into her and per-suaded me to take her on. As I was struggling financially and Kate was on the minimum wage, it seemed a perfect solution for us both.

She took off her jacket, shook out her long blonde hair and presented her right foot for me to admire. 'So, what do you think of my new shoes, Phil?'

'I think they'd look good under a desk while you type,' I answered snappily.

'I got them in a sale on Saturday. Jimmy Choo. Only ninety pounds. Don't you think that's a bargain?'

'I think you were robbed,' I said. 'Or else they're coun-terfeit.'

Her face crumpled. 'No! Do you think they could be?'

I had to smile. 'Probably not. They look lovely. Now can you please get this goddamn report typed up.'

'Oh, the Tapsells one, yes. Shouldn't that have been done last week?'

'Yes, you should have finished it last week.'

'Sorry, I'll get on it right away.' Whatever criticism you might level at Kate, you couldn't dispute that she was always willing and hard-working – once she got started. 'Shall I make coffee first?'

I stood up so she could take my place; a second laptop would have been useful but would have to wait. The rent, Kate's wage, and my divorce legal fees had to come first. 'No, I'll make the coffee, you type,' I said. 'Your father believes it's why God put you on this earth.'

I wandered into the kitchen to the melody of a clacking keyboard that had just become music to my ears. While I waited for the kettle to boil, I turned on the portable radio to catch the latest news.

It had been three weeks' since the raid on Mullah Reda's house and the failed bombings in the West End of London. Thirty-six hours afterwards there was another attempted suicide car bombing at Glasgow Airport. The Jeep Cherokee had burst into flames and the two terrorists had been overwhelmed by bystanders who, thankfully, didn't just stand by. Again, the actual explosion didn't happen. If it had, there would have been carnage. Whatever the reason, it seemed that the gods were smiling on us for once.

Of course, again I wondered if Mullah Reda and his friends might have been connected and played some part in the planning of it all.

But I had no way of knowing because Joe Lassiter had gone to ground and wasn't returning my calls. But then, in fairness, he must have been kept busy with all that was going on. So I'd gone back to work serving writs and carrying out mundane commercial and domestic tasks for my solicitor clients. According to the news, Mullah Reda and his friends were on remand in Belmarsh high-security prison awaiting trial. It would probably be a long wait.

Not surprisingly, my cheque from the Security Service still hadn't arrived but, naturally, the bills from my divorce lawyers had. In fact, they were piling up nicely. Realizing I was broke, they'd politely suggested on pay-as-you-go because they could see it was going to be a long procedure. I now had so many invoices that I considered re-papering the flat's lavatory with them.

I filled two mugs with coffee and took one in to Kate. 'Thanks, Phil.'

'Keep typing with one hand while you drink that,' I warned. 'And be sure to use the spellcheck.'

She giggled. 'Yes, boss.'

At that moment the doorbell rang. I glanced up at the little security monitor. The camera wasn't very well placed, but there was no mistaking that fedora which shielded the face of the man who stood at the basement door.

Kate looked up. 'Shall I see who it is?'

'I know who it is,' I replied sternly. 'Keep typing.'

I wandered into the hallway and opened the door. 'Hallo, Joe, I was just thinking about you.'

He smiled broadly. 'That's nice.'

I ushered him in. 'Not really, I was wondering where the hell my cheque was.'

'Ah, a bit of a delay.' He fished in his inside pocket and

offered me the piece of paper that would keep the bank manager off my back for another couple of weeks. 'Wanted to give it to you personally.'

I resisted the urge to snatch it off him. 'We've got a perfectly good postal service,' I replied, accepting it with more grace than I felt.

'Go on, Phil, look at it.'

I glanced down at the auto-typed figures. 'That's not right, is it?'

Breaking the habit of a lifetime, Lassiter was still smiling broadly. 'It is, but it's a thousand smackers more than you were expecting.'

'How so?'

'The Ice Queen was very pleased with the operation. Very pleased with your part in it.'

Perhaps this woman wasn't quite the dragon that Lassiter was always insisting she was. My second thought was that this unexpected grand meant I would no longer have to share a laptop with Kate.

'Okay if I go in?' Lassiter asked, removing his hat as he stepped into the office. At that moment I'd have granted him any wish he wanted, so I waved him through and followed.

Kate looked up from the desk where she sat. Her mouth dropped. 'Mr Lassiter? It is, isn't it?'

'Hallo, Kate.'

Her smile lit up her face. 'What are you doing here?'

I frowned, suddenly not sure what the hell was going on. 'You two know each other?'

Lassiter dragged his eyes away from her and looked at me. 'We met at the New Forest Show the other day. Kate was in jumping and dressage. A fine horsewoman, looks great in jodhpurs.' He winked and Kate blushed deeply. 'Small world. Bumped into each other by chance. Got chatting in the beer tent and discovered you were a mutual acquaintance.'

Now I knew something was up. I turned to Kate. 'You didn't mention anything.'

She shrugged. 'Slipped my mind. Didn't seem that important.'

'Ah,' Lassiter said. 'So you didn't tell your boss about the lunch date either?'

Kate's hand flew to her mouth. 'Oh, gosh, no. Sorry.'

'What lunch date?' I demanded.

Lassiter placed a hand on my shoulder. 'Calm down, old son. Just planned to take you to lunch today, that's all. As thanks for your help and an apology for the old – er – injury.' He glanced at my left bicep. 'Okay, is it?'

I said, 'Actually it was the other arm. But yes, it's fine now.'

'Anyway, Phil, I was passing and just wanted to give you the cheque and to make sure you're still up for lunch . . .' He glanced at Kate. 'As I hadn't heard.'

'To be honest, I'm a bit busy right now,' I replied churlishly.

Lassiter's unfamiliar smile was starting to look a bit strained. 'Aren't we all, old son. Look, let's put it this way, it would be in the best interests of your bank account to

join me. I need to talk serious business.' He paused, knowing that it really was that easy to manipulate a desperate
man into doing what he wanted. 'Savoy Grill at one
o'clock, okay? I must dash now.'

I opened my mouth, but before I managed to utter a
word, he'd waved goodbye to Kate and disappeared out of
the room.

As the front door slammed, Kate said, 'Isn't he a nice
man, Phil?'

'Isn't he just,' I murmured, wondering just what the
devil Joe Lassiter had planned for me next?

I took the tube to Waterloo and crossed the river bridge
on foot, arriving at the Savoy a few minutes early. Of
course, I realized then it was only a short distance from
Thames House, the headquarters of MI5.

I'd dressed up for the occasion, digging a tie and old
grey suit from my wardrobe. It was now a bit loose around
the waist and was double-breasted. Glancing around the
hotel lobby at all the modern, sharp and shiny three-
button suits on the well-heeled young executive types, I
realized I definitely looked like yesterday's man.

At least I needn't have worried because, true to form,
Joe Lassiter appeared to greet me wearing an equally
unfashionable blue suit that looked as if he'd slept in it. He
carried his shabby raincoat and trusty fedora.

Grabbing my hand, he shook it fiercely as if we hadn't
met for months. 'Glad you could make it, Phil. Got someone I'd like you to meet.'

'You didn't say . . .' I began, but he was already striding towards the restaurant, leaving me to follow him into the august Michelin-star restaurant with its gold-leaf ceiling and rich, brandy-hued panelling.

He made his way straight to a corner table, with starched white linen cloth and heavy silver cutlery, which was set some distance away from all the others.

A woman sat there alone, a slim thirty- or forty-something blonde dressed in a business suit of black Thai silk with a white camisole top peeping out at the neck. She was studying the menu through a small, elegant pair of gold-rimmed reading glasses.

As we approached, she looked up and removed the glasses. Her hair was long and beautifully layered – by a top salon, I guessed – and it framed a perfect almond-shaped face. Her eyes were mesmeric blue and long-lashed, her nose straight and slightly upturned at its tip, and her mouth a luscious pale cherry red that looked good enough to eat.

Lassiter waited impatiently for me to reach the table. 'Phil, I'd like you to meet Felicity Goodall, my boss. Felicity, this is Phil Mason.'

Her eyelids fluttered momentarily in my direction and her smile shone at me as she raised a slender hand. It was smooth and cool to the touch as I reached forward and clasped it in mine.

'Mr Mason, so nice to meet you. I've heard so much about you from Joe here.'

'I'm honoured,' I replied, taking a seat. 'Joe didn't tell me I was going to meet his boss.'

She laughed lightly. 'Oh, Joe likes his little secrets. Now, would you like an aperitif?'

I noticed she just had sparkling mineral water and a twist. 'Campari and soda would be good, thank you.'

Immediately the waiter was there, despite the fact that no one had called him. Felicity gave him the order, which included a whisky and ice for Lassiter but nothing more for herself.

Her eyes fixed me across the table, drawing me in. 'I wanted to thank you for your recent work with us.'

Out of the corner of my eye I saw Lassiter looking at me intensely and I somehow knew he was wondering if I'd complain about being used and shot at. But this didn't seem to be the right moment. 'Glad to have been of assistance.'

'So tell me a little about yourself, Mr Mason.'

I felt awkward at the formality. 'Please, call me Phil.'

That light, slightly breathless laugh again. I wondered absently if she'd laugh that way in bed with her husband or lover? 'Then you must call me Felicity. Things are a lot less formal at the office than they used to be.' Again her eyes focused closely on me. 'So, what about you?'

I shifted a little uncomfortably. 'Not much to tell. Where to start?'

A cloud of irritation dulled the light in her eyes for a moment. 'Well, the beginning is always good. Like *This Is Your Life*. Born in Weymouth, Dorset, in 1962, I understand. Your mother was Spanish, a full-time housewife, and your father a petty officer in the Royal Navy. You spent your childhood playing around in boats and joined the Army Cadets. That gave you a taste for the military and you later joined the Royal Marines at eighteen, serving with 42 Commando in Plymouth.'

I suppose she was trying to impress me, but I just felt annoyed that people like her in MI5 had access to my personal details or anyone else's in the country if they wanted them. I forced a polite smile. 'I think you hardly need ask me then.'

She looked a little amused. 'I'd rather hear it from you, Phil.'

It was as well that the waiter returned then with the drinks. I took a much-needed swallow and decided to get this ordeal over with. 'As I'm sure you're aware, I did a sniper course in my early twenties and passed selection for the Special Boat Service.'

Felicity nodded and smiled warmly at me. 'And you were later seconded to the Intelligence Corps.' She glanced at Lassiter. 'Where you met Joe, working in Northern Ireland?'

'Yes. I was mostly wanted for my surveillance skills.' I pointed out what a lot of people didn't realize. 'The art of sniping isn't just about shooting people. Much of it is observation of the enemy and intelligence gathering.'

That seemed to amuse her. 'But you did some counter-sniper operations in Armagh?'

I didn't really want to be reminded about that. 'Yes.'

'And very successfully?'

If she meant I'd seen an IRA gunman's head burst open

like a ripe watermelon in close-up through the sight of my L96, then yes, it had been successful.

'I got a result,' I replied flatly.

'And over the years, you worked closely with military intelligence in various theatres, including Bosnia?'

She knew it all. I said, 'Yes, I did several specialist tours over the years, but my regular posting was as a senior instructor at the British Army Sniper School.'

'Until you left the Royal Marines just over a year ago . . . after an incident?' I didn't reply and she leaned forward earnestly, placing her hand on my wrist. 'I understand it's difficult, but please tell me . . .'

Just the mention of it started the knot forming in my throat and I felt moisture gather in my eyes. 'I don't talk about it,' I said hoarsely.

Her eyes were very wide and very blue and just inches from mine. 'You should do, it doesn't help to bottle things up.'

Lassiter said suddenly: 'Phil was with a mixed American and British Special Forces group in Afghanistan. They were hunting down and mopping up remnants of the Taliban.'

Felicity glared at him for interrupting, but he steamrollered on. 'Got this gang of fighters holed up in a remote village in the Bora Bora mountains. There was a stand-off. Phil and another sniper began picking some of them off. Then some rag-head got smart, I suppose trying to find out the enemy's location and put his head above the parapet.'

I stared down at the beautiful display of silver cutlery, trying to control my breathing, trying to blank my mind, but in fact seeing the scene replayed in my head like a loop of film, over and over again. I thought that particular nightmare had finally finished. Lassiter said, 'Phil thought it was the gunman's head. But the bastard had got a little girl hostage from the village, put a turban on her and lifted her into his line-of-sight. The bastard knew what would happen. Maybe he just wanted a bad press for us in the world media.' He paused then, and the sudden silence was intense. All I could hear was the solemn clink of knives and forks on the other diners' plates. In a low voice, Lassiter added, 'That is why Phil doesn't like talking about it.'

Felicity squeezed my fist tight and withdrew her hand. 'I'm so sorry, Phil,' she said hoarsely. 'That was unthinking of me.'

Acting out of character like a consummate diplomat, Lassiter lifted his hand and, like a genie from a lamp, the waiter appeared magically at his side. 'We'd like to order now. What'd you like, Felicity?'

'Oh, er . . .' For a second she was thrown, but only for a second. 'Er, just a starter for me. I was thinking the smoked salmon.'

'I'll have the ravioli of king prawns,' Lassiter decided, going for the top of the price list.

Felicity raised an eyebrow. 'Remind me to double-check your expense account next time, Joe.'

Lassiter tilted his head to one side. 'You already do, dear heart. Three times at least.'

I'd recovered my composure somewhat and picked something almost at random from the menu. 'Aberdeen rib of beef, please.'

The waiter was replaced immediately by his wine counterpart from whom Felicity ordered a bottle of Chardonnay without consulting either Lassiter or me.

Once the glasses were filled, Felicity turned to me again. 'Please don't think this insensitive, Phil, but was it after that business in Afghanistan that your marriage started going wrong?'

I blinked, hardly believing what I was being asked. 'What's that got to do with the price of eggs?' I retorted.

That melting smile was back. 'I'm sorry, but if we're going to be doing business, I have to know the sort of person I'm working with. Trust is everything. I'm sure you must understand that?'

I was beginning to realize that the Ice Queen had a very clever way of phrasing things, of wheedling out the answers she wanted. I sighed. 'Well, Afghanistan didn't help. I wasn't much fun to live with. Drank too much and ran up a few debts. But, to be honest, our marriage had been running down for a few years. I was away a lot, too much.'

Felicity nodded sympathetically. 'I know what it's like, Phil, working too many hours, never at home. I was divorced a year ago, a similar scenario. It's all very sad.'

Then the food arrived and we were all distracted by its superb presentation, although despite the exquisite smell and taste I suddenly had no appetite.

After a few mouthfuls of her salmon, Felicity said, 'Tell me, Phil, what do you think about the invasion of Iraq?'

Just like that, out of the blue, and I almost choked on my food. It was most certainly a test and my reply could make or break any deal that might be in the offing for work I desperately needed.

I hedged. 'I don't really have an opinion.'

'Oh, come now, Phil,' Felicity chided, 'everyone has an opinion.'

'I can't have a worthwhile opinion without all the facts,' I countered. 'You probably know them better than me, so what do you think?'

She smiled at that but wasn't falling for it. 'I need to know your view, Phil, the truth. For a start do you believe it was legal?'

I took a sip of wine as I tried to decide how many barrels to fire. 'Possibly, but probably not, from what I've read.'

'And the reasons for the invasion?' she pressed.

'Totally dishonest,' I replied, deciding to go for it. 'Even if we believed there were weapons of mass destruction available to Saddam Hussein, even I knew there would be only a short-range delivery system. On the immediate battlefield or against near-neighbouring countries. So he was never going to use them against Britain unless we turned up on his doorstep.'

'Which we duly obliged,' Lassiter chortled, quite amused at Felicity and I clashing antlers.

I added, 'But I don't know what intelligence SIS had.'

Her expression was deadpan. 'And regime-change to rid the country of an evil tyrant?'

I shook my head. 'There are plenty of them in the world. Do we invade Burma, Zimbabwe, North Korea or China? No, the bottom line is, the decision to invade was the most stupid and ill-conceived political decision I've witnessed in my lifetime.'

'Why?' Felicity asked bluntly.

'If one understands the thinking of Arab nations, it's clear how they'd react to interference from America and Britain in their own internal affairs – however, well-intentioned. It was never going to be in this country's best interests, which should be our government's main concern.' I stopped there. 'I'm sorry if that doesn't square with the depth of loyalty you might be wanting from me.'

The smile returned to her face. 'I don't think your loyalty to your country is in question, Phil. You served in Afghanistan without question, put your life on the line.'

'Not without question,' I corrected quickly. 'I carried out orders because it was my job. Personally, I thought the entire concept of the war on terror was a nonsense.'

She raised an eyebrow. 'Really? How so?'

I seemed to be hammering nails into my own coffin. 'It was a knee-jerk reaction by the USA after 9/11. Washington felt it had to be seen to do something. You don't defeat terrorists by going to war with a conventional army. We might have disrupted their operations and got rid of the Taliban government – which was a bonus – but the al-Qaeda leadership escaped and continues to flourish.'

'How would you have tackled al-Qaeda?' Lassiter asked, mischievously.

I smiled, knowing full well he knew the answer. 'Quietly and covertly, taking time to establish an intelligence network, putting in infiltrators and recruiting agents in place. Then act with surgical precision with special forces to take out the leadership when the moment's right.'

Felicity put her knife and fork on the side of her plate and patted her mouth with her napkin. 'It may surprise you to know, Phil, that I totally agree with all you've said. Most people in the office think the same. But our views and those of our brothers and sisters across the water at the other place' – I gather she was referring to the MI6 headquarters at Vauxhall Cross – 'were ignored by government. Like you, we may question, but still have to follow orders.'

Lassiter leaned forward. 'Despite accusations by the Bush administration, al-Qaeda never had any but the most superficial involvement with Iraq or Saddam. It just never happened. But we knew once a US–UK invasion force went in, al-Qaeda would pile in too – on the other side! The ruling Sunnis under Saddam wanted to hold on to power and welcomed any help they could get. Meanwhile the Iranians saw their opportunity to turn their erstwhile enemies into a friendly fundamentalist Islamic state. So they've been backing the Shi'ites. Quite a mess.'

'More importantly', Felicity intervened, 'our actions seemed – to the Arab world at large – to support what al-Qaeda had been warning them about us all along. It just opened the recruitment floodgates. And that includes here in Britain.'

I nodded. 'As confirmed by that Birmingham operation I was on and that recent bombing attempt in Haymarket . . . Were the two connected, by the way?'

'Our investigations are still ongoing,' Felicity said, 'but we think so. Tenuously at least. Which brings me to why we're talking here now. I'll let Joe put you in the picture.'

Lassiter finished eating and belched lightly. 'Look, Phil, since 9/11 we've been bloody stretched at the office. We'd run down numbers after the Cold War and Northern Ireland, and you can't recruit for our sort of work in a hurry. And Muslims weren't rushing to sign-up. I can tell you, 9/11 was a wake-up call, making us realize that al-Qaeda had the ability to hit us as well as America. Then the invasion of Iraq put us right in the frame too.'

'Those ghastly July 7 bombings in London confirmed it,' Felicity added. 'It changed the political geography, probably for ever. The general public doesn't realize that we at the office have always encouraged leaders of our political enemies, governmental or terrorist, to have residence in Britain – often to the annoyance of the tabloids. It means we know who they are and can keep tabs on them, who they connect with and what they might be planning.'

Lassiter couldn't resist interrupting. 'Plus the covenant of security.'

'What's that?' I asked.

'Terrorists don't like to shit on their own doorstep,'

Lassiter explained and received a scowl of disapproval from Felicity for his choice of language. 'Put simply, Phil, if the UK is their safe haven and headquarters, it's not in their interests to plan attacks on us. It's always worked.'

'That has gone out the window now since the July 7 bombings,' Felicity confirmed. 'On the bright side, we've had a better response from potential Muslim recruits here. But vetting will be doubly hard because we don't want any Trojan horses coming through the gate and, anyway, the training takes a long, long time.'

'Meanwhile,' Lassiter said, 'we need all the help we can get. We've always used private security companies and investigators who have a high military pedigree and intelligence experience. There's going to be a lot more use of those in the short term.'

'People like you,' Felicity said with a dazzling smile.

'I'm flattered,' I said, 'but I was well cut out of the loop on that last operation, as you know. I was shot for my pains.'

'This will be different,' Felicity assured me quickly. 'You'll operate semi-independently, reporting to Joe here. You'll be fully briefed and may have our surveillance officers at your disposal if it's cleared by Joe.'

'You'll be a sort of autonomous orbital unit of the office,' Lassiter explained enthusiastically. 'You'll tackle the tasks in any way you see fit, have access to any information you need.'

I frowned. 'Is that why you were talking to Kate at the New Forest Show? I didn't think it was by chance.'

Lassiter nodded. 'We're in the middle of vetting her. Good family pedigree there, so I don't foresee a problem.'

'I'm a pretty small orbital unit, Joe,' I said. 'It's just me and Kate.'

'I realize that. So it's time for you to expand. And, of course, the terms we offer will be generous. You'll probably also want to upgrade a lot of your equipment at our expense. Apart from that, I've got someone in mind you'd work well with for starters.'

'Who's that?'

'I'll tell you later,' he said enigmatically. 'We'll start you off slowly. Low-grade suspects. A few people who've only just blipped onto our radar. You just investigate them however you think fit and report back.'

Felicity indicated to a waiter to bring the bill and turned back to me. 'What I need to know, Phil, is can we count on you?'

Well, Felicity Goodall knew about my marriage break-up and I've no doubt she'd seen copies of my latest bank statement too. I'm sure she knew exactly what reply she was going to get before I even opened my mouth. 'Of course, it will be my pleasure,' I confirmed.

'Excellent,' she said. 'Now, I'm afraid I have to go, these are hectic times. I'll let Joe fill you in on all the details.'

The waiter returned and she settled the bill with tax-payers' plastic. Moments later Lassiter and I were wistfully watching the sway of those hips beneath the black silk skirt as she left the room.

'She seems very pleasant,' I said.

'That's because the Ice Queen likes you, old son,' Lassiter replied. 'Tough luck.'

'And that stuff about Afghanistan, Joe. I can't believe she didn't know about that.'

'Of course she did, she's got your MoD file.' Lassiter poured the last of the wine into his glass. 'She just wanted to test your mettle, make you sweat a bit.'

I said, 'She did that all right.'

'Then you've had a taste of why she's called the Ice Queen.' He glanced at the empty wine bottle and at his watch. 'I've got to go too, soon. Let's just have a couple of quick cognacs to seal the deal, okay?'

I could hardly refuse and Lassiter went ahead and ordered two large measures of vintage stuff. I warmed the balloon between my palms and asked, 'What's the first assignment, Joe?'

He was already drinking his cognac. 'I'll have the details for you in a few days. Six names. Of course, we couldn't get anything off Mullah Reda's computer, but these names appeared in the records of one of the trio, the Pakistani restaurant owner. They've been computer cross-matched with other references to them from elsewhere. It could be coincidence or they could be players. It'll be up to you to make the initial assessment.'

I nodded. 'Just some straightforward detective work then?'

'Absolutely.'

'And who's this mystery person you think I should invite to join my new orbital unit?'

He ignored the sarcasm in my voice and just reached into his inside breast pocket to produce an envelope. 'Name and address is in there.' He placed it on the table, and drained his cognac. 'Take a tip and don't call first. Just turn up. After five p.m. is usually best.'

Before I could reply, Lassiter was on his feet. 'I'll be in touch, Phil. Glad to have you on board.'

When he was gone, I realized that he'd left me to settle our drinks bill. And two vintage cognacs at the Savoy Grill didn't come cheap.

I reached for the envelope, split it open with my thumbnail, and withdrew the single sheet of typed paper.

I stared at the name in disbelief, and it all came rushing back to me.

The bleak Balkan mid-winter of 1993. Virtually every city, town and village in Bosnia was pockmarked with bullet-holes, walls and roofs collapsed under mortar or artillery fire, as the country was ravaged by a vicious and cruel civil war that was tearing the heart out of the fledgling nation. A nation in rags and without food, and increasingly without homes as one or other of the three warring factions drove out their erstwhile neighbours because they had the wrong ethnic ancestry. Phones were down, electricity was down, and fresh water from blast-ruptured mains spilled wastefully onto the streets.

Refugees with gaunt white faces, mostly the elderly, women and the very young, trudged along the roads carrying all their worldly possessions. Their destination? Anywhere that was away from the fighting.

I was there with the British Army, the largest contingent of the United Nations Protection Force, which was struggling to make a difference. To try to talk some sense into the Serb and Croat warlords who were contesting the ill-equipped Bosnia government forces; trying to get the fighting to stop for long enough to get the UN aid convoys through to the hapless civilian victims.

That morning I stepped out of the Battalion HQ building in Vitez to stretch my legs for a few minutes. It was almost 1200 hours and I was expecting a new arrival to join our small cobbled-together team of intelligence experts drawn from all three arms of the military, including Territorial Army reservists.

It was good to get out into the fresh air for a few minutes. I remember lighting a cigarette and staring up at the surrounding snow-flecked hills and seeing the dirty telltale stains of smoke against the grey wash of sky and knowing that it was the call sign of yet more ethnic cleansing. Another home torched, another family broken and lost, with nowhere to go.

Then the mud-splattered white Land Rover pulled up at the compound gates, headlights ablaze, and I knew it was our new arrival. As the sentries allowed it through, I wondered absently just what she would be like. I'd read the sparse details about her in the signal and automatically envisaged someone resembling a Russian shot-put medallist. After all, she had served in 14 Intelligence Company, one of the toughest covert units of the British Army. That meant a ferocious and gruelling training programme before going on to do undercover work in Northern Ireland.

The Land Rover stopped and a tall, slender figure in DPMs, black hair up and neatly tucked beneath a bright-blue UN beret, sprang out and began manhandling her baggage from the rear tailgate. Despite her slim build, she seemed to have no problem hoisting the huge bergen over one shoulder while she carried another bulging kitbag with her left hand.

She noticed me watching and marched straight across to me. Dark, smouldering eyes with long lashes looked up at me from a perfect almond-shaped face. Her skin was slightly honey-hued.

The full lips parted in an elfin grin. 'Staff?'

I nodded. 'Staff-Sarn't Phil Mason.'

She saluted smartly, her back straight despite the weight she was carrying. 'Corporal Jasmina Alagic, Staff. Your new interpreter.'

And that was Jazz.

From that day on the dismal mountain weather seemed to brighten and the spirits in our little intelligence group lifted, mine especially. Jazz, twenty-six at that time, was always happy and chirpy with a wicked sense of humour that belied her dedication to duty – and her undoubted courage. In fact, the only time I ever saw her depressed was when there was news of another shooting of civilians in Sarajevo by snipers of the Serb forces who were laying siege to the capital.

That hurt her deeply and it was clear why.

Jazz's family were Bosnian Muslims and came from Sarajevo. Her parents had managed to escape the former Yugoslavia and emigrate to Britain during the Cold War before she was born in 1967. Even when the Communist regime relaxed and welcomed holidaymakers, her parents had never felt it safe to return. They still had family members and friends in the area, but only had contact by letter, and in later years, telephone.

'I'm so looking forward to this posting,' she'd told me on the day of her arrival. 'It might give me the chance to meet some aunts and uncles, nieces and nephews I've only ever seen photographs of.'

'Anyone in particular?' I'd asked.

'Oh, yes. Great Aunt Ivana,' Jazz had replied enthusiastically. 'A tall, proud woman, very straight-talking and formidable. You wouldn't want to get on the wrong side of her.'

'And you've never met her?'

'We exchanged a few letters before all this trouble began. But I've had nothing from her recently.'

I'd smiled. 'Then you're with the right outfit to track her down. If you've an address, we should be able to find out if she's still in Sarajevo.'

God, how I came to regret those words. We found Great Aunt Ivana all right. She was buried in the city's main cemetery.

It transpired that the once proud and defiant bastion of middle-class society and former headmistress, like all other citizens, had been reduced to scavenging for food and firewood. One morning she'd taken a bucket to join the queue for water at one of the few functioning standpipes. She hadn't known that a Serb sniper had her in his sights. He was a lousy shot, wounding her in the right lung; the medics tried to save her, but after two days in agony with no morphine, she died.

Of Jazz's other relatives, there was no real news. Older uncles and aunts were thought to have moved away, but no one knew where to. Her niece had been killed in an artillery hit on her family house and her two young nephews were rumoured to be away fighting somewhere.

'How the hell can you do it, Phil?' she'd challenged me, when she discovered that I was a sniper in the Royal Marines.

'I don't shoot civilians,' I'd answered defensively. 'Just enemy soldiers, but I don't like it.'

'Then why do you do it?'

'It just happened. I went on a course and was good at it. That's all. I've never lost any sleep over it,' I lied.

Jazz had glared at me. 'The devil always sleeps well because he has no conscience,' she'd replied testily.

I think it was the only time we'd ever come close to a row. Because, in fact, we became lovers a few weeks after her arrival. We'd become close very quickly. I suppose the dangerous nature of our work and the ever-present risk of imminent death sharpened our appetite for life. My duties were split between dangerous surveillance work behind enemy lines, or sometimes in civilian guise, working alongside Jazz whose upbringing meant she spoke Serbo-Croat fluently.

These close-surveillance assignments were very similar to the work she'd been doing in Northern Ireland, getting close up to major players and monitoring their movements, who they were seeing, what they were doing and where they were going. Only this time the targets tended to be warlords rather than terrorists, although in Bosnia the line between the two definitions became distinctly blurred. Jazz was only five years younger than me, so it suited us – in more ways than one – to often play the role of a courting couple.

I learned that despite her divine femininity, Jazz had always been a tomboy and a daredevil as a child. To her parents' horror she had signed up with the British Army at eighteen. By twenty, wanted for her linguistic skills, she had joined the Intelligence Corps. Getting bored with a desk job, four years' later she applied and passed selection for the army's undercover elite known as 14 Intelligence Company – although its official name changed periodically – for operations in Northern Ireland.

Meanwhile it was proving difficult managing our love affair in Bosnia. If we'd been caught together there'd have been hell to pay. I think we only ever got to bed together some six times in as many months, usually in the house of a befriended local. But those six times were magical and unforgettable and left me with powerful dream-like images of erotica and fantasy that haunt me to the present day. I just cannot believe we did some of the things we did. But then it was at a time when we both knew that each and every day could be our last. In those circumstances there is an almost primeval need to live life to the full.

Given Jazz's impassioned hatred of snipers, when we relaxed and talked together, I was surprised by how often she asked me about it. The skills and techniques needed, what sort of weapons were used.

I was even more surprised, and not a little hurt, when one day she disappeared from Battalion HQ without a word to me, leaving just a short note. *Dear Phil, We've had wonderful times together and I will never forget you, but I am leaving the British Army. Enjoy the rest of your life. Take care. Love Jazz.*

That was it. I tried to find out more, get a forwarding address for her, but no one at Battalion HQ knew anything, and British Forces HQ were very cagey and blanked me.

Thankfully it was summer by this time and the sunny weather helped the heartache along with the fact that our unit was being kept frenetically busy.

It was the following winter when the rumours began. The Bosnian government had deployed a new crackshot in Sarajevo on counter-sniper duties and her name was Jasmina Alagic.

I sensed it was true, and if it was, then she was good, very good. Given a dose of their own medicine, the sniping activities of the Serbs went into rapid decline for a while. Again I tried to track her down, to make contact, but the Bosnian government refused to say anything and the trail soon went cold. It had remained so, until now.

Memories, these and more, flooded my mind as I drove across London in my battered Transit van to the address I'd been given in Putney.

It was a pretty street of Edwardian terraced houses in one of the less-fashionable parts of the district, lined with plane trees in full leaf but marred by rows of parked cars. Following Joe Lassiter's advice, I arrived a few minutes before five o'clock, which was just as well because there were still a few places left in the residents-only bays before everyone returned from work.

I wasn't worried about a parking ticket as I now had the full weight of MI5's powers behind me – well, that's what I assumed. I managed to squeeze into a gap on the same side as Jazz's house, some forty feet away.

Suddenly I was filled with trepidation. When we'd last met we'd been passionate lovers, or so I'd thought. But then she'd walked out without a word and, as far as I was aware, had never attempted to contact me again. So I had no idea what reception I might get.

What would she look like? Would I even recognize her? After all, people can change a lot in fourteen years. She'd been slim, but quite muscular in those days; truly a body I'd have willingly died for back then. Now, at forty, I anticipated she'd probably have added a few pounds, maybe quite a few. She was probably married with kids . . . That bastard Lassiter hadn't even told me that.

When I'd rung him in the afternoon for more information, I just got his voicemail. I could imagine him sitting there, looking at the tiny screen on his mobile with my name on it, and smiling to himself. I thought of 'hiding' my name and dialling again, but decided it wasn't worth the effort.

Then I saw her, there was no doubt.

Jazz had just turned the corner and entered the street. Her hair was a little shorter than I remembered, cut to her shoulders, but still the same lustrous raven's-wing black. She wore a smart tunic top over a light floral dress and small-heeled pumps. Far from having put on weight, I thought she looked rather thin. A little girl of about six held her hand and skipped by her side.

I took a deep breath, climbed out of the van and walked along the pavement towards her. We came face-to-face outside her house. It wasn't until I stopped right in front of her that she appeared to notice me. There was a look of weariness in the beautiful dark-brown eyes that regarded me cautiously, a slight anxiety in her expression. Maybe she thought I might be a mugger.

I said, 'It's all right, it's me.'

Fine lines fractured the smooth surface of her brow. 'Phil? It is, isn't it? I don't believe it!'

I wasn't sure if she was pleased to see me or not; nor, I think, was the little girl, who decided to cling to her mother's dress and stare up at me with distinct uncertainty.

I smiled. 'Yes, Jazz, it's me. I hope you don't mind . . .'

'No one's called me Jazz in years,' she murmured, a

returning smile playing at her lips. 'How did you find me?'

I hedged. 'A bit of a story. Any chance we could chat and I can tell you about it?'

For a moment she seemed flustered and I think then I realized how tired she looked, dark skin beneath her eyes and her cheeks drawn. 'I've just picked Zoë up from the grandparents . . . Er, yes, I suppose . . . why not? If you don't mind, I'll have to get Zoë's tea.'

'Course not,' I said and looked down at the little girl, who was still staring at me sheepishly. There was no mistaking the likeness. 'This must be your daughter . . . Hello, Zoë.'

The child turned her face away and buried it in the folds of her mother's dress.

'Don't be shy, Zoë,' Jazz chided. 'This is Uncle Phil. He's a friend I used to know.' She turned back to me. 'Let's go inside.'

She led the way up the short flight of steps and into the house. The narrow hallway led past a living room with beige walls and contemporary black ash furniture, then a dining-room that was similarly decorated, until we reached the kitchen.

This looked a lot more friendly and lived in, painted in a sunny granary yellow with a large pine refectory table in the centre, and a nice view of a neatly tended back garden.

'So what are you doing nowadays?' I asked conversationally.

She removed her jacket and hung it on the back of a

chair. 'A doctor's receptionist. Only been doing it a couple of weeks.'

'Going well?'

She shrugged. 'There's a lot to learn and there's a lot of jealousy with the other reception girls. I'm the newbee and all that. But I need to make it work . . . before that I was on the check-out at Sainsbury's.'

'Really?'

She smiled tightly at my surprise. 'Like you, Phil, my qualifications from the army were rather limiting.'

I noticed the framed photograph on the dresser shelf: a rather handsome man smiling proudly alongside Jazz, who held a baby in her arms. 'Your husband?' I guessed.

Jazz hesitated. 'Yes, but he's not exactly in a position to support me, if that's what you're thinking.'

Clearly, this was a thorny subject. 'I'm sorry, I didn't mean to pry.'

She turned away and began running water into a kettle. 'No, you weren't to know. I met Ricardo in Bosnia. He was a doctor with Médecins Sans Frontières. We married in ninety-six. Unfortunately he left me three years ago and he hasn't been in touch since.'

'I'm sorry,' I said, lamely.

Without looking back at me, Jazz took two mugs from a cupboard. 'Tea or coffee? It was always black sweet coffee, if I remember correctly. I'm afraid I have nothing stronger in the house.'

'Then you're a reformed character,' I said, trying to lighten the mood, then added, 'Coffee's fine.'

She poured my drink then turned to Zoë and got her seated at the table. There was a brief debate about egg salad versus beans on toast, and beans on toast won.

As Jazz began preparing it, she asked, 'And what about you, Phil, are you married?'

'Barely,' I replied, 'we're in the middle of a divorce.'

She was at the stove and glanced back over her shoulder. 'That's sad. Do you have any children?'

'A boy, Danny. He's eleven now.'

'How's he taken it?'

'I'm not sure he's noticed,' I replied with a degree of honesty. 'If he ever took his nose out of his computer, he might realize.'

'They always notice, Phil,' Jazz said. 'He's probably buried in his computer to blot it out of his mind. You should talk it through with him, make sure he understands it's not his fault. They often think it is, you know?'

'I'm sure you're right,' I answered, wondering if I'd ever manage to get past Nina at the front door and be able to prise Danny from his bedroom. It would be quite an ordeal.

'Was it a mutual thing?' Jazz asked, stirring the saucepan of beans and placing a slice of bread in the toaster.

Very diplomatic, I thought. 'Not really, it was Nina's idea. She'd said for years she was sick of being married to the army, as she put it, but she started the divorce after I'd left. I think she's got someone in the background, the local butcher. But I can't be sure.'

Jazz giggled. 'I'm sorry . . . It's not funny.'

I said, 'That's okay. In truth I realized I wasn't that bothered about it in the end — except for being parted from Danny. I think Nina and I had been drifting apart for years.'

Minutes later, Zoë was served her tea, and Jazz and I wandered into the back garden.

'It's a bit of a mess,' she said. 'I don't have much time.'

'It looks fine to me, better than mine ever was,' I replied. I sipped at my coffee for a moment while I came to a decision to ask the question that had burned at the back of my mind for years. 'I don't want to dig up the past, Jazz, but I wondered why you just went without saying anything to me first?'

She glanced at me for a second then averted her eyes, studying the mug in her hand.

'Cowardice, I suppose. You know what I did?'

'Became a sniper in the Bosnian Army, yes.' My eyes met hers and I smiled. 'That came as a bit of a shock.'

'You'd have tried to stop me.'

'Yes,' I admitted, but I think I'd always known her reason for not telling me before she left. 'But afterwards, I always hoped you'd get back in touch. We had such a good time.'

'Things moved on, Phil. I met Ricardo in Sarajevo and fell in love with him. He was working so hard to save lives in appalling conditions.' I think she could see the hurt in my eyes. 'Sorry.'

I said, 'I understand.'

She regarded me closely. 'There was more to it than

that. When I applied to leave the army, and told them what I wanted to do, at first I was turned down flat. I certainly didn't have the money to buy myself out. Then someone in military intelligence, who knew my background in 14 Int, heard about it. The long and short of it was they agreed to fast-track me out of the army, give me priority sniper training . . . on condition that I spied on the Bosnian government, their officials and their military.'

'Good God,' I said, totally taken aback.

She shrugged and looked sheepish. 'I know, it was horrible. But I was desperate to help out – it had become an absolute obsession with me to become a sniper, to hit back at those Serbs who killed Aunt Ivana. Isn't that crazy? But that's how it was then. And if I wanted to do that I had to go along with them.'

'Did it work out?'

She nodded. 'I guess so. At least I learned that the Bosnian government wasn't exactly squeaky clean. I think the information I gave helped the UN and NATO later. Maybe it saved lives and helped the aid effort, I like to think so. The worst thing was the creep who was my controller. A nasty piece of work, a right lech.'

I raised an eyebrow. 'I couldn't blame anyone for fancying you.'

Jazz frowned. 'In this context, Phil, that is not a compliment. Anyway, he ordered me to have nothing more to do with my old friends in the army. Security and secrecy, he said. But then, by that time I'd met Ricardo and I also remembered you once told me you had a girlfriend waiting for you back home. I suppose that was Nina?'

I nodded. 'So I guess what goes around comes around. Got my comeuppance now.'

Jazz seemed more relaxed having explained all that. 'So if you're out of the army, Phil, what are you doing now?'

It seemed strange uttering the words. 'I'm a private investigator.'

'A gumshoe!' She seemed to find that deeply amusing. 'Goodness me, Phil, that's amazing. Is that how you tracked me down? You must be good.'

'Not really. I've been contracted to do some work for MI5. They gave me your address.'

She stared at me and I could sense the atmosphere between us chill instantly. After a moment, she said, 'The answer's no . . . And you'd better leave now.'

I was perplexed. 'Sorry, Jazz, I don't understand. What's wrong?'

'I know who sent you.' She almost spat the words. 'The same man who was my controller in Bosnia. Joe Lassiter.'

Three

'She threw me out, Joe, that's what happened.'

I'd at last managed to reach Lassiter on his mobile and met up with him at the Morpeth Arms on the Embankment at nine o'clock that evening.

He shrugged, smiled at me and said, 'Well, it was worth a try. Quite a feisty one that.'

'I didn't even know you'd worked in Bosnia,' I challenged. 'And certainly not with Jazz.'

Lassiter gave me one of his sternest of disapproving looks. 'God, the loose talk we get nowadays. I wonder if some of you've ever heard of the Official Secrets Act.' He took a sip of his beer. 'I was still with Army Intelligence then. But, anyway, I don't really think you need to know my full CV, Phil.'

'I don't want to know your bloody CV,' I snapped back. 'I just want to be put in the picture when things affect me. Like that raid on Mullah Reda Rashid, remember? Jazz said you'd already approached her to work for you. Is that true?'

'Er, yes, but I don't seem to be her favourite friendly spook. Thought you might have better luck.'

I said, 'If you'd put me in the picture first, I might have done.'

He drained his beer. 'You're probably right. Still, no harm done. I'd better get off now, been another bloody long day.'

'It's your round,' I said testily.

'Sorry, old son. On me next time. Got a wife to get back to. I'll be in touch.'

That was it. As usual Joe Lassiter managed to leave me seething and punching the air with frustration. Living in his shadowy world, he seemed to have the ability to disappear into thin air whenever it suited him.

Anyway, that had been three days earlier, three days before I got Jazz's phone call out of the blue.

I'd spent the morning in a meeting with the solicitors of Messrs Tapsells trying to persuade them to keep me on, despite the late delivery of my investigation report. I was unsuccessful. In the afternoon, I put the disappointment to the back of my mind and wrote up my wish-list of improved office and surveillance equipment to hand to Lassiter.

It was just gone five in the evening when Kate picked up the telephone. 'Philip Mason Associates. My name's Kate, how may I help you?'

God, how I wish she wouldn't say that! It made us sound like a bloody call-centre.

'It's for you,' Kate said, her hand over the mouthpiece. 'Someone called Jasmina. Very sexy voice.'

Surprised, I reached out and took the offered receiver. 'Hallo.'

There was a breathless giggle at the other end. 'Is that your secretary, Phil? For a moment I thought she said Philip Marlow Associates.'

I smiled. 'What, the Raymond Chandler private eye? I'm not that good.'

She said, 'You left your card on the kitchen table.'

'Careless of me.'

'I'm sorry, I was rude.'

'You were angry, rightly so.'

'Yes, that too. But I should have at least listened to you, let you explain.'

I said quickly, 'We can still do that.'

'Not if it means working with Lassiter.'

'You wouldn't be working with Lassiter, you'd be working with me,' I explained, building a bridge as fast as I could. 'I'd report to him, not you.'

'In that case, I might be interested to hear what you've got to say.'

I frowned. 'I'm curious, Jazz. What's brought about this change of heart?'

There was a hesitation. 'I had a row with one of the receptionists. I'm afraid I walked out.'

Well, it wasn't the best of motives for starting a new job, but that didn't worry me. Maybe I should have thought more about it, but I didn't.

We arranged to meet for lunch the next day at a riverside pub in Chiswick to discuss her job offer. It didn't sound that great, being somewhat sparse on detail. I didn't know how much I was going to be paid by the Security Service, so I couldn't yet give her a salary figure, hours of work or exactly what she'd be doing.

She smiled at me over her prawn salad. 'So what's the wow factor, Phil?'

'You'll be working with me.'

'Mmm,' she responded dubiously. 'When Lassiter approached me before you, he said something about infiltrating Muslim communities in Britain. Is that the sort of thing?'

'Not exactly,' I replied. 'As I understand it, MI5 is overwhelmed with possible al-Qaeda suspects in the UK. We'll be asked to look at a few low-grade assessments so that they can be eliminated from security inquiries. A sort of safety net.'

Her eyes lit up a little. 'If it'll help stop more bombing attempts in London, I'm up for that. That's quite a wow factor.'

'What worries me,' I said, 'is the possibility of long hours and you having to look after your daughter.'

Jazz shrugged. 'We'll have to see. If the money's good then child-minding won't be a problem. And Ricardo's parents love looking after Zoë – any excuse, in fact.'

'It's good you still get on with them,' I said. 'And good for Zoë.'

'Yes, especially as only my mum is alive now and she's very frail. I think it's good for children to relate to grandparents, get spoiled. I regret I never knew mine.'

I said, 'My grandad was a lobster fisherman – I loved going out with him on the boat – and my grandma made the most delicious shortbread you've ever tasted. It melted in the mouth like butter.'

Jazz laughed lightly, then said, 'Okay, Phil, you've sold me on a job I know absolutely nothing about . . . Despite that, when do I start?'

'How about the day after tomorrow? Lassiter's set up a briefing at Thames House at eleven, could you make that?'

'You bet.'

'We'll go through the tradesman's entrance,' Lassiter said, once Jazz and I met him in the reception area of Westminster Hospital, situated just a short distance from Thames House, headquarters of the Security Service, which is on Millbank, overlooking the river. 'God knows which bright spark thought we should tell the world the location of our top two most secret organizations!'

A busy hospital entrance to meet people was a bit more original than the usual hotel lobby, but the principle was the same – to go unnoticed in the crowd.

Lassiter had been on his best behaviour with Jazz, managing to shake hands without a lascivious leer on his face. After brief acknowledgements, we walked with him out of the building into Horseferry Road and, to my surprise, crossed the street to the Magistrates' Court. Jazz, too, looked somewhat bemused as we passed the motley collection of barristers in wigs, smartly suited solicitors and clerks, police officers and ordinary people who were there to stand trial, give evidence and do their civil duty on a jury. We paused outside a nondescript panelled door marked simply 'Private – No Entry' while Lassiter punched a code number into the keypad. We followed him into a short, plain-painted passage which was dimly lit by a single white globe lamp. After a few metres we descended a staircase until we found ourselves confronted by a wooden door with an electronic swipe-card lock.

'Don't be fooled by that,' Lassiter said, 'it's made of bomb-proof steel.'

On the other side we were greeted by a security guard, an older man with white hair and a florid complexion, sitting behind a multi-image CCTV screen. An automatic pistol was holstered on his hip.

Lassiter showed his pass. 'I've got two guests.'

'Right you are, Mr Lassiter,' the guard replied, consulting his day-book. 'Mr Mason and a Miss Alagic?'

'That's correct,' Lassiter confirmed.

The guard handed over two lapel badges. 'Wear these at all times and please don't lose them.' Was there a hint of menace in those smiling eyes? 'Or you'll be in big trouble.'

Once we were pinned up, Lassiter had us pass through the metal-detection arch. 'A mere precaution for all visitors,' he assured us then led us past a small guardroom, through some swing doors and into a wide corridor of ageing white tiles with strip-lighting that reminded me of some of the older Underground stations. Jazz's shoes clacked on the plain concrete floor.

'This is part of the old tunnelling system used during

the war,' he explained. 'Wide enough and high enough to take a small truck. Miles of tunnels under London, you'd be surprised.'

'I see,' Jazz said, 'and of course the Magistrates' Court is a public building.'

Lassiter nodded. 'Plenty of coming and going, so our people can slip in and out. They use the front when the court's open or the back door out of hours; no one would ever suspect.'

I asked, 'Who uses the front entrance to Thames House?'

'Not field officers, that's for sure,' he replied. 'Mostly secretaries and non-controversial visitors. But even that can be a headache in this current climate. Easy enough to photograph people on the steps with a telephoto lens. Follow them home, get a positive ID, and set them up. Blackmail, a honeytrap . . . As I said, I don't know who's bright idea it was to put the place on the map in the first place.'

The corridor was long and straight and seemed to go on for ever. We only passed two people, a couple, coming the other way and they didn't spare us a second glance. At last we reached the brushed aluminium doors of a large and very modern lift which propelled us fast and silently up into the heart of Thames House.

The doors sighed open. 'Second floor,' said Lassiter and stepped out into a small and windowless, steel-walled holding area manned by two guards at a desk. They checked our IDs before allowing us through the security door and into the main body of the building.

It could have been any commercial office anywhere in the world. Grey carpet, magnolia walls, open-plan with low partitioned walls to give a semblance of privacy. I thought what a far cry it was from the slick and shiny space-age look MI5 had been given in the popular *Spooks* TV drama, which I had only ever watched once and never again.

Lassiter led us to one of the partitioned work stations. 'My cubbyhole,' he announced, removing his fedora and raincoat and hanging it on an old-fashioned stand. 'Makes me feel like a battery hen. In the old days I'd have had a proper little office all to myself.'

I looked around at the bland teak desk with its flat-screen computer and three telephones, and on the wall behind it a calendar, a photograph of a woman and child, and a nude picture of the busty celebrity model Jordan. 'Don't the female staff object to that?' I asked lightly, remembering how he'd been complaining that women had virtually taken over the running of the place.

'Yes,' he replied emphatically, 'that's why I put it there. This is my personal space. Just making a point.'

Jazz glanced sideways at me while Lassiter bent to unlock a solid-looking steel filing cabinet. He extracted a file. 'Right, let's go to the briefing room.'

The briefing room was behind partitioned walls and windowless and, Lassiter explained, swept daily for bugging devices. There were ranks of utility plastic-topped tables facing a platform which had display boards on the wall behind it and a large plasma television screen for computerized projections.

Felicity Goodall was standing beside one of the front-row tables and turned her head at our approach. She looked stunning in a beige linen jacket and skirt with a chocolate-coloured blouse. Her fair hair was drawn back severely from her face in a bun, just to let us know she meant business.

With her were two men, who couldn't have looked more different from each other.

'Charles Houseman,' Lassiter introduced the taller man first. 'He's your direct liaison with SIS. That is, of course, the Secret Intelligence Service, or MI6.'

An expensive cream summer suit with hand-stitched lapels showed off a very slim and fit-looking body for someone in his mid-forties. Crinkly dark-blond hair was brushed straight back from the forehead of the perma-tan face, which was lit up by beautifully white teeth that just had to have been capped. His lazy smile did them justice.

'Pleased to meet you, Phil.' His handshake was firm and strong. 'And this charming lady, Jasmina.'

'Down, boy,' Lassiter growled.

Houseman laughed lightly while he stared directly into Jazz's eyes as though trying to hypnotize her. 'I'm totally at your service, any time day or night. I'm an Arabist and my background is the Iraq Desk, but since 9/11 I've been seconded to a special al-Qaeda liaison team. Anything you need to know, just call.'

Lassiter turned to the second man, who didn't wait for the introduction. 'I'm Inspector Ian Proctor, Special Branch. Pleased to meet you both.'

Unlike Houseman, the police officer didn't look as though he'd seen daylight, let alone sunshine, for weeks. His dark hair, greying at the temples, was tousled and it looked as if he'd got up too late for a morning shave, or else hadn't got to bed in the first place. His charcoal suit was certainly creased enough to have been slept in. His eyes looked tired and strained as he added, 'Think of me as your Pet Plod. I'm your official arm of the law, if it's needed. If I can help you on anything MI5 or Six can't, then I'll do my best. We're being kept in the loop on these jokers you're looking at. We make any arrests that are officially sanctioned by the Security Service, and we'll hopefully bale you out if you get arrested by local police during the course of your work.' He smiled thinly. 'But I'd prefer that didn't happen, understand?'

I nodded. 'Perfectly. That wouldn't be my intention.'

Proctor regarded me steadily. 'Good intentions pave the road to hell, Mr Mason, as you know. If any of these jokers are a bad lot, and you get caught, then I could have a corpse on my hands. And I wouldn't want that.'

'We'll be careful,' Jazz assured.

'Miss Alagic,' he acknowledged solemnly. 'You served with 14 Int in Northern Ireland, I believe? Those sort of gung-ho attitudes have no place on the mainland, remember that.'

Felicity Goodall intervened. 'Really, Ian, I'm sure Miss

Alagic and Phil know what they're doing, otherwise we wouldn't have invited them aboard.'

Proctor looked a little abashed. 'Yes, Miss Goodall, I'm sure you're right. I'm tired, a bit tetchy, that's all. Sorry.'

She touched his arm. 'That's fine. And call me Felicity. I'm sure your work is frantic with all the anti-terrorist activities going on.'

He nodded and smiled grimly. 'That and a baby son. Last night was my turn after two shifts back to back.'

'Bless,' Lassiter said without feeling.

Felicity turned to Houseman. 'Would you like to kick off, Chas, with a bit of background? We'll keep all this informal.'

'My pleasure,' the MI6 man replied, and hopped deftly onto the low platform. 'Very briefly, as you'll be aware the man credited with being at the centre of what can only be described as a modern "Jihad" or holy war is Osama bin Laden.'

'Or Bed Linen, as some of us like to call him,' Lassiter muttered and earned a scowl from Felicity.

'From a wealthy Saudi family,' Houseman continued, unfazed, 'bin Laden went to Afghanistan to fight with the Mujahideen against the Soviet invasion in the early eighties and received training from the CIA. Then and subsequently, he and many of his peers began to develop a distaste for the West, which in their eyes, came to include the new Russia.

'Bin Laden and his friends considered these nations morally and socially corrupt – devoted to permissive sexual mores, the amoral entertainment business, guzzling alcohol and drugs with corporate business taking over the commercial world and squeezing profits from the world's poor. All against the teachings of Allah. America was top of the hate list, of course, as they were and are seen to be propping up Israel and keeping millions of Palestinians in poverty and refugee camps.'

Felicity interrupted, 'You have to say that they have a point. Forty per cent of all US civil and military aid is poured into Tel Aviv. The Jewish lobby holds huge sway in Washington.'

I listened with interest. It had struck me over the years that the United States could have put pressure on Israel to give up the Arab lands it had occupied and built on since the '67 and '73 wars. If the Americans had, then it clearly had not been anything like enough.

Houseman said, 'And, of course, the Yanks have always been seen as interfering in the Middle East politically to ensure its thirst for oil is satisfied.'

I raised my hand. 'Wasn't the First Gulf War the trigger to all the trouble?'

'Exactly,' Houseman replied. 'Although not so much the invasion of Kuwait by Iraq and the Gulf War itself, it was the fact that these American infidel forces were based in the holiest of all countries, Saudi Arabia. Bin Laden and his cohorts had always hated the Saudi royals sucking up to Washington, but this was the last straw! War was declared on both Saudi Arabia and America.'

Felicity chipped in with, 'You must remember that the

bin Laden team was still based in Afghanistan and was now well in with the fundamentalist Taliban government who took over after the Russians had been driven out. Bin Laden had support from neighbouring Pakistan, especially elements of the intelligence service and secret police.'

'The bin Laden network is reckoned by some to have been initially founded way back in 1988,' Houseman continued, 'after the Russians retreated from Afghanistan. It began its war against the West in a fairly small way in 1992. Two bombs were set off in Aden. Aimed at hotels where it was thought US troops were staying while in transit to Somalia to assist in an international aid effort. But al-Qaeda hit the wrong hotels and no Americans were killed. Two others were though and seven badly injured.

'Then there was the first attempt to blow up the Twin Towers with a truck bomb in 1993, followed by attacks on the US including the East African embassy bombing in 1998 and the attack on the destroyer USS Cole in 2000.

'Of course you may know, the word "organisation" has always been a misnomer. Bin Laden and his cohorts in al-Qaeda set up training camps in Afghanistan, then mostly mentored and funded Islamic fundamentalist groups in their own countries, providing specialist help and advice if required.'

'More of a network?' I suggested.

Houseman smiled thinly. 'Good description. In fact the word al-Qaeda means "The Foundation". And its operation has been even more like that of a network since 9/11 and the invasion of Afghanistan. It was like trying to break a spider's web with stones. Robbed of a truly safe refuge, bin Laden continued his war on us via the Internet and satellite communications, so we're no closer to finding him.'

'The damage was already done,' Felicity added. 'He'd already had fundamentalist Islam clerics around the world, including here in Britain, preaching and converting young and disconsolate Muslims to his cause.'

'Any Muslim with a grievance,' Lassiter said, 'began to see the US as the root cause of all his woes – however ridiculous that may seem to us. After 9/11 most would have come to regard bin Laden as a sort of Robin Hood hero for striking the enemy in such spectacular fashion.'

Felicity nodded her agreement. 'And the invasion by the US and Britain of Afghanistan and Iraq just seemed to confirm bin Laden's warnings. Now we're seen to be as guilty as America.'

'In this country,' Houseman said, glancing at his watch, 'most recruits will be from Muslim communities, but not exclusively. They've most likely been born here and still have family ties abroad. Arab states across North Africa, the Middle East, south Asian states, Pakistan and down into Indonesia.'

Jazz spoke for the first time. 'Does that apply to the people you want us to take a look at?'

'Yes, Jasmina,' Felicity said, smiling, 'pretty much. I'll go on to that next.' She turned and looked up at Houseman. 'I know you're anxious to get off, Charles. Thanks very much for that.'

He stepped down off the platform. 'Pleasure,' he said, then looked at Jazz and me – although his focus was distinctly more on her. 'Don't forget, call any time you want help or advice, or just to run something past me.' He handed over two calling cards. 'Ring the office number or my mobile if it's urgent.'

As Houseman sauntered from the room, Felicity stood up and took a remote control unit from the front desk. She pressed a button and the giant plasma screen flickered into life, revealing a coloured map of the UK. She said, 'Although you won't hear the politicians saying it, the international situation has indeed become a jihad or holy war between Christians and Muslims.' She turned to Jasmina with a sympathetic smile. 'Sadly that means the enemy is to be found chiefly in the Muslim communities around the country, the majority of which are Pakistani or Bangladeshi. But, of course, that doesn't exclude Arabs, North Africans or converts from the white or black communities. There are currently 1.59 million Muslims in the UK and the recruiting masters for al-Qaeda will ruthlessly exploit any one of them they can get their claws into. And we know there are a lot of potential recruits out there. In fact, there are getting on for two thousand suspects and we currently have some two hundred under full surveillance. Dozens of major terrorist attacks have been thwarted since 9/11.'

Lassiter added, 'Unfortunately, the July 7 one slipped the net.'

'Why', I asked, 'is it proving so easy to recruit these

kids, especially the ones born here? I mean Pakistanis have lived in this country for years. Hard workers, corner shops and all that. There's never been trouble until recently.'

'We can't say it's easy,' Felicity chided. 'Not many people are prepared to blow themselves up, thank God. But there is a huge and growing pool of potential recruits.' She sighed. 'As to the reason for that, it is frighteningly simple. Like West Indians in the fifties, Pakistanis, Bangladeshis and Indians came over to work because we needed them in the cotton and wool mills and clothes manufacturing industries. Places like Bradford, Leicester and Birmingham as well as London. Older generations were poorly educated, many couldn't speak English. There was a big religious and cultural divide between them and the white population and they just didn't integrate well with the rest of society in the same way that the black population gradually has.'

Lassiter smirked. 'Politically incorrect to say so, of course. But then we all remember the Paki-bashing incidents in the sixties and seventies . . . young Muslims didn't grow up here feeling exactly welcomed by the rest of us. And, of course, as is well known, our extreme right-wing political parties haven't helped.'

'As the UK's manufacturing base shrank,' Felicity continued, 'a lot of the industries the Muslims worked in were disappearing. So now we have a lot of unemployed, often poorly educated and disaffected youth, alienated religiously and culturally, who rarely mix outside their own family and community. They turn to drugs and crime.'

'Fertile ground for al-Qaeda's recruiting masters,' Lassiter explained. 'They ensnare the kids at the local mosque, youth clubs, wherever. Blame their woes on the Yanks, of course, and now the British authorities. Tell them how we're persecuting and killing their brother Muslims all over the world. Afghanistan, Palestine, Iraq – a very skewed perspective, but one the kids want to believe, especially when they're shown horrendous video footage of the dead and injured.'

Jazz said, 'I suppose things like the prisoners held without trial at Guantánamo Bay and the torture at Abu Ghraib don't help.'

Lassiter gave her a curious look. 'No, probably not. The recruiters aren't slow to make mileage out of that sort of thing. Then they offer a chance for the young recruits to turn their lives around – and hit back in the name of Allah. They are brought together in small groups. These lads find they have a lot in common and bond together.'

'A bit like regular army training,' Felicity added, 'they become a small band of brothers, protecting each other, not wanting to let their new friends down. Old friends and family become remote, even alien. If they're sent abroad together to terrorist training camps, the bond is all the stronger.'

Lassiter sighed. 'The sad thing is, it works.'

I was starting to see problems just begging to happen. 'Look, Joe, thinking about this, I'm not so sure it's going to work. I'm a Caucasian male and we'll almost certainly be needing to conduct close surveillance work in ethnic neighbourhoods. It won't be like Northern Ireland. I know bugger all about Muslims or the Koran. I'm not sure even Jazz does.'

Jazz flashed one of her disarming smiles. 'I've learnt a lot more in recent years, my husband was quite devout.'

'There you are,' Felicity said. 'I'm sure Miss Alagic can brief you on the basics. There are many lapsed Muslims like there are Catholics. As for looks, you've got black hair, a dark complexion . . .'

Felicity didn't appear concerned. 'Don't forget there are some whites in all areas. You can always pose as a white tradesman or businessman, depending on the situation.'

I must still have looked unhappy, because she added suddenly, 'I've just thought of something . . . or rather someone.'

That took Lassiter by surprise. 'Who? What d'you mean?'

Felicity sucked thoughtfully on the end of her pencil. 'I think they call him Popadom, the little Pakistani chap who works for A4, one of our watchers.'

'I think so,' Lassiter said. 'What about him?'

'Someone was saying in the bar last night, he's broken his leg. He's been desk-bound and hating it. Perhaps we could borrow him for Phil.'

'A4 won't like that.'

'From what I heard, I think they will. Apparently he's useless at paperwork, more trouble than he's worth. I'll chase up on it as soon as we've finished here.'

Great, I thought, an assistant on crutches. Things might have been a little more promising, surely?

I could tell Lassiter knew what I was thinking, and he couldn't keep the smirk from his face. 'Right, let's move on to your hotlist, Phil . . . the six people we'd like you to take a look at . . .'

Two days later, Popadom turned up at my Brixton office.

I could have missed him when I opened the front door. He stood at barely over five feet tall in his highly polished black brogues. Well, only one shoe in fact, because his right foot was in a plaster cast that disappeared up into the trouser leg of a crisp, immaculate navy suit. His white shirt, finished with a tie knotted in a small neat Windsor, seemed to glow in its brilliance. It was a glow that was matched by his even teeth and wide smile set in an agreeable face with big brown puppydog eyes. His jet black hair was gelled and combed with total precision. He hung precariously between a pair of crutches, a bulging leather briefcase held with obvious difficulty in one hand.

'Ah, Mr Phil, I presume?' He struggled to balance as he raised his free hand in an attempt to shake mine. 'I am Popadom.'

'It might be best not to try that,' I said.

He smiled sheepishly. 'Yes, perhaps you are right. I'll be no good to you at all with two broken legs. And I am so grateful to you, you have saved my bacon!' He saw the expression on my face. 'Just a little Islamic joke.'

I stepped back. 'You'd better come in.'

Popadom hopped and swung past me and I ushered him through to my living room, which was fast becoming a makeshift second office, stuffed with a lounge suite, chairs and a battered dining table. Jazz and I had spent the morning laying out documents and photographs of our first six suspects on it.

'Let me take that from you,' she said, relieving the new arrival of his briefcase. 'I really can't call you Popadom, can I? What's your real name?'

He shook his head a fraction. 'My real name is unpronounceable – even to me! I have been Popadom since I was a small boy, even in the army. Or Pops for short.'

I raised an eyebrow in surprise. 'The British Army?'

He turned to me. 'Is there any other? I was a pongo, but as you can guess not in the Guards. I was with the Royal Green Jackets – a fine regiment of foot. Sadly amalgamated thanks to those imbecile civil servants in Whitehall.'

I was beginning to learn that when Popadom was around, you rarely stopped smiling.

'How did you get into MI5?' Jazz asked.

'I volunteered for 14 Int,' he replied. 'That was the start of it.'

'Never!' Jazz exclaimed, taken totally off-guard. 'Me, too. When were you in?'

'From 1986 to 1988.'

Jazz smiled. 'A little before my time.'

'They are a proper regiment now, you know?'

'Really?' I was as surprised to hear that as Jazz.

Popadom grinned proudly. 'The Special Reconnaissance Regiment was formed in 2005 for world-wide
operations. But just now a lot are deployed in London.
Makes me even madder I am stuck behind an infernal
desk! All because of some litter lout!'

I was intrigued. This indomitable little elite warrior
brought down by a litter lout. 'How did that happen?'

'I fell over a bloody damn tin of Coca-Cola left on the
pavement! I went down like a ninepin!' He raised his eyes
to the heavens. 'And I am following someone at the time.
I could not believe it!'

Jazz showed sympathy. 'I think you had better sit down.'

He glanced at the table with the neatly laid-out dossiers
and manoeuvred himself into a straight-backed chair to
look at them. 'Ah, I see you are on the case. I have been
familiarizing myself with the files on these people. On
the surface they do not look like promising candidates.'

'Which, I guess, is why they've been handed to us,' I
said.

Popadom shook his head. 'Do not be so sure, Mr Phil.
My department is trying to keep two hundred people
under surveillance. Few of those will be up to serious no
good, either. Maybe it is no more than an email intercepted to a friend that glorifies some terrorist act. Or a
phone call to someone else who is suspected of having al-
Qaeda connections. These six may be no more or less
likely to be involved. Sometimes it doesn't pay to have too
much intelligence. This was a mistake the former Soviet
Union made.'

'Not seeing the wood for the trees,' Jazz acknowledged.

Popadom nodded. 'The thing about these six are that most have a connection of some kind with the three in custody at Belmarsh. Mullah Reda or the owner of the restaurant chain, Hasan Malik. Or the man who runs the radical Islamic bookshop, Abu Hejah. Even these people may be innocent, of course.'

Jazz frowned. 'Felicity Goodall's damn certain they're not. They could even have some connection with the failed bombings in London and Glasgow.'

Popadom smiled politely. 'That's as maybe, but as yet we cannot be certain we will get a conviction in court,' he said quietly. 'Meanwhile our six only have two points of connection with the accused or two other points of suspicion . . . And for a start, I believe I know that man.'

Everyone's eyes followed the direction of Popadom's pointing finger. The blown-up passport photograph was of a kindly looking, middle-aged Pakistani with a greying moustache and hair.

'Akmal Younis,' I observed. 'Aged sixty and a widower.'

'Like the held suspect Malik, he now runs a chain of curry-houses. Most in London, but a few in Birmingham.'

'How do you know him?' Jazz asked.

'A very, very long time ago I met him. He was a close friend of my late uncle. I was just eleven at the time and Younis had his first little restaurant. I was taken with them to eat there. It was the first time I had ever been taken to eat out. I thought the food was wonderful!'

'So what's Younis' connection?' I muttered, consulting the notes spread out on the table. 'Ah, he's a personal friend of the Merry Mullah and prays at his mosque . . . and his email address was found on Malik's email address list.'

Popadom said, 'Neither of those things should surprise us. Mullah Reda has been at Younis' local mosque for years and Malik has a rival chain of curry-houses.'

'But Malik is also suspected of running an illegal immigrant business,' I pointed out. 'A chain of curry-houses is excellent cover. Maybe the two have that in common, too.'

Popadom shook his head with disapproval. 'That is jumping the gun, Mr Phil, if I may say so.'

I could see his point, but then maybe his childhood memory was clouding his mind to the possibility. 'What are the other connections?' I asked, moving on.

'You could say that the main link is that radical Islamic website called Guardians of Paradise. It is hosted by a theologian called Naved Hussein from Syria. The site promotes extremist views, condemns Israel, America and the West, praises acts of terrorism, and shows videoclips of alleged atrocities committed by allied forces in Iraq and Afghanistan. We know the site is bankrolled by a Saudi with definite al-Qaeda connections.' Popadom looked at me. 'Naved is a long-time personal friend of Mullah Reda who, as you know, always gave the impression of supporting moderation. It was that unlikely friendship that first alerted Felicity Goodall to the possibility that Reda was up to no good.'

Jazz said, 'And that website also has a direct link to Hejah Abu's bookshop. Mail order.'

Popadom nodded. 'Don't forget also that Hejah runs a wide programme of study groups and circles in the Midlands and North East . . . Anyway, website monitoring by our office picked up the next two suspects. The first was Leonard Fryatt.'

I looked down at the picture of a disconsolate-looking young black man with unruly long hair. 'Aged twenty-four,' I read aloud. 'Born here of Jamaican parentage. Lives on some council estate in Lewisham, south London.'

Popadom consulted his own notes. 'Leo is a frequent visitor to the Guardians of Paradise website and he has purchased many titles via the link to Hejah's bookshop. He's also attended a couple of Hejah's study groups.'

Jazz said, 'I thought there had to be two links for each suspect.'

'Ah, quite so,' Popadom replied. 'Leo has also shown up on police files as being a member of Allah's Army. It's a local quasi-religious gang of young Muslim thugs and criminals.'

I pondered that as I began rolling a cigarette. 'He may be a nasty piece of work,' I said, 'but it hardly makes him a likely terror suspect.'

'I agree,' Popadom replied, 'and that also applies to the next suspect even more so, I should think. The woman.'

Jazz leaned over the desk. 'Huda Dahdah' – she stifled a giggle – 'unfortunate name. Syrian apparently. A widow

with a young son. Husband was a suicide bomber killed in
Iraq last year . . . God, how awful.'

'Huda continues to download lots of images from the
Guardians of Paradise website, and a lot of videoclips of
atrocities and suicide bombers taken by al-Qaeda.'

I said, 'Maybe she's trying to find the image of the
moment her husband died.'

Jazz added, 'Or trying to justify her husband's deed in
her own head? A way to cope.'

'Could be,' I agreed. But I'd already moved on to the
next suspect, who had grabbed my attention from the
moment I'd first seen his file. For a start he was Welsh,
white and, I thought, I might have come across him
once.

Popadom saw me looking at the photograph. 'Ah yes,
Mr Phil, I thought he might fascinate you. David Evans.'

'Dave Mohammed Evans,' Jazz corrected. 'Converted
and changed his name by deed poll last year after serving
with the British Army in Afghanistan.'

'Amazing, isn't it?' Popadom said. 'What would make
an experienced Para do such a thing?'

I thought I had an idea, but I really didn't want to think
back to my time in a war theatre just then. Reluctantly I
said, 'I think I might know him?'

Jazz look across the table at me. 'You told me you were
in Afghanistan,' she said. 'Did you see him there?'

'No, I don't think our paths crossed.'

'I can check out his military history,' Popadom said
quickly. 'Maybe that will help jog your memory.'

'Good idea,' I agreed.

'Well, wherever you might have met him, Mohammed Evans appears to know his stuff. He's been giving lectures at some of Hejah's study circles. And I'm not talking about readings from the Koran.'

With that, Popadom produced a very slick, state-of-the-art mobile phone from his pocket, punched a number and was soon talking to someone at the MoD.

'All done,' he announced. 'They'll call me back.'

'That,' Jazz said, 'leaves us with the last two. The first is a corporate accountant and now lecturer in IT and computer science at Imperial College. An Egyptian called Dr Samir Hashim.'

'He is believed to have designed the website for Guardians of Paradise,' Popadom explained. 'He's a friend of the webmaster Naved Hussein. He's also done other website work for a member of the Saudi royal family, who's known to have sent money to al-Qaeda leaders.'

'So guilt by association,' I observed.

'I agree,' Popadom said. 'But then, as the saying goes, you can judge a man by the company he is keeping.'

'Or the job he does?' Jazz suggested mischievously.

But Popadom didn't rise to the bait. 'Finally we come to Akhtar Shahid, a fellow countryman of mine. A twenty-three-year-old student of Dr Samir at Imperial College. This young man runs a private Muslim discussion group at the university, which is very fundamentalist and anti-West. His email address was found in the deleted file on the computer belonging to the bookseller who is in custody. Also last summer Shahid spent several weeks studying at a madrassa in Lahore.'

'What's a madrassa?' I asked.

'I'm sorry, Mr Phil, it is a religious college devoted to Islamic studies. This particular madrassa is known for its radical anti-Western influence.'

At that moment the door opened and Kate appeared carrying a tray. 'Anyone for tea and choccy bics?' she asked with her usual angelic smile.

'Oh, dear me,' Popadom exclaimed. 'I am a martyr to chocolate biscuits. I really am going to enjoy working here—' He was interrupted by the ring of his mobile.

Kate poured out the tea while Popadom listened to the caller and feverishly jotted in his notepad with a pen.

Finally he closed his phone and looked up. 'That was about David Mohammed Evans. I have all the details here, but I think I know the answer, Mr Phil.'

'Yes?'

'In 2002, Paratrooper Sergeant David Evans was on one of your courses at the British Army Sniper School.'

I felt an involuntary shiver like a trickle of icy water down my spine.

Four

It was one of the few nice days of that miserable summer. The sun was high and hot in a sky of porcelain blue. Stained, grey concrete monoliths of sixties tower blocks cast harsh shadows on the surrounding wasteland. Beer cans and polystyrene junk-food wrappers wallowed in the gutters and plastic bags littered the communal lawns that the local council had not bothered to mow. No one here was likely to complain.

I parked my blue Transit alongside a garage block, its rusty up-and-over doors daubed in artless graffiti. There was a repugnant rap poem in red paint that poured scorn and vitriol on the police, women and civilized society in general. There were a surprising number of slogans in Arabic script.

For those who couldn't translate, the central door was devoted to a half-moon symbol in black paint and the legend: This is the land of Allah's Army — Enter at your peril, infidels!

I wound down the window of the van and was immediately aware of the heat and fetid smell of decay. Even the aroma of some spicy Caribbean dish wafting from an open window couldn't disguise the faint hint of dog faeces and human urine in the air; in fact, it just made it worse. From somewhere high above, a ghetto-blaster pumped out an urgent, irritating rhythm and unintelligible words.

So this was the home of Leonard Fryatt, twenty-four-year-old black drug-dealer and urban warrior for Allah.

In front of me, at an oblique angle, was the entrance to the block, guarded by two girls, who were leaning against the wall together, smoking, as they eyed passers-by suspiciously. I could watch them, but they could only see the offside front of my cab. The black girl had big Afro hair like a halo and must have sprayed on the minuscule skirt that clung to her ample hips. Her skinny white friend resembled a living corpse with straggly blonde hair and dark rings beneath her eyes.

It had been two weeks since our initial meeting with Popadom at my office. We had decided to look at our six suspects in relays. As there were only three of us, Popadom, Jazz and I would take it in turns to view each of them, then compare notes. Popadom had begun the process with Leo Fryatt the previous day. Although restricted to his car, the stoic little MI5 operator had managed to clock the young man when he'd left the block of flats where he still lived with his widowed Jamaican mother. Leo was clearly a night owl because he hadn't emerged until noon yesterday and Jazz had seen nothing of him on today's early morning shift before I took over.

Leo was UK-born of Jamaican parents. He'd a history of truancy from school and was in trouble with the police from an early age. His father had died in a pub brawl when Leo was twelve.

As a youngster Leo had achieved no academic qualifications and had apparently only ever held down a job once. He'd been valeting cars for three months when the company's owner reported him to the police for stealing from the customers' vehicles. Since then he'd been drawing the dole although he seemed to have another occupation, given the number of times he was arrested for drug-dealing. Two years earlier he'd spent six months in prison.

Recently he'd been under surveillance by local police investigating a so-called Islamic gang of thugs calling themselves the Army of Allah.

Leo did not appear to have a bank account, but then considering the gang's ethos of using cash – probably stolen – that was hardly surprising. His online book purchases via the Guardians of Paradise website had been paid for using his mother's credit card. She usually had a running debit balance of between minus three and five hundred pounds, and appeared to be struggling to keep her head above financial hot water.

Popadom had already managed to identify a few of Leo's favourite haunts where he'd give a high-five greeting to a group of friends, some black but others Asian or white. That was in a small local park, but he met others in a greasy-spoon café, a community centre and a run-down pub. I wondered where the trail would lead today.

My thoughts were interrupted by the sudden appearance of Leo Fryatt at the entrance to the flats. He was tall, thin and walked with hunched shoulders. Despite the hot day he wore a 'hoody', a dull grey jogging top, over his yellow shirt and a pair of jeans with designer tears in them. His hair had been fine-plaited and had been run back over his scalp to form a small pigtail at the back of his neck.

He paused for a moment, hands thrust deep into the pockets of his top, and scanned his surroundings with an angry scowl.

'Hi, big boy!' the black girl greeted, smiling with bright tombstone teeth. 'How y'doin', Leo?'

The white girl said nothing while he regarded them both with little less than contempt. 'I'm cool, how're you?'

'I'm good.'

'I hope you are,' Leo replied. ''Cos you ain't dressed like you're good. You're dressed like a couple of whores. Look at them skirts you're nearly wearing.'

The white girl sneered. 'Like to take a good look though, don't you, Leo?'

Fryatt ignored that. 'You ain't got no shame before Allah.'

'Think Allah's seen it all before,' the white girl retorted. 'Why don't you run away and play with those Muslim wanker friends of yours.'

Leo's mouth curled into an ugly snarl. 'You won't be so lippy if they catch you dressed like that.'

'Ooh, look at me, I'm trembling with fear!' The white girl turned to her friend. 'C'mon, Sonia, I've had enough of this tosser. Let's go down the shops and get a couple of Red Bulls.'

The young man watched them go with dark, sullen eyes. Then, hands still thrust in the pockets of his top, he loped off in the opposite direction, across the weed-infested paving slabs, to a footpath that would take him to the main road.

I turned the van ignition on, got into gear and drove back out to the main entrance of the estate. There I pulled into a lay-by and climbed out as Leo approached the end of the footpath, some fifty metres further along the main road. He turned right and I crossed the slow-moving line of traffic to follow on the opposite pavement. If he repeated the previous days' pattern, then he was heading for the community centre or the Black Dog pub. Of course, given his broken leg, Popadom had been unable to follow inside either place. I could, but I wondered how the hell I'd handle it if someone from Leo's gang of friends became suspicious and engaged me in conversation.

I had a cover story that might work. The idea had come from another suspect, Dave Evans.

In fact I couldn't decide whether it might not be better to call at his mother's flat as a British Telecom worker or from the electricity company; at least Popadom had provided us with a selection of authentic ID cards from MI5, so we all had a number of options. Leo's mother might welcome the chance to chat to a stranger sorting out a telephone fault and bemoan her wayward son. But then I also surmised that Leo was unlikely to have confided much to her about his more dubious activities.

As it happened the decision was taken out of my hands. Leo suddenly crossed to my side of the road and disappeared. I hurried my pace, thinking he'd gone into a shop. In fact I found he'd turned into an alley between two shops that ran behind the gardens of the houses in the next side-street.

I let the distance between us grow a little more, then sauntered after him. Way in the distance, coming the other way, was a young white woman pushing a pram.

Then, for no apparent reason, Leo glanced behind him and stared straight at me for a couple of seconds, but without slackening his pace. In fact, I was sure he was walking a little quicker. I couldn't respond, because I'd have blown it.

But then, had he sussed me already? Surely not. He'd have no reason to.

Well, he had a reason all right, but not the one I expected. It was to give himself more time as he approached the woman with the pram. Suddenly he flipped up the hood of his jogging top and stepped to one side, blocking the young mother's path. I saw the sunlight flashing on the knife blade.

The woman uttered a scream that was cut short. I couldn't see why, because Leo was in the way.

Acting on instinct, I sprinted forward. My heart was thudding as I ran, and my leg muscles protested at the sudden and unfamiliar burst of exertion. My thick-soled trainers deadened the sound of my fast approach. Leo must have thought he had a lot more time because he didn't even turn round.

As I neared I could see the knife in his right fist pointed at the baby's face. His left hand was outstretched, palm up, as the woman, her face white with fear, began removing her shoulder bag.

At the last moment Leo sensed my arrival and turned, but he was too late. My left arm slipped under his right and jerked hard back, pulling the blade away from the baby. Then I knuckle-punched him in the bicep, the sudden stab of pain sending the knife spinning from his grasp. It was then that the mother's shoulder-bag caught him full force in the face. He gasped and fell back against me as I twisted and jerked his arm high up behind his spine. A thin trickle of blood escaped from his nostril.

The mother stared at me, open-mouthed. 'Thank you,' she muttered, 'thank you so much.'

I nodded. 'Best you go, keep the baby safe.'

She didn't need to be told a second time and hurried away, pushing the pram towards the main road.

When she'd vanished, I kicked the knife well out of reach, and released Leo. He fell back against the fence, nursing his arm and scowling at me.

'Sorry, I couldn't let you do that,' I said evenly.

His frown deepened. 'Who the fuck are you?'

I said, 'Someone who's just saved you from yourself.'

'Fucking smart, aren't you?' he snarled. 'But not so smart when you attack a member of Allah's Army!'

He must have been wearing a belt holster, because when his hand dipped quickly inside his jogging top, it re-emerged carrying an automatic pistol. It pointed straight at my chest.

I didn't have a second to curse my own stupidity in not checking him for other weapons, or even to consider the likelihood that the gun might be a replica. But I'd been here several times before. I said, 'You've left the safety on.'

His mouth and gaze dropped. In that moment of distraction, I knocked aside the gun and grabbed his arm. One quick twist and the automatic clattered to the pavement. Another step forward and once again his arm was half-way up his back.

'Not very good, are you!' I hissed in his ear. 'As much good to Allah as a chocolate soldier!'

'Yeeow! You're hurting me.'

'Hurting you? I'm just considering whether to break your bloody arm.'

'Please, please.'

'Any more weapons?'

He shook his head and winced. Tears were running down his cheeks.

'I said any more?'

'NO!'

I forced him around to face the fence. 'Hands on head!'

This time he obeyed. 'So, who are you?' he asked again as I quickly frisked him. 'You arresting me?'

I laughed. 'I'm not a cop. My name's Ali Khan. I'm new in the area.' I turned his shoulders round so that he faced me again. 'You going to behave?'

'Sure,' he said and began to slowly lower his hands. 'You Pakistani?'

He didn't sound convinced, staring at my blue eyes. 'Pakistani father, English mother,' I explained quickly. 'What's your name?'

After a second's hesitation, reluctantly he said, 'Leo.'

'I'll buy you a drink, Leo.'

He frowned. 'Why would you want to do that?'

I walked across the path and, keeping him in view, picked up the large automatic pistol. It was a 9mm Smith & Wesson 3904 and it wasn't a replica. I checked there was nothing in the breech and removed the magazine, before slipping the weapon into my pocket.

'Because I'm a Muslim,' I said, 'and I don't like what you're doing in the name of Allah. That was an innocent mother and child.'

'She was a Christian white,' Leo retorted with surprising vitriol. 'Dirty and an unbeliever. The Koran says you can take things from people like that.'

I said quietly, 'We'll talk about it over a drink. Tea, coffee, lemonade . . .'

He frowned suddenly. 'I saw you handle that gun. You know about guns.'

He'd just invited me to play my trump card. 'I fought with the Taliban in Afghanistan.'

His mouth dropped open like a goldfish gulping for air. 'Really?'

'Now, are you coming for that drink?' I pressed.

He shrugged, trying to look cool. 'Sure, why not?'

'I wondered about the Black Dog, is that any good?'

'Yeah, it's okay.' He thought for a moment. 'Some of my mates might be there. You won't tell them about this, how you took the gun off me?'

I shook my head. 'Of course not. Let's go?'

The heat of the early afternoon sun cranked up as we walked to the end of the alley and a couple of blocks to the pub. All the time Leo kept glancing sideways at me, an expression resembling awe on his face, as he bombarded me with questions. They weren't clever or pointed, but were asked with excitable enthusiasm. But then I wouldn't have minded if he'd tried to catch me out, because I'd just say I'd been on the opposite side in the battles I'd really fought against Taliban elements. I reckoned I knew enough about the wild borders between Afghanistan and Pakistan to blag my way out of trouble.

'Wish I could fight there,' he said wistfully.

We reached the Black Dog, a dilapidated 1920s corner pub on the apex of two run-down terraced streets. I had a sense the whole area was on borrowed time, just waiting for the arrival of the property developers and the bulldozers. There were two hand-written signs on the swing doors: one insisting shirts must be worn and the other promoting the landlord's home-made Thai curry.

After the bright sunlight, the interior was dark and depressing with bare floorboards and a scattering of unmatched tables and chairs. As my eyes adjusted, I could see that there was just a handful of regulars at the bar, having a monosyllabic conversation about the odds for the afternoon's racing.

I felt a slight relief that none of Leo's mates seemed to be around, because I didn't really want any distractions.

The large, heavy-jowled landlord looked at me with uninterest and didn't even manage a word of welcome.

I turned to Leo. 'What would you like?'

He hesitated. 'A Bacardi and Coke, is that all right?'

I smiled. 'You are a bad boy, aren't you?'

Shifting uncomfortably, he said, 'Allah can't see you in your own home – or your local.'

'Who told you that?'

'We all know it.'

I didn't push the point and placed the order, adding, 'And a tall orange juice with ice for me.'

We found a table where a shaft of sunlight from the sash window cut through the gloom. He pushed his tobacco tin and some Rizlas across the table. 'Help your-self, Mr Khan.'

'What about the smoking ban?' I asked.

'Don't worry, this landlord knows better than to fuck with Allah's Army.'

Helping myself to one of the offered papers and some tobacco, I asked, 'You born here in the UK, Leo?'

'Yeah,' he said, 'me parents come from Trinidad. Me dad's dead now.'

'So not Muslims?'

He chuckled. 'No way. Bloody Baptists.'

'So how come you're Muslim?'

Leo glanced around, checking that no one was in earshot. 'Seen the light, didn't I? There used to be two street gangs around here, both doing stuff. You know, drugs and cars. I was with the Black Dog Boys – this pub was our base, you know. Then the other outfit got a new leader, a Muslim, and they changed their name to Allah's Army. That's when things started getting heavy, know what I mean?'

'A turf war?' I guessed.

'Yeah, and some,' he said as he finished rolling a cigarette. 'These guys had guns?'

'And your gang didn't?'

'No, sure we had some. But we didn't really use them.' He stared down at the cigarette in his hands. 'But Allah's Army fucking did, they didn't . . . don't care about nothing. You get in their way and you get your head blown off.'

'What do the police do about it?'

'The cops? They try, but we always outsmart them. They've nicked about twenty of ours in the past, but we've grown too big for them now.'

'And you decided to join them?'

He shifted awkwardly in his seat and lit the cigarette to give himself some thinking time. 'Yeah, well, I didn't have much option,' he said eventually. 'They visited a mate of mine's home one night. Burst in and stripped him naked in front of his mum. They put a gun in his mouth and said convert to Islam and join us – or in three days we'll be back to pull the trigger.'

'Forced conversion,' I murmured.

'Another mate of mine resisted and was found in a rubbish bin on the estate, shot in the head. Silly fucker.'

'Silly?'

'He should have listened. Allah's Army are real cool. What's Christians ever done for us, living here? Fuck all, that's what. All round the world the Christians try to oppress the poor and the Muslims, 'cos they know we know the truth. I tries to explain to my mum, but she's too blind to see.'

'To see what?' I asked.

'Like how the Bible's been rewritten a dozen times and it's still going on. So God can't have written it, so who has? It's all lies.'

'Who told you that?'

'One of the gang leaders. He does all the religious stuff. He knows the Koran, right? Like you can take things off people, if them's Christians, because they're worse than dogs. And you can kill other drug dealers . . . That way others might stop and think, hey, maybe I'll become Muslim too and then I won't be killed.'

Leo gave the impression he thought all this was a good

idea. I said, 'Maybe this sort of thing could get you killed yourself. By another gang or an armed cop . . . or you fall out with someone in the gang.'

'Allah's Army looks after its own. If anything happened to me, my mum would be taken care of, even though she ain't Muslim. And I go straight to Paradise to fuck celestial virgins because I'd have died in Allah's cause. Can't get a better deal than that.'

I said, 'They tell suicide bombers that.'

Leo scowled at me. 'So what? Don't mean to say it ain't true. I had fuck all before Allah found me, I didn't care about no one or nothing. I was a worthless piece of shit. Now I've got a community of brothers, right? I've got power and I've got respect. No one gets in my way now.'

I couldn't resist it. I said, 'Until I came along.'

He blinked, then smiled slowly. 'Yeah, right.' He thought for a moment, then added, 'But like you're a fellow Muslim, Mr Khan. A real Muslim, like you've killed for Allah. And yet you showed me respect.'

'Of course,' I said. 'Because when it is practised correctly, Islam is a tolerant religion. Did you realize that, Leo?'

There was a look of confusion in his eyes, but I didn't think he was going to argue with his new-found hero. 'Er, yes, Mr Khan.'

I decided to change tack while I was ahead. 'So you've never been to Afghanistan?'

His eyes widened a fraction and his expression froze. 'No.' Emphatic.

It was a curious reaction, as though suddenly he was on his guard. 'Wouldn't you like to go? Maybe get some real military training?'

He shrugged, less than enthusiastic. 'Sure. But I can handle myself already . . .' His mouth formed into a shy grin as he dropped his cigarette butt to the floor and ground it out with the sole of his foot. ''Course not as good as you, Mr Khan.'

I smiled back at him and nodded slowly. 'Well, maybe you could be one day. If you ever decide you'd like to go . . . I've got contacts.'

'Yeah?' Now his interest seemed rekindled a little.

'Sure.' I fished a pen and notebook from my inside pocket and tore off a page. 'Let me give you my mobile number – in case you decide you're interested.' I finished scribbling and shoved the paper across the table. 'Want to give me yours?'

He thought about that for a moment. 'Yeah, why not. I'll give you me private one. The other's for gang business.'

As he ripped the page in half and wrote his own number on the blank part, I'd already decided young Leo might prove useful. It's well known in interrogation and intelligence circles that fanatics are usually the easiest to turn. That's because their heart-felt beliefs are usually ill-founded on lies and misinformation, and they often harbour an underlying fear of those running their own extremist cause.

It was when Leo handed his number to me that the

doors of the pub swung abruptly open. Six or seven men in their late teens to mid-twenties strolled in with all the arrogance and attitude of a gang of Old West gunslingers. Only the football stripes and baseball caps rather spoiled the effect. There was only one white man amongst them, a mean-eyed young man with ginger hair, the rest were of black, Asian or Middle Eastern origins.

The landlord didn't look too pleased to see them initially, but quickly hid his expression and retreated into sullen silence as he served their orders. He clearly knew better than to tangle with them. Quietly the locals at the bar slunk away to find seats and a table elsewhere.

As the drinks appeared on the bar, the gang began shuffling their feet impatiently and looking around the place. The white lad noticed Leo, then frowned when he saw me. He raised his hand in casual greeting. My companion smiled nervously and acknowledged him with a nod of the head.

Then the gang members began whispering to each other and, in turn, glanced over at the two of us. A very tall, thin Arab-looking youngster in a Millwall T-shirt, and wearing a white cotton prayer cap, finished paying at the bar and edged his way through the group. They stepped back deferentially. The young man had all the hallmarks of being the leader. Then he, too, glared at Leo and me. I could see now that he had a sallow complexion and a wispy, immature beard. Eyes as hard and emotionless as black marble scowled from beneath thick dark brows.

'Who's that?' I asked.

'Mustufa.'

The white youngster took out a mobile phone and held it aloft. For a moment I wondered what the hell he was playing at, maybe trying to get a signal. Then I realized he'd just taken a photograph of the two of us. Suddenly the Black Dog didn't seem a very comfortable place to be.

Mustufa began to amble across to our table, his gang trailing in his wake, taking their lead from him.

Leo's smile wavered and he shifted awkwardly in his seat. 'Hi, Mustufa.'

The Arab youth ignored the greeting, and me. His eyes were fixed on Leo. 'Who's this?'

'Mr Khan,' he answered quickly, then added, 'he's a . . . er . . . friend of mine.'

I thought I'd try to ease things and offered my hand. 'You must be Mustufa. Pleased to meet you.'

Mustufa continued to ignore me and my hand. He continued staring at Leo. 'I haven't seen him before. He's not from around here.'

'No, Mustufa, I only met him today. He's new to the area.'

Mustufa shook his head slowly in obvious disapproval. 'You've only just met him and you bring him here. Gossiping like a couple of old women.'

'He's all right, Mustufa,' Leo blurted. 'He's a fellow Muslim, a Pakistani.'

Mustufa spared me a split-second sideways glance. 'He's not Pakistani.'

'Half,' I added quickly, hoping to defuse the antagonism.

'He looks like a cop to me,' Mustufa said.

'No, no,' Leo gabbled, 'he's a freedom fighter. He's fought for the Taliban in Afghanistan.'

'Is that what he told you, eh?' Mustufa replied scornfully. 'Well, before you bring strangers into our midst, you ask me first. Got it?'

'Yes, yes, of course, Mustufa.' There was a feeble, ingratiating smile trying to reach Leo's lips. 'I'm sorry, it won't happen again.'

'No, it won't,' Mustufa said, and straightened his back.

Then, for the first time, he turned his attention to me. 'Now we'll see if this Mr Khan is the warrior he thinks he is . . .'

To give him his due, Mustufa sprang at me with the speed of a cobra, so fast I barely caught the flash of the gleaming knife blade in his right hand as his left fist grabbed the collar of my shirt and hauled me half-way across the table towards him.

His face was in mine, so close I could see the pores on the greasy skin and each individual wisp of the beard he was trying to grow. But I was more concerned with the sharp prick of the knife blade pressed under my chin.

'So, Mr Khan, is it cop or killer for Allah?!' he hissed. His breath smelled of cheap mouthwash.

I looked into his eyes and smiled. 'Allah akbar,' I said softly. God is Great. 'So you are the leader of His army? I bet He's pleased to have you on His side.'

For the first time I could detect something in those cold stone eyes, maybe curiosity, maybe uncertainty. Why didn't I flinch, why wasn't I cowed, why didn't I fight back? Then he noticed the slow movement of my arm and glanced down, blinking, just in time to see the barrel of Leo's Smith & Wesson automatic rising up in the gap between us until it was under his chin.

'Drop the knife, big boy,' I said quietly, 'or I blow your fuckin' head off.'

Instantly his grip on my collar relaxed and the weapon clattered onto the table. It was my turn to move fast, grabbing his right wrist with my free hand and moving round the small table so that I could force his arm up into the small of his back. The gang members gasped and took an involuntary step back as they saw the gun now jammed into Mustufa's temple.

The landlord looked over at the sudden, violent movement. 'Hey, what the hell d'you think . . .!'

'Don't worry, we've stopped smoking. Get me the front door keys – pronto!' I snapped. 'Unless you want blood all over your floor!'

He hesitated, gawping.

'DO IT!' I shouted, 'or you'll get the next round!'

That was enough to get the landlord to move his heavy, slack body faster than I guess it had moved in years. He lifted the hinged flap on the bar and came through at a pace.

'Bolt the second door and wait outside!'

He nodded as I started backing towards the double

doors with Mustufa remaining in my grip and the pistol still at his temple. I took one last step outside into the bright daylight and stuffed the gun into my jacket pocket.

'Key!' I demanded of the landlord and held out my hand.

As soon it was in my grasp, I propelled Mustufa forward, back into the pub with his arm still trapped high up in the small of his back. He tripped and fell, the momentum taking him several feet across the floor to land in a heap at the feet of his mighty, and now totally demoralized, army.

'See you around, Leo!' I called out before slamming the door shut and twisting the key in the lock.

The landlord stared at me with an expression that hovered between bemusement and anger. 'Who the fuck are you? A copper?'

I tapped the side of my nose, suddenly filled with elation and the adrenalin rush of getting out of a tight corner by the skin of my teeth. 'No, Batman.'

But I had no time to wallow in smug self-congratulation. It might have taken only minutes, even seconds, for Mustufa's gang to break down the door or to find a way out at the back of the pub. And, if Leo was right, some might even be armed with guns and not hesitate to use them.

I sprinted to the nearest side-street, diving and taking turn after turn until I was sweating profusely and my lungs were heaving. There were even tears of strain and exhaustion in my eyes. I was so out of condition, it was pitiful.

When I finally got back to my parked van in the hot afternoon sun, I was literally hobbling.

'You did what?' Popadom exclaimed.

I was seated at the table in the little converted 'ops room' of my flat with Popadom, Jazz and young Kate.

I shrugged and took another swig from the chilled bottle of beer. 'It seemed like a good idea at the time. It still does.'

'MI5 work is not about brawling on the streets,' Popadom admonished with a little shake of his head.

Jazz chimed in. 'Phil couldn't let Leo mug that woman and child.'

I said, 'The incident broke the ice. Gave me a chance to use the cover story.'

'Going to that pub was a high-risk strategy,' Popadom persisted.

'I didn't know his mates were going to turn up,' I said defensively, 'and react in the hostile way they did.'

Popadom was still shaking his head. 'And then to be threatening the gang with a gun! Talk about making discreet inquiries.'

'The gun wasn't loaded,' I said.

'What about Leo using the Guardians of Paradise website?' Jazz asked.

'I'd only just met him, I couldn't go into all that,' I replied. 'Anyway, my guess is all those young yobbos use it . . . or do if they've got a computer. I certainly don't think Leonard Fryatt is any kind of terror threat. He's just a rather sad, ill-educated victim of modern society who thinks he's found a reason for life and for living. Now he's got a little bit of power.'

'And a gun,' Kate chimed in brightly.

'They all have,' I replied, dismissing it lightly. 'In fact, my thought was to turn young Leo into an agent to work for us.'

Popadom stared at me. 'Are you out of your mind, Mr Phil? We are supposed to be doing a little discreet surveillance and assessment, not recruiting a network of spies.'

'I thought you'd like the idea,' I said. 'I told him I had a contact who could get him to train in Afghanistan. You could be that contact.'

'This is getting worse by the minute.'

I disagreed. 'Once word got round, we'd soon find out who in that gang was seriously motivated. And if any of them were already connected with al-Qaeda, they'd also want to know what was going on.'

Jazz was listening intently. 'Lassiter told us that the gang has chapters and contacts in most Muslim communities in the UK. I can't see what harm it would do. Something might crawl out of the woodwork.'

Popadom remained unconvinced. 'Well, Mr Phil, you must be doing as you see fit, but I think it wiser to stick to our exact remit.'

I said, 'I was told to operate in any way I felt best. My inclination is to run with it and see if it's got legs.'

Jazz placed a consoling hand on Popadom's shoulder. 'Don't worry, Phil knows what he's doing. He won't take silly risks.'

I hoped I did know what I was doing and wasn't just trying to fly without an aircraft. But now we'd dealt with Leo, I wanted to see how Popadom and Jazz had got on with our other suspects.

'What happened with Popadom's favourite curry-house owner?' I asked Jazz.

From the corner of my eye I noticed a sullen expression settle over Popadom's face. It was still a sore point with him. He had wanted to meet the friend of his late uncle again and felt he'd have a natural rapport with him. But Jazz had been very insistent that an older man would more likely fall for her feminine charms. Given our history and my experience of her, I could hardly disagree with that. Besides, I felt that given his personal family connection with Akmal Younis, Popadom's assessment might be less objective. We had settled on a compromise whereby Popadom kept Younis under surveillance for a couple of days and tried to build up a pattern of where he went, whom he saw, as he had with Leonard Fryatt. Then Jazz would go in for a closer inspection – in this case, quite literally.

'Younis was an absolute pussycat,' she declared. 'A charming old boy, an absolute gentleman. He couldn't have been nicer – and me going in as a health and safety inspector doing a spot check! Mind you the kitchen of the curry-house in north London I visited looked immaculate. He said I was the most pleasant inspector he'd ever come across.'

'I bet,' I said.

'He even invited me to join him for a meal and we had lunch. Damn good it was too.'

'Told you,' Popadom muttered darkly. 'That was my lunch you ate, Miss Jazz, so I'm glad you enjoyed it!'

'I was on difficult ground though,' Jazz explained, 'because he knew Mullah Reda and the rival curry-house owner Hasan Malik – and they're both on remand in Belmarsh. He'd have smelled a rat. So I said I was Muslim and I'd recently relocated from Birmingham. I said I'd known Reda at my mosque there, and would like to find such an excellent imam around north London.'

'Did he mention Reda's arrest?' I asked.

'No, and I didn't detect any special reaction.'

'And which mullah did he recommend?'

'One in Finchley, but I've checked him out and he appears to be a moderate.'

'Like Reda was supposed to be,' Popadom pointed out.

Jazz added quickly, 'But interestingly, when we were talking about his business and the trade, he mentioned Malik. Said how terrible that he'd been arrested and how he thought it would all prove to be just a terrible mistake.'

'So they are friends?' I pressed.

'I think more like business acquaintances and friendly rivals. That would explain why his email address was on Malik's computer.' Jazz smiled. 'I certainly don't think

Younis is really a likely suspect. I think we'd be quite safe to drop him from the list.'

Like Leo, Akmal Younis seemed like another dead end. I was almost disappointed, which was ridiculous because our job was to safely eliminate minor suspects and save MI5 time, resources and money.

I turned to Popadom. 'You followed Younis for a couple of days. Any pattern emerge?'

'Well, I gather his wife died years ago and he now lives alone with his dog, a black Labrador. Nice house, but small. I'm sure he could afford something bigger and more elaborate if he wished to.' Popadom didn't need to consult his notes. 'Takes his dog for a walk in the park every morning at about a quarter to eight. Then drives to his office at the Spirit of India restaurant, that's his flagship in Hampstead. Or else he visits one of the other outlets. The dog goes everywhere with him. Late afternoon he takes it for a walk again – wherever he happens to be, I'd guess. Then he'll eat at one of his own outlets before going home. On the two days I followed him, he was back before ten. Lights were out by eleven.'

'Is it worth continuing?' Jazz asked.

I shrugged. 'Hard to tell. This is all very hit and miss. But we should at least run all these surveillances over a weekend. Patterns could be a lot different then, more socializing.'

Kate looked at her roster. 'Popadom is due to follow Younis tomorrow, Saturday.'

'That still okay with you, Pops?' I asked him.

He smiled gently. 'I have nothing else planned.'

'And Jazz is due to try and make contact with the Syrian lady,' Kate reminded. 'Mrs Huda Dahdah.'

'Ah, yes,' Jazz said thoughtfully. 'The wife of the suicide bomber who died in Iraq. I'll be walking on eggshells. Not looking forward to that one.'

'You'll cope,' I assured.

'And you, boss,' Kate said, 'are going to take a look at Dave Evans.'

I nodded, but still felt uneasy about it. A former Para who'd converted to Islam after serving in Afghanistan and was now taking part in theology discussion circles, giving them the benefit of his military experience. We knew each other – just – but I wasn't at all certain what sort of reception I'd get.

Still that was tomorrow.

I glanced at my watch. It was now gone five. 'Anyone fancy a drink?' I asked.

'I'll have to hobble off home, Mr Phil,' Popadom said. I'd learned that his wife hated cooking and he hated what she cooked, so they'd come to the perfect arrangement. He cooked and she ate.

Kate said, 'I want to get to the stables tonight and get a ride in.'

'Seems like I'm your last hope,' Jazz said with a smile.

'What about Zoë?'

'She doesn't drink,' Jazz answered mischievously. 'Besides it's her ballet class tonight. I won't have to collect her until seven.'

When, a few minutes later, we were strolling together in the afternoon sunshine, I realized we'd spent no time alone together since she'd called me up after her change of heart and we'd met to discuss my job offer.

'So how are you enjoying being a gumshoe?' I asked.

'The truth?'

I frowned. 'Of course.'

She laughed at my look of concern. 'Don't worry, I'm loving it! It's been great being a housewife and mum, but I'd forgotten what a buzz this sort of work can be.'

'Not exactly cutting-edge Northern Ireland stuff,' I said.

'I think I'm too old for that sort of thing now. This is quite exciting enough for me, and the money's going to be very handy.'

'No mention of the charming company,' I replied, sounding miffed.

'Ahhhh.' She slipped her arm in mine and looked up. 'The company is as fun as it always was, Phil. It's nice to be working with you again.'

We reached the pub. It was a bit run-down, but the landlord was friendly and made his own range of excellent pies, and it had a pleasant if rather overgrown beer garden with a couple of gnarled old apple trees.

I bought a beer and a J2O for Jazz before joining her at a table. 'So you really are off the booze?'

'Ricardo, my husband, was quite strict and didn't like me drinking,' she replied. 'I sort of got out of the habit. I don't really find I need it now. And I feel better for it.'

I smiled. 'I seem to remember we put away quite a lot in Bosnia.'

'That's what life on the edge does for you,' she replied and lifted her glass. 'Cheers. To a friendship rekindled.'

God, I suddenly realized just how beautiful she still was. Her long black hair splashed over the shoulders of her white cotton blouse, those enticing eyes with their long lashes regarding me over the rim of her glass.

I remembered how gaunt and troubled she'd looked when I'd first met her again, but she seemed happier and more relaxed now. 'To us,' I said.

'To us,' she repeated softly.

'I've often thought about you. Wondered where you were, what you were doing? I wanted to come after you.'

'I'm glad you didn't.'

'You covered your tracks too well.'

She placed her glass on the table. 'Better to let things run their natural course.'

'And now?' I asked, trying to play it cool.

'Things have run their course, haven't they, Phil? Fate has brought us back together again.'

'Meaning?'

I knew I shouldn't have pushed it. She sat back in her seat. 'Just that. Let's see how it goes.'

I wanted her then, I knew. The passing years had changed nothing. Images flashed through my mind, her tender naked body beneath me, her squeals of abandoned laughter and wild pleasure. It was as though a warm and sultry breeze had gently blown aside the blue mists of time, and suddenly it seemed like only yesterday. It was as though she could read my mind, like she always had. She leaned forward again and placed her hand on my wrist. 'That isn't rejection, Phil. It's not anything, not yet. I have to put Zoë first in my life now.'

I was just about to say 'Of course' when my mobile began its irritating and jaunty tune, shattering the moment. I really must work out how the hell to change it, I thought, and lifted it to my ear.

'Hi, man,' the deep male voice said. 'It's me, Leo. Allah akbar!'

'Hallo, Leo, how are you?' I replied. Jazz raised her eyebrows, surprised and curious, as I continued, 'Hope you didn't have too much hassle with your friends after I left.'

The voice at the other end laughed. 'No, man, it was like cool. Like they was seriously impressed. They didn't say as much, but they was all a bit shocked. Mustufa's reputation took a bit of a knock, but it didn't harm me street-cred. Got a bit more respect, I think.'

'Good,' I said flatly, nothing more. I wanted Leo to make the first move.

There was an awkward pause. 'I wondered if we might like meet up again sometime?'

Five

I left home early the next morning, Saturday.

At five in the morning the roads were fairly clear and I had a good run up to Leicester where Dave Mohammed Evans lived in a bedsit. The sky had clouded over, acting like a lid on a saucepan. It was hot and sticky in the old van and, for once, I longed for the comfort of a decent, air-conditioned car.

The drive gave me an opportunity to think about Leo and the best way to handle him. So far I'd just promised to get back in touch. After all, I didn't want to waste a lot of time on him if all his mates in Allah's Army were just misguided criminal yobs like him. But, according to the police, the gang had long since stretched its tentacles out of London to as far as Bristol, the Midlands and Yorkshire. So there were plenty of possibilities.

But each time I began concentrating on Leo, my thoughts kept drifting away again to Jazz. And, frequently, I didn't have the willpower or inclination to drag them back. I didn't want to risk pushing too hard or too soon with her. As I was seeing her at work every day, I decided that time was on my side. Rather like fishing to get the big one, get the right time and place, have infinite patience and then reel in slowly.

By the time I reached the outskirts of Leicester, the traffic was thickening fast, probably with everyone trying to get the shopping chores out of the way early in order to make the most of a rare warm afternoon. Later on I guessed the suburban streets would be heavy with the smell of barbecue coals and charred meat as dads had their once-a-year crack at cooking.

But, as I turned into Dave Evans' run-down neighbourhood, I had a feeling that barbecues would be few and far between there. It was a dilapidated bedsit-land of tall, converted Edwardian houses, left to fall into disrepair by absentee landlords interested only in collecting the weekly rent in cash. It was the sort of place you lived when you were down on your luck and had nowhere else to go.

I found a parking space in view of Dave Evans' place. Through a pair of pocket binoculars, I studied the building. The brickwork needed repointing and so much faded paint had flaked from the front door that it was impossible to tell the original colour. Grimy net curtains hung from windows that looked as though they hadn't been cleaned in years.

As I focused on the third floor, the closed curtains were sudenly flung open. A bare-topped figure struggled with the sash window. Finally he managed to release it and then he leaned out to survey the street and take a breath of fresh morning air. The face was identical to the one in the photograph that lay on the passenger seat beside me. Drawn and sunken-eyed, the unshaven chin had been left to become a short black beard. His unwashed hair was long and drawn back in a ponytail.

He sat on the windowsill in pyjama bottoms with a mug of something hot and smoked a cigarette, idly watching passers-by and seemingly enjoying the sun. After a few minutes he tossed his cigarette butt far into the middle of the street and went back inside. At least he was up, so hopefully I wouldn't have to spend half the day sweltering in my van. I settled down to wait, and poured myself a coffee from the flask I'd taken with me.

In fact, I had less time to wait than I'd been expecting. I'd barely finished my drink when he appeared at the front door and trotted down the steps. I'd already clocked his car, a battered old M-reg Vauxhall, parked further down the street and so I waited until he'd walked past it before deciding to follow on foot.

I thrust my hands in my jeans pockets in that sort of 'amble mode' people adopt when they've nowhere in particular to go and sauntered along on the opposite side of the street. If Evans knew any counter-surveillance techniques, he didn't use any. He walked quite purpose-fully and I speeded up a gear as he made his way towards the local high street. He stopped at the corner shop to purchase some groceries. The Asian owner seemed to know him and they chatted amiably for several minutes until they were interrupted by the arrival of another customer.

Evans then continued down the high street. Here it became clear that this was a distinctly ethnic neighbourhood, the low-rent shops full of signs in various languages as well as English. A video shop specialized in Bollywood and Chinese titles, another outlet specialized in unusual herbs and spices, others carpet remnants and second-hand furniture. Muslim women in chadors or hijabs walked with their young children, and many men wore prayer hats and other items of Asian dress.

At last Evans entered a coffee shop. Only when I reached the entrance and saw that he wasn't in the shop, did I realize he must have gone straight ahead up a steep flight of stairs. The wall sign showed a painted hand pointing up to the Starburst Internet Café on the first floor.

I kept on walking, across the mouth of the next side-street, where I lingered at a second-hand bookshop, flicking idly through the paperbacks on the pavement stall. Evans' stop at the Internet café could prove interesting. I'd pass on its location to Lassiter and they'd be able to monitor any emails Evans sent from there.

It was twenty minutes before my quarry re-emerged. He turned left and passed behind me on his journey down the high street. After picking up a paper at a newsagent, he continued on to a café that had a scattering of tables and chairs on the pavement. It was hardly continental chic, but it was fairly adventurous for this part of Leicester. I watched from across the road in the reflection of a charity shop window until he came out with a cup of

coffee and a fried egg sandwich. When he took a seat and
unfurled his newspaper, I made my decision.

Taking care that his back was slightly towards me, in
case he saw me and decided to cut and run, I crossed back
over to his side of the street and approached the tables. As
I passed close to him, he glanced up.

I did an immediate double-take and halted. 'Good
God, I don't believe it! Dave, isn't it? Er . . . Dave Evans?'

He frowned, alarm obvious in his eyes. 'You're mistaken, mate,' he answered sharply.

But I was already sitting down opposite him at the
table, smiling amiably. Pretending not to have heard his
initial response, I blustered on. 'Remember me? Phil
Mason. Your instructor at Sniper School. Never forget a
face.'

He looked a little less concerned now. 'I looked nothing like this then,' he replied warily. 'Surprised you . . .'

'It's a gift. Having to put so many new names to faces
on each course. Mind if I join you?'

He still hadn't smiled. 'It's a free country.'

'And a small one,' I said. 'I'm doing freelance courier
work. Man with white van. Just stopped off for brunch.
And bingo, here you are!'

Just then a teenage girl emerged from the café in a
skimpy skirt and tank-top that revealed a tacky piece of
jewellery hanging from her navel. She began clearing the
other tables.

'Excuse me, sweetheart. Any chance of a black coffee
and a bacon roll?'

She looked at me and scowled. Despite my oodles of charm, it didn't work. 'This ain't waitress service. Order inside.'

Sod it! Given Evans' less than warm reception, if I had to go inside, the chances were odds on he would do a runner. And if I didn't go and order, it would look extremely suspicious.

So I used the old army maxim when dealing with women: if charm doesn't work, throw money at them. 'A quid tip for a favour. Be an angel.'

She seemed to focus on me properly for the first time, then noticed Evans sitting next to me. 'Oh, hi, Mo? This a friend of yours?'

'You could say that, Sal,' he answered non-committally.

'In that case, I don't mind.' Then a half-smile cracked her sour face. 'Just tell him I ain't that cheap.'

Still without looking at me, the non-waitress disappeared inside with her tray of dirty crockery.

I turned back to Evans. 'Mo? Did I hear right? Don't remember anyone calling you that.'

He looked extremely uncomfortable. 'I converted to Islam. Took Mohammed as a middle name. Helps you get on, living in this neck of the woods.'

I tried to show an expression of mild surprise. 'I read the Koran when I was in Afghanistan,' I said. 'Interesting stuff. Viewed the Arabs differently after that.'

For the first time he showed a glimmer of interest. 'You served in Afghanistan?'

'Yep. That's what finally decided me to quit the army.

Didn't like the way the allies were going about things. There and in Iraq.'

Evans actually smiled. It was a grudging, sullen sort of smile, but it was a smile. 'Me, too. Shame we didn't meet over there.'

I upped the stakes and laughed. 'We might have gone AWOL together!'

'Yeah, maybe.' I appeared to have set him thinking. After a pause, he said, 'Of course, the youngsters are always up for a scrap, but a lot of senior NCOs and officers had serious doubts about a lot of things.'

I changed tack. 'So what you doin' now?'

Wariness crept back into his expression. 'You know, a bit of this and a bit of that. Scraping a living.'

I kept smiling. 'Yeah, but what? I found it difficult to settle when I came out. Not sure this courier work is for me. A lot of night driving, young man's game.'

Evans said, 'I'm a sort of odd–job man. Make a living, word gets round. Was always handy with DIY. My ex-wife made sure of that.'

'You two split, like me and mine?'

He nodded. 'Divorced.'

As I smiled in commiseration, I recalled his file said that he was 'separated'. That was either a slip of the tongue or the file was out of date. Probably the latter.

'Fancy a pint at lunchtime?' I asked, feeling I was slowly making progress in winning over his confidence.

'Not really, I'm Muslim,' he replied flatly. 'And I've a busy day.'

At that point Sal arrived with my coffee and bacon roll. As I paid out some loose change I was frantically wondering how to win Evans over.

When she'd gone, I said, 'I'm up this way several times a week nowadays. It would be good to meet up for a chat. Compare notes. We could maybe go for a pizza, or something.'

His hard grey eyes appraised me for a moment. 'Yeah, I guess we could.'

'Got a mobile number?'

He rattled it off while I jotted it down on a paper napkin. I wrote mine on another section and tore it off for him. 'Feel free, Mo – is that what you prefer to be called nowadays?'

'It's what I'm known as round here.'

'Mo it is then.'

He frowned. 'And your name again?'

'Phil Mason.'

'I remember you now. Yeah, one of the instructors. We spoke once, some piss-up in a local after we finished the course.'

'Happier times,' I said.

That elusive smile hovered again. 'You can say that again . . .' His voice trailed off as his eyes averted to some point behind my shoulder. He added tersely, 'You'll have to forgive me, Phil. Got some business to attend to.'

Even as I turned I became aware of the man's presence as he paused beside us, casting a shadow across the table.

'Good morning, Mo. Allah akbar.' He inclined his head towards me. 'And who is this gentleman?'

The voice was cultured, almost hiding the foreign accent. It seemed to go with the expensive grey silk summer suit and open-necked, dark-green shirt. His hair was wavy black and neatly coiffured, as tidy as the tooth-brush of hairs above his upper lip.

'Allah akbar,' Evans rejoined. 'This is Phil, an old army mate of mine. We just bumped into each other.'

'How nice,' the man said. I wondered if there wasn't an edge of sarcasm in the way he said it. He was smiling, but his eyes remained cold and without any obvious expression or emotion.

I stood up and shook the man's hand. 'Pleased to meet you—'

'Hussein.'

Evans said quickly, 'Phil was just going.'

I picked up my half-eaten roll. 'Yes, forgive me. In a bit of a hurry. See you around, Mo.'

I turned and headed back down the high street, my head reeling. Hussein, Hussein, Hussein. Hussein who? Damn it, I knew that face.

'What in the hell d'you think you're playing at, Phil?'

Joe Lassiter was waiting for me when I arrived back at the office in the late afternoon. Jazz and Popadom were already there, looking decidedly apprehensive.

'Who's been pulling your tail?' I asked as I removed my jacket.

'You have, Phil. I've just read your report on your encounter with Leo Fryatt yesterday. D'you realize the local police have been running around like headless chickens looking for a mad gunman!'

I smiled. 'Just using my initiative, Joe.'

Lassiter puffed up his chest in indignation, making him look dumpier than ever. His specs magnified his eyes into big moist prunes. 'Don't be funny with me, Phil. The Ice Queen's livid. Your inquiries are supposed to be discreet. Your target, this Leo lad, was even interviewed by the local cops. That'll put him and his mates even more on their guard. Not exactly what we're trying to achieve, is it?'

I took a seat and sighed wearily. 'Look, I admit things didn't go as planned, but then I didn't know he was going to hold up some woman and baby at knifepoint.'

'He was hardly likely to actually stab them,' Lassiter retorted acidly.

I said, 'I don't take chances with a knife pointed at a baby's face.'

'Good for you,' Jazz said. Absently I thought how stunning she looked in her lemon-yellow summer suit, very elegant. It showed off her honey skin tone and flared nicely on her hips.

Lassiter just sent her a withering glance. 'Spare me the applause, sweetheart, and keep out of this.' His attention returned to me. 'And where's that knife and the gun now?'

'In the Thames,' I lied.

'Jesus.'

'Look, Joe,' I said. 'It wasn't textbook, but Leo sees me as some sort of hero now. I think we could use that.'

'Oh, yes, and so now you want to recruit your own agents? Give me strength.'

My anger grew. 'Look, you told me to handle these investigations as I see fit. Allah's Army is a big grouping with elements in all the big ethnic conurbations. Leo could be well placed to know if anything's going down.'

'Oh yes,' Lassiter said, 'I forgot you are now a holy al-Qaeda warrior!'

'Well, it impressed Leo. It might give me the opportunity to get to know him and his gang a little better.'

Popadom spoke for the first time. 'I have been thinking over Mr Phil's suggestion. On consideration, it could be most useful in the longer term. I know that is not our remit, but then we can be keeping Leo on the back burner, so to speak, while we continue looking at other low-grade suspects.'

Jazz added, 'If Leo comes up with nothing, then we quietly drop him. If he gets us results your office can take over, Joe.'

Lassiter said grumpily, 'I can see you lot are sticking together.'

I smiled. 'Put it like that, Joe, and the Ice Queen might even buy it.'

'I suppose, if I let her think it's her idea . . .'

Kate saw her opportunity to turn the temporary ceasefire into permanent peace. She picked up the tray of biscuits from the table. 'Anyone for a Hob Nob?'

While Lassiter took one and surreptitiously slipped two more into his pocket, I wandered over to the table and picked up one of the files. I flicked it open at the first page with the obligatory photograph. I was right, it was his coiffured hair that had stuck in my memory.

'That's him,' I said aloud, 'I'm sure of it.'

'Who?' Jazz asked.

'The man I saw with Dave Evans this morning.'

'How did that go?' Lassiter asked.

'All right. I managed to have a brief chat with Evans. He was cagey, but at least we swapped phone numbers. Then this man turned up. Naved Hussein.'

Lassiter looked up sharply. 'Impossible,' he said through a mouthful of biscuit. 'He's not in the country.'

'Who is this Naved Hussein?' Jazz asked. 'Remind me.'

'Runs the Guardians of Paradise website,' Lassiter replied.

'Oh, yes,' Jazz said, 'I remember. He's a friend of Mullah Reda.'

'Runs the site from Syria,' Lassiter continued. 'And that's where he is now. If he'd entered the country, Immigration would have let us know.'

I said, 'You're assuming he's travelling under his own name.'

'Mmm, fair point,' Lassiter conceded grudgingly. 'Although his mug shot and details are on the Suspects Index.'

I couldn't resist it. 'Maybe he was in disguise.'

Lassiter had the good grace to smile. 'Could be truer than you know. However it suggests to me he didn't come in via Heathrow or Gatwick.'

He pulled out his fancy mobile phone, searched for a number, and in a couple of seconds was talking to his special contact at the Harmondsworth centre. At the other end it took only a few minutes to trawl through the more than twenty thousand names of suspect terrorists, subversives and drug traffickers, held on the 'Ivan' computer, for anyone who may have passed through any of Britain's five hundred terminals at ports and airports in the previous month.

Lassiter grimaced as he snapped his phone shut. 'Nothing. They're going to have to run a visual and that'll take time.'

'A visual?' Jazz asked.

'Everyone is secretly photographed as they enter the country nowadays. It's all computerized, but these aren't portraits so the quality is patchy. That means someone has to go through every single picture to try and spot our friend. It's a long job with no guarantees.'

I said, 'But I'm damn sure it's him.'

Lassiter considered for a moment. 'Okay, but we need to know the name he's travelling under.'

'Maybe Dave Evans knows,' I suggested.

'Was Naved actually introduced to you?'

I nodded. 'Just as Hussein.'

'Well, that fits. But then every other bugger in the

Middle East has Hussein as his first name. And I can't believe he'd tell someone like Evans his cover name.'

'Or names,' Popadom added. 'He could be using more than one passport.'

I said, 'At least we seem to have hit pay dirt. Naved Hussein is at the centre of this possible spider's web and the only one with almost certain al-Qaeda connections.'

'So why's he here?' Lassiter thought aloud. 'And why was he meeting Evans?'

'Evans has been talking to study groups run by the bookseller Abu Hejah,' Popadom reminded. 'These study groups are typically attended by gullible youngsters.'

'Leo Fryatt attended a couple in North London,' I added. 'So maybe Evans has been looking out for likely al-Qaeda recruits.'

'It's beginning to look that way,' Lassiter agreed. 'Certainly possible. Evans would know the sort of young-ster with the right potential.'

I said, 'I think I need to chase up on Evans quickly.'

Lassiter shook his head. 'Don't appear too eager, Phil, you'll frighten him off. Anyway, he's not going to open up to you just like that. Did you say you've got a phone number for him?'

'His mobile, yes. And one for Leo Fryatt.'

'Excellent, let me have them.'

As I copied them out for him, Lassiter said, 'We'll have their mobile calls intercepted. Then I'll clear it with the Ice Queen to get an A4 surveillance team on Evans right away and get the System X boys at Oswestry plugged into his landline. Hopefully Evans'll lead us to Naved Hussein sooner rather than later.'

It really was all a bit scary how no communications were private nowadays, I thought.

'I was due to take over on Evans tomorrow,' Popadom reminded, the tone of disappointment clear in his voice.

'Sorry, Pops,' Lassiter said. 'Assuming I get clearance, a team will be dispatched immediately. Now it seems Evans really is a player, we can't risk continuing to cover him half-heartedly. You concentrate on the others on your list.' He turned to me. 'Except you, Phil, if you reckon you can get close to him.'

I nodded. 'It won't be easy, but I think it's worth a personal follow-up.'

Lassiter picked up his hat and raincoat from the chair. For once he wasn't actually wearing either, but it seemed he just couldn't bear to leave them at home. 'Well done, all. Our first result.'

When he left I think we all felt a bit deflated. As soon as we got something really interesting, the case was removed from us. I know that was always the name of the game, but that didn't help. At least I still had a remit to try to get to know Evans better.

I shoved the disappointment from my mind and turned to Jazz, wondering how she'd got on with the widow of the suicide bomber who'd died in Iraq. 'Did you make contact with Mrs Dahdah today?'

Jazz's smile melted. 'Yes, it was just so sad. The poor woman is eaten up with grief. I posed as a British

Telecom engineer with a reported mystery fault in the street. When she opened the door wearing her scarf, I told her I came from a Muslim background too. Before I knew it we were drinking mint tea together.'

'So she opened up to you?' I asked.

'She just poured it out. It was all tea and tears. I don't think she really has any friends in London. I think I was just the excuse she needed.'

'Did she mention her husband?'

'No, but I saw his photograph and asked her who he was.'

'Did she say he was a suicide bomber?'

Jazz gave me a strange look. 'Of course not, Phil. She said he'd died in an accident in Iraq. Apparently she didn't even know he was there. She thought he was in Damascus on business.'

'Did you find out why she is visiting the Guardians of Paradise website?' Popadom asked.

Jazz's smile returned. 'Can't just drop that into a conversation, Pops. But I kicked off by saying how awful the Americans were behaving in Iraq. She agreed. Then I said I wish I had some way of knowing what was going on over there, how you cannot trust the British media.'

'She told you about the website?' I guessed.

'She told me about the Al-Jazeera news website and the Guardians of Paradise. Apparently she only discovered them on her husband's computer listed under his "Favourites" after he died. To be honest, I think she's trying to justify her husband's actions to herself. After all, he left her and three children. I really don't think Huda Dahdah is any kind of threat.'

I nodded. 'I'm sure you're right. At least we'll put her at the bottom of the pile.' I turned to Popadom. 'And what about your favourite restaurateur? Any change to Younis' routine today?'

Popadom said, 'Just variations on a theme, Mr Phil. Being Saturday he has a lie-in, takes his dog for a walk – meeting no one else – then he did some gardening. There was a Tesco online delivery of groceries, but there were no other visitors to his house. He finally left for his restaurant at around four in the afternoon.'

'Does it open on Sundays?'

'I do not believe so.'

I turned to Kate. 'Who's on the roster for Younis tomorrow?'

'Roster? Oh, my God!' A hand flew to her mouth. 'I've completely forgotten. I am *sooo* sorry. I'll work it out now.'

It would be a good forty-five minutes' work, sorting out who was or wasn't available for each job on each given day. In addition we were due to take a look at the last two suspects on Lassiter's list, the lecturer at Imperial College and one of his students.

'I've got to go, Kate,' Jazz said. 'I'm collecting Zoë from her grandparents. Can you telephone the details to me later?'

'Sure thing,' Kate promised.

Jazz turned to me. 'I need to change into something casual. Can I use your bedroom?'

'Of course,' I said, and risked a crooked sort of smile. 'I thought you'd never ask.'

She picked up a hessian carry-bag and, with a half-grin on her face, rapped me lightly on the arm with her fist as she passed. 'You should be so lucky,' she whispered provocatively.

'You're right, I should,' I answered.

Then she was gone. Popadom reached out for his crutches and struggled to stand up. 'I, too, must go. I have a veritable feast to prepare for my good lady. Kashmiri chicken.'

'Sounds good,' I said, thinking I'd probably be eating something out of a tin, yet again. Still, it helped save a little cash.

'I'll phone you, too, Pops,' Kate called out as she settled down before her laptop.

Popadom hobbled towards the corridor and the front door. As he opened it, I heard his gasp of surprise. 'Oh, hello! Can I help you?'

'Does Philip Mason live here?' The voice was stern and female – and all too familiar.

'Indeed . . .' Popadom replied, then called out, 'Mr Phil, there is a lady here to see you!'

I wondered for a brief, fanciful second if I could get to the front door and slam it shut before Nina could get in.

No chance. Typically she'd already marched straight into the hallway so that I came face-to-face with her at

the office door. She was tall and almost painfully Atkins-
diet thin, wearing a very expensive-looking beige trouser
suit I'd never seen before. It went well with her long and
wavy auburn hair that suggested she had just paid another
visit to Toni & Guy's.

Nina had never been given much to smiling, and her
rather over-made-up face certainly wasn't smiling now.
'Working on a Saturday?'

'We're very busy just now,' I explained. 'A lot of work
on.'

'Well, you certainly seem to be doing all right for
yourself,' she said. I noticed that her bright-red lipstick
had leeched into the tiny lines around her mouth. 'I've
just bumped into Joe Lassiter on the street. Didn't know
you still associated with that little slimeball. Said you were
doing work for him. That's a government contract, I suppose?'

'Just bits and pieces,' I replied.

She brushed past me and stood in the middle of the
room. Ignoring Kate completely, she looked around and
I could see her taking in all the new office and communications equipment Lassiter had provided. 'Those bits
and pieces must be paying very well, I'd say.'

'This is Brixton, Nina, not Knightsbridge,' I retorted,
'and this office is only rented by the month.'

She didn't seem to, or want to, hear that. I saw Kate
gawping as Nina turned on her high heels and pushed
past me again as she returned to the hallway, turning
sharply left, leaving me to trail after her.

Throwing open the living-room door, she glanced at the mess of papers, photographs and maps. 'You always were an untidy bastard,' she snapped disdainfully, then headed towards the bedroom.

'That's enough, Nina!' I said loudly. 'I'd like you to leave!'

I'd just caught up with her as she threw open the door. Over Nina's shoulder I saw Jazz standing by the bed, her mouth dropping open in surprise. She was balanced awkwardly on one leg, naked except for a black thong, as she endeavoured to pull on a pair of dark-blue Levi's.

It's hard to know who was the most surprised of the three of us. My shock was the unexpected sight of Jazz's pert and youthful breasts again, whipping at my senses, after all these years. But the memory flash was short-lived, as she snatched a blouse from the bed to cover herself.

Nina stood and stared. 'Very cosy.' She turned to me. 'Who is this?'

'Jazz,' I said, grabbing the handle and closing the bedroom door quickly, 'an old friend.'

There was no apology forthcoming from Nina as she turned her back on the bedroom. 'Jazz? I remember that name. Some girl you met in Bosnia.'

I said, 'Yes, she was in the army, before you and I were married.'

'Then you certainly haven't wasted any time,' she retorted.

'Jazz is working for me, that's all.' I wondered why the hell Nina always seemed able to put me on the defensive.

She held her chin high. 'Next you'll be telling me you haven't been seeing her during our marriage.'

'Well, I haven't,' I retorted. 'She's married with a kid.'

'And since when would that have stopped you?'

I decided not to dignify that with yet another denial. 'Look, Nina, what the hell are you doing coming round here? If you've anything to say, say it to my solicitors.'

'I've been trying that. All this week.'

I was puzzled. As I began leading the way back down the hall, I said, 'I've heard nothing from them.'

'Maybe that's because they haven't been paid.'

'What? Is that what they told you?'

'It's the inference my solicitors got from talking to yours.'

'That's rubbish,' I said, although the truth was I had been struggling to meet the torrent of bills. Apparently Nina was making hard work of our divorce settlement, and that was expensive. 'In fact I got Kate to post a cheque . . .'

I'd reached the office. 'Kate,' I called, 'd'you remember that cheque I asked you to post a couple of weeks ago? The one to my solicitors?'

She swivelled her chair around and smiled up at me. 'Of course, Phil, you said it was very important.'

'Do you actually remember posting it?'

'Yes, of course. The box at the end of the street . . .'

Her voice trailed off. 'Was that the night I was rushing to get to the cinema?'

I took a deep breath. 'I don't know. You tell me?'

Her smile became a little fixed before her lips reformed into a sort of apologetic pout. 'Oh, my God . . .' She reached for her shoulder bag and rummaged in it for a few seconds. Then she plucked out the crumpled envelope like a rabbit from a hat. 'I was going to post it the West End and—'

'Forgot?' I suggested.

'Phil, I'm *sooo* sorry.'

I took it from her and turned away, only to find Nina standing, arms folded across her chest, gloating in silence. 'I just hope that's not an example of how you run your business, otherwise you're not going to have much of a future.'

She could have added 'by the time I've finished with you', but didn't. She didn't really have to.

I'd had enough. I put a hand to her shoulder and steered her towards the front door.

'We can talk outside,' I said as we went out towards the warm summer evening air and up the steps to street level.

Something was niggling me, something wasn't quite right. Nina didn't want to talk to me face-to-face, she'd hired a ruthless female solicitor to do that for her. If she'd come all the way to Brixton, it was for a purpose.

I stopped by the railings. 'So what d'you want to talk about?'

'My solicitor thinks I should be entitled to part of your future earnings.'

I swallowed hard. 'Does she now? You've already got the house and been promised a generous allowance for Danny.'

She tilted her head to one side. 'But you have a job, Phil, a livelihood. I don't. I haven't worked since we married.'

I said, 'Danny is eleven. I'm sure you can start again now, at least part-time.'

Nina looked skyward. 'I'm much too old, no one would want me. I'd have to retrain or something ghastly.' She smiled a sugary smile. 'And, of course, if you've been having a relationship with that Jazz woman during our marriage, that could make a big difference.'

Now I understood. This was just a fishing expedition to see how my business was going, see how much she could push for. Finding Jazz there was just what she needed, the icing on the cake.

'An adulterous husband,' she said, just to confirm my thoughts, 'with a thriving future. Looks like you've already got a staff of three . . . Why should I have to suffer while you enjoy a life of Riley?'

I wasn't going to argue with her, the lawyers would end up arguing for her anyway.

I said, 'Well, get your solicitors to speak to mine.' I held out the envelope. 'Be an angel and post this for me.' She hesitated about accepting it, so I added, 'That way you can be sure mine will reply to yours next week.'

There was a flicker of a smile, or was it a suppressed snarl, on her red gash of a mouth as she finally took the envelope. She'd been had, she clearly realized, and didn't like being fooled into dancing to my tune.

She went to go, then hesitated and turned back. 'Oh, by the way, you can tell that Jazz woman she's much too old to be wearing a thong. Mutton dressed as lamb. Very unbecoming.'

I watched glumly as her figure receded down the street. As I turned to go back inside, Jazz was climbing the steps from the basement, having now changed into jeans and a blouse.

'And who the hell was that, Phil?' she asked with a frown. 'Your wife?'

'Afraid so. I'm sorry about that.'

'It's all right. Just took me back for a minute.' She pulled a sympathetic smile. 'I only saw her for a second, but she seemed like a bit of a dragon.'

'Just somewhat,' I agreed. 'I should have asked you to marry me back in Bosnia and saved myself a lot of grief.'

Her smile remained. 'I was too young then. I'd have turned you down.'

'And now?'

Her dark eyes regarded me closely. 'That's a silly game to play, Phil.'

I hesitated for a moment. 'Yes, of course,' I said. But I wasn't at all sure I was playing a game.

'Goodnight, Phil. See you at the next debrief.' She looked thoughtful for a second, then, as if on a sudden impulse, reached forward and kissed me quickly, but firmly on the lips.

Then she was gone, walking purposefully up the street.

For a moment or two I watched her, thinking how good she looked in the snug-fitting jeans. Then I dragged my eyes away, and began walking in the opposite direction. I needed to get some provisions in; typically I'd run out of basics again. Luckily there was a small parade of shops a couple of streets away and I stocked up on tea, coffee, milk and chocolate biscuits. Since Popadom had arrived on the scene, we seemed to get through a prodigious amount of those.

When I returned to the flat, I found that Kate had gone home, leaving the new roster open on my desk. I ran my forefinger down the Sunday column. I was due to keep an eye on the elderly owner of the curry-house chain, Akmal Younis. If nothing unusual occurred, he'd also be put at the bottom of the pile with Mrs Huda Dahdah.

Popadom and Jazz had a more interesting day in prospect, taking an initial look at the Egyptian lecturer in IT at Imperial College, Dr Samir Hashim, and his student, a Pakistani called Shahid Akhtar.

I decided on an early night. As usual, Saturday TV was rubbish so, after making some beans and egg on toast, I watched an old DVD of *Patton: Lust for Glory* in the company of a bottle of Scotch. Finally I crashed at around ten.

But I couldn't sleep. Tossing and turning, I seemed

only to be able to think of Nina's earlier visit and the prospect of a crucifying divorce settlement.

I must have got to sleep eventually, but only to wake up around dawn in a cold sweat. After a mug of strong, sweet tea and some toast and marmalade, I felt a lot better. It's strange how problems magnify when you're in bed at night, how the demons crowd in on you like they've got little sticks that they keep poking in your brain whenever you seem on the brink of dropping off. I'd never been brilliant with finances and, since leaving the security of army life, I'd become increasingly paranoid about finding myself suddenly without money. The divorce settlement was always going to be a tough one for me to manage, and that was even before I realized that Nina was going to squeeze me for every last penny she could get.

Still, with daylight now streaming in through the bed-room window and the back garden full of birdsong things suddenly didn't seem so bad. If I could hang on to this MI5 contract for a few months, I should be able to get my embryonic company onto a less wobbly financial footing.

By six-thirty, I was on the road, taking the ring road westward before eventually driving off north on the A404 towards Pinner on the north-west outskirts of London. I'd seen Popadom's photographs of Akmal Younis' house, and I found it easily enough in a very pleasant, very sub-urban and leafy street of 1930s houses. They were a mix of semis and detached properties with little Tudor flour-ishes by the architect that didn't really work. Virtually all the front gardens were neat and well tended and, although many had garages, the street was still lined with parked cars. There was a red Volvo estate parked in Younis' drive.

All those vehicles made it difficult to find a parking space for my van, but I managed to squeeze into a tight gap a few houses down on the opposite side of the road. I took out a newspaper and spread it over the steering wheel, so it would appear to any passer-by that I was reading. Surveillance in suburban residential areas is always a nightmare; anything out of the ordinary is so easy to spot by residents, twitching at their net curtains.

It was almost eight o'clock now and I decided it was time to play with my new toy, which Lassiter had delivered a couple of days earlier. It was a state-of-the-art Cellular Interceptor, which resembled a normal mobile phone. But this little baby was a lot more than that. To be honest, I found it simpler to operate than *my* over-complex mobile phone. Maybe that was because it just did what was asked of it! Add a target's mobile number to its memory and it would let me know every time that person made or received a call and the number of the phone at the other end. I could then listen to both sides of the conversation or read off text exchanges. I'd already programmed Younis' number, along with those of Leo Fryatt – Dave Mo Evans was now being monitored direct by MI5's communications spooks – although I couldn't pick up Leo's today because my machine only had a range of ten miles. Still, I reasoned, you can't have everything.

There was also a small digital recorder which I placed on the passenger seat and plugged into the Interceptor. Conversations might be in any language and need to be translated by experts. At least I'd once done a crash course in Arabic, but that was now decidedly rusty.

I settled down with the Sunday rag and wondered if the gadget would give me some entertainment.

I didn't have long to wait. At just gone eight-thirty my Interceptor bleeped and Younis' mobile number began flashing on the small screen along with a new number from the person calling him. It was from another mobile. I just remembered to save the new number to memory, when I realized, with some disappointment, that it was a text message. I struggled to switch 'mode' and bring the message up on my own screen. It read simply 993.

I waited. Would Younis reply? After a pause, he did. Even more simply, just 0. Then the Interceptor died, the exchange of messages finished.

I stared down at the receiver in my palm. What the hell was all that about?

No one exchanged numbers like that in text messages. Surely it would make no sense unless both parties knew what the numbers meant? I swear it took a full minute for the penny to drop. I think it was probably because both Popadom and Jazz were already so convinced that the genial and gentlemanly Younis was an innocent party, that I'd subconsciously accepted it as a fact myself.

But for two people to exchange and understand

numbers like that, it had to be a predetermined code. And I don't think there are many curry-house owners who use text-message codes in their everyday lives.

I felt a sudden surge of excitement. Of course, there was no way of knowing what 993 meant. But a simple reply of 0 suggested to me a confirmation or acknowledgement, hence no need for further messages.

Still puzzling on this, I suddenly caught sight of a Muslim woman in my near-side wing mirror. She wore a hijab headscarf and a long skirt and was pushing a pram with its hood up to protect the child from the sun. As she approached along the pavement beside my van, I absently noted that she had a rather attractive face, despite her eyes being hidden behind a pair of sunglasses. She almost looked familiar, but I couldn't think how . . .

I frowned and studied her more intensely as she drew level with the van.

My God, I thought suddenly, I don't believe this.

I hit the button to lower the near-side window just as she passed. 'Jazz!'

The woman froze, her shoulders stiffening, and I knew she was as taken aback as I was, wondering whether or not she knew the voice, if she should break cover to acknowledge it?

'It's me, Phil,' I called, lowering my voice.

I saw her shoulders relax and she backed up a couple of steps until she was level with the window. She looked perplexed, almost angry. 'I didn't recognize your van. What the hell are you doing here?'

'Watching Younis, of course.'

'That's my job today.'

Suddenly I realized. 'Don't tell me . . .'

'Kate phoned me last night with the rota details. You're supposed to be watching Shahid Akhtar, that student at Imperial College.'

'I'll kill that girl,' I muttered darkly.

'She got it mixed up?'

'Again,' I confirmed wearily. 'That's what *you* should have been doing.'

Jazz nodded. 'I'll make myself scarce then.' She smiled. 'Nice Muslim girls shouldn't be chatty with hoary old van drivers.'

'Not so much of the old,' I scolded.

'I can try and track down Shahid this afternoon. It'll be better than nothing.'

I indicated the pram. 'Boy or a girl?'

'My packed lunch.'

I laughed. 'I could never eat a whole one.'

Then Jazz turned the pram around and began walking slowly back down the street. It took a few minutes for me to stop thinking of the best way to fire Kate and to settle down again. My thoughts were suddenly concentrated as the Interceptor began bleeping and Younis' mobile number flashed on the screen again. It was a new number, another mobile. I switched 'mode' to bring up the text message he was receiving.

'XXX,' I muttered. It was then followed by a full stop and the letter H. Then the line went dead.

God, all this code stuff was so infuriating. It was being so near to discovering something and yet so far.

I'd barely overcome my frustration when the Interceptor came alive again. This time it was Younis making the call, and this time on voice. My spirits leapt.

'It is Dog here,' the Pakistani said. He sounded nervous.

'Use code!' the male voice at the other end snapped.

'I have just received a triple X.'

'Damn, from whom?'

'From Dove.'

A pause. 'Then we must pay heed.'

'But I need to see you,' Younis pleaded. 'It is really most urgent.'

I could almost sense the irritation in the other man's voice. 'It will have to be a different venue. Place 11. We met there once before, remember?'

'I remember.'

'In one hour, no two. Use the time wisely, do you understand?'

Younis seemed unsure. 'What? Oh, yes, of course.'

'You must be certain, or it will be another triple X. You understand me?'

'Thank you so much, I am so very grateful.'

'Now you must destroy the phone you are using. Only use a new one from now on. I just hope you have not compromised us.'

'I am sorry,' Younis said.

The other party hung up. The screen on the

Interceptor confirmed that Younis had phoned back the original caller.

It was all starting to make some kind of sense. A man had called Younis to suggest a meeting and Younis had confirmed it. Then another caller had sent the enigmatic XXX, which was some kind of warning to abort the meeting. But Younis sounded seriously anxious to meet anyway, so they agreed on a new time and venue.

This could be tricky. Younis would now be on his guard. Maybe that's what the caller had meant by 'use the time wisely'. Make sure he wasn't followed.

Well, that wouldn't be difficult with me being single-handed rather than the usual requirement of a team of four. I wished to hell the XXX call had come before Jazz turned up, not after she'd gone. We could have teamed up with a slightly better chance.

I wondered if she was still nearby? How far away had she parked her car? I snatched up my mobile and thumbed her number. It came up on voicemail, dammit. I didn't bother leaving a message.

Time could be running short and I had to take decisive action because I didn't want to be close by when Younis left his house, whether on foot or in his car. I started the van's engine, pulled out of the line of parked cars and drove past his house to the T-junction at the far end. I turned left and pulled immediately into the kerb. I stopped, climbed out and walked back to the corner. The garden fence topped with a wildly overgrown clematis gave me perfect cover to look back down the street towards Younis' house.

This way I had everything covered, whether he left home by car or on foot. I wouldn't follow from immediately outside his place; he'd spot that immediately. If he went the other way or came towards me, I was in a perfect position. I leaned against the fence, half-hidden by the clematis, pulled the folded Sunday tabloid from my back trouser pocket and pretended to read.

I didn't have long to wait. It was almost ten when Akmal Younis appeared at his front door with his chocolate Labrador on a lead. The man looked nervous, agitated, as he walked past the red Volvo estate that was parked in his drive and looked carefully up and down the street. Then he returned to the rear of the vehicle, opened the hatchback and waited for his dog to jump in. Slamming the hatch shut, he moved to the driver's door, climbed in and kicked over the engine before reversing out.

I watched anxiously to see which way he would turn, my heartbeat changing rapidly from a trot to a canter. The brake lights blinked at me.

He was heading in the opposite direction. That was fine. There was only one way he could go, and I would pick him up at the next intersection and thereby offer no clue that I might be following.

I sprinted back to my van, started it up, and drove straight off. I accelerated hard for a few hundred metres then threw a hard left into a street that ran parallel to the one in which Younis lived.

I'd almost reached the T-junction when the red Volvo flashed across in front of me, travelling left to right.

I resisted the urge to pull straight out and waited for another car to pass by and then I followed behind that. It was a risky but necessary strategy. If I sat immediately in Younis' rear-view mirror he'd smell a rat and that would be it. He'd abort his rendezvous. This way, although I stood a chance of losing him, at least there was an equal likelihood of success. It certainly helped being high up in the van's driving position, so I could see over the roofs of any cars between us.

During the next half-hour he tried it on, attempting to discover if he had a tail. The usual tricks, turning a corner and pulling up hard, so a tail would overshoot on the main road or follow him round and be forced to carrying on past for fear of blowing his cover. Younis later drove into a supermarket car park, went round a couple of times and came out again. He also suddenly drove into a residential cul-de-sac, which nearly caught me out.

But as I was always one or two cars behind him, I managed to avoid these sneaky little fieldcraft tricks. I think the truth was Younis wasn't very good and not very well trained, assuming, that is, that he'd been trained at all. It's one thing being told how to do these things, but quite another when it comes to putting them into practice.

I was thankful for that, because I was fast discovering that my skills were decidedly rusty. If I'd known we'd be following a 'confirmed' suspicious terrorist quarry, who actually suspected he was being followed, I'd have handed it over to Lassiter's pros in MI5. As it was, I had to do the best I could.

At last Younis seemed satisfied he was in the clear and stopped playing games. An hour after it started, I found myself following him at three cars' distance towards one of those leafy little Regency public parks scattered around the London suburbs that are often described as the lungs of the capital. I estimated we were about ten miles from his house.

As Younis pulled into the parking-area lay-by in front of black wrought-iron gates, I drove on past and, once out of sight, quickly tucked into a parking bay that was free. I pulled on a garish baseball cap, grabbed my bag of tricks and leapt out. When I stopped at the corner pillar of the park railings, I was just in time to see Younis sauntering through the gates with his chocolate Lab trotting at his side.

Allowing a few seconds for him to get ahead, I followed along a short pathway that led to a T-junction some fifty metres ahead. To my right was a single-storey mock-Tudor building that housed the park's public conveniences. Outside the door of the Gents stood Younis, staring straight at me.

Damn it!

I just managed to check my faltering steps and ambled on. The trouble was he'd clocked me and had the advantage now of being behind me. Of course, as far as I was aware, there was no reason for him to know who I was or to even suspect I was shadowing him . . . unless he came across me again in the park. That was assuming he wasn't going to turn right round and get back into his car, leaving me high and dry. It was time to gamble. I reached the T-junction where the pathway split left and right beside flowering borders. If Younis was to be following into the park shortly, I needed to know which way he'd turn. Straight ahead of me was a slope where people were sitting on the grass, mostly courting couples or families with young children having picnics.

Without actually rushing, I climbed briskly up the hill towards the patch of trees and rhododendrons at its summit. Half-way up I paused, pretending to be out of breath, and looked back down towards the park gates. I couldn't see Younis at the lavatory entrance, because of the positioning of nearby bushes, but I could see his dog.

Satisfied, I completed the short distance to the summit. There I dropped down on the grass in the shade of some trees. I had no intention of hiding and looking suspicious, but I was anyway certain Younis would be unable to detect me in the shadows. All part of my sniper background.

I waited impatiently for him to make his move. Five minutes passed. Then suddenly he was on the move, heading towards the T-junction with his dog at his side. He turned to his left and ambled on, still looking anxiously about him.

Once he had his back to me, I climbed to my feet and followed along the edge of the glossy rhododendron bushes, keeping my quarry in view some hundred metres distant, down on the path. Then I lost him as he turned a bend into the shelter of some overhanging willows. I moved forward more urgently, waiting for him to reappear beyond the trees. He didn't.

I cursed. I quickened my pace and took a course down the slope that would get me to the path some distance beyond the willows. When I finally reached the path, I was perspiring heavily with exertion and an adrenalin rush.

When I glanced back towards the willows, I could just determine Younis, seated on a bench with another man. I took a step back behind a shrub, which hid me from his view.

From my bag I extracted one of the new toys that Lassiter had provided, a very smart Pentax digital camera. I put it to my eye and adjusted the focus, peering through the leaves of the shrub.

I zoomed in until I had both men in the frame, took a snap, then tightened the focus on Younis. He looked extremely unhappy and was sweating profusely.

After another snap, I swung the lens slowly until I had the other man's face in tight focus. He was possibly an Arab, and probably in his early forties. His thick black wavy hair was very shiny and neatly cut, like the moustache above his upper lip.

As I took a picture of him, I decided I didn't recognize him . . . and yet, those very dark eyes with their almost malevolent expression seemed to ring an alarm bell somewhere deep in my subconscious.

I lowered the camera and looked down at the last image I'd taken in the viewfinder. Then suddenly I had it.

In the photograph I'd seen of him, he'd had a beard and had been wearing thick tortoiseshell-rimmed spectacles.

Goddammit, was it possible? I swear my heart skipped a couple of beats.

Younis was only talking to Dr Samir Hashim, the IT lecturer from Imperial College – who Popadom was supposed to have been following this very afternoon.

And, as far as MI5 had been aware, the two men didn't even know each other.

Six

Suddenly I heard Younis' voice raised in anger.

'That's it, I've had enough!' were the words I think he said.

I glanced up from the camera, just in time to see him stand up and stalk off down the path with his dog towards the park gates, leaving the other man staring after him from the bench.

I wasn't sure what was the best action to take. I decided not to take my eye off the ball and to stick with Younis as best I could. Dropping my camera back into my bag, I began sauntering along the path towards the willows. As I passed the bench Dr Samir was so engrossed in an animated conversation on his mobile phone that he didn't even notice me. Unfortunately he was talking in Arabic and I could barely make out a word.

As I rounded the bend in the path, I realized that Younis was much further ahead than I'd thought. He was walking so fast that it was almost a trot. He was a good hundred metres ahead when he and his dog reached the junction and turned right towards the gates.

I arrived at the entrance just in time to see his car

reversing out of its parking space and then accelerate away.

There was no time to get to my van, turn it around and give chase. The best I could do was to return to his house and hope to find his car already there. Feeling deflated, I headed back to my van.

A familiar figure was standing in the shade, leaning with his back against the near-side wing.

Popadom raised one of his crutches. 'Bloody things, Mr Phil!' he exclaimed in frustration.

I realized what had happened. 'Of course, you were following Dr Samir . . .'

'Yes, but there was no way I could be following when he got out of his taxi! It is really, truly maddening!'

'You saw Younis and his dog?' I asked.

'Yes, just now. So the two men are connected in some way?'

'Well, they had a meeting.'

'That is what I am thinking. Dr Samir had some sort of coded text exchange and then a brief conversation with someone. Now I realize it was Younis. It suggested a rendezvous.'

Of course, I was forgetting that Popadom also had an Interceptor machine and would have been listening to any calls Dr Samir made.

'We've missed a trick,' I said. 'We should have assumed that any of the six people on our list might know each other and logged all their known mobile numbers in the Interceptors.'

Popadom smiled and shook his head slightly. 'Ah, that is wisdom after the event, Mr Phil. We will not be making that mistake again.'

I suddenly thought of something. 'It seemed that Younis and Dr Samir had a bit of a row. Younis stormed off, then Dr Samir was on his phone. Did you pick up anything on your Interceptor? The number he was calling?'

'No,' Popadom replied. 'I think he was destroying his old phone after talking to Younis. It will be a new pay-as-you-go number that we do not have.'

'Ah yes, of course.'

'Perhaps you should return to the park and try to pick up a tail on my Dr Samir,' Popadom suggested.

Of course, the old MI5 pro was right. 'Good thinking, Pops. Call me if he comes out this way.'

'Certainly.'

Then I left, walking as fast as I could back towards the bench under the willows. Hardly surprisingly Dr Samir was no longer there, but then I hadn't passed him on my way in. I continued on around the path until I eventually came to another gate. I had a nasty feeling that had been Dr Samir's route out. I continued on the circular path until I was back at the main entrance.

Popadom was waiting expectantly.

I shook my head. 'Lost him.'

Ten o'clock the next morning saw Popadom and me at Thames House for a meeting with Joe Lassiter.

I'd telephoned him at his home the night before to tell him about the meeting between the curry-house owner Younis and the Imperial College lecturer Dr Samir and their coded text-message exchange. Lassiter's obvious irritation at having his evening in front of the television disturbed soon gave way to unveiled excitement. He insisted on me going into MI5's headquarters to see him the next day.

Meeting us at the security desk, he rushed towards us enthusiastically, perspiring from the unfamiliar exertion. The sleeves of his crumpled striped shirt were rolled and his tie askew. I had the feeling he'd got into the office very early that morning.

The expression in the eyes behind the pebble-lensed spectacles for once actually matched the fat smile on his face. 'Phil, great to see you!' he greeted with unusual warmth. 'You, too, Pops. Looks like we might have a result.'

I played it cagey. 'Well, two of our suspects know each other, Joe, that's all.'

Lassiter showed disappointment at my reticence. 'Yes, but used a coded text exchange and set up a highly suspicious rendezvous. That's why you're here. And I've set up a meeting with the Ice Queen. Felicity's waiting for us now.'

He led the way alongside the open-plan office where I remembered he had his work station and down a plain-walled corridor, past a series of bland, teak-veneered doors. He stopped at one marked Briefing Room 6 and knocked.

'Come,' a female voice ordered from the other side.

Lassiter opened the door and stepped aside to allow us to enter. Felicity Goodall sat at the only table in the small, windowless room. She was wearing a blue linen skirt and jacket. From the doorway I couldn't help noticing the long, tanned legs elegantly crossed beneath the table and a pair of designer high heels that Kate would have died for. The Ice Queen was a picture of cool.

She looked up from reading the contents of a single, slim folder, which was the only item on the desk, and peered over the top of her natty gold-rimmed reading glasses.

'Hallo, Phil,' she said with a smile and a flutter of those long lashes. 'Nice to see you again.' She transferred her gaze to Popadom. 'You, too, Pops. How's the leg?'

'A damn bloody nuisance, boss, pardon me,' he replied, adding, 'at least the plaster is due to be coming off tomorrow.'

She removed her glasses. 'You'll be pleased, I bet. Must itch like fury.'

He gave a little shake of his head. 'Then I am getting back to doing some proper work.'

Felicity gave one of her light, slightly breathless laughs. 'Oh, I think we might hold on to you here for a little while. Make sure you're really fit before we hand you back to the watchers.'

I think she saw Popadom's protest coming and quickly indicated the stack of modern upright chairs, matching the desk in black ash with chrome legs. Lassiter began pulling them off the top of the pile and placing them on the floor to face the desk.

As we took our seats, Felicity said, 'Well, gentlemen, this is quite an interesting development. Let me see now if I remember correctly. Your team is currently tasked with having a look at six possible terrorist suspects.

'Mrs Huda Dahdah, widow of an insurgent suicide bomber killed in Iraq, whom you report as being very unlikely material. Leonard Fryatt, a black youth who's a member of the Allah's Army gang in south London. You think he's just a petty criminal and a wannabee jihadist. You think he poses no real threat, but he could be a useful informer?'

I nodded. 'I don't think he's the right material, but he could give us an insight into what, if anything, members of Allah's Army might be planning.'

'Low-level?' Felicity asked.

'Very. I thought I could just keep in touch, befriend him.'

A frown creased her brow. 'Oh, yes. I gather you made quite an impression on him.' There was a distinct hint of disapproval in her voice. 'I trust we won't see any recurrence of that sort of thing?'

I smiled. 'Of course not. But the situation did put me in a good position to keep in touch with him.'

Felicity almost sighed, I thought. 'Well, if you think you have the time and it could be worthwhile, I'd have no objections.' She glanced back down at the open folder. 'Moving on, there is this former Welsh soldier called

Evans. You've done well, there, Phil. He's definitely up to something and he is now an official suspect. The watchers from A4 began moving in on him yesterday. I gather you know him from the past?'

'Didn't exactly know him,' I explained. 'He passed through Sniper School when I was there.'

'And you'd be happy to meet up with him again?'

'If he agrees,' I said. 'He was a bit cagey at the time, but we swapped phone numbers.'

'Not surprising he was cagey,' Felicity replied, 'knowing our friend Naved Hussein was about to turn up – assuming you're right, of course. He's the one I'm really after. Most definitely linked to al-Qaeda, and suspected of being one of their facilitators. If he's in the country we must find him.'

'I understand that.'

'Well, meet Evans if you can. But for God's sake tread carefully, he could be a very dangerous man . . . And don't do or say anything to arouse his suspicions or upset our watchers' operations. Remember they're now monitoring all calls on his mobile phone and any emails he sends from that local Internet café.'

'I'll be very discreet,' I assured. 'I won't rush things.'

Felicity nodded and referred back to our list. 'That brings us to a British-born student of Pakistani origins at Imperial College. Young man called Akhtar Shahid.'

I said, 'Jasmina visited his place yesterday afternoon. She didn't get much time there because we had an operational blip.' I really didn't want the Ice Queen knowing exactly how incompetent a member of my staff had been. 'But I have spoken to her briefly. Apparently Shahid shares a house with a half a dozen other male students. Most are from Pakistani families. Jasmina posed as an employment agent that specializes in offering well-paid part-time jobs for undergraduates.'

Felicity raised her eyebrows. 'That's a neat one.'

'Went there looking for a name that didn't exist,' I explained. 'Said she must have the wrong address, but maybe they'd be interested themselves? As it turned out, the lads were quite keen. It was a good way to get chatting and for them to give personal information.'

'And Shahid was there?'

'Yes.'

Felicity looked intrigued. 'And what jobs did she offer? She must have had to think fast.'

I shook my head. 'No, she did it the other way round. Asked them what sort of job would suit them best. She'd go back to her agency and see what was available or keep them on the books for when something suitable turned up. Of course, she had to ask a lot of personal questions and take down telephone contact numbers.'

'Including Shahid's?'

'Apparently. I'll have all the details later today.'

'And what sort of job was he interested in?'

'Jazz gave them a few options. I think he said kitchen work or helping out in a care home.'

Felicity looked surprised at that. 'And her general impression?'

'Well, the flat was bit of a tip, typical all boys together, plates of unfinished food around, takeaway cartons and such. She even spotted a few empty beer cans, so they didn't appear to be radicalized Muslims. There was a copy of the Koran on a bookshelf, but also a pile of lads' mags. No prayer caps in evidence.'

'And Shahid himself?'

'Quiet apparently, very polite. Jazz thought maybe shy in the presence of a woman. She'll try to get to know him a bit more, but first impressions are that he's an unlikely candidate.'

Felicity smiled. 'Well, I'm impressed with Jasmina's methodology. Might use the technique in some of our other investigations. I'll look into it. But then we mustn't lose sight of the fact that Shahid has purchased inflammatory anti-West literature over the Internet and has taken part in radical study groups.'

'Hardly surprising, given the leanings of his tutor,' I pointed out.

'Ah, yes, Dr Samir Hashim . . .' Felicity said. 'That brings us to this meeting yesterday. Joe here believes it to be of great significance, I gather.'

I said, 'First it came as a surprise that Dr Samir and Younis even knew each other. And it was definitely a bit suspicious. There was an undoubted use of coded text messages between them. In view of events, it seems that was to set up a meeting at a predetermined place.'

'Then later Younis got another text from a different number,' Lassiter explained eagerly. 'Not a number known to us. The message was just "XXX" – very enigmatic, but it seems it was an abort message, a warning from someone.'

Felicity frowned. 'Who could that have been?'

I shrugged. 'I've no idea. It's possible I was spotted, but I don't think so as I successfully tailed Younis later. Maybe someone else was just afraid that they'd be compromised.'

'Anyway, Younis was clearly anxious to go ahead with a meet,' Lassiter went on. 'He called Dr Samir on voice, asked to go ahead with the meet at a different RV and time.'

'Not very professional,' Felicity observed.

'Dr Samir was pretty pissed off about it,' Lassiter agreed. 'Scolded Younis and told him not to use that mobile again.'

Felicity had picked up a pencil from the desk and idly chewed at the rubber end, deep in thought. She said, 'And they had this meeting?'

'Phil followed Younis to a park,' Lassiter confirmed. 'Meanwhile, unbeknown to him, Pops was following Dr Samir to the same park.'

She looked directly at me. 'I suppose you've no idea what happened?'

'They met at a park bench,' I replied. 'All I know is that Younis was very agitated and angry. He shouted at Dr Samir. "That's it. I've had enough" or something like that. Then he stormed off.'

Felicity puffed out her cheeks and tapped her pencil on the desk. 'Mmm, I see.' She turned to Lassiter. 'So what's your take on this?'

Lassiter leaned forward eagerly, resting his elbows on his knees and rubbing his hands together. 'Shine a light on the both of them. Get A4 surveillance in place.'

'You know how stretched the watchers are, Joe?'

'I know, but this is a hot one, I feel it.'

'Because of the coded text messages?'

'And a secret RV. They bloody well didn't want to be observed.'

Felicity turned to Popadom. 'I gather you've known Akmal Younis for a long time?'

'I was meeting him a few times as a child, he was a friend of my late uncle's. We ate at his curry-house. But that was many years ago.'

'You've already reported that, in your view, he's a very respectable businessman.'

She turned to me. 'And Jasmina, posing as a public health inspector, has interviewed him at some length, is that right, Phil?'

'Considered him to be an unlikely threat of any kind,' I confirmed. 'He's only on our list because he prayed at Mullah Reda's mosque and knows another of the suspected co-conspirators. But both men are in the curry-house business, so it should be no great surprise. And Younis has freely acknowledged he knows Malik Hasan.'

Lassiter could see the situation slipping from his grasp. 'But Jasmina and Popadom could be wrong. Yesterday's events are so suspicious!'

Felicity took a deep breath. 'Joe, you must consider that Akmal Younis is sixty years old. He's been in this country since he was twenty. He's run a successful business for years, as Popadom here well knows. He was even a personal friend of Pop's uncle who, according to our records, was more British in his attitudes than most of us around this table. Younis is hardly radical Muslim firebrand material.'

'But those coded calls,' Lassiter protested, 'the secret meeting . . .'

Felicity smiled sympathetically. 'There's something of which you won't be aware. It only came to our attention on Friday afternoon last week. Apparently Younis is under investigation by Customs and Inland Revenue, suspected of false accounting. Given the size of his curry-house empire, it could involve substantial amounts of money. Dr Samir, as well as being an IT lecturer, is also a fully qualified accountant and economist.'

I could see Felicity's thinking. 'You mean that could be the reason for the coded calls, the secret meeting?' I asked. 'Wanting professional advice from a friend?'

Lassiter fell back against his seat, looking like a boxer who knew he faced defeat in the next round. 'I had no idea,' he murmured.

'Of course not,' Felicity said, 'I'm sorry, Joe, but I'm going to have to turn down your request. We've got two hundred suspects under full investigation at the moment, and we're adding to them by the hour. Most are just wannabees, just discussing terrorist attacks in theory or making half-baked plans. But if we hear about them, we have to follow up.'

'I'm aware of that,' Lassiter said testily, a poor loser as always.

'I'm afraid I just do not have the resources to follow up Younis on the evidence so far.'

But Lassiter wasn't about to give up so easily. The boxer in him took one last swing. 'What about Dr Samir?'

Felicity pursed her lips. Very kissable lips, I thought suddenly, and almost missed the words they were speaking. 'Give yourself some more time on him. We know Dr Samir's a friend of Naved Hussein and Samir helped him set up his Guardians of Paradise website. Naved is al-Qaeda connected and, if Phil is right and he's in the UK, he may try to contact Dr Samir. Because of that, I've already put Samir under electronic surveillance.'

'How exactly?' I asked.

'His landline and known mobile calls are being monitored,' she explained with unexpected patience. 'And we've got a live CCTV relay on his front door from a car parked outside – just in case Naved turns up.'

I thought how things had moved on from my days in Northern Ireland. Then a car headlamp would conceal a camera to take a fuzzy black-and-white picture every time an infra-red beam was broken. Someone retrieved the film every day. Now it was wide-screen technicolour live action to a remote MI5 monitoring station – no doubt with a plasma screen and full quadraphonic sound.

'But is that enough?' Lassiter pressed.

'Same story, Joe,' Felicity replied, a tone of exasperation

creeping into her voice. 'Dr Samir may have radical Islamic sympathies, but it doesn't make him a terrorist. I have to prioritize. If Phil and his team come up with more, obviously I'll reconsider.' She glanced at the slim gold Cartier on her wrist. 'Now, if you'll excuse me, I have another meeting to attend – suspects with a little more evidence to warrant action than yours, I'm afraid, Joe.'

Lassiter finally threw in the towel and rose to his feet as Felicity made her way to the door. 'Well done, anyway, lads,' was her parting crumb of comfort as she disappeared.

'Bloody woman,' Lassiter breathed as Popadom and I followed him out into the corridor. 'Prioritize, my arse. Today's buzz-word. Seems I never hear anything else.'

When we reached the security check-out, I asked, 'How do you want us to proceed, Joe?'

Lassiter was obviously still seething at having his plan of action thwarted and it seemed to take several seconds for him to get his mind into gear. 'Well, I think we can write off Mrs Huda and the black guy Leo Fryatt, although you can keep in touch with him if you think it's worthwhile.'

I nodded. 'Dave Evans is ongoing and we've only just started to look at the student Shahid Akhtar . . . what about Younis and Dr Hashim? D'you want us to drop them, move on to some new suspects?'

Lassiter glared at me as though I was mad. 'The Ice Queen didn't say drop them, Phil, she's just not prepared to hand the investigation over to Service staff . . . yet.' He said it with the distinct implication that one day she would. 'I'm the field controller on this and I know when I smell a rat.'

'So what do you want me to do about it?' I repeated.

He grunted. 'Let me have a think about it. I'll be in touch.'

Popadom watched as Lassiter stomped off down the corridor. 'I am thinking that is one very unhappy bunny.'

'And what do you feel, Pops? About Felicity's decision.'

He sighed. 'In the old days, Mr Phil, before half the Muslim population of this country became terrorist suspects, Dr Samir and Younis would definitely have been under full MI5 scrutiny.'

I felt a kind of inexplicable shiver as he spoke the words.

I'd arranged to meet Leo Fryatt at lunchtime.

Deciding to give the Black Dog pub a wide berth, I suggested a rendezvous in the lobby of the Ritz Hotel on Piccadilly.

Leo had almost choked on his mobile phone. 'You takin' the piss or what, Mr Khan?'

I'd smiled to myself at his reaction and answered the question with one of my own. 'What's the matter, Leo, isn't a good Muslim warrior worthy of the good life in this world?'

'Yeah, of course, but the Ritz . . . that's a swanky job up west, innit?'

'You've heard of it, then?'

'Course.'

'Have you got a suit?'

'Now you really are takin' the piss!'

'All right then, Leo. Smart casual. No jeans and no trainers. Can you manage that? I'll meet you in the lobby at one. There's a nice Lebanese restaurant nearby. Lunch on me, okay?'

'Er, yeah, sure . . .'

I'd said, 'There's more to life than the Black Dog and a McDonald's.' Then I hung up.

At one o'clock I was waiting for him in the lobby of the Ritz. Meeting in hotel lobbies is a favourite trick of intelligence officers as, with all the comings and goings, two people meeting briefly are unlikely to be conspicuous or even remembered. Also most large London hotels have at least one member of staff, perhaps a manager or concierge, who is on MI5's payroll, to help them keep an eye on the movement of any suspect residents and help gain access to their rooms. Of course, I had no idea who that might be at the Ritz.

When Leo turned up, I was pleasantly surprised that he had actually made an effort. He was wearing a smart rainbow-coloured shirt with short sleeves, chinos and a pair of suede loafers. The smart effect was rather spoiled by the plaited black hair and short pigtail, but it was a start.

As I approached he was glancing around nervously as though half-expecting to be pounced on by a security man at any moment and booted out. I was wearing trousers and a light linen jacket and Leo didn't recognize me until we were face to face.

'Hallo, Leo.'

'Oh, hi, Mr Khan.' He frowned. 'You said we ain't eating here?'

'That's right. D'you like Lebanese food?'

'Never 'ad it.'

'Best Arabic food ever.'

His eyes lit up at that. 'What like Muslim food?'

'Muslims and Christians live in Lebanon,' I replied as we walked back towards the entrance.

We crossed over Piccadilly to the Fakhreldine, which was on the first floor with a panoramic view over Green Park. Leo's jaw dropped and his eyes widened at the opulence of the restaurant, all mirrors, gilt and red-leather upholstery.

'Hey, awesome. You come here a lot, Mr Khan?'

'Once in a blue moon,' I replied honestly. 'First came years ago for a business lunch on expenses. Always liked the food and staff.' I didn't add that there was no way I had even been able to afford West End restaurant prices on my military pay.

The maître d' smiled, took care not to notice Leo's radical hairstyle, and led us to a window table where we could look out over the grass and trees of Green Park.

As he handed us the menus, I asked, 'What d'you recommend today?'

'I would suggest the beef in pomegranate sauce,' he replied without hesitation.

I looked at Leo. 'Fancy that?'

The macho mini-mobster looked terrified, but tried to put on a brave face. 'Yeah, why not?'

I settled for lamb casserole with pinenuts and ordered a bottle of white wine.

'Wine?' Leo queried as the maître d' disappeared. 'I thought you didn't drink no alcohol? Like when we was at the pub.'

'I only drink wine with food, Leo. It's part of the meal. I don't buy all this fundamentalist crap.' I smiled gently at the look of astonishment on his face. 'Why should drinking fermented fruit juice be a sin . . . unless it takes over your life?'

'That's not what the imams say?'

'Radical imams say a lot of things,' I retorted. 'Like it's fine for us to blow ourselves up, to kill and maim innocent people because they are not of our religion. Like most religions in history at one time or another, Islam has been hijacked by some of its clergy to give themselves power and wealth.' I held Leo's gaze steadily across the table. 'When did you ever hear of a mullah volunteering to be a suicide bomber?'

At that point the wine waiter appeared with a chilled bottle of Lebanese wine and filled our two glasses. When he'd gone, Leo picked up his drink. 'So you're sure this *is* okay, like?'

I nodded and raised my glass. 'To Allah the Merciful.'

Leo smiled awkwardly and took a sip. Judging by the sour expression on his face he didn't have much of a taste for wine.

'Yeah, to Allah.'

'So why did you want to see me, Leo?'

'You said you had contacts. That maybe they could get me some . . .' he lowered his voice conspiratorially '. . . like proper military training.'

I pursed my lips. 'Oooh, yes, I think I did mention that.'

'So you didn't mean it?' The disappointment in his voice was unmistakable.

'I meant it all right, Leo. It's just not that simple.'

'What d'you mean, Mr Khan?'

'You have to prove yourself to the organization. That you are trustworthy, have honour and integrity – and courage.'

Leo looked puzzled. 'What organization?'

I allowed myself an enigmatic smile. 'I think you know who I'm talking about.'

His eyes widened. 'You mean . . .' he checked the volume of his voice, lowering it to scarcely a whisper '. . . al-Qaeda?'

I didn't answer directly. 'Your help is needed.'

'Mine? How can I help?' He frowned suddenly. 'I don't want to be no suicide bomber.'

I raised my finger to my lips as I saw the waiter approach with our meals. Once he'd gone, I said, 'You do understand that the organization of which I speak is, in truth, more of a network. At the centre the leadership can organize strategy, but mostly the tactics are the work of others in their own countries. Sometimes the leadership is asked to sanction activities and help out with expertise, but much that is done in its name is outside its control.'

Leo prodded a fork suspiciously at a chunk of beef on his plate. 'No, not sure I knew that, Mr Khan.'

'Well, Leo, increasingly the leadership does not like what is done in its name. The point was well made at 9/11 – the greatest terror attack of all time.' I paused, trying to make my argument sound convincing. 'So the leadership thinks the bombings in London and Madrid may have started to become counter-productive.'

Having overcome his initial reluctance, Leo was now devouring his beef in pomegranate sauce with gusto. With his mouth full, he mumbled, 'Like how is it counter . . . what you said?'

'Starting to alienate other Muslims in these countries, making them feel isolated,' I said. 'The leadership needs people with their ears to the ground in the radical Muslim community. Trustworthy people who can keep their eyes open and their mouths shut. People like you.'

'Me? I don't know nothin'.'

'You're in Allah's Army. If some hothead is planning something stupid, the leadership wants to know about it. Then it can be stopped – or the people can be helped to get it right by our experts.'

Leo had already demolished his meal and pushed his plate away. 'That sounds like spying on my brothers, Mr Khan.'

I shook my head. 'No, helping them, Leo. And helping

the leadership. Helping the cause of Islam. Not like those criminal friends of yours at the Black Dog.'

That went down well. I could see Leo liked the idea of being regarded more highly by the al-Qaeda leadership than his cronies like Mustufa. 'So you want me to infiltrate like, yeah?'

'No, think of it as being a secret liaison officer for the leadership. Put yourself about a bit, could you do that?'

Surprisingly, Leo helped himself to more wine. 'Sure, Mr Khan, I reckon I could be your man.'

I had just said goodbye to my new recruit, when my mobile rang.

It was Joe Lassiter. 'Where are you, Phil?'

'Standing in Piccadilly', I replied, 'watching the girls go by.'

'You free to meet? I've been thinking.'

That sounded ominous. 'I've nothing much planned for the rest of the afternoon. Must do the VAT soon . . .'

Lassiter took that as a yes. 'Look, I could do with some fresh air.' He named a little backstreet pub in Westminster. 'I'll see you there in half an hour.' Then he hung up before I had a chance to wriggle out of it.

I found Lassiter sitting at a small table under an awning outside the pub, with a single pint of lager in front of him.

He looked up and grinned at me. 'Grab yourself a drink, Phil. Looks like you need one.' As I moved towards the door, he added, 'Oh, and I could do with a refill. Cheers.'

Neatly stitched up yet again by Lassiter, I bought another lager for him and a long Coke and ice for me. I'd had enough alcohol for the time being. Of course, Lassiter spotted it straight away. 'Not Lent, is it?'

'If you're up to something, Joe,' I replied, 'I want to be able to think in a straight line.'

He smiled at that. 'So what have you been doing since our meeting with the Ice Queen this morning?'

'Had lunch with Leo Fryatt.'

'The black kid.'

'As you know, he thinks I'm connected to al-Qaeda. He's offered to be an informer on whatever mischief the Allah's Army gang might be planning . . . in return for military training if he proves himself.'

Lassiter nodded. 'Might turn out to be useful. And recruited under a false flag, I like that.'

I took a mouthful of iced drink, then said, 'You said you'd been thinking, Joe. Thinking what exactly?'

He sampled the fresh glass of lager, giving himself a moustache of foam in the process. 'Felicity won't upgrade and hand over Akmal Younis' case to the office without more evidence. So let's keep him in our sights and get it.'

'What about the fact that he's being investigated by the Revenue?'

Lassiter shook his head, adamant. 'That's one of the things I've been thinking about. I don't see that as a reason for the secrecy and suspicious behaviour we witnessed. Businessmen are always being investigated by the Revenue, it's what happens. And everyone has some little thing to hide. Even if it's something bigger, they don't make coded phone calls and have secret meetings on park benches with advisers. It's all pretty open in my experience.'

I'd known Joe Lassiter for a long time and, despite his many faults and irritating manner, he was basically good at his job and had a nose for such things. I said, 'I'm not sure we can get more at the level of surveillance we can offer. I mean, Jazz even managed a long lunch with him and got absolutely nothing. And if Jazz can't get a sniff of something wrong, then no one can.'

'I agree,' Lassiter said, 'that's why I want to up the ante.'

'What d'you have in mind?'

'Break in to his house and have a nose.'

That took me by surprise. 'A break-in? By who?'

'You.'

I nearly sprayed a mouthful of Coke over him. 'What? I don't believe you just said that. That's the whole point of wanting Felicity to hand it over to your boys. The professionals.'

'You can do it, I know that.' Adamant.

'Spare me the false flattery, Joe,' I snapped back. 'I could do it. I have done that sort of thing a couple of times in Northern Ireland. But I'm pretty rusty—'

'Take Jazz with you,' he replied glibly. 'She was in the Det. It'll be like riding a bike for her. She won't have forgotten.'

'I'm not at all sure Jazz would agree to that,' I replied.

'She's not in the army now. And I certainly can't believe Felicity would sanction such an action.'

Lassiter looked suddenly grim-faced. 'The Ice Queen doesn't have to, Phil. I'm your liaison with the office, not her. Let me deal with her . . . after the event.'

'You're barking,' I replied bluntly.

Lassiter's magnified eyes narrowed behind his pebble-glass lenses. 'Did you see footage of those injured in the London bombings?'

I nodded. 'Some stuff on TV.'

'They won't have shown on the box what I've seen, matey.' For a moment Lassiter looked very pale and, for once in his life, his emotional anger seemed totally genuine. 'Hospital footage. Mutilated faces, arms and legs blown off . . . innocent people facing a life of utter purgatory. By comparison, maybe the dead victims were the lucky ones.'

I shook my head. 'That's moral blackmail, Joe, and you know it.'

'Moral blackmail is the least thing I'd use to stop another bombing,' he growled back at me. 'Younis is somehow involved in things, even if it's on the periphery. I feel it in my water.'

'You may well be right,' I said, 'but I still think you need to persuade your own boss first.'

He spared me a look of pure exasperation. 'Have you any idea what it's like at the office? Because, Phil, I don't think you do. First they're running round like headless chickens, swamped with supposed terrorist suspect leads from the police and public. The office simply can't cope, and then there's the inter-department feuding and rowing as always – made worse by the number of women involved now!'

Lassiter was back on a favourite hobby horse and I wasn't going to be able to stop him. 'I've told you Felicity is at loggerheads with "Medusa" – Melissa Thornton, her Head of Desk. Felicity wants her job and Melissa knows it. She just can't wait for Felicity to put a foot wrong! Felicity got away with the Mullah Reda raid – but only because she got a result! That's why our darling Ice Queen won't risk a bollocking by committing resources without sufficient evidence.'

I could understand that. 'But what about you, Joe?'

'Felicity doesn't like me, simple as that. Women don't act and think like men. That's a good enough reason to prise me out. Have me transferred to the Registry or something. The only reason I'm still here is because we're so bloody short-staffed.' He paused to take another gulp of lager. 'But if I can get a result for Felicity . . .'

'You might become best mates?' I suggested.

He scowled at my sarcasm. 'I might just keep my frigging job.'

I drained my Coke and swirled the clinking ice cubes around the glass. 'I understand, Joe. Just wish I could oblige.'

A strained and ominous silence developed between us. I took out my tobacco tin and began making a roll-up. Suddenly Lassiter said, 'I bumped into Nina the other day, just as I left your office. Did I mention it?'

The words struck me like a thunderbolt. I knew his angle immediately. 'No, but she did.'

Lassiter was all smiles. 'Mentioned you were working for me. She seemed very interested. Wondered how much we were paying you.'

'Did you tell her?' I expect he could detect the note of near panic in my voice.

'Course not, matey. Mind you, that Nina of yours can be a very persuasive woman. She's invited me to have a drink with her sometime this week.'

'Are you going to?'

'Depends really.'

Why was it I knew exactly what it depended on.

'Joe,' I said, 'were you born a complete bastard, or did you have to work at it?'

Lassiter just smiled and raised his glass. 'I've time for one more, I think.'

Seven

It was under a dull and starless sky that I drove to Jazz's place in Putney on Wednesday night.

I glanced at the clock on the van's dash. It was approaching midnight and Jazz would be expecting me. She didn't know why she was wanted, but I'd told her yesterday that I might be needing her for something important. I said I couldn't go into details. She'd pulled one of those cute expressions of hers that told me I was an idiot for playing at secret squirrels and not trusting her fully.

Normally she'd have been right. But what I didn't tell her was that I couldn't go into details because I was too damn sure she'd say no.

'Wear black,' I'd said enigmatically.

'My cocktail number?' she'd asked cheekily. 'Or jeans and trainers?'

'I can't afford cocktails, so it'll be jeans and trainers.'

I double-parked outside her house, but before I could get out of the van Jazz opened her front door and trotted down the steps. As she climbed in I saw she had her hair up in a clasp and wore no make-up. She still looked stunning. She'd added a long-sleeved black cotton top to the jeans and trainers.

She grinned. 'Are we doing a Milk Tray commercial?'

'Something like that,' I replied, driving off.

'Are you going to fill me in now?'

'That's the best offer I've had all week.'

She hit me playfully on the arm. It didn't hurt, but you could sense the power behind it. I reckoned Jazz was still pretty fit. 'So tell me, Phil.'

I said, 'When we get there.' Then I changed the subject. 'No trouble getting a babysitter for Zoë?'

'No, I told you, Ricardo's parents are always up for looking after their little darling. Spoil her rotten.'

Conversationally, I said, 'You still haven't heard from your husband?'

'No,' she replied hoarsely.

'Haven't his parents heard from him?'

'No, they'd have told me.'

'Seems strange. Obviously a caring man, a doctor . . .'

'It happens, Phil, all the time. Some men bottle up their problems, can't cope, then just vanish. Police files are full of missing persons, you know that.'

'Had you thought about divorce?'

'Look, Phil, I don't want to talk about it.' There was an edge of irritation to her voice now. 'Okay?'

I nodded. 'Of course, I'm sorry.'

She reached across and touched my knee. 'I'm sorry, too, believe me. Didn't mean to snap.'

I gave her a quick sideways glance. 'I still care about you, you know? A lot.'

Although I was back watching the road, I knew she was smiling. 'I know.'

We lapsed into silence as I drove north, the traffic beginning to thin out as the capital began closing down for the night. Eerily I noticed how often I heard the distant wail of police-car sirens as they raced this way or that. Perhaps it was my imagination, but there seemed to be a lot of activity going on.

Eventually Jazz said, 'Where are we going, Phil? This is the way to Akmal Younis' place.'

There was no point in denying it now. 'Lassiter wants us to take a closer look.'

'You told me his section chief had pulled the plug on it.'

'Not according to Joe,' I replied. 'She just won't recommend MI5 taking over without more concrete evidence. All to do with office politics apparently.'

'I don't trust that man.'

'He's okay,' I lied to reassure her.

We were very close to Younis' house now, entering the residential estate. Jazz seemed agitated. 'You say Lassiter wants us to take a closer look. What exactly do you mean?'

I tried to sound casual, as though it was the most natural thing in the world. 'Look around his house.'

'What? Break in?' She was astounded. 'Is Younis there?'

'Yes, Popadom is on watch. He's had his plaster off

and he's keen to do some proper work. Younis is no doubt sleeping like a baby. According to his medical notes, he takes a Zopiclone every night for his insomnia.'

'How did you get his medical notes?'

'Through Lassiter.'

I pulled in at the end of the street and killed the engine.

Jazz glared at me. 'I want no part of this, Phil. It's unprofessional and stupid. And it could be dangerous.'

'You assessed Younis as being a non-threat,' I pointed out, somewhat unfairly.

'But what if I'm wrong? I'm a single mum, have you overlooked that?'

'Younis is a pussycat, we all know that. Even if he is mixed up with anything, he's not the violent type.'

She bit her lower lip. 'I don't know, this is all a bit of a surprise. I think you'd better leave me out of this.'

'Can't, Jazz, we need you.'

'What for?'

I held up the leather wrap and opened it, revealing the row of pockets holding ten different lock-picking instruments. 'I'm rubbish at this, you're not.'

'Younis has a dog,' she countered.

'A Labrador. He might just lick us to death. Besides . . .' I held up a soggy plastic bag. 'It'll be taken care of. Laced meat. It'll get a treat and its best night's sleep ever.'

She shook her head. 'You really are serious about this, aren't you?'

'Yes, and I'm sorry, Jazz, but you can pick but can't choose in work like ours.' She didn't appreciate my joke, so I added, 'We need your expertise. And you know I'd never put you in harm's way.'

She didn't answer but folded her arms across her chest and stared forward out of the windscreen. I took the opportunity to pick up our newly acquired short-range radio transceivers.

'Ace Cabs to Delta One. Over . . .'

Popadom's voice came back in the separate earpiece. 'Delta One receiving. Over.'

'Come in now, Delta One. Over.'

'Roger that. Be right with you. Out.'

Moments later Popadom appeared at the corner and approached our van. I opened my door. 'How's the land lying, Pops?'

He was all smiles. 'It is all very quiet, Mr Phil. All neighbours who went out earlier have returned.'

'And how's the leg?'

'Wonderful, just a little stiff.' He peered into the cab. 'Glad to have you with us, Miss Jazz. Mr Phil is thinking you may let us down.'

Jazz scowled at me. 'Does he now?'

'Don't worry. I am sure it is safe. The dog roams free in the house.' He looked at me. 'Do you have the meat? Ah, good, then I am suggesting I put it in the front letter box. We are waiting fifteen minutes before you go in. If the dog barks, we are waiting thirty until all is quiet again.'

I said, 'As we discussed? Over the side fence and into the rear kitchen door.'

Popadom nodded as he took the bag of meat from me. 'That is still best. Shall I be starting now?'

I glanced back at Jazz. 'Yes?'

'I suppose so,' she replied grudgingly.

As Popadom set off enthusiastically on his mission, I reached into the glovebox and pulled out two black woollen balaclavas and handed her one, which she stuffed into the back pocket of her jeans. 'I won't forgive you for this, Philip Mason.'

I looked at her, aware of my childish grin. 'You love me really.'

'Do I?' The dimples in her cheeks were deepening, suggesting a smile was trying to force its way onto her face. 'Let's just keep quiet, Phil, before you say something we both regret.'

I shrugged. She probably had a point. We settled down to wait. After five minutes Popadom confirmed over the radio that the meat had been delivered. The dog had not barked. Our man remained on station, hidden from view by next door's hedge.

The digital clock on the dash blinked ever more slowly, it seemed, as we waited an eternity for the fifteen minutes to pass. An occasional car passed us by, but none turned into the street where Younis lived. There was nobody about.

At last I nodded to Jazz. 'Let's go.'

We slipped out into the chill night air and walked

together down the pavement. I took her hand in mine. 'Take it slow, like lovers,' I said. 'We'll have a clinch just past his house. In those deep shadows.'

She slipped her arm around my waist. 'Okay.'

The sky was still filled with low, brooding cloud that blotted out the stars. Only the streetlamps provided low light and created shadows around hedges, trees and gate pillars. In one or two house windows there was the tell-tale blue flicker of a TV screen or computer being used by those who could not sleep. It was silent but for the spasmodic, distant sound of a motor vehicle. In someone's back garden a cat screeched momentarily before the quiet returned.

Younis' house was in darkness as we passed and then stopped beneath an overhanging tree, turning to face each other. I took Jazz in my arms, feeling her slender waist beneath my hands. Her eyes were very close, very wide and very beautiful. They seemed to bore into my skull with their penetrating gaze, as though Jazz was trying to transmit her unspoken thoughts. Before I realized my mouth crushed down on hers. She did not resist, her lips yielding to mine as her grip on my arms tightened.

'God, it's been so long,' I heard myself breathe.

'So long,' she echoed.

Popadom's voice cut in to my radio earpiece. 'All is clear. Go, go, go!'

I cursed silently and pulled back, the taste of her still on my mouth. Jazz looked at me with a half-smile and nodded. I turned and vaulted the low ornamental hedge and, keeping tight into the shadow of the garden side fence, edged across the lawn. I was aware of Jazz close behind me.

Our path was blocked by a locked side gate and another fence topped with a strip of trellis. In the corner, where the two fences joined, two dustbins had been conveniently placed. I sprang up on one of them, then heaved myself up and over the trellis. It swayed and creaked but held firm until I was over and able to drop to the lawn on the other side.

I crouched and watched the side of the house for any sign of life while I waited for Jazz to follow me over. In a few seconds she landed lightly beside me. Without exchanging a word, we both pulled on our balaclava masks.

There were two side windows opposite us, the lower sitting room and an upper bedroom, both with curtains shut. There was a kitchen window to the rear and a door just by the corner. That would be our way in.

I felt the fear a rat must feel when it leaves the safety of the shadows and sprinted across the back lawn to a paved patio area. We already knew there was no security light or burglar alarm at this building, which made our mission a lot easier. In fact, the lack of security at Younis' house had been another of Jazz's earlier arguments that he was unlikely to be a serious player in the terror game. And, I must say, I had tended to agree.

When we reached the kitchen door, I held the penlight to give a pinpoint beam on the keyhole.

'At least it's a bog-standard make,' she said. 'You have to keep up to speed on this sort of stuff, you know.'

Jazz deftly inserted one of the repertoire of lock-picks. She fiddled and twisted with it for several seconds, those seconds slowly dragging to a full minute, then two.

'Is that the right pick?' I whispered.

'It's been a long time,' she muttered.

'Let me try,' I said, taking the instrument from her.

I pushed the hook in, rotated it and almost immediately, to my surprise, heard the tumblers click. 'Your lucky day,' Jazz said. 'Seems I've lost my touch.'

As I twisted the handle, the door yawned open to reveal expensive terracotta tile flooring and oak-finished kitchen units. I stepped inside and scanned quickly with the penlight. The chocolate Labrador was lying flat out on the floor, fast asleep.

'One contented pooch,' I murmured, aware that Jazz was close behind me.

I was certain that a man like Younis, who ran a thriving business, would have to have a small office or study at home. I'd learn most about his activities from computer files or papers left around the place. But first I had to find them.

I opened the inner kitchen door and stepped into a hallway. It was tastefully decorated with occasional items of antique furniture. Asian pottery and small sculptures were much in evidence, and landscapes of wild and dusty mountain terrain that could have been Kashmir, seemingly by the same artist, hung on the walls. I turned the brass handle of the first side door and flashed the penlight beam around a dining room with a magnificent mahogany table that would have easily seated twelve guests. My quick inspection discovered cupboards loaded with fine porcelain crockery and glasses of every description, and drawers for cutlery, place mats and coasters and all the other paraphernalia for entertaining.

But there was likely to be nothing of interest here. The next door in the hallway gave onto a living room with three comfortable, plump leather sofas gathered around a coffee table. There was a very large plasma screen television in the far corner. Next to it was an old writing cabinet. Its hinged desktop was open and covered in papers. I reached for a pocket in my black cargo trousers and extracted a small Polaroid camera, taking a quick snap of the desktop flap and its contents. This was so all items could be replaced as they were found. I placed the print on top of the television and began rifling through the papers and documents while Jazz held the torch. A cursory glance told me that Felicity Goodall's information about Younis' financial affairs was correct. There were half a dozen letters from Customs and Inland Revenue and others from his own accountants and solicitors.

I attempted to leave everything as I found it before moving on to the cubbyholes and drawers at the back of the cabinet. A box drawer of pens, pencils, paperclips and the like. Other sections were filled with utility bills, personal handwritten letters which looked as if they came from family and relatives in Pakistan, car registration papers, insurance policy documents, receipts for the purchase of household items and miscellaneous domestic paperwork. There was no computer.

I glanced at Jazz and shook my head. This seemed to be all Younis' personal administration. Anything to do with his business or any dubious activities must be elsewhere. Referring to the Polaroid snap, I replaced everything where I'd found it and stuffed the photograph back in my pocket.

We moved back into the hall and I indicated silently to Jazz that we were going upstairs. Of course, for a properly authorized MI5 operation they would have secretly obtained architect's plans of the house from Younis' building society or his solicitors but, as Joe Lassiter was taking a flyer on this one, I just had to guess on the first-floor layout. My guess was that there were three largish bedrooms, one of which was likely to be used as some sort of office.

I reached the bottom of the stairs and began my ascent, placing my feet on the outer edges of each step where the timber would be less likely to creak. In an ungainly bow-legged motion I quickly reached the landing. I knew that the first closed door I came to would be Younis' bedroom because its light, viewed from the front of the house, was always the last to be turned off at night.

Next to it I could see an open door to the bathroom. If there was an office up here, then it would be behind one of the remaining two doors. Aware that Jazz was close behind me, I edged across the carpet and placed my palm on the handle of the door, gently easing it open.

I don't know who was more surprised, me or the figure in dark clothing who was standing in front of the small desk, apparently in the middle of unplugging the laptop computer. He turned his head sharply in my direction, but I couldn't make out any real detail of his face in the darkness. I think he gasped, but it could have been me. Then he snatched at the computer, ripping it free from its socket, and charged straight at me.

His shoulder caught me full in the chest, throwing me hard back against the open door, and he raced past, throwing Jazz roughly aside. I recovered quickly, ignoring the pain, and launched myself after him in a rugby tackle. My arms snapped tight around his calves and he slammed down onto the carpeted landing like a felled tree. I was vaguely aware of the laptop spinning out of his hands and crashing loudly down the staircase.

As I gasped for breath I must have loosened my grip around the man's legs, because the next thing I felt was his boot in my face. If he hadn't been wearing rubber soles, I think I'd have lost my front teeth. As it was, all I tasted was the warmth of the blood as it ran from my nose.

Then he was on his feet again and rushing for the stairs while I staggered to my feet and followed him as swiftly as I could. But, by the time I reached the lower hallway, I was just in time to hear the slamming of the front door.

I drew to a halt, heaving air into my lungs. Christ,

what a disaster! Even dosed with sleeping pills, Younis could never have slept through this.

Turning, I glanced back up the stairs. Where the hell was Jazz? Didn't she realize we'd have to run for it? For all we knew, Younis could be armed.

'COME DOWN NOW!' I shouted, throwing caution to the wind.

Suddenly, to my surprise, the top landing light came on. Jazz was standing at the top of the stairs, looking down at me.

Her face was very pale. 'Phil, I think you'd better come up here.'

I scrambled back up the stairs. Jazz was standing at the now open door of Younis' bedroom. 'What is it?' I asked.

'Take a look,' she said hoarsely.

I stepped past her. Younis lay flat on his back in the centre of a double bed, wearing grey silk pyjamas. He was staring at the ceiling, his face like white marble against the background of a sodden vermilion pillow. The neatly drilled hole in his forehead said it all. Flashburns to the flesh suggested he'd been shot at very close range. The exit wound would be horrendous and now I could see the wriggly grey matter amidst the thick layer of blood.

'Sweet Jesus,' I muttered.

Jazz said, 'I doubt he had time to realize what was happening. I guess that's some consolation.'

I glanced at her. 'Looks like Joe was right. He is involved with the terrorists. Somehow.'

'He's also a human being, Phil.' She turned away. 'And fundamentally a decent man, I think.'

I wasn't going to argue with her. I guess women have a different perspective from men sometimes. Instead I plucked the mobile from my pocket and called Lassiter. He answered immediately.

'Look, Joe, we're in situ. It's all gone belly up. We got in and found our man dead.'

'Shit!' Then a pause. I could almost hear the cogs of the brain clicking. 'Suicide?'

'No. We disturbed an intruder, who got away. What d'you want us to do?'

There was a long pause. I wondered if he was thinking how the hell he'd explain all this to the Ice Queen and still keep his job. 'Stay put, Phil. I'll get Special Branch to work with the local woodentops on this. Don't touch anything.'

With that he hung up. I turned to Jazz. 'We're to wait.'

She didn't look happy. 'I knew this was a bad idea.'

'I'm sorry.'

'That's okay,' she said, forcing a smile of reassurance. 'Neither of us knew this was going to happen.' Then she noticed the state of my face. 'God, Phil, are you all right?'

'Just a nose bleed, nothing broken. I think it's stopped now.'

'You'll have a right bruise tomorrow.'

I moved back out to the landing. 'Let's go down and get Pops in here.'

When we reached the bottom of the staircase, I found the laptop that the intruder had dropped when I'd tackled him. The lid had detached itself from the keyboard and the screen was shattered. Jazz stooped to retrieve it.

'Better leave that for the cops,' I said. 'DNA and all that.'

Then I noticed the lump of meat by the front door. The same steak that Popadom had pushed through the letter box earlier, uneaten. I turned the lock and opened it. Almost immediately Popadom appeared at the gate and scurried down the path towards me.

'Goodness, Mr Phil, what in the hell is happening, please?'

'Did you see the man who rushed out?' I asked, ushering him in.

'Of course. At first I thought it was you.'

'Did you see his face?' I asked as I closed the door.

'I am afraid not. It is much too dark.'

'And you didn't give chase?'

He gave me a strange look. 'Of course not.'

I was forgetting. Spooks are like rats, staying in the shadows where they can't be seen. A churlish thought, but I was in a churlish mood.

I said, 'Younis has been murdered in his bed. We just found the body.'

Popadom stared at me, his jaw dropping. 'You're jo . . . No, no, of course you are not joking! . . . And that man . . .?'

'An intruder,' Jazz explained. 'We disturbed him while he was trying to take Younis' laptop. Presumably he was the killer.'

I added, 'I've spoken to Lassiter. He's sending the Special Branch boys around.'

Popadom nodded. 'Of course. How astonishing.'

'Haven't got a hip flask on you, I suppose?' I asked suddenly.

'Mr Phil, I am Pakistani. A Muslim.'

I turned and headed towards the kitchen. 'Then I'm going to make a cup of tea. I need something.'

Popadom scurried after me. 'Is that wise? You may contaminate evidence.'

'I doubt the intruder made a pot. I'll take the risk.'

As I stepped into the kitchen and turned on the light I remembered the dog. It was still lying where it had been earlier, only this time I could see the pool of blood. It hadn't fancied our laced steak because it was too dead to eat. And now I could also see the open kitchen window, the wooden frame disfigured where someone had used a jemmy to wrench it open.

There was already water in the electric kettle, so I just threw the switch. As I'd guessed, once the brew was actually on, no one was going to decline a mug of tea. We stood around, clutching our mugs and sipping the hot liquid for comfort, not talking, each of us alone with our innermost thoughts.

It was perhaps another five minutes before we heard the approaching banshee wail of the first police-car siren. More joined it, adding to a manic cacophony of noise drawing ever closer as the circus arrived.

'I'd better open the front door,' I said and sauntered into the hallway.

But I'd left it too late. I could see the gyrating pulses of blue light through the glass of the door just before it crashed open under the force of a two-man metal ram. Then the firearms officers raced in, helmeted and in flak jackets, yelling, 'ARMED POLICE! ARMED POLICE!'

I stood still, bemused, clutching my mug of tea.

The first officer waved his Heckler & Koch at me. 'ON THE FLOOR! NOW!'

'Oh piss off,' I said, laconically, 'the killer's long gone.'

But the officer was having none of it. 'NOW!' he yelled.

Reluctantly I eased myself down, only to have the mug of tea kicked from my grip before I was unceremoniously flipped onto my stomach and my legs spread. Urgent fingers began frisking me for weapons.

Finally I managed to look up as Popadom strolled forward, holding out his MI5 security pass. 'Security Service,' he said softly. 'It's all right, this man is with me.'

I saw the smirk on his face as he glanced down. Behind him, Jazz was creased up with suppressed laughter.

It crossed my mind that if Popadom hadn't been with us, Joe Lassiter might just have let Jazz and me stew to save his own hide. I wouldn't have put it past him.

A few minutes later I had my dignity restored and met the local detective superintendent, a short, stocky man with a balding head of grey hair and a moustache as thick as a dead ferret. His name was Potter and he viewed us with deep suspicion while Popadom did all the talking.

'I am understanding that Special Branch is on its way,' Popadom told him. 'I am afraid I cannot answer any questions until they arrive. I'm sure that you are understanding, national security, yes?'

Potter clearly wasn't understanding at all. He was wearing what looked like a deceased man's suit from an Oxfam shop, and I noticed that his shirt beneath it looked suspiciously like a pyjama top. He said, 'Well, if it's all right with you, my men will continue sealing off the street and I shall look at the scene of the crime for myself?'

Popadom gave a little shake of his head and smiled. 'Of course. Upstairs, first door on the left.'

Potter grunted and headed for the staircase. 'Bloody fishy,' he was heard muttering under his breath.

Police officers and scene of crime experts were now starting to fill the house; enough of them to throw a party.

Then the Special Branch contingent arrived, arrogant and swaggering in their street-cred casuals. They were led by Inspector Ian Proctor, the officer we'd met at Thames House at our first briefing. He was still tousle-haired, unshaven and obviously still hadn't seen daylight since our last encounter.

He went straight for me. 'What did I tell you, Mr Mason? There's no place for gung-ho attitudes on the mainland, remember?'

I nodded, smiled and said nothing.

'So what's this? Illegal breaking and entering? Then you find the corpse of a terrorist suspect. That's a fine bloody mess for me to sort out.'

'Just following orders,' I replied evenly.

'Whose?' He gave a snort of derision. 'Don't tell me . . . Lassiter's. Man's a bloody menace, a loose cannon. I have a good mind to let Potter here bang you three up for the night on suspicion. Just to teach you and Lassiter a lesson.'

Before I could reply another voice answered for me. 'Taking my name in vain again, Ian?'

Proctor turned, looking just a little sheepish. 'Hallo, Joe. Just saying your friends here are lucky they're not being arrested as murder suspects. You really should keep them on a tighter rein.'

Surprisingly, Lassiter seemed to be in a very good mood. 'Yeah well, Ian, they can get a bit over-enthusiastic. I'll show them a yellow card.'

The Special Branch man grunted. 'And I'll want them at Paddington Green to be interviewed at nine tomorrow morning, sharp.'

I groaned inwardly, but Lassiter wasn't perturbed at our inconvenience. 'No problem, Ian.'

He then turned to Jazz, Popadom and me and indicated for us to follow him into the dining room, which was so far clear of police. Proctor followed us in as Lassiter switched on the light, perched himself on the edge of the table and announced, 'I've spoken to the Ice Queen and she's on her way. Wasn't pleased at first, but then she was half-asleep. Then the penny dropped that this was pretty much confirmation that Akmal Younis has been involved in something seriously shady after all.'

'So you're off the hook?' I observed sarcastically.

He gave a smug smile. 'Might even have won a Brownie point or two. So just bring the inspector and me up to speed on exactly what happened.'

I ran through the sequence of events quickly.

Lassiter scratched at his unshaven chin. 'So someone had broken in, even though Popadom had been watching outside since nightfall?'

The Pakistani officer nodded. 'I saw nothing, Joe. He must have climbed in over the rear fence. It backs onto a pedestrian walkway.'

'Does that mean he saw you? Realized you had Younis under surveillance?'

Popadom shrugged. 'There is no way of telling.'

Proctor interrupted. 'And you didn't see the killer properly when he ran out of the front door?'

'No, the light was too poor. Just that he was of medium height and slim build. I am thinking he was a young man. Fit, probably under forty.'

Proctor turned to me. 'You collided with him, Mr Mason, can't you remember anything?'

'There was only ambient light from the streetlamps outside,' I explained, 'and it was only a split-second before he barged into me.'

'Could he have been Middle Eastern or Asian?'

'Sorry, couldn't say.'

'I didn't see his face either,' Jazz added. 'I just noticed he seemed pretty much dressed in black. Maybe a boiler suit.'

Lassiter said, 'So you reckon when you arrived, he'd already broken in and shot the dog?'

'Looks that way,' I confirmed.

'I'm surprised the shot didn't wake Younis, even if the dog didn't,' Proctor muttered thoughtfully. 'So I suspect the murder weapon was used with a silencer.'

'And Younis takes sleeping pills each night,' I pointed out.

'So the intruder mounts the stairs,' Lassiter went on, 'shot Younis dead in his bed, then proceeded to disconnect the laptop . . . when you two turned up. Must have scared the life out of him.'

'Us too,' I added.

'At least he dropped the damn thing.' Lassiter turned to Proctor. 'I'll need the hard drive, Ian. Can your forensic people do their stuff pronto and get it over to me?'

'Not a problem, Joe.'

Lassiter looked at me. 'Seems to me, Phil, this could all be connected to that row you witnessed in the park between Younis and that lecturer Dr Samir. What was it you thought he said, that he'd had enough?'

'Enough of what?' Proctor asked.

'That's the question,' Lassiter replied. 'Enough involvement with a terror cell? Was he being coerced, blackmailed in some way into working with them?'

'You're jumping to conclusions,' Proctor chided.

I said, 'But would it be serious enough to explain tonight's events? If Younis was going wobbly on them, just what would their probable reaction be?'

Lassiter smiled slowly. 'To get rid of him and any

incriminating material he might have in his possession. Like a computer.'

Proctor shook his head, disapproving of all the wild speculation. 'And who exactly was this man Younis supposed to have met?'

'Dr Samir Hashim,' I told him, 'a senior lecturer in economics and IT at Imperial College. He's got past connections with Naved Hussein.'

'Ah, Naved,' Proctor said. 'The Syrian you believe you saw in Leicester the other day. Al-Qaeda connected.'

'It could all be connected,' Lassiter rejoined.

'Are you suggesting this Dr Samir is the prime suspect for murdering Younis?'

'Well, if my hunch is right, certainly,' Lassiter answered. 'Maybe not physically, but perhaps he ordered it. Trouble is we've only just started looking at him, so we've no idea what role he might be playing in all of this.'

Just then there was a knock on the door. It was opened by a uniformed officer, who stood back to allow Felicity Goodall to enter, carrying a neat leather attaché case. Even though she had been called from her bed urgently in the small hours of the morning, the Ice Queen still managed to look stunning, crisp and sparkly as though she'd come straight out of the box. The blonde hair was down to her shoulders and her smart linen power-suit in powder-blue was matched by her high-heeled shoes. Her make-up was faultless.

She didn't mess about and went straight for Lassiter. 'Right, Joe, you'd better make this good.'

For his part Lassiter launched enthusiastically into the night's events and summed up the conclusions we had all been starting to reach. Felicity listened attentively and without interrupting.

'Well,' she said finally, 'seems you were right after all, Joe. We've certainly now got all the circumstantial evidence we need to make this an official Security Service inquiry.' She turned to Proctor. 'We already have Dr Samir under electronic surveillance. If you agree, Ian, I'd like to see a co-ordinated dawn raid on the home of Dr Samir. Also all the properties in Younis' curry-house chain. All his staff will have to be interviewed.'

Proctor said, 'I can certainly take Dr Samir in for questioning at first light. But I suggest we move on the curry-houses around midday. By then all the kitchen staff and waiters are likely to be at work. Otherwise word will get round and someone could do a runner.'

'Good point.' Felicity placed her attaché case on the dining table and flipped it open. 'I have a list here of all the branch addresses and telephone numbers.'

Proctor took the offered sheet of paper and glanced at his watch. 'I'll get moving straight away and keep you posted.'

As he left the room, Felicity smiled and regarded the remaining four of us. 'Well done, all of you. I can't condone Joe's approach – as he well knows. For someone outside the Service to break into property is downright illegal – besides that sort of thing is best left to our experts and done with proper sanction. But at least it seems we could be onto something. Early days though.'

I said, 'If this is part of a terrorist cell, hopefully we might have prevented another bombing.'

Felicity looked at me closely. 'A nice thought, but there are sure to be others . . . Good Lord, Phil, what have you done to your face?'

'The intruder put his foot in it.'

She winced. 'It looks painful. You're not paid to be an all-action hero, Phil, do remember that in future. Now, I suppose you three wouldn't feel up to coming with us to Dr Samir's home, would you?'

I smiled. 'You bet,' I said, although Popadom didn't look as though he quite shared my enthusiasm.

Jazz stifled a yawn. 'Sorry, guys, I can't join you. I'm all in, I need to get home.'

'Take the van,' I said, 'I'll catch a minicab later.'

'Thanks for that,' Jazz replied. 'See you tomorrow, guys.'

'Well done,' Felicity said as she left, then turned back to Popadom and me. 'This has been your case up to now, so I'm pleased you're able to come. You might spot something that Special Branch could overlook.' She looked at her elegant gold wristwatch. 'I expect Ian will organize it for around five, so not long to wait.'

Popadom said, 'I really must phone my wife and tell her not to be worrying. If she wakes up and finds I am still not in the house, there will be not a little hell to pay.'

*

I should have been feeling shattered after the night's events, but now the adrenalin had kicked in.

I sat beside Felicity in her dark-blue Mercedes with its darkened windows while Popadom took a back seat. She drove fast, almost fiercely, talking all the time on her hands-free phone. First she contacted her surveillance control centre to check on any movements picked up on the CCTV camera hidden in a vehicle parked outside Dr Samir's house. The monitors confirmed that he hadn't left the house since returning from work the previous evening. It was assumed he was asleep in the house along with his wife and child. There had been no suspicious calls on his landline or the only pay-as-you-go mobile number we had for him, although we knew that was probably obsolete now anyway. Apparently, trawling through service providers' customer lists had not revealed any other numbers taken out in his name.

Then Felicity was talking to Inspector Proctor, updating herself on Special Branch's plans for the raid, then her Head of Desk and dreaded rival, Melissa Thornton. No doubt news of the impending arrest would be passed on to the Home Office, in readiness for any media briefings later in the day.

It was a quarter to five when we arrived at the police marshalling area, a pub car park half a mile from Dr Samir's house. There were vehicles and officers everywhere, some in bright-yellow traffic jackets and others from the firearms unit in dark-blue body armour and NATO-style helmets. Proctor recognized Felicity's

Mercedes, detached himself from a group of chatting plain-clothes detectives and walked over to us.

'We go in at five,' he confirmed to Felicity. 'The assault elements are just ready to get into position. Marksmen are already covering front and back. But with his wife and child in the house we're not really anticipating any trouble. Worst case scenario is that Dr Samir tries to use them as a human shield.'

'God forbid,' Felicity said.

'Anyway, if you wait here, I'll call you as soon as the house is secured. Okay?'

Felicity nodded and we began an irritating wait as most of the car park began to empty of vehicles as the police closed in on their target. The clock on the dash seemed to go into slow motion as I watched the digital countdown to five o'clock. Outside the sky was lightening noticeably and the dawn chorus was beginning in earnest.

The Merc's radio was patched into the police net although there had been total silence as the plan went into operation.

Then suddenly: *Leader to Blue Section. GO, GO, GO!*

In my mind's eye I saw the firearms team, crouched behind the high outside wall of the three-storey Victorian building that Dr Samir rented, suddenly sprinting through the gate, across the small garden and up the steps to the front porch. Officers standing aside, Heckler & Kochs at port, while the other two were about to smash an iron ram into the lock . . .

HOLD FIRE! WHAT THE . . .?

Suddenly Proctor's voice cut in. 'What's happened?

Woman and child at door . . . Then the officer snapped back into assault mode.

ARMED POLICE! ARMED POLICE! DO NOT MOVE!

Then there was a sudden silence. 'Damn!' Felicity said and switched on the ignition. 'I'm getting down there.'

A few minutes later we turned into Dr Samir's street and pulled up in front of the police tape that cordoned off the road. There were already a number of bystanders, most wearing dressing gowns, their sleep having been rudely disturbed by the sudden influx of police vehicles and personnel.

Blue lights pulsed eerily as we ducked under the tape and made our way through the officers standing around. Proctor came out of the front gate of Dr Samir's house just as we reached it.

'Ah, Felicity, the house has just been secured.' There was a bemused expression on his face. 'Well, that was a first. Dr Samir's wife was waiting for us. Just opened the door. Cool as you like, she took one look at the gun pointing at her and invited the officer in for tea!'

'Cheeky minx,' Felicity said, then she frowned. 'And Dr Samir, don't tell me . . .?'

'Flown the nest, it seems. As you had the front covered on CCTV, he must have got out some other way.'

'What else did the wife have to say?'

'Nothing yet. A special female team are just taking the young daughter away.'

Even as he spoke two female officers appeared at the gate, one carrying a three-year-old with tear-stained cheeks. The lolly she held in one small hand seemed to be having a soothing effect because her crying had stopped.

'Right, let's get on,' Proctor said. Popadom and I dutifully traipsed in behind him and Felicity.

Dr Samir's wife was seated on the sofa in her front room, with a detective sergeant and a female uniformed officer standing over her. She was a petite and demure woman in her thirties, dressed in a long dress and traditional black hijab headscarf. The face it framed wore a very placid expression and was beautifully made up with lipstick, mascara and eyeliner. She certainly hadn't just got out of bed.

'I'm Detective Superintendent Proctor from Special Branch,' the policeman announced, then indicated the rest of us. 'These people are from the Security Service.'

Her expression didn't change. 'I am very pleased to meet you. I have offered your colleagues a cup of tea but they have declined. I offer the same to you.'

Was this a wind-up or what, I thought?

'We are not here to drink tea, Mrs Samir,' Proctor returned, barely concealing his anger. 'We are here to arrest your husband on suspicion of terrorist activities.'

There was a ghost of a smile on her face. 'He is not here and he is not a terrorist.'

'Then where is he?'

'I do not know.'

'We know he arrived home yesterday evening after college,' Proctor countered. 'When did he leave again?'

She looked down at her wristwatch. 'About an hour . . . no, more like an hour and a half ago.'

Felicity frowned. 'Did he leave by the front door?'

'I do not know, I was still in bed.'

The police sergeant interrupted. 'Ma'am, it's likely he scaled a front side wall into another garden.'

'That would explain why the CCTV didn't pick him up,' Lassiter added.

'Did he say anything to you before he left?' Proctor continued.

'That I should expect the police to call soon. To be ready and dressed and to co-operate.' She looked directly at Proctor. 'Not to tell any lies.'

Felicity looked extremely concerned now, and I could understand the reason. 'Why should your husband expect a police raid?'

'Because he received a phone call. It woke us up.'

'On the house phone?' Proctor asked.

'No, on one of his mobiles. He uses two or three for work. One each for a different type of business. College, his IT consultancy and some accountancy work that he does.'

'Which call was this on?'

'I do not know and he did not say who the call was from.'

Felicity asked, 'Didn't you think all of this was a bit suspicious?'

'At first,' the woman replied calmly, 'as I know my husband is not a terrorist. But he explained to me that you English police are very nervous and suspicious of we Muslims since that first horrible bombing in London and everything else since. Hashim said because of some business acquaintances in his past you might think he was somehow connected with the jihad.'

Felicity smiled but there was a flinty gleam in her eyes. 'Then if you are so certain of your husband's innocence, why do you think he was so afraid to be interviewed by the police?'

'Not Hashim,' she said, her face colouring with indignation, 'he is not afraid of anyone or anything. He just does not want to be kept under arrest for months without trial, or be sent by the Americans on a secret flight to be tortured abroad.'

'That would not happen,' Proctor assured.

'But not to risk it is safer. You English seem to do anything the Americans ask.' She gave a demure smile. 'When will I see my daughter again? Where have you taken her?'

'She is safe with Social Services,' Proctor answered evenly. 'Meanwhile I should like you to accompany me to the police station for further questioning.'

'Of course.'

'If you go with my sergeant, I shall speak to you again later.'

Dr Samir's wife rose to her feet and left with the policeman and the uniformed female officer.

Proctor watched as they disappeared through the door. 'She knows exactly what Samir is up to,' he said quietly. 'But can I prove it?'

'And can we find Dr Samir himself?' Felicity asked.

'We'll alert all cars, put a watch on railway stations, tube lines and airports, ports . . . usual stuff. But so far the evidence against him remains very circumstantial.'

I glanced around the room. 'Maybe you'll find something here.'

'Oh, believe me, Phil,' Proctor assured. 'I'm going to take this house apart brick by frigging brick.'

'There's something else of even deeper concern to me,' Felicity said.

Popadom spoke for the first time. 'That the late Akmal Younis received a warning that he was being followed to that meeting with Dr Samir? And now Samir is warned of this police raid?'

The same thought had occurred to me. 'Is it possible,' I asked, 'that al-Qaeda has got an insider in the Met?'

Proctor's eyes met mine. 'That has always been one of our greatest fears.'

Of course it was my imagination, but I could have sworn the temperature in the room dropped suddenly by several degrees.

Eight

'Smug little bitch,' Felicity Goodall said, stirring a single sugar lump into her black coffee with a silver spoon. 'She didn't bat an eyelid. Knows we can't touch her.'

Lassiter's section boss had invited him, Popadom and me to join her for breakfast at St Ermin's Hotel, just a short distance from New Scotland Yard. After the adrenalin rush of raised expectations and the shattering disappointment when we found that Dr Samir had flown the nest, I think we all felt a need to chill out and take stock of the situation.

'His missus didn't even hide the fact he'd had a tip-off by phone,' Lassiter recalled acidly. 'She was gloating on it, enjoying every minute.'

'She won't be gloating when we catch him,' Felicity said and stabbed at her scrambled egg and smoked salmon.

'What are the chances?' I asked.

Felicity glared at me as though I'd just made an improper suggestion. 'We'll get him.'

Lassiter shoved away his empty plate. 'Sorry, boss, but it might not be that easy. If he has got al-Qaeda resources, then he could have genuine documents for a new false identity. Then, will he try to get out of the country or have reason to go to ground somewhere here?'

I said, 'You mean until he's finished whatever operation he might be planning?'

Popadom answered for him. 'Dr Samir could disappear easily into any of the Muslim communities in this country. If he is quiet and minds his own business, no one will notice him or ask questions. These communities are feeling very isolated now. Indeed it is questionable how many people would grass on him – even if they suspected he was a jihadi.'

'Bloody right,' Lassiter agreed. 'The Yanks reckon they know how to fight the war on terror. Then the Muslims in America and Europe see the news . . . Afghanistan, Iraq, Abu Ghraib, Guantánamo Bay . . . the list seems endless to them. It all just drives young radicals into joining up to fight their perceived enemy. Us! The number of possible suspects we're having to look at now runs into thousands.'

'Yes, yes, Joe,' Felicity said irritably, 'we all know we've got our work cut out. And it's pointless to speculate exactly when and how we'll catch up with Samir. The police have only just started searching his home and his office . . . Meanwhile I'm more concerned about the tip-off he received. It's got to have come through someone in the Met while the raid was being organized. There are a considerable number of Muslims in the police now and it only takes one bad apple . . .'

Felicity's voice trailed off as she looked beyond our

table towards the restaurant entrance. The woman who had just entered was all in black. Glossy black hair, swept up into a clipped bundle at the back of her head, black trouser suit, black silk shirt, and black high heels. She was tall and slim and carried herself with all the confidence and elegance of a *Vogue* model.

Lassiter turned round in his seat. 'I see trouble,' he whispered to me. 'Medusa cometh . . . No love lost between the two of them.'

Felicity rose to her feet. 'Phil, this Melissa Thornton, my Head of Desk.'

Dark, long-lashed eyes regarded me from a pale-skinned face spoiled by a streak of crimson lipgloss. 'I've heard about you and your team, Mr Mason.' She didn't make it sound like a compliment, and I was about to find out why as she occupied an empty seat next to Felicity. 'And I heard what's happened the moment I stepped into the office this morning. An unauthorized break-in, discovery of a body and then a suspect is tipped off about a police raid. What the hell's been going on?'

'The break-in was Lassiter's bright idea,' Felicity retorted without hesitation in pointing the finger. 'Thought Phil Mason's people could do it unofficially.'

'*Mea culpa*,' Lassiter agreed meekly.

But Melissa Thornton still had her rival in her sights. 'Why didn't you sanction our people to do it?'

'Because I didn't think there was enough evidence yet to suggest there was a definite terrorist link.'

'But Lassiter did?'

Felicity nodded. 'One of his infamous hunches that are usually wrong.'

'But this time he was right, is that it?'

'It looks like it.'

'Who was the dead man?'

'A man called Akmal Younis, an apparently respectable Pakistani restaurateur. Late middle-aged. Very low-level suspect and really only by association.'

'And this Dr Samir who did a runner?'

'Another low-level suspect that Phil's team was investigating. They discovered that Younis and Dr Samir knew each other and had a clandestine meeting a couple of days ago. Circumstances made us believe Dr Samir may have had Younis murdered.'

'Why should Dr Samir want him killed?'

I interrupted. 'I observed them at a clandestine meeting. If they are part of a terror cell, it's possible Younis couldn't take the pressure any more and wanted out.'

Melissa turned to Felicity and frowned. 'D'you think Samir actually murdered the victim himself?'

'Very unlikely,' Felicity replied, shaking her head. 'Just arranged it.'

'Then you should have sanctioned full surveillance of Dr Samir, for goodness' sake. Not send in the Size Tens!'

'The murder made that one tricky,' Felicity pointed out. 'Our people were at the scene and Dr Samir is so far the only suspect. The police are obliged to follow it up.'

'So how was Samir tipped off?'

'We were just discussing that. A phone call, according to his wife.'

Melissa's green eyes narrowed like a cat's. 'That is disturbing. Is she likely to be charged?'

Felicity pursed her lips. 'Well, unless something incriminating her is unearthed in the house search, we've nothing that will stick. She's a cool customer, just playing it straight and denying everything. But if she remains free, there's a chance she'll get too cocky for her own good.'

'And make contact with her husband?'

'Or another cell member.' Felicity's smile was a little sheepish, I thought. 'I have arranged surveillance for when she's released from Paddington Green.'

Melissa's expression said it was all a bit late for that. 'Well, if this is a new cell, there's no point in speculating what they might be up to until Samir's home and office are searched.'

Lassiter added, 'There'll be raids on all of Younis' curry-houses later today as well.'

Melissa rose from her chair. 'Well, I just hope there isn't going to be a tip-off about that as well.' She looked at Felicity. 'Do be sure to keep me well up to speed on all this, won't you? Don't forget, it's me who carries the can.'

She didn't actually *meeow*, but she might as well have done before she turned sharply on those black high heels and strode out of the restaurant and into the courtyard.

*

Felicity Goodall and I were the last ones to leave the hotel. Outside the weather was cloudy and promised another dismal day.

'Where do you live?' she asked as we walked across St Ermin's Hotel car park. 'Brixton, isn't it?'

Why was it I felt a bit embarrassed about that? 'It''s an up-and-coming district,' I joked.

She laughed lightly. 'I know it is. People just remember its old reputation. Black ghettos and the riots. That was a long time ago. Anyway, let me give you a lift.'

'That's okay, thanks, I can grab a cab.'

She touched my arm lightly. 'Nonsense, it's not out of my way. Or is it just that my driving makes you nervous?'

'Not that much,' I lied. 'Where do you live?'

She lifted her electronic ignition key and fired it at her Mercedes, which blinked its lights in instant obedience. 'A little pad in Clapham, overlooking the common.'

'Nice.'

'Yes, it is,' she said as she opened her door. 'Good views of joggers and muggers – oh, and gays, of course. Bought the place after my divorce.'

That hit a raw nerve with me as I slipped into the passenger seat. 'So was your husband left with anything?' I asked.

She threw me a mock scowl as she started the car. At least I think it was mock. 'Enough. More than he deserved, anyway.'

I said, 'As long as he's not living in a cardboard box and surviving on broken biscuits.'

She laughed lightly as we drove out into the streaming early morning traffic. 'Oh, not my Edmund. Big in the city and lots of little nest eggs buried all over the place. I'm sure my solicitor only discovered half of them.'

'Wish I'd thought to do that,' I muttered.

'Ah, that suggests at least you're an honest man.'

'Yeah, honest and skint.'

'Your wife giving you a hard time?'

'Nina's not one to take prisoners. Not where money's concerned.'

She gave me a quick sideways glance. 'Don't mean to pry, but who wanted the divorce? Or was it a joint decision?'

'It was Nina's decision.' I scratched the stubble on my chin as I thought about it. 'But to be honest I was fairly happy to go along with it. Our marriage had been rocky for years.'

She came back with a light laugh. 'Until you found out how much it was going to cost you?'

I smiled a grim little smile. 'I must say I've been a bit shocked to see how much she might be entitled to . . . a cut of future earnings and all that. Wasn't really expecting that.'

'She's not working then.'

'Nina's allergic to work.'

'Then we'll have to make sure we can keep you gainfully employed, won't we? You've certainly made a promising start. Joe said you were good.'

My spirits struggled to get off the deck; they weren't

going to soar any time soon, but at least it seemed Lassiter's boss was happy enough with my efforts so far.

I said, 'I gather you've got a lot of work on.'

She shook her head in a gesture of despair. 'You would hardly believe it. Over two thousand people being investigated and new tip-offs coming in all the time from the Muslim communities. People suspicious of friends and neighbours. I think the whole country's paranoid. But it's so difficult to separate the wheat from the chaff. Not to mention time-consuming and expensive.'

We were over Lambeth Bridge now and heading towards Brixton. Actually Felicity's driving was pretty good, relaxed but also sharp and focused, although a bit too fast for the city road conditions. She seemed to anticipate well, switching lanes quickly whenever she saw a developing situation that would gain her a couple of seconds of journey time.

Suddenly she said, 'Phil, I've been thinking. Dr Samir has done a runner, right? What is the one suspicious connection he is already known to have?'

'I suppose that's his past association with Naved Hussein who runs the Guardians of Paradise website,' I replied. 'Designed it for him.'

'Exactly. The same Naved you are certain met with that ex-soldier, Dave Evans. So if Evans can lead us to Naved, there's a good chance he'll also lead us to Dr Samir.'

I considered that for a moment. It made good sense. 'If Samir and Naved are old buddies, it might be likely.'

'What worries me, Phil, is that something big could be

going down. I know it's just supposition. Something freaked out the curry-house owner Akmal Younis and something was important enough for him to be murdered for wanting out. Dr Samir goes to ground at the same time we believe Naved Hussein has entered the country illegally. And we know that Naved is a facilitator for al-Qaeda.'

I said, 'Well, at least you've now got a full surveillance team on Evans.'

We were entering Brixton High Street and I began giving her directions as we threaded our way through the narrow residential streets until we pulled up outside my flat.

She turned off the engine. 'Thing is, Phil, you actually know Evans, don't you?'

'That's putting it a bit strong. He passed through one of my Sniper School courses, that's all. When I met him last week he was pretty edgy, didn't exactly welcome me with open arms.'

'I imagine not as he was just about to meet Naved.' She raised one eyebrow. 'He did give you his phone number, though. It's very likely he's feeling pretty lonely just now, throwing in his lot with these Muslim radicals. However much he may empathize with their cause, they are not his own people. And if he's getting deeply involved in something dangerous . . . Maybe meeting an old ex-army oppo is just what he needs.'

I said, 'Evans isn't the sort for loose talk.'

That glorious smile was back on her face. 'You may not know it, Phil, but it's a psychological fact that virtually all men have to share their darkest secret with at least one other person. Women, on the other hand, don't.'

'That's scary,' I said lightly.

'So maybe catching up with Evans should be a priority.'

'Sure,' I agreed.

'Are you going to invite me in for coffee?'

I hadn't been expecting that. 'Er, yes, of course.'

She followed me down the basement steps while I went ahead and opened the door. I could hear the faint tap of a computer keyboard as I led the way into the front office.

'Hiya, Phil,' Kate greeted, looking up.

'This is my secretary and girl Friday, Kate,' I said.

Felicity looked a bit taken aback, as though she hadn't expected anyone to be there. 'Pleased to meet you. I'm Felicity. A work friend of your boss.'

'I'll put the kettle on—' I began.

'Oh look, Phil, on second thoughts, I ought to get home and get some sleep. You must need it too, you look exhausted.'

To be honest I felt as bad as I must have looked. I just wanted to crash. 'If you're sure . . .?'

'Another time. In fact come over to my place for a drink one evening.'

I said, 'That would be good.' And I meant it.

'I'll call you.'

With that she turned and left the flat, closing the door quietly behind her.

'Who's that glamour-puss?' Kate asked. 'A new girl-friend?'

'That, young lady, is Joe's boss. The infamous Ice Queen.'

Kate laughed. 'I'd watch her if I were you. If she melts she'll wash you clear away!'

After Felicity Goodall left I lay flat out on my bed and died. It wasn't until late afternoon that my slow resurrection began. I could hear voices in the front office as I pulled on my clothes and went to the kitchen to make a sweet black coffee and a bacon wedge.

I pushed open the office door to find Popadom chatting with Jazz and Kate. He turned towards me, grinning, 'You are sleeping the sleep of the extremely righteous, I think, Mr Phil.'

He'd clearly been there a while and looked as bright and dapper as always.

'The sleep of the bloody knackered,' I muttered gruffly. 'How come you're so chirpy?'

'Clean living,' he answered. Irritatingly, I thought he might have a point.

Jazz asked, 'How's the face? It still looks a bit swollen and the bruises are coming out.'

I rubbed my tender cheekbone and the bridge of my nose. 'I'm sure I'll live. Now have we heard anything about the curry-house raids?'

Popadom nodded. 'I have spoken with Inspector Proctor. It all goes like clockwork. Many arrests, many suspected illegal workers.'

'So no tip-offs this time?' I asked.

As he shook his head, Jazz asked, 'Tip-offs?'

'Haven't you heard? When the police went to arrest Dr Samir this morning, he'd vanished. Had a warning phone call, according to his wife. There might be a leak somewhere in the Met.'

Jazz frowned. 'That's a worry. Does anyone have any idea who?'

Popadom answered, 'The police have begun an investigation. But that will take time. Like the results of the curry-house raids.'

'Meanwhile,' I said, 'we have to move on. I was talking to Felicity this morning and she wants me to have a crack at getting closer to Dave Evans as a priority. On the basis that he could lead us to Dr Samir and Naved Hussein.'

'Evans is already under Service surveillance,' Popadom pointed out, sounding concerned. 'You could be jeopardizing their operation.'

I shook my head. 'I have no intention of doing that, Pops. Just an ex-army acquaintance meeting up for a drink. He might give something away.'

He said thoughtfully, 'Then I think you should be meeting up with the watchers on the case, so everyone knows what is going on. We cannot be affording mistakes.'

I nodded in agreement. 'Do you know who they are?'

'Not specifically, but I can find out. Leave it with me.'

I left it with Popadom and an hour later he had a name for me. 'Jeff King. I worked on his team at one time in the past. A good man, pleasant man. I have just spoken to him. He is now finished his day shift and says he'd be happy to meet us.'

'When?' I asked.

'This evening. We can meet at his hotel. He'll arrange rooms for us.'

I glanced at my watch. It was just gone five. 'Should be possible to get to Leicester around eight to eight-thirty. Have you got to go home and pack?'

Popadom shook his head. 'I am always keeping a bag in my car. I am ready now.'

I said, 'Just give me five minutes.'

I returned to my bedroom, threw a change of clothes and my spare toilet-bag into a small case. As I zipped it up, Jazz knocked on the door and came in. 'What do you want me to do tomorrow, Phil?'

'Well,' I replied, 'as Dr Samir's turning into such a hot potato, maybe you should follow up on that student of his, Shahid Akhtar. I know you didn't think he was the right material, but we daren't dismiss him out of hand. As you got on so well, it might be worth probing a bit more. Maybe coax him along, express some radical thoughts of your own. See how he reacts.'

'He's very shy of women.'

I picked up my case and moved towards the door, placing my left hand on her arm. 'Then be gentle with him.'

Then I kissed her fleetingly on the lips. She did not pull back or turn away, she just smiled. 'I will. Do please take care.'

I nodded. 'See you soon.'

'Taxi's here!' Kate called out.

Then Popadom and I were on our way through the rainy London streets, heading to Euston Station. An hour later the crowded Intercity train was pulling out of the terminal, racing north.

By eight-thirty we were signing in at the Ramada Hotel on Granby Street in Leicester city centre. After dropping off luggage in our respective rooms, we made our way down to the rather splendid bar area. It was all pale oak and padded leather settees and club chairs.

Popadom spotted Jeff King immediately. He was sitting alone in an alcove to the right of the bar, reading a newspaper.

As we approached, he looked up and smiled broadly. 'Hi, Pops, you ol' bastard,' he greeted, rising to his feet. 'How the devil are you?'

They shook hands. 'I am fine now, thank you.'

King glanced down at Popadom's legs. 'Ah, I see the plaster's gone. No more skiving for you then.'

The Pakistani officer smiled politely and nodded in my direction. 'This is Phil Mason.'

King regarded me coolly for a moment. He was about five-ten with broad shoulders, dressed in a blue casual shirt and chinos. His neatly cropped and brushed fair hair and moustache hinted at a military background and the clean-shaven face wore an unnervingly impassive expression as we shook hands.

'I'm Jeff,' he said, with only a hint of a smile. 'Can I get you a drink?'

'Best offer I've had today,' I replied.

Minutes later we were settled down in the alcove, well out of earshot of the other customers.

'So you're a freelancer,' King said with a tone that suggested mild disapproval.

I decided to put him straight. 'Ex-SBS and Intelligence Corps.'

'A cabbage-hat,' he said, smiling for the first time. 'Still can't have everything. I'm ex-Gloucesters.'

I added, 'Now I'm running a small detective agency.'

'With a nice little contract from Lassiter, no doubt,' he said, regarding me over the rim of his beer glass. 'And you're the outfit that sussed David Mo Evans?'

I nodded. 'We're just looking at people low on the suspect list. It's all a bit hit and miss, I'm afraid. But it's better than nothing, I suppose.'

'Yeah, I suppose,' he agreed. 'Thames House is struggling. They just can't give everyone the full works. Suspects run into hundreds, I'm told. I hear they're hiring all the agencies that have a former military presence. People they can trust.'

'So how's it been going with Evans?'

King lay back against the brown leather upholstery of the alcove seat. 'Well, he's been a good boy so far. We've got eight operatives running a round-the-clock four-man box. I'm on the day shift, heading up Alpha Section. Beta Section's on standby throughout the night.'

'What's Evans doing now?' I asked.

Glancing at his watch, King replied, 'Having a quiet

drink in a pub. Non-alcoholic, of course. Usually alone. If
he talks to anyone, it appears to be casually with bar staff
or one of the regulars. That's the pattern so far. Before the
pub, he usually goes out for a cheap meal, a greasy-spoon,
an Indian or a Chinese, sometimes a burger bar. Then on
to a pub for a couple of drinks while he reads the papers.
Home and tucked up in bed around ten.'

'And during the day?' Popadom asked.

'Bit of an odd-job man. Bit of decorating, household
repairs and so on. We know about a dozen of his customers now, monitoring the mobile phone number you
got. Of course, any of them could be part of a cell network, but somehow I doubt it. Nevertheless they're all
under scrutiny now. Evans isn't exactly flogging himself to
death with work. More concerned with preserving a
cover story, it seems to me.'

'Is he still going to that Internet café?' I asked.

King nodded. 'Most afternoons for about an hour or
so. All his emails, sent and received, are being intercepted.
I've been told he's got about a dozen Hotmail and Yahoo
addresses. Probably uses them in a pre-agreed rotation
with other cell members. Although I've not heard from
Lassiter that anything of significance has been intercepted.
So maybe he's just emailing friends and family.'

'And his mobile phone?' I pressed.

'Well, our teams are doing close contact on that. He
seems to call just customers and what appear to be genuine relatives or friends – of course, they're all being
monitored as they're added to the list.'

Popadom said, 'I think he would be most certainly keeping a clean pay-as-you-go for any dirty business.'

'That's what we think,' King agreed. 'We had a couple of A Branch bods gain entry last night while Evans was at the pub. Sadly, if he had another phone, he'd kept it with him.' He reached into his inside pocket and produced a small plastic envelope. 'You might like to have a look at these.'

I opened the envelope and looked at the Polaroid photographs of Evans' bedsit. Before touching anything they had taken pictures with an instant camera in the same way that I had done in Akmal Younis' house. Mo Evans' bedsit was a drab and depressing little room. I could see the threadbare carpet and stained curtains, and patches of bare plaster where the paper had peeled away from the damp walls. The furniture was lumpen post-war utility stuff, the varnished finish long faded. At least the sheets and blankets on the narrow, single bed had been made up with military precision.

There was an alarm clock on the bedside table, an English language copy of the Koran in paperback and some magazines. It looked like he had an interest in handguns and sea-fishing.

'Personally,' King said, 'I find it hard to believe a guy like Evans could go all Muslim.'

I shrugged. 'It takes all sorts. He witnessed a lot of bad shit in Afghanistan and Iraq.'

'So do a lot of our boys,' King replied, 'but they don't all switch faiths and start addressing radical Muslim groups.'

I handed back the photographs. 'Talking of which, I don't suppose Naved Hussein has appeared on the radar?'

King smiled at that. 'I wish. That's the big prize we're waiting for. I gather it was you who clocked him with Evans?' When I nodded, he added, 'And you're positive it was him?'

'I've questioned myself a hundred times, and I'm as sure as I can be.'

'Then maybe we'll get lucky sooner or later,' King replied. 'And tell me, when have you got in mind meeting up with our Mr Evans?'

I'd been giving the matter some thought. 'I'm afraid if I phone him first, it'll give him an excuse to turn me down.'

'That's true enough,' King said. 'So how about just bumping into him again?'

'Well, if we know where Evans is now, there's no time like the present.'

The team leader glanced at his watch. 'It's just gone nine, so we'd better get moving.'

His car was in the hotel car park. I was surprised that it was just a dark-blue Ford Mondeo that looked due to be put through the car wash.

'Don't let looks fool you,' King said as we approached it. 'Souped up and a sixteen-valve turbocharged engine giving nought to sixty in under seven seconds, plus modified suspension.'

He opened the driver's door and indicated for me to sit next to him while Popadom scrambled into the back seat.

'Bullet-proof glass,' King continued, tapping the wind-screen and starting the engine. 'Quick-change magnetic false plates, UHF aerials concealed in the rear parcel shelf and VHF in the wing mirrors. That box of tricks by your feet is a CCTV monitor, standard and image-intensifying for night-time. Cameras are in the headlamps.'

Even driving in the car park I could feel the Mondeo's surge of restrained power. As we reached the street, King threw a switch on the dash, clearly enjoying showing off all these hi-tech gizmos as a head-up display map appeared in the glass of the windscreen, just like in a modern jet-fighter. 'We've got an electronic beacon hidden in Evans' car. That map shows it and the sur-rounding streets using GPS technology. It will also show the position of all our vehicles when we're following.' He grinned. 'Handy for not crashing into each other in our enthusiasm.'

There was some sort of hands-free radio transmitter in the car, but all King did next was press an unmarked button on the dash and spoke aloud. 'Alpha Taxi A1 to all B call-signs. I have a male passenger who will shortly be joining your client. All okay and cleared. Say if there is a problem please, Beta Taxi A1. Over.'

'We usually use taxi or ambulance speak,' Popadom explained helpfully. 'One cannot be too careful with frequency scanners in use today.'

'Out,' King said as he received his reply and ended radio contact with the Beta team on surveillance night shift. 'No problem, Phil. Evans is alone. At his usual table.

Far left-hand corner as you enter. He'll be able to see you as you enter and approach the bar.'

We were nearing the run-down city suburbs where Evans lived in his bedsit. The high street was fairly quiet at this time. It was an essentially Muslim neighbourhood and the inhabitants were not renowned for their wild nightlife. There was a crowd of sullen-looking youths hanging around outside a kebab shop, but they did not appear to be particularly noisy or troublesome.

King swung left into a side-street and pulled in. 'Continue up the high street and you'll find the Star on your right.' He looked at me directly. 'Don't get into trouble, Phil. If Evans really doesn't want to see you, then accept it. Walk away. Remember you'll have members of Beta watching you at all times.'

'Thanks for your help, Jeff.'

'Just don't make me regret it,' he replied bleakly.

I exchanged a smile with Popadom and climbed out of the car. For a moment I stood and watched as it drove off. It was unsettling knowing that the professionals were concerned that I could somehow mess up their operation.

Retracing the half-dozen paces back to the high street, in my mind I ran over once again how I was going to handle this situation. I couldn't exactly plan it, because it would all depend on Evans' reaction. But in my head I'd run through countless imaginary conversations and hoped I'd covered all the most likely responses I'd meet. It started to rain as I crossed the road and a few minutes later reached the Star. On the corner of a side-street it was run-down, the once-white rendering grubby and weather-stained, and the paintwork peeling away. I climbed the single step and pushed open the door with its old-fashioned etched window.

I guessed it was the last refuge of the remaining white or non-Muslim inhabitants of the area. There were no more than a dozen people in the place, all Caucasian males apart from one bleary-eyed West Indian propping up the bar, who looked like he came with the furniture and fittings. He was talking to the publican.

Most of the other customers were middle-aged and drably-dressed, except for Dave Evans. As predicted, he sat to the left of the bar in the far corner beside a door marked 'Toilets'. Although I deliberately avoided looking in his direction, from the corner of my eye I saw him glance up instantly from the redtop newspaper he was reading. He was certainly sharp, or was it just edgy? Was it no accident that he'd adopted a real professional's position in which to sit each night? Back to a wall and a full view of everyone who entered, plus a convenient escape route through the door to the lavatories, should it be necessary.

I crossed the dirty, beer-stained carpet to the bar. The publican, a big man with a spider-veined face and wisps of white hair sprouting from an almost bald head, reluctantly interrupted his conversation with the West Indian to shuffle over to me. His beer belly was hidden by a large, crumpled shirt and supported by colourful paisley braces.

'Yes, skip?' he asked without enthusiasm.

I viewed the row of porcelain pump handles. 'A pint of Pedigree, please.'

'Anything else, skip?' he asked as he drew off the ale.

I shook my head and placed a fiver on the bar.

'Hallo, Phil.'

The sudden sound of Evans' voice right behind me took me by surprise. If anything I thought he might have slipped out while my back was turned, or at least given me a hostile reaction. Not that he was exactly exuding warmth.

'Good God, Dave!' I said, mopping up the spilt beer with a towel mat. 'Made me jump. Didn't know this was a haunt of yours.'

'Your nerves are bad,' he said. It sounded like an accusation.

'Hoped I might find you somewhere round here.'

'Why didn't you phone me, then? You took my number.'

I shrugged. 'Lost it, I'm afraid. Still, a happy coincidence, eh?'

The eyes were still dark, sunken and wary. 'Yeah, I guess.'

'Let me get you a drink.'

He hesitated, glanced at the clock behind the bar. I realized then I'd cut it very fine as the hands edged towards five to ten. 'Go on, then. But I'm a bit sick of fruit juice.'

'Still sticking with it, then? The no-alcohol thing.'

'It's not a choice, Phil.'

'A coffee?' I suggested.

'No, not here. Some sparkling mineral water will do, cheers. Ice and a slice.'

While the landlord dealt with the order, Evans whispered, 'Bert's coffee's disgusting. Ditchwater. Makes army coffee taste good.'

As I followed him back to his table, I noticed the hair and ponytail was still unwashed. He again sat with his back against the wall while I took the chair facing him.

'Still doing your courier work?' he asked.

I nodded. 'Till I can find something better.'

'It's not easy getting back into civvy life,' he said.

'Trouble with the infantry,' I said. 'You're only qualified to kill people.'

A half-smile showed on his unshaven face. 'True enough.'

'Can't say I don't miss the army. Now each day's a grind.' I remembered the picture of the magazines in his room. 'Can't wait to get a long weekend away. A spot of sea-fishing.'

He raised an eyebrow. 'Really, sea-fishing?'

'Darset boy, born and bred,' I answered, adopting the accent I'd lost years ago having been mercilessly teased about it in the Royal Marines. 'Spent most of my childhood fishing off Weymouth.'

'Never fished there,' he said. 'Mostly off Pembrokeshire.'

I smiled. 'That's one hell of a lot of coast . . . I fished out of St David's once with an uncle of mine. Nearly landed a baby shark.'

Evans actually chuckled. 'The one that got away, eh? Now you're talking.'

'Best ever,' I said. 'Was once five months off Florida courtesy of the Royal Marines.'

'How d'you wangle that? I knew you cabbage hats had it easy . . .'

'I volunteered for a six-month exchange with the US Marines. Playing at platoon commander.'

He winced. 'That deserves a medal in itself.'

'When I got there, the Yank OC and I soon realized that everything was so different,' I explained. 'Weapons, drill, radios, they way they did everything was totally alien. In the end the OC decided I'd take charge of the Marines' daily physical training programme. About the only thing I could do.'

Evans seemed genuinely intrigued. 'How did that work out?'

'Fine, I thought at the time. But after a few weeks the OC called me in. Said he'd received a tirade of complaints.'

'About what?'

'About me working them too hard. Said I'd exhausted the poor mites. Suggested I took the rest of the time off and go fishing, as he put it. So I took him at his word. Got a loan of someone's boat and had a fantastic time. Marlin, swordfish, barracuda . . . all sorts. Also made a few bob taking out tourists.'

Now Evans was actually laughing. 'Maybe that's what I should do. Take a new direction in life.'

'Why not? Cheap to live in the States and Yanks aren't all that bad when you get to know them.'

His smile faded. 'I'm a bit committed at the moment. But sometime later maybe.'

'We could be partners.'

Evans downed the last of his mineral water. 'There's a thought.'

'Another drink?' I asked.

He shook his head. 'Not for me. But come back to my place for a coffee, if you like. It's not far. I think I might even have a bottle of medicinal brandy somewhere.'

This was a turn-up I hadn't been expecting. 'Sure, thanks.'

As we stood up to leave, I wondered who in the bar was an A4 watcher? None of them looked remotely suspicious, but then I suppose that is the general idea. Again, once we were outside, there was nothing and no one to indicate we were under surveillance. Almost as if reading my mind, Evans was keeping his eyes open, glancing at each parked car we passed and every vehicle that drove by us.

It only took ten minutes, down the wet, near-deserted high street then branching off into the side-streets, to reach his digs.

When we climbed the front steps to the dilapidated house, he produced a key. 'I'm afraid it's not up to much. My missus got the house.'

The front door swung open to reveal an old-fashioned black-and-white chequered mosaic floor with lots of tiny tiles missing and patched up with cement. There was a pungent pot pourri of must, cat's pee and cooking fish in the air. A pushchair and a mountain bike were parked at the bottom of carpetless stairs up which Evans led the way.

When we reached the next floor landing, he turned to the door on the left and produced a second key on the ring to open the Yale lock. Instead of pushing it open wide, he just eased it a few inches, hunkered down and carefully squeezed his right hand through the gap. When he stood up and opened the door I saw he was holding an old training shoe, in which was a glass tumbler of what looked like lemonade. He clearly must have put the two items as close as he could behind the door when he'd left earlier. It took a moment for me to realize why he'd done that: anyone else entering the room in his absence would have sent both trainer and glass flying, never knowing the configuration in which they'd been left or what the tumbler had contained. Evans would be certain to know there'd been an intruder.

That made me feel distinctly uncomfortable. But I just said lightly, 'You paranoid or what, Dave?'

He just grunted and stared around the gloomy little room. 'Primitive but effective,' he said. 'Can't be too careful nowadays.'

Closing the door behind us, he crossed to a chest of drawers and bent to examine the top one closely. 'An old James Bond trick,' he said, 'a damp hair across the join of a drawer where it opens.'

'My God,' I said. 'You really are taking this seriously.'

Satisfied that the hair was still in place, he straightened his back. 'Got a feeling someone got in here the other night.'

'A thief?'

He shook his head. 'No, someone checking me out?'

'For what?'

'Well, I've been involved with a few radical Muslims,' he said cautiously, turning towards me. 'Attended a few meetings, trying to understand them a bit more, get into the Islamic head. If a white man does that sort of thing . . . well, people can get suspicious.'

I decided to take the bull by the horns. 'You mean Special Branch . . . or the security boys?'

Oddly, he gave a terse little smile at that. 'Yeah, maybe them. But I was thinking more of some of these Muslim hotheads. They might not think I'm really what I am. They can get suspicious of outsiders, those like me who want to convert.'

'I suppose so.' It was one aspect that I hadn't really considered. 'But you told them why? Your experience in Iraq and Afghanistan.'

'I could just be making that up.'

I nodded. 'Well, as you know, I was there too. Felt much the same as you. In fact I wouldn't mind meeting some of them, get their perspective. Their fellow Muslims have had a pretty rough deal overseas.'

Evans' eyes bored into mine. 'Not a good idea, Phil. Leave it alone. I think you can guess their perspective.

Don't get involved with those people unless you're fully committed.'

Had I pushed it too far? I back-pedalled. 'I'm sure you're right. Nevertheless I'd be up for it.'

He opened his bedside cabinet and rummaged for a couple of moments before extracting a half-bottle of brandy. 'Maybe,' he muttered, 'once I feel I've been properly accepted myself . . . And if you still feel the same way then.'

Having kicked the idea into the long grass, he crossed to the far corner of his room where there was a curtained-off kitchenette comprising a sink, a minuscule worktop with a two-ring electric appliance and a small fridge. He put a kettle on, added coffee to a couple of mugs, then picked up two tumblers. He gave one to me then dropped down onto the bed.

I pulled over a hard chair, sat down and accepted the bottle from him, slurping an inch of brandy into the tumbler. 'Are you going to be tempted?' I asked, nodding towards the glass in his hand.

'Haven't touched a drop in two months.' He gave a wry smile. 'Think Allah would forgive me one little lapse?'

I nodded. 'He's very understanding, I believe.'

I poured some brandy into his glass. He took a small sip. 'Dammit, that's good. But I don't think my Muslim friends would agree with me.'

'Like that guy who arrived when we first met at the café?' I asked. 'What was his name, Hussein? Why is every other Muslim called Hussein?'

Evans' eyes hardened. 'Oh, him. Just an acquaintance.'

'Seemed nice enough. Very sophisticated.'

'Wealthy businessman,' Evans replied flatly. 'I rarely see him. He's mostly out of the country.'

'You doing business with him?'

Suddenly I could see the anger in Evans' eyes. 'No, Phil, I'm a bloody odd-job man. Just met Hussein at a local mosque once. We talked and he was interested in my views on Bush and Blair's wars. End of story. What's with the inquisition?'

I smiled. 'Sorry, Dave, didn't mean to pry. Just making conversation.'

Suddenly, Evans placed his tumbler on the floor at his feet. 'Look, maybe this wasn't such a good idea, Phil. I'm feeling a bit tired and I've got to make an early start tomorrow.'

I swallowed my brandy. 'Sure, Dave, didn't mean to get your back up.'

He shook his head. 'No, no, you haven't. As I said, I'm a bit tired, bit tetchy. Sorry.'

Evans was on the edge, anxious and paranoid, and I could tell his nerves were starting to betray him.

I stood up. 'Anyway, Dave, nice chatting. Can I look you up again next time I'm in town?'

He showed me to the door. 'Sure, sure. We can talk fishing. But leave it a couple of weeks, eh? I'm a bit busy just now.'

'Thanks for the drink,' I said and started down the stairs.

It was a relief to step out into cool, damp air. Dammit, had I seriously aroused his suspicions? I expected to get it in the neck from Jeff King when I arrived back at the hotel.

But, having hailed a passing taxi, there was no fall-out from the man when I got to the Ramada. King was still sitting in the alcove in the bar with Popadom.

He waved me over. 'Hi, Phil, something's just happened.' He seemed unusually cheerful. 'Someone's just phoned Evans' mobile.'

'Oh?'

'Didn't show up on our monitors, so it must have been a pay-as-you-go phone that we suspected he had.'

'How do you know then?' I asked.

He stared at me as though I was the dunce of the class and Popadom shook his head in disbelief at my naivety. 'Because', King said, 'we bugged his room during the break-in, of course.'

I felt a complete idiot for not having made that assumption myself.

'So we only got one side of the conversation,' King continued. 'But Evans called the guy who phoned "Hussein", and ended his conversation with "See you then".'

My mouth dropped. 'You think . . .?'

Popadom said, 'Yes, Mr Phil. It is looking like Mr Evans will maybe soon meet our most wanted man, the very elusive Naved Hussein.'

Nine

I met Popadom in the hotel restaurant for breakfast. We'd just sat down and ordered from the waitress when my mobile rang. I snatched it from the table.

It was Jeff King. 'Sorry to interrupt your bacon and eggs, Phil, but chummy's on the go.'

'What d'you mean?'

'He's just left his digs, straight into his car and heading south,' King replied rapidly. 'He wasn't wearing his usual overalls, so this doesn't look like a normal working day for our friend. If you want to join us, my car's out the front and ready to go.'

'I'll be straight with you,' I replied and switched off. As I stood up, I turned to Popadom. 'I'm joining Jeff. They think Evans could be on a mission . . .'

He raised his eyebrows in surprise. 'To meet Naved? If so then maybe this is being our lucky day.'

'Hope so.'

'What would you like me to do?'

'You may as well head back to London. I'll join you as soon as I can.'

'Very well, Mr Phil.' He grinned. 'And I am wishing you very good luck.'

I snatched up my overnight bag from the floor and headed for the door. Jeff King was waiting in his special dark-blue Mondeo, the engine running. As I scrambled into the passenger seat and shut the door, he took off immediately.

'Evans left just before seven,' King said, 'at the very moment our two teams were changing over. Caught us a bit on the hop. Looks like he could be heading for Junction 21 on the M1. So he could be going south towards London – or picking up the M69 towards Coventry. Either way our team has got him covered.'

Once away from the precincts of the hotel, King handed me a small device like a hearing aid. 'Wear that to listen to our radio traffic.' Then he lowered his electric side window, reached out and slapped a magnetic blue flashing light on the roof, before switching on a police-style siren.

That was it, King became a man transformed. His driving was confident, slick and fast. A bit too fast for my liking, but at least he handled the car expertly and with sharp anticipation skills as cars eased aside to let us pass. Soon we'd cleared the congestion of the inner city and were whistling down a dual carriageway through the south-western suburbs.

'Ambulance callsign Alpha Zulu,' King spoke to the hands-free radio transceiver. 'How's the patient?'

A male voice came over the loudspeaker. 'He's fine,

stabilized, nice and steady. Just approaching Junction 21 and we're . . . oh, right, we're going straight over the roundabout and . . . turning onto the M69.'

'Roger that,' King said crisply. 'We'll be joining the party soon. Out.'

I'd found a road map in the side-door pocket. 'So maybe Coventry or Brum,' I said, opening the spread on the West Midlands. 'A lot of Muslim communities.'

'Doesn't do to make any assumptions in this game,' King scolded. 'That's when it all goes wrong.'

We slowed down as we ourselves approached Junction 21, and slipped into the torrent of swirling traffic, before veering off onto the M69. King pushed his foot to the floor and I felt the surge of unbridled power pushing me back into my seat as the speedo spun towards 120 m.p.h.

King flicked on the head-up display that suddenly appeared within the windscreen glass. It was a rolling map of the M69. On and around it were four small moving circles. One in red, and some distance in front of it, another in blue. Some distance behind it were two more blue circles.

'Red is from the beacon we placed in Evans' car,' King explained. 'We've now got one vehicle – a silver Honda Civic – ahead of him, which he shouldn't suspect of being part of any surveillance team. There's a white van and a motorcycle some way behind him. With this technology we no longer have to get too close and risk compromising the operation.' King now switched off the siren, opened his window and retrieved the flashing light. Then he jabbed a finger at the display. 'If you watch, you'll see as this car comes into frame.'

Sure enough, at the bottom of the rolling map, a new moving blue circle edged into view.

King now slowed to just below seventy and tucked into the middle lane, behind a National Express coach. 'Now it's just a waiting game,' he said.

But it turned out we didn't have long to wait. After some five miles, the radio came on. 'Alpha One to Ambulance Control, we're approaching Junction 2 with patient . . . yes, yes, turned off down slip road at last minute! No signal! Shit . . . it's all right, I can follow. Over.'

Our Honda Civic – Alpha Three – ahead of Evans' car had overshot the slip road.

'Roger that,' King snapped. 'Alpha Two take over from Alpha One as lead vehicle as soon as you can.'

Alpha Two came on air. A female voice. 'Roger, Alpha Zulu. Out.'

King added, 'Alpha Three – continue on. Stop on hard shoulder just before Junction 1. I'll call for you to rejoin us when we know what's going on.'

I looked down at the map as we, too, reached the Junction 2 slip road and followed.

'This doesn't go anywhere. Countryside and a dozen villages.'

King said, 'He's checking to see if he's got a tail.'

We were now on the B road. 'Heading to Sapcote,' I advised.

Suddenly it was the female voice again. 'Alpha Two to Control, he's hanging a left, hanging a left!'

King glanced at the display. 'Go straight on! Go straight on!'

The red circle representing Evans' car had turned left up a country lane and continued towards the village of Stoney Stanton about a mile further on. We also now crossed the mouth of the turn-off, and kept on going. After travelling another quarter of a mile we came across a scruffy unmarked white van pulled over at the side of the road. A motorcyclist in black leathers and black bone-dome was standing on the road, talking to the driver. King signalled and tucked in behind the van. The motor-cyclist saw us and immediately walked quickly up to King's open window.

The visor was flipped up and a pair of beautiful green eyes gazed in at us. 'Hi, Jeff, what's the score?'

'He's checking for a tail, using the country lanes,' King said, then glanced at me. 'This is Cass, earning her spurs with us.'

The green eyes smiled. 'Still?'

'If you want to play with the big boys . . .?'

'Male chauvinist pigs, you mean,' she returned lightly. 'How d'you want to play this, Jeff?'

He was watching the screen carefully. The red circle had reached Stoney Stanton, then turned right onto a road that ran parallel to the one we were on . . . Then it suddenly stopped.

'Ah,' King said. 'There we are, just as I thought. He's

stopped to see if anything's followed. Let's wait and see what he does next.'

After a few minutes, Evans must have felt satisfied because his car began moving again, continuing east along the B581 towards the villages of Primethorpe and Broughton Astley. There he repeated his anti-surveillance manoeuvre by suddenly turning off and stopping to see if any following vehicle slowed to see where he'd gone or else followed and was then forced to go ahead of him.

'I've a feeling he's going south,' King said. 'Let's move. I'll take the lead for a bit.'

'See you,' Cass replied, snapping down her visor and heading for the motorcycle parked in front of the van.

King started the Mondeo's engine and we set off in hot pursuit once again with our white van and Cass' motorcycle close behind.

The team leader of the watchers was quickly proved right. As we swiftly gained on him, Evans had now picked up the A426 that ran south adjacent to the M1 motorway towards the historic market town of Lutterworth. By the time he turned onto the southbound carriageway our Mondeo was just three cars behind him.

King called up Alpha Three to get going again, turn east onto the A5 and to join us on the M1 as soon as they could at the end of the queue.

Evans had settled down at just under 70 m.p.h. and soon we were cruising past the outskirts of Rugby towards the Watford Gap service station. It was there that we nearly came unstuck, when Evans braked suddenly and turned off without signalling, driving up to one of the petrol pumps.

King followed him, talking rapidly on the radio to the rest of our team. 'He's stopping for petrol. Cass, come in with me. Alpha One and Three keep going in the slow lane . . .' He glanced at me. 'I'm not sure about this, Phil . . .'

'Has he clocked us?' I asked myself aloud.

'Must have,' King said. 'We were the first vehicle in after him.'

I was thankful for the very dark-tinted windows as our Mondeo pulled up at another pump on the next row, where it was mostly hidden from Evans' view. Our quarry was out of his car now and looking back to see which other vehicles might be following him in. Sure enough, Cass obliged, but smartly rode her motorcycle to a far corner of the forecourt, where she dismounted and began examining the rear wheel for some imagined problem.

Suddenly, without getting petrol, Evans climbed into his car and began driving out back onto the motorway.

'Damn!' King cursed. 'Crafty bastard.'

'What now?' I asked.

'We'll have to wait a bit. He'll soon catch up with Alpha One and Three. They can take over again. We'll keep out of sight for a while.'

But Evans hadn't finished yet. As King drove slowly away from the pumps to park nearer the exit, I noticed on the head-up display that suddenly the red circle was stationary on the motorway – just a short distance from the service area.

It was suddenly clear what he'd done. After driving about a mile, Evans must have pulled onto the hard shoulder, probably put his hazard flashers on, lifted up the car's bonnet, then waited.

Effectively he'd broken up our team and our four-vehicle 'box'. Alpha One and Three were crawling inexorably south towards Northampton in the slow lane. We and Cass were in a quandary. He'd seen us enter the service station immediately after him; if we didn't pass him again on the motorway in the next few minutes, he'd guess there was something fishy going on and be on the lookout for us later.

King studied the display. 'Where's the next junction?' he asked.

I looked at the map. 'Junction 16 for Northampton.'

'Alpha Zulu to One and Three,' he snapped into the radio. 'Pull over on the Junction 16 roundabout and wait. Our patient has stopped on the motorway, doing an A–S routine. Two and I will join you . . . Did you get that, Cass?'

'Roger, Alpha Zulu,' her voice came back.

King muttered some obscenity under his breath and we drove off to join the southbound carriageway. Sure enough, we passed Evans a few minutes later, standing by the uplifted bonnet of his car, watching to see if we'd make an appearance. Our Mondeo zoomed by in the fast lane with Cass following a few minutes later.

It was a full twenty minutes before Evans finished his waiting game, hopefully satisfied that neither the Mondeo nor the motorcycle were a tail after all. That was the time it took before he eventually drove past Junction 16, allowing us at last to re-establish ourselves with our white van – Alpha One – again just a few vehicles behind him.

Evans didn't try any more tricks. He just went back to a good steady speed as he passed through Milton Keynes and Luton to the northern suburbs of London. Finally, at Junction 2, he slipped left off the motorway and took the road to Finchley. After a few turns he stopped outside a row of shops. King pulled into the kerb and ordered Cass ahead to observe from a discreet distance.

Her voice suddenly filled the interior of our car. 'Alpha Two to Zulu, subject is feeding the meter. I think he's taking a hike. Walking east on the north side of the street.'

'Roger, Alpha Two, stay with him,' King snapped, 'until I can get a box in place.'

'Roger, out,' she confirmed.

King then called up the rest of the team. 'You heard Alpha Two. Deploy on foot. Alpha Three, you're closest. Get either side of him. Alpha One, take up position as soon as you can.'

As the rest of the team confirmed, King explained, 'Our white van and silver Civic each have four people with them apart from the drivers. Our teams are usually twelve in total with a mix of four vehicles. They'll have Evans "boxed" in a matter of minutes.'

Sure enough, the first two watchers called in to their

team leader moments later to confirm that they were in position, one ahead of Evans as he walked and another behind him. Within another three minutes, two more watchers from the Civic were deployed on the two opposite streets that ran parallel to the street the target was on. At any moment they could cut in to replace the others if there was any danger of them being compromised. Whichever way he went, Evans would be covered.

Five minutes passed before a voice came over the radio again. 'Alpha Three to Zulu. Subject has entered grounds of an office block, heading for the entrance.'

King frowned. 'Single company office?'

'Er, no, there's a sign in the grounds by the entrance. Multi-occupancy. Er, insurance brokers, some sort of medical outfit, import-export, and several others . . . I'm in pursuit.'

'No!' King said sharply. 'Do not approach. Repeat, do not approach! Pull back well out of sight of the building.'

'Roger that. Out.'

'What's going on?' I asked.

King grimaced. 'Evans knows his counter-surveillance drill, right? And this looks like a classic. Go into a tall office building containing several companies. Seek a vantage point and watch as your tail goes into a panic to try and discover which company or floor you've gone to. Then he'll either abort his planned rendezvous or try another way of shaking you off.'

'I see.'

Going back on the radio, King asked, 'Alpha Three, is

there anywhere in the vicinity I can park with a view of the office?'

'Er, yes. Parade of shops opposite. Couple of parking bays free. Limited waiting.'

'Okay, I'll be there in a few minutes.'

King started the Mondeo and pulled out, moving quickly through a succession of side-streets until we were in sight of the office block where Evans had taken refuge. King signalled right, then swung across the road and into one of the parking bays. He first checked to see he could see the main entrance across the street, then glanced along the row of shops. 'I'd better do this, in case he recognizes you. I'm going to that newsagent to buy a paper. Keep your eyes peeled for Evans leaving that building.'

I nodded, realizing that, assuming our target was watching us, King was demonstrating an innocent reason as to why the Mondeo had stopped.

While King left the car and sauntered along the pavement, I studied the office block floor by floor. In a window on the fifth, which I assumed to be part of the stairwell, I caught sight of a shadow. It was the silhouette of a man. It looked as though King was right again; Evans was waiting and watching for any tail to give itself away.

King emerged from the shop, glancing at his watch, a copy of a tabloid in his hand. As he rejoined the car, I saw a black taxicab turn into the grounds of the office block and stop on the forecourt outside the entrance. Moments later the glass doors swung open and Evans emerged. He made straight for the taxi and climbed in.

'Crafty bastard,' I hissed.

'Alpha Zulu to all units,' King said rapidly. 'Subject has left the building and got in a taxi. Black cab . . .' He read out the registration number as it edged out of the grounds and into the street. 'Heading east . . . Calling Alpha Two. Come in now and pick up the tail.'

Cass' voice piped up, 'Roger, Zulu. Out.'

Seconds later, the black leather-clad figure flashed past our Mondeo in pursuit of the taxi. We followed while the white van and Civic picked up the scattered watchers and joined the chase. Soon our surveillance pattern was re-established as our quarry moved south. But now our proximity to the taxicab had to be much closer as there was no radio beacon attached to it. Suddenly the brilliant modern technology was made redundant.

When the taxi reached Willesden, it suddenly stopped and Evans alighted, paying off the driver. Our Mondeo happened to be the lead vehicle and King swung off right down a side-street before coming to a halt. We were parked alongside the wrought-iron railings of a church graveyard which occupied the corner plot.

King said, 'Get out and take a look, Phil. See which way he's going while I deploy the team on foot.'

'Right,' I said, opening the door.

'Don't get spotted,' King warned sternly.

I crossed the pavement and peered through the railings, looking across the graveyard to where another set of railings ran alongside the main street and entrance gate to the church. I could just determine the figure of Evans crossing the road. He hesitated at the stone pillars of the church gate and glanced left and right. Seemingly satis-fied, he pushed open the gate and entered.

Suddenly my eye caught a movement to the right. A black-haired woman wearing sunglasses and dressed in a blue summer suit rose from a wooden bench on the path that ran between the tombstones.

As Evans approached, she removed her sunglasses and smiled.

I blinked in a double-take. Could I be wrong? I'd only ever met her once, but then once was enough. Melissa Thornton was not the sort of woman you forgot in a hurry.

'Who?' King looked puzzled.

'Melissa Thornton.'

'Who's she?'

'Head of Desk, G Branch,' I replied, amazed that he didn't know her name. 'Have a look yourself.'

King shook his head. 'No point,' he said thoughtfully. 'I'll take some photos, of course, but I've never even met her. She'll be based at Thames House and we're in the Capital Radio building on Euston Road. Wanted to move us in with them, but thankfully it's too low-lying for our radio reception needs. Her sort don't mix well with pond-life like us. We usually just get to meet case officers like Lassiter.'

'What are we going to do?' I asked.

'We?' There was a half-smile on his face. 'I'm doing nothing. Just keep watching and following Evans. Then

I'll report back to Lassiter about anyone and everyone he's met today.'

'Including Thornton?' I asked.

'Of course. If you're convinced it's her, Phil, then I'll tell Lassiter exactly that.'

King's complacency was starting to irk a little. 'You don't sound concerned. Don't you think it's just a bit strange that he should be meeting her?'

He nodded. 'On the face of it, sure. But this is the intelligence game, Phil, and it's all played in shadowland. I learned long ago just to get on with the job.'

And that's just what King and his team continued to do. Evans' meeting with the woman, whom I was convinced was Melissa Thornton, lasted another ten minutes. Then Evans stood up from the bench and sauntered back to the street.

As King started his car, I made a decision and opened the door. 'Thanks for everything, Jeff. But I think I'll get back to base now.'

He shrugged. 'Fine. I've enjoyed the company.'

I climbed out and watched as he drove off, wondering what the hell to do? I felt a huge temptation to approach Thornton and ask her what was going on? Why was she meeting up with one of our prime suspects?

Then another thought occurred to me and I didn't like it one little bit. I took an easier option and hailed a passing taxi to take me back to my office. I needed time to think.

*

I arrived just minutes after Joe Lassiter had turned up with confirmation that the al-Qaeda facilitator, the enigmatic Naved Hussein, was indeed believed to have entered the country back in July.

Kate had just mastered our snazzy new coffee machine and was handing mugs out to Jazz and Popadom. 'Would you like one, Phil?'

'Just black and sweet, none of that frothy stuff,' I replied and turned to Lassiter. 'I thought that would take weeks – if you got anything at all.'

Lassiter looked pleased with himself. 'Got a result quicker than expected. New computer software that matches existing facial photographs with CCTV footage. Came up with an eighty-seven per cent match on a certain Jawad Nasrallah, travelling on a Jordanian passport. Came over to Holyhead on the Dublin ferry as a foot passenger. Thought you'd like to know.'

Although I'd been certain, it was good to have near-solid confirmation that I hadn't been sending MI5 on a wild goose chase. 'Do we have anything else?'

'Not yet. We're contacting Irish Intelligence and we'll be doing credit-card checks and all the rest of it on the new identity . . . takes a little time. And what about you? I thought you were with the watchers on the Evans case?'

I took the offered mug from Kate. 'Ah, yes. Something a bit odd happened. That's why I decided to get back.'

Lassiter looked perplexed. 'What d'you mean by odd?'

'Well, Evans came south after trying to shake off any

tails . . . But finally he didn't meet up with Naved Hussein or any other suspects. He met a woman – Melissa Thornton.'

The case officer nearly choked on his coffee. 'I don't believe that, Phil! Not for a minute!'

'I'm sure.'

'Couldn't be.'

'I was right about Naved,' I insisted, sticking my neck out. 'I'm good on faces. It was Melissa Thornton or her absolute doppelgänger.'

'Does this Melissa have a twin sister?' Kate asked brightly.

'Not to my knowledge,' Lassiter replied with irritation.

Jazz asked, 'Why should she be talking to Evans?'

'No idea.' I decided to bite the bullet. 'I had a really crazy thought, Joe. The leaks and tip-offs, this notion that there's information being leaked from the police . . . or maybe from somewhere else.'

Lassiter stared at me as though I was some sort of escaped lunatic. 'I really don't see Melissa Thornton as a converted Islamic extremist, d'you?'

I was starting to wish I hadn't mentioned it. 'No, but she clearly knows Evans. They must have met somewhere, got to know each other. Maybe she let some things slip to him.'

Lassiter gave one of his sickly, lascivious smiles. 'D'you mean pillow talk?'

'How the hell should I know? It happens.'

Popadom had been listening intently. 'It is true. Where there is a willy, there is always a way.'

Lassiter raised his palm. 'Okay, okay. No point in us guessing. I'll have to pass this on to Felicity Goodall. If Phil's right on identification, she'll have to take it further. If he's wrong, you lot are probably out of a job.'

Just then his mobile rang and he answered it. After listening for a few minutes, he snapped it shut and announced: 'That was the A4 Ops Centre. King's team say it looks like Dave Evans is heading for home. They'll stay with him, of course, but it looks unlikely he'll be meeting up with Naved Hussein today after all.'

Disappointment hung heavily in the air of the front office. 'Maybe tomorrow,' I said.

'Maybe,' Lassiter echoed. 'And talking of tomorrow, Phil, maybe you'd like to come down to Thames House around eleven. We're due to have a briefing from the electronic boffins on the contents of the late Akmal Younis' laptop that you retrieved. And a few other updates.'

'Sure,' I agreed. 'I'll be there.'

It was the next morning, while in a taxi with Jazz on our way to Thames House, before I remembered to ask her if she'd managed to see Dr Samir's student, Shahid Akhtar, the previous day.

'A very shy, sweet boy,' she replied. 'Doesn't like to look me straight in the eyes, too embarrassed. When I pushed him a bit more about part-time work, he didn't seem as keen as his housemates. Claimed he'd like the extra money, but was too busy with his studies.'

I said, 'Presumably you saw that note from the Immigration Service? Shahid went to Pakistan for four weeks last summer.'

Jazz nodded. 'I asked him about that. He said he went to visit his extended family.'

'Nothing more? Did you ask if he'd attended a madrassa while he was there?'

'Of course. He sort of hesitated and said no. I told him I was a Bosnian Muslim and that I would love to attend a madrassa and wondered what it would be like. That's when he admitted he had paid a visit to one. He couldn't remember which. He said he'd like to return there when he'd finished his studies in England.'

'And you still think he's an unlikely suspect?' I pressed.

'It's just my personal view, Phil. Sorry.'

It crossed my mind she was feeling a bit sorry for the lad. I made a mental note to get Popadom to meet Shahid Akhtar for a second opinion. After all, the student was young and impressionable, had been under the influence of Dr Samir and we knew he had attended radical group meetings in the UK.

Just then the taxi pulled up outside the Horseferry Road Magistrates Court where Joe Lassiter was waiting for us. Minutes later we were through the secret entrance and along the corridor to MI5's Thames House headquarters.

As we went up in the security elevator, Lassiter said,

'Well, I told the Ice Queen about Melissa Thornton and Evans first thing this morning – and, just in case, I checked out the photographs that the watchers took of the meeting. Got to agree, old son, that sure looks like Melissa.'

'What did Felicity say about it?' I asked.

'As puzzled as all of us. She's decided to call Melissa into our meeting and just play it with a straight question.'

'Melissa is Felicity's boss, right?' Jazz asked. 'Couldn't that be a bit tricky for her?'

Lassiter eyed Jazz closely, too closely. 'Such beauty – and brains, too.'

Jazz met his gaze with a hard glare. 'Careful, Joe. This isn't Bosnia. I've grown up a bit since then.'

Lassiter feigned innocence. 'Sorry, didn't mean to upset your sensibilities. Look, you're right. That's why Felicity's going to keep it in the open with us as witnesses to Melissa's response. Should also ensure she doesn't get a carpeting.'

The lift stopped and the doors opened with an asthmatic wheeze. Lassiter led the way through the office to one of the small conference rooms. The door tag had already been flipped to 'Engaged' and sure enough Felicity Goodall was waiting for us, seated at a small table with papers and photographs spread before her.

She glanced up as we entered. 'Hi, Phil . . . Jasmina. Nice to see you both again.'

And it was good seeing the Ice Queen again. Despite

Lassiter's dark warnings, I found her intriguing company. As always she managed to look demure, business–like, smart and stunning all at the same time.

She wore an unusually tense expression on her face as we shook hands and exchanged pleasantries. When we sat down, she said, 'Well, Phil, you've certainly dropped an unusual one on my plate. The lady who met up with Evans is most definitely Melissa. Even better than her DNA . . .' She hesitated for effect. 'I recognize the clothes she was wearing.'

Lassiter gave a snorty little chuckle. 'Ah, never thought of that. A woman would, wouldn't she.'

Felicity ignored him. 'I'm sure there's a perfectly rational explanation for this, it's just that I can't think of one off the top of my head.'

There was a sharp rap of knuckles on the door, which was opened without waiting for a response. As when I'd last met her, Melissa Thornton was all in black, although this time she was wearing a sleek pencil skirt rather than trousers. Again she had her hair up and looked as if she'd stepped out of a fashion shoot.

She dumped the pile of papers she was carrying on the desk in front of us. 'I hope we can make this quick, Felicity,' she said as she accepted the seat Lassiter offered her. 'I've got a report to finish for the COBRA meeting this afternoon.'

Felicity smiled awkwardly. 'Well, Melissa, I hope this will only take a minute or two, but it's something I really do have to ask you.'

Melissa hardly bothered to hide her irritation. 'Well?'

'Phil Mason here was out with one of our surveillance teams yesterday. They were following a suspect.'

'Yes, Felicity, of course. It's what they do.'

The Ice Queen pushed a grainy photograph of Dave Mo Evans across the table. 'This man. Do you recognize him?'

'What?' As she stared down at the close-up picture that had been taken with a long-distance lens, I could see the pale porcelain skin pale even more. 'Where did you get this?'

Felicity frowned. 'Get it? I got it from the file. He's one of the six suspects Phil Mason is looking at. Dave Evans, a former British soldier.'

'Yes, yes. I know who he is,' Melissa snapped. 'Why the hell wasn't I told about this?'

'You were routinely copied a file-note summary on . . .' Felicity consulted her notes. 'Exactly a week ago. Last Saturday.'

Melissa was now glaring at the photograph with such intensity I was almost expecting it to burst into flames. 'Dammit, I was in the States. That bloody "War on Terror" Conference in Washington. A total waste of time . . . And I've been in meetings all week . . . Notes on over two hundred suspects . . .'

'You mean it's probably still in your in-tray?' Felicity suggested. She could have been sympathizing, although I had the feeling it might have been gloating. Extracting another photograph from the file, she placed that in front of Melissa too. 'This was taken of Evans yesterday. Are we right, that's you with him?'

Melissa lifted her eyes and aimed her glare directly at Felicity. 'You can see damn well it is. And who's got him under surveillance? A4 or these . . .' She didn't finish her sentence, but I think she was about to say 'cowboys'.

'A4,' Felicity answered. 'Phil handed over once we knew Evans had a known al-Qaeda contact . . . You won't know then, that contact was Naved Hussein.'

'Of course, I bloody know. And I want you to pull the A4 surveillance off immediately! D'you hear?'

Felicity looked flustered. 'Excuse me. Why?'

Melissa Thornton took a deep breath, lent back against her chair and closed her eyes. 'Because Dave Evans isn't a suspect,' she said in little more than a whisper. 'I'm running him.'

I noticed Lassiter's jaw drop and I'm sure mine did too. 'What?' Felicity breathed once she'd overcome the shock.

But her boss' eyes were open again and she was back on the attack. 'You heard. And don't you all sit around gawping. I'm running Evans. He's in deep and he's found a conduit into the al-Qaeda network.'

Felicity's eyes hardened. 'Shouldn't I have been informed?'

There was the hint of a sneer on those glossy lips. 'No, not you, Felicity. I informed upwards. My action was cleared by the DD-G himself.' She hesitated, perhaps realizing that she had let her true feelings about Felicity show in front of outsiders. She smiled stiffly. 'It was too delicate, too risky to have it generally known within the Service. The DD-G agreed with my decision to run Evans myself . . . for the time being, at least.'

Lassiter shook his head slowly, clearly finding it hard to believe what he was hearing. I remembered him telling me once that the deputy director-general had the hots for Melissa Thornton.

'How did this all happen, boss?' Lassiter asked.

It was unusual to see Melissa smile, but there was a hint of one on her glossy lips now. 'Like so many things in life, a chance encounter. It was after the July 7 bombings in London. We sent officers to the various attack sites to assess what exactly had happened, exactly who was responsible. Later I went to the Royal London Hospital to talk to survivors. That's where I met Dave . . . Dave Evans.'

'He was one of the injured?' Felicity asked.

Melissa shook her head. 'Not really. He'd been lucky, just a few cuts from flying glass. He'd been travelling on the tube at Edgware Road. It was a Circle Line train travelling in the opposite direction that exploded right alongside them. He spent over an hour with others, helping the dying and maimed before the rescue services finally got to them.'

'God, how awful,' Felicity murmured.

'He was still covered in blood and dirt when I met him. Sitting at the bedside of this horribly-injured teenage girl, saying her name over and over again, trying to comfort her, trying to reassure her.' Melissa took a deep breath as she recalled the horror of the moment. 'The girl died while I was there. I went outside with Evans, we both needed some fresh air. And a cigarette and a drink. That's when I discovered who he was, an ex-soldier out of work. He told me the irony was that the dead girl had been Muslim. A language student from Jordan.'

I was puzzled. 'Is Dave Evans a genuine convert?'

Melissa shook her head. 'Not really. But he'd genuinely left the army in disgust at our involvement in Iraq and Afghanistan. And he did take the trouble to read the Koran out of real interest. Of course, he didn't know who I was when he told me he'd attended anti-war rallies and meetings in London. Said he'd got quite friendly with local Islamic groups as a result.'

'And that gave you the idea to run him as an agent?' Felicity asked.

'After another couple of meetings,' Melissa confirmed. 'Evans was angry with the American and British governments, but even more incensed at the radical clerics who hijacked the Koran and twisted meanings to fire up ignorant young hotheads. He told me he still had nightmares about Amal, the girl on the train. The way her charred arm had come away in his hands.'

'Oh, my God,' Jazz murmured.

'By that time he'd got involved on the fringes of Mullah Reda's clique. Of course Reda was thought to be a moderate at the time. Evans had been invited to one of his study-circle meetings to talk about his experiences fighting in Muslim countries. By the time I put the proposal to him, I think he was beginning to realize things weren't quite what they seemed with the Merry Mullah. I had no trouble persuading him.'

'But now he's in really deep?' Lassiter pushed.

Melissa nodded. 'They gradually accepted him because he seemed – no, is – genuinely interested in the theology of Islam, and also because of his military expertise. They valued him for being able to spot the best potential recruits for operations, here and abroad. Those leads have been vital to us. No one knows it, but his information has enabled us to prevent a dozen terrorist operations. Evans could even be the reason some suspects are on your list.'

I closed my eyes momentarily. God, did things ever change in the murky world of intelligence? The bluffs and double bluffs, the one hand not knowing what the other was doing? Just like all the dirty dealings I'd witnessed during the secret war in Northern Ireland. No one and nothing is as they seem. You had to ask yourself sometimes if that was honestly the best way to go about things, or was it really all about personal power and egos?

'Does Evans know where Naved Hussein is now?' Felicity asked.

'Al-Qaeda people aren't stupid,' Melissa replied tartly, 'you should know that. Evans has met him a few times and is getting closer, but he doesn't know his address or have any phone numbers. Contact is made by Naved from a public phone and a rendezvous arranged – then that RV is usually changed several times at the last minute until Naved's henchmen are sure he's not being followed.'

Felicity frowned. 'Are you sure you want me to pull out the A4 team, Melissa? If al-Qaeda tumbles Evans, then they might be useful for his own safety.'

'You know that's not A4's remit. They won't break cover. They're more likely to be the reason he's tumbled.'

I added, 'Evans told me he thought someone might have broken into his room. I thought it odd that his concern was that it might be his Muslim friends checking him out – rather than British security.'

'Now you know why,' Lassiter said.

Melissa stared at me. 'You've actually spoken to Evans? My God, this gets worse by the second.'

'I've met up with him a couple of times,' I replied defensively. 'We knew each other vaguely from way back in the army.'

'I sanctioned Phil's contact with him, Melissa,' Felicity added. 'Clearly I wouldn't have done so if I'd been kept in the loop.'

Melissa was still staring at me. 'Well, no more old soldiers' reunions, okay? Keep well away from him. Understood?'

Before I could reply, Felicity cut in. 'What about technical surveillance?'

'What's in place exactly?'

Lassiter knew the full details. 'CCTV live-relay in a car outside Evans' digs, the room's bugged, the public payphone on the landing, plus one of his mobile phones –

and we're patched into the email addresses he uses from the local Internet café.'

Melissa thought hard for a moment. 'I suppose that's all right . . . but I wish to hell you hadn't bugged his room. One of his Muslim contacts could check that out and find it . . .'

Felicity looked puzzled. 'Look, Melissa, surely our top priority is to arrest Naved Hussein. He's in the country illegally and that could signal something big is going down.'

Melissa almost snarled as she replied, 'Find Naved, yes. Not arrest him for God's sake! What are you thinking of? Evans is getting ever closer to Naved, expecting another meet to be arranged at any time now. When we locate the little scrote then you can put A4 on him with the full works until we know all his contacts and what the hell he's up to. Arrest him and he'll just be replaced by another al-Qaeda facilitator who we don't know.'

Felicity turned to Lassiter. 'Can you get on to A4 Control please, Joe, and call off the surveillance teams immediately.'

Lassiter rose to his feet. 'D'you want Technical Branch to take the bug out of Evans' digs?'

'No,' Melissa interrupted sharply, 'Naved's boys could have Evans under surveillance themselves. As he's an ex-soldier, they're always going to have slight reservations about him. So keep well away. Let me have the details and location of the bugging equipment used. I'll phone Dave and tell him. He can dispose of it quietly.'

'I'll arrange it, boss,' Lassiter said and left the room.

Melissa stood up from the table and gathered her papers. 'At least let's hope no harm's done. Now if you'll excuse me.'

She turned sharply on those elegant black high-heeled shoes and disappeared out through the door.

Felicity puffed out her cheeks and pursed her lips. 'Whew! That was all a bit tense . . . And that wasn't any sort of apology I heard on the way out, was it?'

My eyes met hers and I smiled. 'Don't think so.'

Jazz said, 'Forgive me for asking, Felicity, but do you think she might be – er – quite close to Dave Evans?'

'What makes you say that?'

'Just feminine intuition,' Jazz replied, 'or maybe I'm wrong. She called him Dave rather than Evans in the beginning and corrected herself. Then called him Dave again at the end. Just the tone of her voice when she talked about the time they met.'

'It's possible,' Felicity conceded. 'But it's more than my job's worth to go down that road. She got the blessing of the DD-G on this, so I'm certainly not going to rock the boat.' She glanced down at her Cartier wristwatch. 'Ah, time for our visitors.'

Barely a second later, the door opened and Lassiter re-entered the room, followed by Inspector Proctor of Special Branch and a man I hadn't met before.

Lassiter ushered them in and invited them to take seats at the table. 'I think you all know Inspector Proctor . . . and this is Professor Peter Schneider, head boffin of our IT department, G-TAC.'

Wild, curly hair sprouted in abandon around his shiny bald pate and the thick lenses in his spectacle frames suggested he'd perhaps spent too much of his sixty-odd years glued to a computer screen. I immediately sensed his life was his work to the exclusion of everything else, certainly of any interest in clothes. The threadbare corduroy trousers and ancient tweed hacking-jacket with open-necked lumberjack shirt suggested comfort dressing rather than any kind of fashion passion. A ready but nervous smile played on the lumpy and elongated face.

'Pleased to meet you, gentlemen — and ladies,' he said in an amused voice that had just a hint of a German accent. 'Not often I'm allowed out of the workshop. Or even have any visitors — unless someone wants their Nintendo repaired or for me to wipe all signs of naughty websites they've visited from their laptops.'

'Good thought, Prof,' Lassiter said. 'I'd better give you a call sometime.'

'Thank you, Joe,' Felicity interrupted coldly. 'Now let's get on. Ian, how are you?'

'Fine, thanks,' the inspector replied. And, in truth, he looked a little less like a zombie than when we'd previously met. At least this time he had shaved and wore a sharply pressed suit, although his eyes still lacked any inner light. 'My baby son's stopped teething for the moment. A couple of nights' respite.' He glanced around the table. 'Now, I've got a few interesting things to share with you. But first the bad news . . . our search of Dr Samir Hashim's house proved totally negative. He's either as clean as a whistle or one very professional, clever man.'

I frowned. 'He's an IT lecturer. Didn't he have a computer or laptop?'

'His wife said he did have a laptop, but must have taken it with him.' Proctor shrugged. 'Along with all his CDs, apparently. Interestingly, she said he never went online at home, did all his Internet work at Imperial College.'

'Have you . . .?' Felicity began.

'Of course, we raided Imperial College immediately after we tried to arrest him. We took all the computers Dr Samir's believed to have had access to. Not too popular with the college authorities, I can tell you. Professor Schneider's boys are going through them.'

'Is Mrs Samir still playing Miss Goody Twoshoes?' Felicity asked.

'Yes, and I've got nothing to hold her on. I'm going to have to release her.'

Felicity nodded solemnly. 'Can you liaise with Joe, Ian? I want an A4 team on her round the clock.'

'If we've got a team left,' Lassiter muttered to himself.

Felicity smiled icily. 'Of course you have, Joe. Sharpen up. You've just taken one off the Dave Evans case.'

Proctor continued, 'The slightly better news is the results of the raids on the late Mr Younis' curry-house empire. We rounded up some sixty personnel in the dragnet, most of Pakistani origins, some born there, some native British. Waiters, chefs, kitchen hands, cleaners. We think three may be Afghani. Younis' general manager is being very helpful. He willingly gave us immediate and full access to staff records. As a result, we were able to go to the homes of those working on different shifts. All their homes have been searched. Only one disappeared before local police arrived at his digs, but we're on to him.'

Lassiter asked, 'Are you surprised the general manager is being so co-operative?'

'Not when he explained the situation,' Proctor replied. 'He says he was aware the company was in financial difficulties, but there was nothing he could do about it. He had a good idea what was going on, but he had no actual evidence. Younis ran a very patriarchal business, keeping tight control of finances and personnel recruitment. The manager says he was afraid he'd lose his job if he asked too many questions. He also had doubts about some of the staff.'

'Doubts?' Felicity pressed.

'He suspected some might be illegal immigrants but, again, says he had no evidence.'

'Was he right?' Lassiter asked.

Proctor nodded. 'About fifteen on false documents, we think. Word soon got out about the arrests and we had two firms of Pakistani-community solicitors banging on the door straight away. The suspects are still being held, but no one's saying much yet. The general manager's been released without charge. You might find it helpful to talk to him.'

I said, 'Can you arrange that?'

'I'll ask him. As I say, he's been helpful so far. I think he's hoping to take over the business.'

'You've searched the houses of these fifteen?' Felicity asked.

'Yes. No weapons or explosives or bomb-making equipment found. Three of them had some radical Islamic videos or books, but nothing more to suggest membership of an al-Qaeda cell. None of them had computers, they don't appear to earn enough to own one.' Proctor rubbed his chin. 'All the other staff have been interviewed. The majority have been employed for a year or more.'

'So not too much progress,' Felicity observed stiffly.

Proctor gave a slight smile. 'Well, you could say it's progress to find there isn't a latent terror cell in that lot.'

It was Felicity's turn to allow herself a slight smile as she turned to Professor Schneider. 'And, Peter, are you also going to tell me the good news that the late Mr Younis was also not part of a terror cell?'

The professor peered at her over the top of his glasses. 'Dear lady, wish that I could . . . The truth is, I suspect the dead gentleman did indeed have something to hide. Firstly, all the live documents and spreadsheets on his laptop related – or genuinely appear to be related – to his business or family correspondence and domestic affairs. He seems to have been more scrupulous than most in deleting his incoming and sent emails, and also in empty-ing his electronic wastebin.'

Felicity looked impatient. 'So you didn't find anything?'

'Oh yes, dear lady, but we have to go from the proverbial wastebin to the dustbin and then the landfill site, if you get my meaning. We probed deep into the hard drive with our specialist retrieval software.' Probably because he wasn't allowed out of his laboratory too often, the professor was making the most of the opportunity to explain his black arts. 'There were a number of emails of interest and a number of documents. Many were encrypted, but we've been able to unscramble them. Software technology today makes it all so much easier. But some, I'm afraid, were in one-off code. That is where only the sender and recipient know the code which is only ever used once and discarded. Some of the emails came from remote mailboxes like Hotmail and Yahoo! Which, as you know, anyone can have access from any computer in the world, making the true identity of the sender virtually impossible to verify.'

'And others?' Lassiter interrupted, beginning to share Felicity's impatience.

'Others,' Schneider said slowly, 'appear to have been sent from Pakistani government computers.'

'Known individuals?' Felicity asked.

The professor shook his head. 'No, impossible to tell that. But, as you know, many believe there is a powerful lobby of support for both the Taliban in Afghanistan and the al-Qaeda network within the ISI.'

'What's that?' I asked.

Lassiter chipped in. 'The Directorate for Inter-Services Intelligence – the biggest of Pakistan's intelligence agencies. Under President Musharraf, it's engaged in Bush's war on terror at some levels, but a lot of people in the intelligence community believe there's a strong rogue element of Muslim radicals that goes its own way. The ISI's a bit of a monster by some accounts, and not always under proper political control.'

'It is my best guess,' said Schneider, 'that such people may be the source of some communications with Mr Younis. Most of the direct messages to Mr Younis seem to be referring to people, but proper names aren't used, just codenames. Mostly animal world and minerals. Like diamond and gem, or giraffe and dove . . .'

My ears pricked up. 'Did you say dove? Was that actually one of them?'

Schneider considered for a moment. 'I do believe it was.'

'What's the significance of that?' Felicity asked.

'Someone with that codename texted Younis a warning before he had that fateful meeting with Dr Samir.'

Lassiter was on to it. 'It could be the codename of their informer.'

Schneider wasn't pleased with the interruption. 'As I was saying, these exchanges are in open-code, but I get the feeling they referred to people coming to the UK from abroad. Questions of their identity, their flight times, arrival arrangements . . . that's my best guess. It is all detailed in my report.'

Proctor said, 'Excellent, Professor, maybe I can tie those references in with some of Younis' employees.'

Schneider nodded. 'Indeed, and this is perhaps where Mr Younis' obvious inexperience in this sort of field may help you. There is one Word document – not an email – that was deleted and binned, that we were able to recover. It is a list of names that matches some of his past employees. In brackets beside each is one or more other names.'

'Aliases?' Proctor asked.

'That would seem to be one possible explanation, although there could be others.' The professor smiled gently. 'But remember, by far the majority of Younis' received emails were just copied to him for reference. The original recipient was someone called Blackwidow at a remote Hotmail address.'

'As in spider,' Felicity said.

'Centre of the web,' Lassiter murmured. 'I'll get on to the Yanks, see if we can't get something on the identity of the mailbox owner.'

'One copied email to this mailbox owner was of special interest, I thought. It came from Pakistan, sent very late at night there, and was unusually badly typed, full of spelling errors. The sort of thing we might do after a few too many drinks.'

'Pakistan is dry,' Jazz pointed out.

Schneider allowed himself a smile. 'That doesn't necessarily mean the sender was at the time. It rather comes under the heading of emails you wish you'd never sent. It was certainly indiscreet.' He picked up a sheaf of paper from the table and handed it to Felicity.

She put on those cute gold school–marm specs of hers

and began reading aloud. 'Dear Blackwidow, such a small yet deadly creature to ensnare the biggest leader of the evil infidel empire is desecrating our holy lands of the mid-east. To kill him on the land of his beloved and despised poodle – giving back the shock and awe they perpetrated on Iraq. We will all love to see the Al Jazeera footage of the secrets agents running round like headless turkeys screaming in panic "President down! President down!" as he lies broken and bleeding as Allah takes his revenge with sweetness. Signed, Hawk.' She finished reading and looked up. 'When was this sent?'

'A few days before Mr Younis was killed,' Schneider replied.

I said, 'Could it have been that email that spooked Younis? Sounds like some nutter talking about killing President Bush – that could be why he was talking about wanting out of his relationship with Dr Samir.'

'Dr Samir could well be Blackwidow,' Proctor added.

'But wait a minute,' Lassiter said, 'as far as I'm aware, there are no plans for the US president to visit the UK. And this sounds like it's referring to an assassination attempt here on British soil.'

Felicity looked quite pale suddenly. Slowly she removed her reading spectacles. 'It's top secret. President Bush is coming over to the UK, but on a strictly private visit.'

Lassiter's mouth dropped. 'God, really? When?'

'In four weeks' time.'

Ten

The man looked around nervously as he entered the interview room. He was about five foot seven, of slight build and he wore a light-grey suit and open-necked shirt.

'Brings back bad memories,' he said, smiling awkwardly. The overhead strip-lights gave a sheen to the man's wavy black hair and dark complexion. 'I was petrified when I was first brought here.'

It was Monday morning and Inspector Proctor and I had been waiting for the restaurant general manager Firoz Dogar in the basement holding area at Paddington Green Police Station.

'Understandable,' Proctor said sympathetically. 'It's good of you to come back.'

There was uncertainty in the man's dark eyes. 'And you are not going to charge me with anything?'

Proctor gave a reassuring smile. 'No, that's not the plan. You've come here of your own free will, and that's appreciated. You can have a solicitor if you wish, but you will not be under caution.'

'Then why here? Why not at the restaurant office or my local police station?'

'Because, as I'm sure you realize, this is a matter of national security. So it's best no one local to you knows you're talking to us. Besides this is a padded, sound-proof room.'

Dogar nodded. 'So this isn't just about the boss' murder or illegal immigrants?'

'It could be something more,' Proctor admitted cautiously. He turned to me. 'This is Phil, the gentleman I was telling you about. He's a security consultant.'

I offered my hand to Dogar who shook it less than enthusiastically. 'Pleased to meet you, Firoz,' I said. 'Take a seat.'

The three of us gathered around the table. There were no tape recorders or cameras operating. 'Can you tell me a bit about the late Mr Younis' business?' I began.

'Sure,' Dogar said. 'He started it about five years after he arrived in this country with his wife. I think they came from Pakistan about forty years ago. He told me they both worked very hard for five years to afford their first little curry-house in north London. Not far from where the Spirit of Bombay is now.'

'Did they have any children?' I asked.

'Yes, three. A girl who sadly died of illness when she was four. Then two sons.'

'But they don't work in the family business?'

'No, Mr Younis gave up on his sons. The eldest had an expensive education and thought he was too good for the restaurant trade. He had a top job as an accountant in the City and finally met a Pakistani woman, married her and emigrated with her to Pakistan. He runs a very big business over there. Mr Younis used to say that I was his son now.'

'What about the second, younger son?'

'Huh!' Dogar didn't hide the contempt in his voice. 'Ali is a little shit. He's thirty-five now and a total waster. He's probably the reason our business started to fail. He was a piss-artist, snorted cocaine and ran up huge gambling debts.'

'Could that be anything to do with when his mother died?' Proctor asked. 'About ten years ago?'

Dogar shrugged. 'Maybe, but he never did a stroke of work before, either. His father joked he was allergic to it. The Pakistani community does not like shirkers, we have a strong work ethic, as you know. Anyway, Mr Younis was always baling him out of trouble. Then finally he had enough – he cut him off and had nothing more to do with him.'

I wondered if I was seeing the pattern emerge. 'When was that?'

'About two years ago.'

'But it was too late for the business then?'

Dogar nodded. 'As I've already told the police, I was not allowed anywhere near the accounts. But about then I noticed that some suppliers were complaining their bills hadn't been paid. Some would not deliver the goods. Mr Younis complained about the tax bills and how the restaurant turnover was dropping. He blamed Gordon Brown, the then chancellor. Said no one had any spare money left in their pockets.'

'But he survived until now,' Proctor observed.

'It seemed to get better when Dr Samir came on the scene,' Dogar replied, 'about two years ago.'

Dr Samir! Our missing IT lecturer and former accountant from Imperial College. The same man I'd seen at the secret rendezvous with Akmal Younis. Trying to keep the tone in my voice neutral, I asked casually, 'And how did that come about?'

'Mr Younis had known Mullah Reda and a rival restaurant owner, Hasan Malik, for many years. They met at the mosque sometimes. They were acquaintances rather than friends . . .'

Proctor said, 'You do know that both those men are currently being held in custody, charged with terrorist offences?'

'Of course,' Dogar replied stiffly, 'our community pays close attention to these things. Personally I think it is another high-handed police error. I'm sorry, it's just what I and most people think. And I am certain Mr Younis would have had nothing to do with such matters . . . Anyway, back then it had become common knowledge that Mr Younis was in financial difficulties. I understand his rival Hasan Malik put him in touch with Dr Samir. Apparently he has a formidable intellect, a lecturer in advanced computer technology as well as being a corporate accountant some years back.'

'And how did Dr Samir help?' I asked.

Dogar shrugged. 'I don't know exactly, Mr Younis never told me. Dr Samir was often coming to our office and the two of them would go out. After a while our suppliers seemed happier and there was again always money to pay our wages. I think there was still some dispute with the taxman, their officials called once or twice a year. Even now. But everything got much better.'

Proctor suddenly raised an eyebrow. 'And what's happened to the younger son, Ali?'

Dogar shrugged. 'Probably on Dr Samir's advice, Mr Younis told him to go and not come back. He didn't.'

'Did that surprise you?' Proctor asked.

The general manager gave a half-smile. 'Knowing Ali, yes, very much. He always knew his father was a soft touch.'

'Do you know where Ali lives?'

Dogar shook his head. 'Not now. He did have a flat over the Spirit of Bombay at the time. I came into work the next day and he'd gone. Furniture, clothes, the lot. I haven't seen him since and I don't think Mr Younis did either; I know he'd have told me. Ali just disappeared.'

I said, 'When did Dr Samir last come to the office?'

'Ages ago. Maybe a year and a half. Not since Ali vanished and things got better.'

'Do you think Samir may have put money into the business?'

'I wouldn't be surprised, but I don't know. I mean, somehow things suddenly got better.'

I thought I detected a certain distaste in Dogar's expression whenever he mentioned Dr Samir. 'Would I be right to think you didn't care for him too much?'

Dogar shrugged. 'Not much. He seemed very arrogant and full of himself, albeit in a quiet way. And . . . maybe it's not connected . . . but after he got involved in helping Mr Younis . . . that's when I started having doubts about some of the staff Mr Younis was employing.'

'Why exactly?'

Dogar gave a dry laugh. 'They weren't any damn good! Some hardly spoke English, most clearly knew nothing of the restaurant trade and there was a high turnover of staff . . . The thing is, in all the years I knew him, Mr Younis had always been wonderful at choosing excellent people.' He added with a wide grin, 'After all, he hired me!'

I said, 'And do you know what's going to happen to the restaurants now?'

'I wish I did,' Dogar answered with a wan smile. 'I want to be in touch with the executors of Mr Younis' will, his older son and family in Pakistan. I am hoping maybe I could be managing director of the chain and run it for them. Or at least to buy the Spirit of Bombay to run with my wife. But it may be hard for me to raise the money.'

'Well, good luck,' I said and meant it. 'Thanks so much for your time.'

Dogar nodded graciously. 'If there's anything else, just call me. But, please, not at this place again.'

By the time Firoz Dogar left it was lunchtime and Inspector Proctor suggested we went out for a beer and a sandwich.

It was good to step out of the oppressive atmosphere

and air-conditioning of Paddington Green and into day-light, even though the sky was overcast. As we took our drinks and food to one of the outside tables at a nearby pub, Proctor said, 'Did you see any pattern emerging from that chat with young Dogar?'

I nodded. 'I was on that surveillance operation when Mullah Reda, the restaurant owner Hasan Malik and the bookshop owner were arrested. I understand that Malik's curry-house chain was believed to be a possible conduit for illegal immigrants, is that right?'

'*Was* is the operative word,' Proctor replied. 'I can tell you that from his records as employer, there were a number of highly dubious staff members who've since dis-appeared into the community. But he's been squeaky clean on that front for . . .' He paused for effect. 'About sixteen months.'

So I was right. 'About the time that Dr Samir began assisting Younis at the Spirit of Bombay.'

'Exactly.'

'Popadom's family had known Younis for years, Ian, and Pops swore the man was squeaky clean, the model hard-working Asian immigrant, building up a new life from nothing.'

Proctor raised his index finger. 'Until his wife dies. He is distraught and spoils his youngest son, Ali, who goes off the rails and builds up huge debts – which, being a loving father, he feels obliged to wipe out. The business starts to go belly-up.'

'Enter rival restaurateur Hasan Malik,' I said rather

dramatically, 'who sees an opportunity for a new conduit for illegal immigrants – and possible terrorist operators. Risking someone else's business instead of his own.'

'Immigration has been interested in his operation for a long time,' Proctor confirmed. 'Perfect chance for him to clean up his act and get someone else to do the dirty work.'

I said, 'A desperate Younis is introduced to Dr Samir – the spider at the centre of the web, we've heard say – and walks into the trap.'

'But what sort of trap, we have to ask ourselves?'

'Help to clean up Younis' financial mess,' I suggested, 'but at a price. Maybe blackmailed in some way, perhaps over tax evasion.'

'Ensnared into taking over and running Hasan Malik's illegal immigration operation – if that's what it was.'

'You're thinking it's a way of bringing al-Qaeda recruits in from abroad?'

'Maybe, or maybe a mix. It's all the same business, false identities, passports, etc. You heard what Dogar said just now. A lot of the new staff were useless and didn't stay long. How about disappeared into the community with new identities?'

'It fits,' I said, rolling up a cigarette.

'You haven't had a chance to go through that list of names Professor Schneider gave us yesterday, I suppose?'

I shook my head and lit up. 'Popadom was going over that at the office this morning.'

'My people are running all the computer checks and

matches today. Hopefully we'll come up with something solid.'

I said, 'I can only guess it all became too much for Younis and he freaked out.'

Proctor took a sip of his lager top. 'Especially if there's any mileage in this assassination threat. Imagine Dr Samir *was* behind it and thought Younis might squeal, put his hands up to the police or whatever . . . there's your motive for his killing.'

'It would make sense.'

'What do you make of that email on Younis' laptop, about an asasssination attempt on the US president, Phil? That used to be your line of business, didn't it?'

I smiled thinly. 'Not exactly assassination, Ian. I've never murdered unarmed civilians.'

Even as the words left my lips the vision sprang instantly into my mind. Trying to focus the crosshairs of the sniper's rifle amid the dust and gun smoke in the Afghan air and the glare of the sun, the small head appearing momentarily above the baked mud wall. I could even feel my finger against the trigger and the sudden recoil into my shoulder, and hear the whipcrack as the lethal bullet sped on its way. An image of the aftermath replaced it. When the firefight was over and I saw the crumpled heap of the little girl, her shattered skull and the pool of her blood and brain-matter already congealed in the heat of the day. I felt sick.

'You okay, Phil?'

I tried to clear my head. 'What? Oh, sorry.'

'You look pale.'

'I'm all right. Lost in the past for a minute.' I took two long gulps of beer and gave myself time to think. 'Anyway, that email, it was all a bit vague. Sounded like the rantings of a lunatic or some fantasist. I imagine a lot of radicalized Muslims exchange wish-list messages like that.'

'Maybe, but it'll have to be taken seriously.'

I considered the prospect for a moment. 'And, of course, if there is anything really being planned, it could just as well be attempted by a suicide bomber as a sniper.'

'True,' Proctor agreed thoughtfully and began demolishing his triple-deck sandwich. I'd lost my appetite, still shaken by the unwanted images that had haunted my dreams for such a long time. Thankfully the nightmares were occurring much less frequently nowadays. After a few mouthfuls I pushed my plate away and it was just then that the irritating ringtone of my mobile began.

I glanced down at the tiny screen and saw the name as I picked it up. 'Hi, Pops, how's it going?'

'Very, very well, thank you, Mr Phil,' the ever cheerful voice said. 'And I have something that may make you feel very, very well too.'

'What's that?'

'First thing this morning I am going through all the copies of documents from Professor Schneider. And what do I find? In the staff records a Mr L Fryatt was employed as a part-time kitchen porter at one of his curry-houses. It was last year, but only for a few weeks.'

I was stunned. 'You think it could be Leo Fryatt?'

'Well, I could not be telling for certain from those records because he was casual staff and paid cash in hand. But remember the other encrypted name-list the professor found?'

'The one with other names in brackets.'

'Indeed, Mr Phil. He is listed as Leonard Fryatt on that – and there is just one other name in parenthesis beside it. The name of Moussa Diawara.'

'Is that an Arabic name?'

'It's an African name, Mr Phil. I immediately contacted Mr Lassiter and he ran it through our computer link checks with the Immigration Service. A Mr Moussa Diawara travelled to Pakistan last year on a French passport. The name is Senegalese, a former French colony and largely Muslim, do you see? And he returned to the UK four weeks later.'

I could hardly imagine Leo Fryatt managing to get himself a false passport, let alone fund a trip to Pakistan. 'Perhaps the names in brackets aren't aliases. Maybe they're the names of employees' references . . .'

'I haven't finished, Mr Phil.' For once Popadom seemed mildly irritated that I'd interrupted his flow. 'You see on the same PIA flight there was travelling one Shahid Akhtar no less!'

Shahid Akhtar – Dr Samir's butter-wouldn't-melt student, coy and shy when Jazz had spoken to him. And Leo Fryatt, you lying little scrote, I thought savagely, although I was more angry with myself for having been so taken in by him.

'Anything else?' I asked.

'I am thinking that is enough for now, Mr Phil!' he replied triumphantly before I switched off the mobile.

'Interesting?' Proctor asked.

'Very. We appear to have established a link between one of Dr Samir's students, Shahid Akhtar, and another suspect on our shortlist.'

'Which one?'

'Leo Fryatt.'

'The black guy from south London?'

I nodded. 'Apparently they travelled on the same flight to Pakistan around a year ago. Fryatt used a false passport in the name of Moussa Diawara. Fryatt had also been employed as casual labour at one of Younis' curry-houses about that time.'

'Looks like you're on to something, whatever it might be,' Proctor said. I had the feeling he'd heard all this sort of thing many times before. After all, according to Lassiter, MI5 had already unearthed some two hundred networks plotting over thirty different acts of terror between them. 'I'm afraid I've got to be off, Phil. But keep me fully in the loop, won't you?'

We shook hands. 'Of course.'

He left and I ordered another beer. I needed to think. Could I turn this privileged information to advantage in some way? By the time I'd drained my glass, I had made my decision.

I phoned Leo Fryatt on my mobile.

'Yo, Mr Khan, you all right?' He sounded pleased to hear from me.

'I'm fine, Leo. We need to talk.'

'Cool, man. You name it.'

I named it. 'You free this afternoon?'

'Can be. Where you wanna meet?'

'How about Battersea Park, on the Embankment?'

We agreed the details. I finished by saying: 'I'll be seated on an empty bench, reading a paper. You come along and sit casually at the other end.'

I wanted to get him engaged, to feel both important and secretive. I knew it had worked when he said, 'Like in a spy movie?'

'Sure thing, Mr Bond,' I quipped.

He loved that. 'Cool, man. See ya.'

I'd allowed a couple of hours before our rendezvous, so I decided I had time to stretch my legs before hailing a cab. Exercise was something pretty much missing from my life recently and I made a pledge to myself to get just a little fitter and leaner. Six-pack abs and running marathons were not on the cards any more, but I decided I really should make more of an effort.

I hadn't been walking long when my idle thoughts were interrupted by my mobile's maddening melody. The screen read 'Private number'.

I pressed the button. 'Hallo.'

'Is that you, Phil?'

I thought I recognized the voice. 'Yes. Miss Goodall?'

Her laughter was as light as champagne bubbles. 'Felicity, yes. Don't be so formal . . . Hope it's all right to call, I got your number from Joe.'

'Of course, it's all right. What can I do for you?'

'That drink we talked about, at my place, you remember?'

'Of course.'

'Are you doing anything this evening?'

If only, I thought. Either I'd be catching up on office paperwork or watching dire TV with a takeway pizza on my lap. 'Nothing I can't change.'

'How about seven tonight? Give me time to get home and take a shower.'

A vision of water cascading over that slender naked body flashed across my mind in a split-second like one of those illegal subliminal telly commercials. 'Seven would be great.'

She gave me her address and directions and hung up, leaving me smiling gently to myself as I decided that was enough exercise for now. I bought an early evening edition of the *Standard* before hailing a cab to take me back to Brixton. Once home, I went straight to the bathroom to freshen up, then I had Kate call a local minicab to take me to Battersea Park.

I arrived early at the north gate before walking along the riverside path beneath the rustling leaves of the plane trees. I found an empty bench facing the Embankment wall. Sitting down, I rolled a cigarette and flicked through the pages of the newspaper.

It was ten minutes before I saw Leo Fryatt approaching. He was ambling along with his hands thrust deep in the pockets of his baggy, half-length cargo-pants and was whistling to the music plugged into his ear from a – no doubt stolen – iPod. I could just see the small pigtail swing behind the head of braided hair.

He played the part well as he recognized me. Slowing, he glanced down at his chunky Rolex watch and then looked around as though looking for someone he was about to meet. He shrugged and sat down at the opposite end of the bench, slipped out his mobile phone and pretended to be looking at his text messages.

'Hi, Mr Khan,' he said out of the corner of his mouth, doing a very poor impression of a ventriloquist.

'Hallo, Leo . . . just wondering if you've really changed your ways?'

'Hey, man, what y'mean? I don't do no more muggin'.'

'The Rolex?'

'It's a fake, man.'

'And the iPod?'

He pouted his lips. 'Yeah, well, that's like history. Can't give it back 'cos I don't know who it was I took it off. But, I tell you, I'm good.'

'And the drugs?'

'What's on with you, Mr Khan? I gotta live on somethin'. Unless you gonna pay me for information I give you.'

I said quietly, 'But you haven't given me information yet, Leo.'

'Ain't been nothin' to give. I gotta be careful, can't be nosy, ask too many questions.'

'You know my people demand total honesty, Leo, don't you? Have to be able to trust you.'

He shrugged. 'Sure, I know that, man. That's cool.'

'Then why did you tell me you hadn't been to Pakistan?'

Instantly his eyes widened with fear. 'I didn't.'

'Yes you did, when we first met.'

'I didn't understand what you meant. Anyway, I ain't been. No way.'

'Don't lie to me, Leo.' I added menacingly, 'It's a punishable offence.'

He glared at me. 'You *are* a fuckin' cop!'

'Don't talk to me like that, Leo. My brother's a general in the ISI.'

'What's that?'

'The Pakistani intelligence service. Some of their units have links with my people, you understand me? They have links with al-Qaeda and they've been checking up on you.'

Despite the fact the weather was quite cool, I noticed beads of sweat breaking out on Leo's face. Now he looked really scared. 'Yeah, well, maybe I just paid a visit. On holiday like.'

I ignored that. 'They don't mind that you went – they're encouraged by that. But they are not at all happy that you lied to me. Because Leo – or should I call you Moussa – they know you went to Pakistan with a student called Akhtar Shahid. Do you want me to tell you the PIA flights you travelled on, the times and dates?'

'Okay, man, but am I in trouble?'

'Big trouble if you lie to me any more.'

'I won't lie no more, I swear in the name of Allah.'

I stood up. 'C'mon, let's walk.'

Reluctantly he climbed to his feet and fell into step beside me as I ambled alongside the slow green flow of the Thames.

'So talk, Leo. Persuade me I can trust you. Tell me about Akhtar Shahid.'

'I ain't seen Akhtar for ages. I first met him at a mosque in north London. He was very quiet, didn't say much to no one. But when I got to know him in a study group, man, did he get fired up! He was real bonkers like. Dead keen to blow himself up and kill as many people as possible. Guess I got carried away a bit.' Leo looked down at his feet as we walked.

'Then one day he says he's going to Afghanistan to learn to fight and stuff. Did I want to go too, like? I said cool – it sounded great – but I ain't got that sort of money, I told him. Then he says, no problem. He knew people who would pay for me . . . I was cool with that.'

'What about the name change?'

Leo glanced sideways at me. 'He said it would raise suspicions if a black guy from a Jamaican family went to Pakistan – he told me we'd have to go to Pakistan to get to Afghanistan. Hey man, I didn't know where them places was. I didn't do much school. Akhtar said if my cover was broken, they wouldn't be able to use me in operations later. So they got me a new passport. French, man, like cool. Akhtar reckoned they make 'em in Thailand.'

'How did you get it?'

'Some contact of Akhtar's, some old bloke who runs an Indian restaurant in north London. He arranged it all, knew people.'

'A man called Akmal Younis?'

'I don't remember. Sounded somethin' like that.' Leo sniffed heavily and sighed, as though it wasn't a pleasant memory. 'And I had to work for him for a while, in the kitchens.'

I frowned. 'Was that a major career move?'

He missed my sarcasm. 'A bad one, if it was. Akhtar was worried 'cos I did some heroin and crack back then. He thought his contacts in Pakistan wouldn't like that. I said I could take it or leave it. So he gets this job for me to prove I was clean and could do regular work, fit in with society, like. I hated it. I always stank of fuckin' curry.'

'But you got to Pakistan?'

'Yeah, for four weeks. First we goes to this madrassa, you know a religious school. Man, that was weird, a real bore. Then we goes up into the mountains for some military training. I don't know if it was Pakistan or Afghanistan, somewhere way out on the borders, nothing for miles.'

'What sort of military training?' I asked.

'We does a week using all sorts of firearms, you know, like handguns and rifles – that was cool. Then a week learning about explosives and how to make and use them. We finished with a week of lectures. How to run cells, communicate amongst members, select targets . . . That was all a bit of a drag.'

I think I was getting the picture. 'So you didn't like the academic side, the lectures?'

'Never been my scene, man. The guns was good, but I couldn't remember all that textbook stuff, not in that short time. It was so intense! And I was dyin' for a fix, that didn't help my concentration any.'

'So what happened?'

'When we got back here, Akhtar told me I'd been binned. The lecturers and instructors decided I wasn't the right material, too unreliable. Fuckin' cheek!'

'Why didn't you tell me any of this before?'

'I thought you were going to give me a second chance, that's why I didn't say nothin'.' He glanced sideways at me. 'I guess that's out of the question now?'

I came to a halt and faced him. 'Not necessarily, Leo. I appreciate it that you've come clean at last. Four weeks isn't long to expect someone to master so much. Not everyone can be a fast learner.'

'I'll try harder, much harder next time. And I'm off heroin and crack. Just do the odd bit of weed, like.'

I nodded in mock sympathy. 'That's good – well, better. And what you have to remember, Leo, is that those instructors were not part of our organization.'

That threw him. 'No?'

'There are many radical Muslim groups doing their own thing all around the world. You remember I explained to you that our organization needs to know what others are doing in its name. People like this Akhtar Shahid, a young hothead. Just say he planned to plant a bomb on a London bus . . . imagine your mother happened to be on it, maybe going shopping. How would you feel, tell me?'

Leo pouted for a second as he thought about it. 'I'd fuckin' kill him, man.'

'Exactly. You'd come to hate everything he stood for and everyone would assume he worked for our organization. We'd be blamed and no one would understand why we did it. Acts of terror have to be very carefully selected and thought through.'

He concentrated hard for a moment. 'Yeah, I can see that.'

I wasn't sure he could, but it didn't really matter as long as he believed what I was telling him. I said, 'So you still want to prove yourself to the organization?'

'Sure, man. Just give me the word.'

'Okay, Leo, I'd like you to get back in touch with Akhtar. Can you do that for me?'

He shrugged. 'Yeah, I guess. We didn't part best mates, but I can try.'

I said, 'I want you to get friendly with him again, find out as much as you can about what he's up to, any illegal activities. Give the impression you still want to help, find out who his friends and contacts are, that sort of thing.'

'Sure, I'll do that. Why not?'

I stopped walking and held out my hand to Leo. 'Thanks. Your help will be appreciated. I've got to go now. Call me as soon as possible with whatever you've got. Allah akbar, Leo.'

The young man grinned widely, his eyes large and bright with pleasure. 'Allah akbar, Mr Khan.'

I got home and quickly devoured a cold chicken with pickle sandwich before taking a shower and changing into some chinos and clean short-sleeved shirt.

Miraculously the taxi from the local minicab firm I regularly used actually arrived on time.

Felicity Goodall's penthouse flat was on the top floor of a salubrious Edwardian mansion block overlooking the north side of Clapham Common. The high wrought-iron gate opened onto a paved garden filled with a glorious display of flowering shrubs that wouldn't have looked out of place at the Chelsea Flower Show. Once past the entry-phone, an ancient cage lift winched me slowly and noisily to the top floor.

As I struggled to slide open the metal concertina gate, Felicity opened the door of her apartment. 'Hallo, Phil, good to see you. Do please come in.'

It was good to see her, too, looking stunning in a hip-hugging, tobacco-coloured skirt and a cream blouse. 'Thanks for the invite,' I said.

She stepped aside, allowing me to enter the hallway. It was hardly the 'little pad in Clapham' that she'd described to me when she'd given me a lift back to Brixton.

The high-coved ceilings and spacious dimensions lent themselves well to the minimalist modern style in which the apartment had been decorated. I followed the fitted deep-pile beige carpet through to the lounge which was furnished with two expensive, stressed-leather sofas and huge occasional ceramic pots filled either with rubber plants or ornate dried twigs, and an enormous circular coffee table with a smoked-glass top. Net curtains jigged in the slight breeze where the double glass doors opened onto a balcony. There, to my surprise, Joe Lassiter stood with a glass in his hand. Why had I assumed this would be pleasure, not business?

Felicity said, 'I've just made some fresh Pimm's if you fancy one? I always think that's hard to beat on a summer day.'

It had been a long time since I'd had one, I'd almost forgotten the taste. 'That would be good,' I replied.

'Blue gin, orange, some grapes and a sprig of mint . . . That okay with you?'

She poured the fruit cocktail from a tall glass jug into a large tumbler and handed it to me just as Lassiter wandered in from the balcony. 'Hallo, Phil. Pity we haven't got the weather to go with the drink.'

I agreed. 'Can't remember a summer as miserable as this one.'

'Tell me about it,' Lassiter said with feeling. 'Can't say this global warming stuff is such a bad thing. Bring it on!'

'Sorry, Joe,' Felicity said lightly. 'Global warming's just a blip in the earth's usual thirty-year weather cycle. Down to extra solar activity, I understand. It'll be cooling down again by 2010 apparently.'

Lassiter gave a half-smile. 'Bloody cool enough now. By 2010 we'll all be cycling to work and going blind trying to see by those ghastly low-energy light bulbs.'

'Can't see the Americans going far down that road,' Felicity said, then looked at me. 'Talking of whom, that's one of the reasons I asked you over this evening.'

I nodded. 'I see. This supposed assassination attempt on the president?'

Felicity picked up on the scepticism in my voice. 'Supposed or not, Phil, we're obliged to take it seriously. You can imagine the embarrassment and political fall-out if anything did happen on British soil.'

'Of course,' I said. 'But how can I assist?'

Lassiter helped himself to another Pimm's. 'Felicity and I have been chatting about how best to handle this threat – however unlikely. Of course, the VIP protection boys will be doing all the routine work. But your team indirectly unearthed this and you're closest to some of the parties who *could* be involved.'

'Moreover,' Felicity added, 'you used to be a sniper. Just the man to get into the mind of any potential assassin. We'd like your team to think outside the box, so to speak. Of course, that would be in addition to anything we or the police will be doing.'

I said, 'To be honest, I'm not sure a sniper would be the best or only option. I imagine the president will be pretty well protected with bodyguards, armoured limousines and the like. So a bomb or suicide-bomber would be just as likely.'

Lassiter scratched at his chin, 'You've got a good point there. Any suggestions?'

'Well, if you're serious about me taking this on, it

would be useful to have someone on the team from EOD.'

'EOD?' Felicity echoed.

'321 Explosive Ordnance Disposal Squadron,' Lassiter explained. 'Royal Logistics Corps. The terrorist bomb disposal guys.'

'Ah, yes, I see. An excellent idea.'

I said, 'I've an old friend from the army, Gerry Shaw. Met him on a sniper course years ago. But he eventually moved on to EOD. I also worked with him in Northern Ireland and in Bosnia. He's semi-retired now, lecturing on the subject round the world, so he's still pretty much up to speed on the latest developments.'

'So this could be right up his street?' Felicity asked.

'If he's not tied into anything else, Gerry would jump at it, if I know anything about him. I could give him a call.'

Felicity glanced at Lassiter for his agreement. 'That's settled then,' she said. 'Now let's sit down and I'll tell you as much as I know about the president's planned visit.'

I made myself comfortable on one of the sofas while Felicity and Lassiter sat opposite me. 'It's all a bit sketchy at the moment,' she began, 'but basically George W. is coming over here in September with his wife, Laura, and one of their twin daughters, Barbara. It's a private visit. Apparently Barbara studied Humanities before graduating in 2004 and has since been working at a Smithsonian museum in New York, the Cooper-Hewitt. All forms of historic and contemporary design, I gather. Now she's thinking of taking a PhD in Fine Arts at Cambridge.'

I frowned, trying to remember what I'd heard about Bush's girls, or the 'First Twins' as the media liked to call them. 'Weren't those two a bit on the wild side?'

Felicity laughed. 'Aren't all students? I think they were caught drinking under age or something, and were known for trying to throw off their Secret Service bodyguards. But they've both done some charity work overseas and the other daughter, Jenna, is writing a novel.'

'How old are they?' Lassiter asked.

'Mid-to-late twenties, I think.'

'So why's Daddy coming over?'

'You've got a daughter, Joe, aren't you still protective of her?'

'My daughter hasn't wanted to know me for years.'

'Yes, well, maybe George W. is more caring than any of us thought. Besides, I gather he's also looking forward to a private meeting with our new prime minister away from the glare of media attention. This would provide the ideal opportunity.'

I said, 'I'll need to know his itinerary, where they'll be staying and their travel plans in detail.'

Felicity nodded and poured herself and me another drink. She replaced the empty jug on the table. 'I'll speak to Grosvenor Square. Get someone from the embassy to talk to you.'

Lassiter stared at the empty jug. 'Very moreish, that Pimm's.'

'Oh, Joe, I'm so sorry, but that's the last of it.' I noticed her glance very quickly at me before looking back to

Lassiter. 'Anyway, shouldn't you be going home to that lovely wife of yours? She can hardly be seeing anything of you lately.'

Why was it something told me that Mrs Lassiter would be quite happy with that particular situation?

Recognizing defeat, Lassiter prised himself from his seat and picked up his jacket and trusty raincoat from the back of the sofa. 'Of course, you're right, boss. I'll see you in the morning.'

He nodded his farewell to me and let himself out. As we heard the door shut Felicity said, 'Oh, he really can be a tedious little man. Now he's gone, I'll make some more Pimm's . . . unless you'd like something else.'

'No, that's fine.'

'Come with me to the kitchen,' she said, leading the way. 'When Joe visits it's like having a kid in the house, having to hide all the sweeties. Although in his case it's any bottles of alcohol lying around. He's got more front than Blackpool when it comes to asking you outright, or even helping himself.'

'I'd noticed,' I said.

The kitchen was austere with gleaming stainless-steel units and fittings and a grey marble worktop. I had the distinct impression it wasn't used much for cooking.

'Drink's always been a problem with people in the Service, especially the men,' she said. 'I guess it's all that stress and not being able to tell anyone what they're doing. That's why we've got the Pig and Eye.'

'Pig and . . .?' I asked, not understanding, as she opened

one of the steel cupboards where she kept her secret hoard of bottles hidden from Lassiter.

A beautifully manicured index finger pointed to one of her crystal-blue eyes. 'Pig and Eye. Our bar at the office, to encourage our people to drink with workmates rather than get loose-tongued at some local London pub.'

I said, 'Well, you can say what you like about Joe, I've never known him to give anything away – even when he should have done because I was working with him! Secret squirrel syndrome we used to call it in the army.'

Felicity held up a new bottle of Pimm's. 'Shall I just make two glasses rather than a jug? I mean, I wonder, have you eaten?'

'Just a sandwich.'

'How about we go out for a meal. A working supper on the Service. My treat.'

My spirits soared distinctly at the prospect of a meal for two with Felicity. 'That sounds good.'

'There are some nice places now along Lavender Hill. It's just a ten-minute walk.' She'd made up the drink and dropped in some ice cubes from the freezer. 'Do you miss the army life?' she asked suddenly.

I took the offered tumbler. 'I miss the camaraderie – and knowing what I was doing. Civvy Street can be a bit of a steep learning curve. But no, I think it was time for me to get out. Morale is pretty low in the forces now, and too many frontline troops are badly equipped. And with piss-poor support.'

She nodded. 'I've heard. It's an utter disgrace.' Then she

smiled and led the way to a door set in the far wall. 'Shall we sit outside?'

The door opened onto a small roof patio that looked over the leafy rear gardens of neighbouring properties. In addition to the array of potted shrubs there was also a wrought-iron table and two matching chairs.

'Very nice,' I said.

'I like to unwind here on summer evenings,' she said, sitting down. 'Sometimes it's hard to believe you're in the middle of the hustle and bustle of London.'

The sound of traffic was muted and the air filled with evening birdsong. 'You're very lucky.'

'I only won enough to buy this after a hard fight with Edmund.' She laughed that breathless little laugh of hers. 'If you look closely you can still see the bloodstains on the carpet . . . Talking of which, how's your divorce going, if you don't mind me asking?'

'Grinding on.'

Suddenly she placed her hand over mine. It was cool and soft. 'I'm sorry, Phil. Just make sure it doesn't crush you. If your own solicitors aren't up to it . . . well, I've got the best. I'll put you in touch.'

'Thanks, but they're probably too pricey for me.'

'Their senior partner is a personal friend of mine, you'll be all right.' There was something in the way she said it that made me wonder exactly what she meant by the term. Maybe I was right in my suspicion, because she continued, 'What I was saying earlier, about being in the Service. Not being able to tell anyone about what you do, being unable to share your worries . . . It can get very lonely. So it's nice to be able to talk to you.'

'Thanks,' I said, then added teasingly, 'better talking to me than a bottle of Pimm's.'

She threw back her head and laughed. 'Yes, Phil, very observant. It's not just the men who drink too much! But I keep it in moderation.'

'I'm sure you do.'

Just then her mobile phone trilled and she picked it up from the table. 'Hallo, Melissa?' A frown suddenly creased Felicity's forehead. 'Come over, what now? Well, yes, I was about to go out, but . . . Sure, about ten minutes.'

'Melissa Thornton?' I asked as she switched off.

'Yes. Sounded in a bit of a state. Very unlike her. Already on her way. I'm sorry about this. I hope you don't mind.'

'Of course not,' I lied.

Hearing mention of the dreaded 'Medusa', as Lassiter called her, reminded me of Popadom's discovery earlier in the day. I said, 'By the way, we found out something of interest today. Although I'm not sure how relevant it might be.'

Felicity still seemed distracted. 'Oh, what, I'm sorry. What did you find out?'

'Dr Samir's student, Akhtar Shahid, went to Pakistan with the black south London lad Leo Fryatt some thirteen months ago. And they both underwent military training at a camp on the border.'

'Good grief, how interesting?'

'And the late Akmal Younis provided the false pass-ports and other documentation. It seems like Dr Samir somehow blackmailed him into this role. I was talking to Inspector Proctor earlier. We wondered, if there's any mileage in the assassination of the US president rumour, could that be the reason Younis wanted out?'

Felicity had her finger on it straight away. 'And the reason why he was killed?'

'It could fit,' I said.

'Have you done anything about it?'

'I spoke to Leo earlier today. I put him on the spot and he admitted everything.'

'You did what?'

I raised my hand defensively. 'It's all right, he still thinks I'm with al-Qaeda and that I got my information from Pakistani intelligence. Apparently he didn't make the grade in training and hasn't seen Akhtar for a while. But now he's going to get back in touch and keep me informed.'

Felicity nodded slowly. 'That could be useful. But for God's sake don't take any chances, Phil. No heroics and no playing cowboys and Indians.'

'I promise.'

It was then that we heard the chime of the doorbell from the apartment. Felicity went inside and some minutes later returned to the patio with Melissa Thornton.

She looked as smart as ever in a dark-blue silk summer skirt and top, but her hair was a little dishevelled and her mascara had run.

As she saw me she did a double-take. 'I didn't know he was here.'

Felicity said, 'You didn't give me a chance to tell you. We're just discussing the case files Phil is working on.' She placed a hand on her colleague's arm. 'For goodness' sake, Melissa, what's this all about?'

Melissa looked at me again and I could tell she was running something through her mind, trying to make a quick decision. 'Look, Mr Mason, it's about Dave Evans. You knew him in the army, he can look after himself, right?'

That threw me. 'Er, I'm afraid I hardly knew him at all. What's happened?'

'I don't know.' She sounded on the verge of tears. 'I telephoned him on his mobile, but he's not answering. Not even voicemail.'

Felicity said, 'That could be a technical hitch.'

'I think it could be more than that. I contacted Technical Branch who are monitoring the remote CCTV camera in the car parked outside his bedsit. Three men, Arab-like in appearance, visited the house earlier this evening. They left after fifteen minutes. And they weren't residents of any of the bedsits.'

'That doesn't mean anything,' Felicity said, 'unless you know they actually visited Dave Evans.'

'You don't understand. I was phoning to warn him about the bug in his room. That bug is no longer sending a signal.'

Eleven

I said, 'You know, Melissa, I'm not sure this is such a good idea.'

We were seated in the rear of the police car as it screamed north up the M1 motorway with blue lights pulsing and its siren wailing like a soul in torment.

'Nonsense, Phil, you're the ideal person for this.'

Now that she wanted me for something, we were suddenly on first-name terms and the best of mates.

'Couldn't you just send the local police round to check he's all right?' I suggested. Of course, if she'd kept Jeff King's team on the job she wouldn't be in such a panic now.

Melissa shook her head. 'That's a not a bright idea if all is well and there's a simple explanation. Dave was certain that Naved's team were keeping watch on him. They will already know you're a friend of his. It'll be the most natural thing in the world for you to turn up. And he'll be able to keep his cover intact.'

I had to agree she had a point and I realized she wasn't going to take no for an answer. We lapsed into an uneasy silence until the car finally stopped a couple of streets from Dave Evans' digs.

Melissa looked decidedly nervous as I stepped out of the car. 'Don't worry,' I said reassuringly, 'I'm sure everything will be fine.'

It was getting dark as I made my way along the pavement. There were few people about on the streets of the run-down neighbourhood of Edwardian houses. A noisy trio of youths were making their way home, loaded down with six-packs of lager, a woman in a hijab hastily crossing the road to avoid them; an old man in a flat cap walked his dog.

Although I maintained a nonchalant air as I walked, I was watching carefully for a sign of anyone in the rows of parked cars or standing around who might have been keeping an eye on the entrance to Evans' flat. The only suspect was a boy of about eleven sitting on the steps of a house opposite, eating from a packet of crisps. Not a likely al-Qaeda recruit.

I mounted the steps to Evans' place. Melissa had given me a spare set of keys, but to keep up the pretence I pressed the plastic entry-phone marked 'Flat 5'. It didn't work. Then I realized that the front door was ajar and pushed it open. The pushchair and mountain bike were still in the hall, but this time the smell of curry was added to the nauseous aroma of must and cat's pee. From somewhere above me came the base thud of some heavy rock music.

Moments later I was on the first-floor landing and could just detect the burbling of a radio coming from beyond the door of Evans' flat. I relaxed and smiled to myself about Melissa's almost hysterical paranoia before knocking loudly. There was no reply. I rapped again, louder, and waited. There was still no response. The radio continued playing.

Now my own concerns came back in a rush.

Evans had last been monitored returning to his flat at around five in the afternoon, at which time the bug was still transmitting. Technical Branch was adamant that Evans had not been picked up leaving the house again on the secret CCTV camera in the car parked outside. Even so, Melissa had made them double-check the footage as we were driving up to Leicester. I knew it was his usual routine to go out in the evening for a bite to eat and a drink, but maybe he had a reason to stay in tonight. He may have simply not been feeling well and taken to his bed with a couple of sleeping pills.

There was only one thing for it. I inserted the key in the lock and eased open the door, remembering his little security device of a tumbler in a trainer I'd witnessed on my last visit. It wasn't there. That meant that Evans himself should be in.

The hinges creaked as the door swung open and I peered in warily. Dim light from a bedside lamp illuminated the dowdy little room. Evans was sprawled face-down on the bed itself, fully clothed. I smiled to myself as I immediately scanned the room for a bottle of alcohol. Perhaps I'd got him back into bad habits after my visit?

Then I smelt it. It was only faint in the warm air, but it wasn't a smell that I was ever going to mistake. Cordite.

'Christ, he's topped himself,' I breathed and rushed in.

As I reached the bed I could see the blood dripping steadily from the bedspread to form a vermilion pool on the threadbare carpet. His face was turned towards the bedside lamp and the huge exit wound in the rear of his skull had been in shadow.

God, I thought, he's paid the price. Thought he could handle it and then he found he couldn't. Suddenly it was all too late to ask for help. I'd seen it enough in Northern Ireland, amongst undercover soldiers and RUC policemen alike. I had even been fleetingly tempted myself once, but had managed to draw back from the precipice.

I frowned. Where was the gun? With a wound like that he'd have been dead instantly; he certainly wouldn't have moved anywhere. The gun would be on the bed or on the floor . . . but then? Suddenly I realized this wasn't making any sense. He was totally in the wrong position for suicide to have been possible.

I felt a sensation like ice water trickling down my spine and the hairs on the back of my neck rose. Evans had been shot in the mouth all right, but by somebody else. Then, I guessed, he'd been thrown onto the bed.

The vomit began its sudden rush and it was all I could do to hold it down. I thought I'd left this sort of dreadful sight behind me, all this senseless killing. I reached for the main light switch and, when the single bulb came on, I saw it. On the mirror above the bricked-up fireplace, the words smeared in blood. Dave Evans' blood.

Die spy! In the name of Allah.

Again I only just managed to stop myself from throwing up. Then I backed towards the door, glancing at the figure on the bed. 'Sorry, mate,' I whispered.

Closing the door quietly, I descended the stairs as quickly as I could, anxious to get into the street and breathe some fresh air. As I made my way back towards the waiting police car, I cursed my own complacency. I thought I'd finally persuaded Melissa that her agent and lover was almost certainly fine. Now I'd have the unwelcome task of telling her that I was wrong and he was dead. Not just dead, but brutally murdered. What goes through your head when you're made to kneel before a man who puts a gun in your mouth?

I knew the answer to that. There hadn't just been the lingering smell of cordite in that room; Evans had soiled himself.

The police car was parked with its lights out. I went straight to the rear passenger door and climbed in.

'Well?' Melissa asked anxiously.

'Not good, I'm afraid,' I said, then blurted out, 'Dave is dead. He's been shot. I'm so sorry.'

Her mouth fell open and I saw the look in those dark eyes, the utter disbelief and horror. 'No! . . . Oh, no, tell me it isn't true.'

I grimaced. 'I'm so sorry, Melissa,' I repeated.

She glanced down at her hands, clasped together in her

lap as she tried to grapple with the situation. Her decision was made in a split second. 'I must go to him.'

She was half-way out of the door as I grabbed her arm. 'Melissa, no, that isn't a good idea. It's not a pretty sight.'

'What d'you mean?' she demanded. 'I've seen bodies before.'

'He's been shot in the head. Someone put a gun to his mouth.'

'Oh, God.'

The police officers in the front seats had both turned round and were listening intently. The sergeant in the front passenger seat said, 'You want me to call the local force, ma'am, get the street sealed off?'

Melissa was in a daze. 'What? Oh, yes, of course.' She thought for a moment. 'But nothing should be touched at the crime scene until we've got Special Branch officers involved.'

The sergeant picked up the radio transceiver. 'I'll arrange that, too, ma'am.'

She turned back to me. 'Do you think the killers did anything to him before he died? You know, hurt him, questioned him?'

'I can't be certain, but it didn't look like it.'

Melissa bit her lower lip. 'But I don't know why? Dave seemed to be getting on so well with Naved and his gang. He thought he'd really been accepted. And we were so careful.'

I wasn't sure how to put this. 'I'm afraid you weren't quite careful enough. There were words written on the mirror in the room. They said "Die spy! In the name of Allah".' I didn't tell her they'd used Evans' blood for ink.

She stared at me. 'So they did know – and wanted us to know that they did.'

That made me think. 'How many people were actually aware of what Dave was doing?'

'I told you at that meeting the other day. Until then just three people. Me, the DD-G and Dave himself.'

She wasn't going to like this. 'I was with the A4 team that managed to follow him all the way to London for his meeting with you. If we could do it, couldn't Naved Hussein's boys have done the same? Or similar?'

'Don't be ridiculous, Phil. Al-Qaeda hasn't got the technical resources of A4. They might be good, but they're not that good.'

I had to agree she had a point. If she was right, then the only other people who knew that the ex–soldier was an agent were Lassiter and Felicity and my motley crew. None of those were likely to go running to the enemy. Our problem was that we couldn't even *find* the enemy!

Melissa said, 'I can only think that somehow Dave gave himself away, some chance remark.'

I nodded. 'It happens.'

The sergeant turned round again in his seat. 'All organized, ma'am. Local force officers will be there in a few minutes.'

'Thank you.' She sighed wearily. 'Let's get back to London.'

*

The news of the death of Dave Evans left everyone in our small office in shock and created a depressing atmosphere for the next few days. He'd started on our file as a prime terror suspect and turned out to be a superhero. An under-cover operator who, according to Melissa Thornton, was doing dangerous work connecting with embryonic terror cells and secretly tipping off MI5 so that it could intervene. His selfless actions could have saved God only knew how many lives.

What really nagged at the back of my mind was the possibility that I had contributed to his bloody fate. After I'd engineered that supposedly 'chance' meeting at the Star pub and left his flat later, I'd made no real attempt to hide my tracks when I returned the Ramada Hotel and met up with Jeff King and Popadom. If Naved Hussein's boys had their suspicions about Evans and had been keeping him under surveillance, it wouldn't have taken too much savvy to work out that Evans' old soldier friend was up to something. They might not have been sure what, but then they may have even put a tag on King or Popadom, or some other member of the team. The problem when you're following someone, is that you don't tend to think that someone else may be fol-lowing you.

Thankfully everyone's mood lifted with the unex-pected arrival of Gerry Shaw. I'd been trying to reach Gerry, leaving messages on his answerphone about a very interesting job that had just turned up. About a month's work for a seriously fat cheque. I gave him my new address and said it would be great to meet up anyway sometime, even if he wasn't able to take up my offer.

Typical Gerry, he just turned up unannounced, carrying a duty-free bag from one of the ferry companies. As I opened the front door, he thrust the bag into my hands.

'Greetings, you old bugger!' he said, grinning widely. 'Looks like you could do with a drink. Nice bottle of Jameson's for old times' sake. Got a couple of glasses?'

I shook his hand firmly. 'God, Gerry, you haven't changed. Don't you ever give someone any warning?'

'Sorry, spur of the moment,' he replied stepping over the threshold. 'Anyways, warnings are for IRA bombers – and you can never trust them.' He then began chuckling at his own joke.

Gerry was an irrepressible optimist. Unlike during his army days, his jovial and florid face now sported a short grey beard to match an unruly but full crop of hair. Even if he wasn't smiling, which was rare, you could bet on your mother's life that there'd be laughter in those pale-blue eyes.

He indicated the technicolour beach shirt and long blue yacht shorts that concealed his short, stocky body. 'Just got back from Cyprus. Two weeks with the missus! Enough to make the angels weep. Made the mistake of telling her I haven't got another lecture tour until October. Suddenly the house is falling down, the fence needs repairing, and the garden's full of weeds.' He grinned. 'Your message was an answer to my prayers.'

'And how is Rose, by the way?' I asked, showing the way into the hall.

'Fine, same as always. Still the bane of my life,' he chuckled. 'Still God-bothering with her chums at the church, making jam and chutney. Still trying to ban me from the local. D'you know, I think she dragged me round every bloody church on Cyprus.'

In fact Rose was a saint, a little old-fashioned for her age, but tolerant and undemanding of the impulsive and unpredictable Gerry, who never seemed to plan for anything in his domestic life. But beneath that carefree façade, Gerry Shaw was a man with nerves of steel. In fact one of the bravest men I knew when he was on tour in Northern Ireland with 321 Explosives Ordnance Disposal Squadron of the Royal Logistics Corps.

I'll never forget the time that the Provisional IRA had placed a bomb inside a stolen milk-tanker and left it parked outside a fortified police station in a residential area. After detecting and detaching a trembler-switch booby-trap device in the cab, he'd had to remove his protective armoured bomb suit to enable him to climb down through the hatch of the tanker to operate in that dark and claustrophobic world. It would have been a feat for a slimmer man, but for poor old Gerry it was a really tight squeeze.

Having a drink with him later he'd confessed cheerily, 'Thought I really wasn't going to make that one, Phil. Like potholing inside the bomb itself.'

And I suppose it was.

Everyone looked up as we entered the front office. Jazz, Kate and Popadom were there, sitting around during one of their rare tea breaks. I was a hard taskmaster. 'Got an unexpected guest. This is Gerry Shaw, an old friend of mine from the army. A former bomb–disposal man.'

'Ooh,' Kate said, 'gosh, you must be so brave.'

Gerry took her hand and pressed it to his lips. 'Hallo, Petal, and what's your name?'

'I'm Kate,' said Kate. 'I'm the girl Friday.'

'Only work one day a week, eh? Never mind, I expect you run the place really.' He finally let go of her hand. 'Tell you what, Petal, why don't you grab some glasses. The boss has got a nice bottle of Jameson's that'll go well with that tea.' As Kate, blushing, rose to her feet, he added, 'Oh, and I'm not so brave. We used a lot of clever devices to keep us safe.'

His eyes followed her appreciatively as she headed to the kitchen.

'She's too young for you, Gerry,' Jazz said.

He turned back to look at her, but it took him a second or two to recognize her. 'I know that voice. Good Lord, it's . . . it's . . . Jazz! How could I forget that name, or that gorgeous face!'

'We only met a couple of times, Gerry,' she laughed, 'so you are forgiven.'

He kissed her on the cheek. 'You still look the same.'

'I don't think so, a few more lines.'

'Then my eyesight's going.' He glanced back at me. 'But wait a minute, Phil, are you and Nina still . . .?'

I shook my head. 'Between nisi and absolute.'

Gerry looked puzzled. 'You and Jazz were an item once, back in Bosnia, wasn't it?'

'That's history, Gerry,' I said quickly. 'Jazz is on my staff.'

Gerry looked relieved that he hadn't opened his mouth and put his sandalled foot in it. 'Staff? Yes, so what is this? That sign on the door. Philip Mason Associates — private bloody investigators. You pulling my leg?'

'Thanks for that vote of confidence, Gerry. And yes, we are.' And I added with more confidence than I felt, 'And we're bloody good, too?'

Gerry looked abashed, momentarily. 'I'm sure.'

'And this is another associate, Popadom.'

Typically the neatly dressed little Pakistani had been sitting unobtrusively, watching and listening to the banter. Now he rose to his feet and shook hands. 'I am so, so pleased to be meeting you, Mr Gerry.'

'Popadom? Like in . . .?'

'Yes, like in your local takeaway,' he chortled. 'And no, it is not racist. I named myself because my real name is so long and complicated I can hardly pronounce it myself.'

At that point Kate returned with some glasses and I distributed the whiskey which, to my mild surprise, Popadom also accepted.

Gerry found himself a seat and said, 'So what's this all about?'

'Well, I'd not long started this agency, working alone

with just Kate – usual sort of stuff for solicitors and insurance companies – when a man called Joe Lassiter from the
Security Service looked me up. He used to be in army
intelligence, not sure if you know him?'

Gerry shook his head. 'Don't think so.'

'Well, seems like Five is stretched to breaking point
with all these al-Qaeda threats. It's been pulling in all the
help it can get from the outside. Security firms, detective
agencies, those with good military pedigrees to help out
on the more low-level operations. Part of a cell we
unearthed *could* be planning an assassination attempt on
George W.'

Gerry shook his head and smiled. 'And you want me
to make the bomb? You're on!'

'Shut up, Gerry,' I admonished lightly. 'This could be
real. The president's coming over here on a private visit in
a few weeks' time. He'll have all the usual protection and
precautions, but in addition we've been asked to think
into the mind of al-Qaeda. Think of the most likely way
they'll try. Jazz and I from the sniper viewpoint, you
from . . .'

Gerry nodded. 'The big bang perspective? Sounds fun.'

'You'll even get paid,' I added.

'Even better, but I'd do that for nothing.'

'Then you're earning too much.'

'I'm available as from now. Do I get a briefing?'

'Of course. I'll run over the case with you now – such
as it is. And tomorrow a briefing's been set up with the
Americans at Grosvenor Square.'

I ran over the bare bones of what we knew. That a highly suspected al-Qaeda facilitator called Naved Hussein, usually based in Syria, was known to be in the country under a false identity, which suggested something big could be going down. At the centre of an apparent cell seemed to be an Egyptian, Dr Samir, a lecturer in IT (and former corporate accountant) at Imperial College, who had disappeared having been tipped off about a police raid. That lecturer was thought to be behind the murder of an elderly and respectable curry-house owner, Akmal Younis, who appeared to have been a reluctant accomplice in providing cover for illegal immigrants who could be al-Qaeda connected. He wanted out, but was killed to shut him up. However, it was from his laptop that reference to the planned assassination was extracted by MI5 boffins.

Meanwhile, a former British soldier in deep cover for the Security Service had managed to connect with Naved himself and other cell members before he was murdered, apparently suspected of spying on them.

Two other young people being investigated by us had received some elementary military training in the Afghanistan area, but there was no strong evidence they were part of any cell or other terrorist activity.

'Did I hear that right?' Gerry asked. 'This cell – for want of a better word – has bumped off two people. One of their own and one of our undercover boys?'

'It seems that way,' Jazz said.

'Then I'd say this cell reckons it's got something pretty

serious to protect,' Gerry said thoughtfully. 'That suggests to me this assassination theory could have legs.'

The next morning Gerry and I agreed to meet up with
Lassiter for a coffee at a nearby hotel before going on to
the US Embassy in Grosvenor Square.

Lassiter was already there when I arrived, sitting alone
at a table and tucking into an expense-account breakfast
of lavish proportions. He barely glanced at me as I sat
down, all too intent on feeding his face.

'Morning, Phil,' he mumbled with his mouth full and
indicated the white china jug on the table. 'Help yourself
to coffee.'

Just to annoy him, I reached across and took one of the
fat Cumberland sausages he was about to stab. 'That looks
nice, Joe. Didn't have a chance to eat.'

He glowered at me as I put the sausage on my empty
plate and helped myself to a cup of black coffee. 'Would
you like to order a meal of your own?' he asked.

'Is that an offer?'

'No, it is not.'

I picked up the sausage with my fingers and took a
bite. 'I can't afford the prices here.'

'And I'm not a charity.'

I smiled as he drew his left arm protectively around his
plate to prevent any further thefts. 'Who are we seeing at
the embassy, Joe?'

'Some Yank by the unlikely name of Herbert J.
Weatherspoon. At least he's not Junior, Senior, the Third

or any other rubbish. He's something to do with their Secret Service.' Lassiter glanced at his watch without moving his arm from around the plate. 'We've still got twenty minutes or so.'

I wanted to ask Lassiter something before Gerry Shaw showed up. 'Joe, I've been thinking . . .'

'Oh yes?'

'How long have you known Popadom?'

Lassiter had cleared his plate in record time and wiped his mouth on the napkin. 'First bumped into him about three years ago. As you probably now realize, we case officers don't often get to meet the watchers. Hardly knew him at all until he joined your team.'

'He told me he'd been in the Service about five years.'

'So?'

'Isn't that about the time al-Qaeda started kicking off big time over here?'

'Probably before then . . . But what's making you suddenly ask about him?'

'I got to thinking when we were driving back after Dave Evans was murdered. Only my team knew that Evans was under cover.'

Lassiter shook his head. 'Is this because Popadom is Pakistani?'

'It had crossed my mind.'

'Look, Pakistani or not, Popadom comes with excellent credentials. He's been in this country since he was a small boy. In the army with 14 Int, half a dozen gongs for bravery, cleared to work with SIS as well as the Security Service. Fully vetted and squeaky clean.'

'I just wondered,' I said defensively.

'Wonder on this then, Phil. Once Medusa revealed all about her lover-boy, the secret was out. Not just your team, but I knew and so did the Ice Queen. Even the DD-G knew. I think I even mentioned it to A4 Control when I was asked to pull Jeff King's team off.'

That incensed me. 'You did what?'

Lassiter waved my protest aside. 'Oh, not in so many words, but I think it was pretty obvious. No one can resist a story like that. There's bound to be talk or specu-lation. The point is no one in our lot is going to be tipping off al-Qaeda. The most likely reason Evans got topped was by a mistake he made himself.'

Well, of course, that was always a possibility, but I had other concerns. 'There was also that tip-off when Younis was about to have his secret RV with Dr Samir. Then later Dr Samir also got warned about the police raid.'

Lassiter sighed. 'Look, Younis was an amateur. Are we talking tip-off or just a warning by others in his cell to do things right? Terrorists have been known to be pretty paranoid. And anyone in the Met, maybe some Asian officer or civilian, could have had misplaced allegiances and have given Dr Samir the word.'

That actually made me feel better. 'I guess you're right.'

'Trust me, old son.' One of those rare smiles appeared on his face. 'But if you really want Popadom off your staff . . .'

I shook my head. 'No, no. I'm sure you're right. I'm just getting paranoid too.'

'So you are, Phil. But for your peace of mind, I'll put him down for a vetting update, okay?'

'Will he know about that?'

'No, as usual we'll be like rats in the shadows.' He glanced up suddenly, looking over my shoulder. 'I do believe this must be your friend.'

Gerry Shaw had just wandered into the room. Unlike the previous day, he looked almost dapper in a well-cut grey suit that added an impression of height to his stout frame. He looked around pensively, caught my eye, and headed for our table.

After brief introductions, Gerry just had time to swallow a coffee quickly before we set off across the square to the US Embassy.

Herbert J. Weatherspoon was waiting for us at the top of the front steps, carrying a large briefcase. He was a very tall, slim all-American boy with over-developed biceps and shoulders that his sharp, slate-grey suit struggled to contain. His likely age was difficult to discern because of the ostentatious wrap-around sunglasses. The clean-shaven, finely chiselled features and military-style cropped hair suggested a soldier-boy who never really wanted to grow up. But I reckoned he had, and was now aged somewhere between his late-thirties and early forties.

The resonant, velvet sound of an advertising commercial voice-over rather confirmed it. 'Hi, guys. I'm Weatherspoon, you can call me Herbie.' The dazzling teeth in the broad smile suggested he'd come straight from a polish by his dental hygienist. After we shook hands with him, we were commanded to 'Follow me!'

We didn't escape the ritual metal-detector and thorough check for weapons of mass destruction, but Weatherspoon, still wearing his shades, briskly steered us through the rest of the security process that had us issued with nametags incorporating digital photographs taken and printed on the spot.

As he led the way along endless corridors and down in a lift deep into the bowels of the building, he explained, 'This issue is too sensitive to discuss in the normal offices. I'm taking you to a secure "bubble" where we can talk. Lead-lined and white noise constantly passing through the twin-layered walls.' He really did sound quite proud of it.

'Have al-Qaeda really got sophisticated eavesdropping equipment?' Gerry asked with mischievous innocence.

'Hell, no, Mr Shaw. But other nations have, who may not wish us well. They could pass on any information if they had a mind.'

Gerry gave me the wink and I knew he was thinking that those could be sadly the majority of nations on the planet in recent years.

We finally arrived at the 'bubble', just a square box-like construction in the middle of a larger concreted area. There was an armed US Marine guarding its steel door, who stepped aside to let us enter. It was larger inside than one imagined, with blank walls surrounding a huge conference table and chairs, all set out with water jugs, pens and paper ready for the next emergency briefing. At the far end was a communications centre with telephones and radio equipment and a whole bank of television monitors, all switched off.

Following Weatherspoon's invitation we took our seats around one end of the table while our host filled a water jug from a little machine set in the wall.

'Just like the US Navy, I see,' Gerry whispered to me. 'A dry ship.'

Weatherspoon placed the jug on the table and took a seat for himself. 'Right, gentlemen, I understand you've been tasked to look at security issues concerning our president's forthcoming private trip to the UK. I understand this is in addition to measures already being taken by ourselves, your protection police and MI5?'

'Quite so,' Lassiter said. 'Phil Mason is a former instructor at the British Army School of Sniping, with a lot of experience in various theatres, including Afghanistan. Also worked in Army Intelligence. Gerry Shaw — also once sniper trained — is an experienced former bomb-disposal operator. Worked within our Royal Logistics Corps and later with the Metropolitan Police unit here in London. He now lectures around the world.'

'Ah, I see,' Weatherspoon said without managing to look very impressed. 'Trying to think how the enemy might go about assassinating our president?'

I said, 'If we work out how we'd do it ourselves, then there's a better chance we'll pick up on anything others might have missed.'

'Our boys don't miss too much,' Weatherspoon replied, just a little icily.

'Of course not,' Lassiter jumped in quickly. 'So would you just like to run through the plan and itinerary with us?'

Weatherspoon placed his heavy briefcase on the table. It was only then that I realized it was handcuffed to his wrist. After removing the cuff, he undid the combination locks and opened the lid. He handed across three documents to us.

'I don't wanna hear these have been left in taxis or pubs, right,' he warned darkly. 'Keep under strict lock and key. Authorized eyes only.'

Something told me our Secret Service friend wasn't too impressed with British security.

'President Bush is arriving on Air Force One for a private visit in September. ETA will be 1100 hours on the Saturday. He'll be with his wife Laura and daughter Barbara. The visit will be just before the start of the Michaelmas term, so it'll be quiet with no students around. Barbara's thinking of doing a PhD in Fine Arts at Girton College, Cambridge.'

Weatherspoon continued: 'Air Force One will be landing at RAF Larkheath. Of course, this is a US Air Force Europe base and the airforce colonel there has his personal quarters at an old country house within the grounds of the base. He's an old friend of the president and First Lady, and they will be staying with him.

'The president also wants to use this visit to meet your

new prime minister again – informally – and talk through some issues. You've noticed relations between our two nations have cooled a little of late.'

'Will he only be staying at RAF Larkheath?' I asked.

'That may ultimately depend on any security risk assessment at the time. But I'm told he's privately interested in visiting Cambridge himself and may just go with his daughter out of courtesy to meet the university vice-chancellor over that weekend. He has also invited his old friend Tony Blair and his wife to a small dinner party during his stay. Plan is to fly out again on the following Tuesday morning.'

Lassiter said, 'It would be helpful if the president could be persuaded to stay within the base for the duration.'

For the first time Weatherspoon removed his sunglasses to reveal hard green eyes. 'Mr Lassiter, the president of the United States doesn't take kindly to being told what he can and can't do. And certainly not when his actions are dictated by a bunch of rag-head terrorists. The chief does what he wants and it's our job in the Secret Service to make sure he's safe doing it.'

'I know, I know,' Lassiter replied. 'But a journey between RAF Larkheath and Cambridge gives a lot more opportunity for any terrorist to strike.'

'Actually those opportunities are limited,' I countered. 'I'm sure Herbie's boys can find a number of alternative routes between the two places. A sniper or bomber has to be certain when and where a vehicle will pass. That means he would still have to opt for a location close to the airfield that the president *has* to use – or close to the destination at Girton College.'

Weatherspoon considered for a moment. 'I can see the logic in that.' He paused and gave a thin-lipped smile. 'But anyway, RAF Larkheath is an air-force base, so we'd have in mind to fly the Bushes out and back by helicopter. There are plenty of grounds at Girton College for it to land.'

Lassiter said, 'Well, we've certainly no indicators that any jihadists in the UK may have access to surface-to-air missiles.'

That made me laugh. There were still plenty of them in Afghanistan and Iran and other countries where al-Qaeda was welcomed. If the target was important enough and they had specific intelligence, it would be far from impossible to smuggle some missiles into the UK in bits for reassembly here. They certainly had the resources. But I said, 'You don't need a missile to bring down a chopper. A heavy-duty sniper rifle can do the job, aimed at the tail rotor.' I added, 'But the same principle applies, the main risk will be leaving and returning to the airfield or landing and leaving the college grounds.'

Gerry Shaw said, 'Tell us a bit about RAF Larkheath.'

'Well, it's probably not as well known as its sisters in the region, Mildenhall and Lakenheath. And frankly we like it that way.'

I frowned. 'Why's that?'

Lassiter leaned sideways towards me in a conspiratorial manner. 'Useful for extraordinary rendition and other dubious activities.'

Weatherspoon looked irritated. 'Larkheath is also a little smaller. There are no fighter aircraft based there, mostly Hercules and Galaxy transports and various helicopters. So it doesn't attract too much media or public interest.

'It's some twenty miles from Cambridge. An old wartime overspill station. It was taken over for much the same purpose by Strategic Air Command in 1953 – in support of our forces in West Germany during the Cold War. It's administered by an RAF wing commander, but it's run operationally by a USAFE colonel. It's home to some one thousand two fifty military personnel. Together with families and civilian support staff, there are around two thousand two fifty Americans in the surrounding area.'

'Still pretty big then,' Gerry observed.

'And security?' Lassiter asked.

'Usual arrangement. For diplomatic purposes, inside the fence is considered to be US soil – similar to an embassy – so it's patrolled by armed USAFE police in armed vehicles. Your own Ministry of Defence police, also armed, operate both sides of the wire as an interface between military and civilian personnel.' He paused. 'There are details and maps in your dossiers. I imagine you'd like to visit sometime soon. When you're ready, just give me a call.' Weatherspoon plucked a very impressively embossed calling card from his top pocket. 'Just call on my direct line and all doors shall be opened to you.'

'Thanks,' I said.

'Just before you go, gentlemen.' Weatherspoon fixed his gaze on Lassiter. 'Nothing much has trickled down to us from either the CIA or the Department of Homeland Security about the full nature and source of this threat. So I don't know if you MI5 people are sharing all with us – as we would hope and expect?'

Lassiter shrugged and forced a smile. 'Oh, I'm sure we are, Herbie. It just stems from something our boys found on a suspect's computer. Nothing specific.'

'Specific enough to have you guys sitting with me now. What was the suspect's name? I'll have the DHS run it through their database. See what we've on the guy.'

Lassiter's cheeks reddened and I noticed he was perspiring lightly. 'Have to get clearance on that, Herbie, from the boss. I'm just a humble foot-soldier.'

The hell you are, Weatherspoon's expression said, but his words were, 'Is this suspect in custody?'

Lassiter beamed widely. 'Put it this way, Herbie, he's not going anywhere any time soon.'

He was right there. Akmal Younis was now either in a mortuary freezer or buried under six foot of earth in a cemetery at a north London mosque.

A few minutes later the three of us were back out on the street. The air might have been chilly with a threat of rain, but it was still more pleasant than the sterile, air-conditioned security 'bubble' we had just left.

'Why didn't you tell Weatherspoon about Younis, Joe, or our other suspects?' I asked Lassiter as we stood waiting for taxis.

He tapped the side of his nose. 'We like to do things our way, Phil. Give the Yanks the names of our suspects and the CIA will be snatching them off the streets without a by your leave. Then spiriting them away to have their fingernails pulled out in some foreign jail. Or else find themselves in Guantánamo Bay. That's no good to us.'

'You mean you'd rather let them run . . .?'

He nodded. 'For a while. Until we find out what they're up to and can get other members of any cell.'

'You wouldn't rather lock up suspects for three months?' Gerry asked. 'Give the cops time to investigate properly. That's what a lot of politicians want.'

Lassiter looked pained. 'Look, the majority of these so-called suspects are young, stupid Walter Mittys, all fired up by jihadist clerics who want to blame the woes of the Muslim world on anyone but themselves. Most suspects couldn't blow their own noses, let alone blow up a bomb. Put an innocent man in prison for three months and, if he wasn't a terrorist when he was arrested, he sure as hell will be after. No one's learned the lessons of internment in Northern Ireland. It was the IRA's best recruiting sergeant.'

'For what it's worth,' I said, 'I think you're right.'

Just then two taxis turned the corner. Lassiter took one back to Thames House while Gerry and I returned to the office in the second.

I had been feeling in reasonably good spirits until I walked through the door. Kate, alone in the room, looked up with an unusually glum expression. 'There's a letter waiting for you, Phil. Sorry, I opened it by mistake.'

'From who?'

'Your wife's solicitors.'

'And did you also read it by mistake?' I growled.

'Sorry,' she repeated with a limp smile. 'It's your wife's final settlement demand. Would you like a cup of tea?'

I glanced down at the letter on the desk. The figures leapt out at me from the page. I suddenly needed something a damn sight stronger than tea.

Twelve

'How much?' Jazz asked, incredulous.

I repeated the figure and the percentages. I'd actually waited until lunchtime for that drink I so desperately needed, and had persuaded Jazz to join me for a snack at our local.

'That's outrageous,' she said, as we sat in the courtyard garden. 'I can't see any judge agreeing to that.'

I shrugged. 'I'm not so sure. Neither is my solicitor. A child involved, you see, and Nina hasn't had a job for years. Reckons now she's unemployable.'

'But didn't you say that she's got a boyfriend?'

'Allegedly the butcher, a man called Frank. I've met him once or twice at friends' parties in the past. But I don't know if they're actually cohabiting.'

Jazz shook her head. 'For goodness' sake, Phil, you're supposed to be a private eye.'

'I can't go snooping on my own wife.'

'That's all very noble, but it's also your future at stake.'

I said, 'I thought I might go round and try to reason with her.'

'Is that really a good idea?'

'Probably not, but I think it's all got a lot more acri-monious since solicitors became involved. Maybe I can talk her round – if she'll even listen.'

Jazz smiled gently and placed her hand on mine. 'Well, at least look out for any signs of a butcher in the house. It's called clues and that's what detectives do for a living.'

I nodded, knowing she was right. 'You haven't got caught up in this divorce nightmare stuff?'

'No. If my husband ever turns up again . . . but there seems little point at the moment. I've got more important things on my mind.'

I nodded. 'Like earning a living?'

She smiled. 'And that's become so much easier because of you, Phil. I'm very grateful.'

'Nonsense, it was the best business decision I've made yet.'

'Perhaps you'd like to come round one evening. Let me cook you something.'

That took me by surprise. 'Sounds good.'

'Do you still like curry?'

'I eat other things now, too. But I remember those curries you cooked up on the naphtha stove in Bosnia.'

'Oh, Phil, they were dreadful! I only made curry to disguise what was in the meal.'

'They were still delicious.'

'You thought that because you were just a little bit in love with me at the time.'

I laughed. 'Probably. Anyway, the curry idea still sounds good.'

'Are you doing anything on Saturday evening?'

'Nothing planned.'

'Then let's do it.'

I floated through the rest of the afternoon at the office. Gerry and I pored over the documents provided by Herbie Weatherspoon and pulled some area maps down off the Internet. Frankly, the itinerary was still patchy, various meetings pencilled in. Saturday, the date of the president's arrival, would be spent going with his wife and daughter from RAF Larkheath to Girton College to meet the vice-chancellor, senior tutor and head of department. Then a return to the airfield grounds and home of a senior USAFE colonel for an informal drinks and dinner party. The invited list of guests were a mix of English and American – some political and some military, then a number of industrialists and media chiefs. To be honest I recognized only a handful of names, including those of the Conservative and Lib Dem opposition leaders, and the ex-PM and his wife, Tony and Cherie Blair. It was suggested in the margin that the couple might stay overnight.

The next day would be the turn of the newly appointed Prime Minister Gordon Brown. He and his wife were coming for lunch, after the departure of the Blairs. The two men would be holding private, informal talks in the afternoon. Those to be followed by a light supper, the new man in Number 10 apparently eager for an early night before starting work again on the Monday morning. It seemed Mr Brown was taking his new job very seriously. The US president and his family were due to fly out of RAF Larkheath for home during late morning.

Gerry said, 'Any terror cell's going to be hard-pressed to get a crack at George W on this itinerary. Most of his time's behind the wire at the colonel's house.'

'A shame we can't persuade him to stay there and not visit Girton College,' I said.

'But to be honest,' Gerry replied, 'if he's flying in there by chopper, they'd have to get lucky or have extremely good intelligence to get a bead on him. The college is going to be closed for the day, no students in residence and just a few of the university's great and good to meet them.'

I added, 'And I'm sure the American Secret Service boys will be swarming all over the campus.'

Gerry nodded, 'Maybe this is just an al-Qaeda wet dream after all.'

'I hope you're right.'

I hadn't heard the door open behind me. 'What's all this about wet dreams?' Jazz asked, laughing. 'Leave you boys alone for a couple of minutes and the talk gets dirty.'

Turning round, I said, 'Don't creep up on me like that – you're not in 14 Int now.'

She poked her tongue out at me, then glanced down at the open dossier. 'Is that the stuff from the Americans?'

'Yes,' I replied. 'And the good news is any al-Qaeda cell is going to have some damn good inside intelligence to have a snowball's chance.'

'Don't be too complacent, Phil,' she warned. 'You know there's no such thing as a hundred per cent security.'

'I know that. But most of the president's time is going to be spent inside RAF Larkheath.'

'Not sure I've heard of that. Where is it?'

'Closer to Ely than Cambridge, and pretty remote. Apparently it's not much used except for the Yanks' sneaky-beaky stuff.'

'Ah, I recall it now,' Jazz said. 'I think I remember USAFE announcing they were going to close it around the same time as Greenham Common. I suppose I just assumed they had.'

'Maybe that was the idea,' Gerry added.

'Anyway,' I said, 'the sooner we take a look at the place the better. I'll give Weatherspoon a call.'

'Should I come, too?' Jazz asked.

I felt that the atmosphere between us had warmed of late. 'As a fellow former sniper?'

'Two heads and all that . . .'

'Of course. How's your workload?'

'Quiet – until Lassiter brings those new suspect names over.'

'Then I'll see if we can't visit RAF Larkheath tomorrow.'

Jazz smiled. 'That's fine for me.'

'Good, I'll phone Weatherspoon, then call it a day. Think I'll go over and see Nina.'

Jazz raised an eyebrow. 'Want some company?'

'You mean, you think I might need a shoulder to cry on?' I hesitated. 'Sure, thanks.'

Herbie J. Weatherspoon was the typically over-polite American gentleman when he answered his phone and had no hesitation in agreeing for Jazz, Gerry and I to visit RAF Larkheath the next day at noon. Having taken down our details in full, he promised to talk to the USAFE base police, who would arrange for us to be met by a member of the British MoD police. We would need Security Service photo ID. Having just joined us, Gerry Shaw didn't yet have that. But a quick call to Joe Lassiter resolved the problem: the personnel security section would have it delivered to my office by nine the next morning.

With the job done, Jazz and I went out to my van to begin the journey across London to my former family home in the Surrey suburb of Worcester Park.

As we neared our destination, Jazz said, 'You didn't think Popadom should come with us tomorrow?'

'Best to keep someone in reserve at the office,' I replied absently.

'Maybe just as well,' she murmured, looking out of the side window at the passing high street shops.

That rather surprised me. 'Meaning?'

She shrugged, not turning to face me. 'Oh nothing really . . . I just wonder about him sometimes.'

'Wonder about what?'

At last she turned. 'Don't get me wrong, he's a lovely guy . . .'

'But?'

'I know he's lived here since he was a child and even served in the army. But you can never know where people's deepest personal loyalties really lie.'

I was amazed that Jazz had the same niggling reservations that I'd felt. I tried to be as diplomatic as I could. 'You think recent world events could have changed his perspective of things?'

She took a deep breath. 'Well, it has changed the perspective of a lot of Muslims in this country and across the world, Phil. Guantánamo Bay, the invasion of Iraq and Afghanistan, torture at Abu Ghraib, extraordinary rendition . . . I'd never thought of Popadom like that, but it was when you said that Younis had a tip-off that time, then Dr Samir . . . and poor Dave Evans the other day.'

I smiled grimly. 'You won't believe this, Jazz. I raised the same worries to Lassiter only this morning.'

Her eyes widened. 'Really? And what did he say?'

'Basically dismissed it out of hand. Said there's no reason at all to suppose any leaks came from our outfit – and I know he's right.' I signalled left into one of the narrow suburban streets of the 1930s garden estate with its irritating speed humps every few yards. 'And I know anyone of Asian or Arab descent working with MI5 would have been re-vetted since 9/11.'

Jazz nodded. 'Yes, I'm being silly really. It just worries me that's all. Wouldn't it be a disaster if one of their new Muslim recruits turned out to be an agent?'

'Well, I think Pops has really stood the test of time. But

on this presidential visit issue, I'll discreetly keep him as out of the loop as possible, without upsetting him.'

She smiled. 'I guess there'll be plenty to keep him busy with Lassiter's new list.'

As we approached my former mock-Tudor, semi-detached home, I pulled into a gap in the line of parked cars. Most houses had a garage in the rear garden, but it meant negotiating narrow side and rear alleys, so few people bothered. And nowadays it seemed each family owned at least two cars.

I turned off the engine. 'If you don't mind waiting?'

'I've got a book in my handbag. I'll read that. You take as long as you like.' She smiled. 'Good luck.'

Realizing that I'd no doubt need it, I climbed down from the van and walked the fifty or so metres to the wrought-iron gate. It opened onto a small front garden which, frankly, looked a bit of a mess. Neither Nina nor I had green fingers, but at least between us we'd managed to keep the lawns looking tidy, pruned the roses and dead-headed the other flowers. When I was home on leave, it could actually be quite therapeutic. I saw that now part of the low front wall had been removed and some of the lawn replaced with a strip of tarmac for a vehicle to park.

It was strange walking up the familiar crazy paving path to the front of the semi with its white pebbledash, Tudor beams and obligatory bay window. And it was strange because it no longer *felt* familiar. Although it was the same house, it didn't quite look the same. Even in the tatty garden there was a different atmosphere about the place. I looked up and wondered if Danny would be in his room, no doubt playing on his computer.

I stepped up to the door with its small, circular stained-glass window. It may have been regarded as a special feature to estate agents but, oddly, I'd always hated it. I pushed the button to hear the old-fashioned ding-dong chimes resonate deep in the house.

Moments later, the door opened and Nina was standing there in a designer T-shirt and jogging pants. Devoid of her usual layers of make-up, she was looking her age.

She did a double-take. 'Oh, it's you. What do you want?'

'We need to talk.'

'Oh, the letter from my solicitors. Took that to bring you round here, did it?'

'What d'you mean?'

'You're not here to visit your son, are you?'

That rather wrongfooted me. 'Well, I hoped I might see Danny while I'm here.'

'You know my rules, Phil, no visits without pre-agreement.'

'But you never do agree, Nina; that's the problem. Every time I ask, you have some damn reason why it's not possible.'

We both knew she was playing mind games and considered the divorce to be a power struggle. 'Anyway, he doesn't want to see you, you know that. He still thinks you walked out on us.'

'And have you put Danny right? Told him it was you who wanted the divorce?'

She gave an ugly little twist of a smile. 'Don't lecture me on how to bring up my son. You were never here to help with that. Anyway, he's out with Frank getting a takeaway.'

I feigned puzzlement. 'Frank? Who's Frank?'

Nina's cheeks flushed. 'You know Frank. Frank Grint. You've met him.'

'The butcher?'

She tilted her chin. 'Hardly. He owns a meat-packing factory.'

'So why's he out with Danny?'

'Because he's a friend and they get on well.'

'And do you and Frank get on well?'

I could see the anger in her eyes. 'That's none of your damn business, Phil. We're getting divorced and I'm allowed to have friends.'

'So if Danny and Frank are out, can we talk?'

'I've nothing to say to you.'

'About the letter, your demands.'

'Ah, so it is about the letter.' She sounded triumphant. 'My solicitor told me not to discuss that with you. You'll have to go through your own solicitor.'

'They're costing a fortune and getting us nowhere.'

'My solicitor seems to have got you here. Pleading, by the look of it.' She raised an eyebrow. 'You ruined my life, Phil, and now you're going to pay for it.'

At that moment a flashy four-by-four with huge

chrome bull-bars swung off the road and on to the parking strip in the garden. Instantly the passenger door flew open and Danny raced towards me. 'Hi, Dad! Dad! Are you coming back?!'

Before I could answer he launched himself at me and I had him in my arms in a mutual hug, swirling him around in a circle. 'Great to see you, Danny. Gosh, you've grown.'

I placed him down in front of me. A skinny, fair-haired eleven-year-old who was a little too tall for his age. You could see he had some of Nina's features, but I liked to think he'd inherited the best parts of my personality. 'I knew you'd come home, Dad. Frank's all right. But I preferred you living here.'

'Frank lives here?'

'Yes, Mum says she's going to marry him.'

'ENOUGH, DANNY!' shouted a deep, angry voice.

Frank Grint was standing by the driver's door of the four-by-four, wearing baggy deck-trousers and a red polo shirt. It was the wrong colour for the florid complexion of the broad face and too tight to disguise his beer belly. He was how I remembered him: shaven-headed, a frame the size of the bulls he chopped up for a living, tanned and heavily tattooed.

Nina reached for Danny. 'Go inside now, there's a dear.'

Danny turned to me, a look of disappointment on his face. 'You're not coming back, are you, Dad?'

I smiled. 'Can't really if Frank's living here, can I? But we'll go out together soon, eh? Maybe do some fishing?'

His smile didn't quite manage to hide the sadness in his eyes. 'That would be great, Dad.'

As Danny slipped past his mother and disappeared inside the house, Grint strode over to me. 'What d'you think you're doing here?'

'Ah, Mr Grint,' I said with a forced smile. 'I think you know who I am. I'm talking to my wife.'

'Well, she don't want to talk to you. So piss off!'

'Leave it, Frank,' Nina interjected. 'Phil was just leaving.'

Well, it certainly didn't look like there was any point in staying, unless I wanted a brawl with Frank Grint. I thought about it seriously for a long moment before deciding that wouldn't really be in the best interests of Danny – or my divorce settlement. While Grint stood in front of me with his fists clenched like two ham hocks, I called over his shoulder to Nina. 'I'll ring you about a date to see Danny.'

'Sure.'

Grint couldn't leave it there. 'Now fuck off, and if I catch you sniffing around here again, you're dead meat.'

I smiled. 'Can't get enough of it, can you?'

'What?'

'Dead meat.'

I turned abruptly and left the garden, seething with anger that I had chosen not to take him on. I certainly didn't like the idea of my son being brought up by an oafish bully like Grint. When I glanced back both Nina and her boyfriend had gone inside the house and closed the door.

Jazz looked up as I reached my van and climbed into the driver's seat.

She put her book down. 'Oh dear.'

'Is it that obvious?'

'That you've just swallowed a wasp? Afraid so. Was it really bad?'

'Pretty much how you predicted, yes. At least I saw Danny for a minute.'

'Was that Danny in that silver Jeep thing that pulled in? I couldn't quite see from here.'

'Yes, Danny and the butcher, Frank. He's not the nicest of humans on the planet.'

'I'm sorry. How was Danny?'

'A bit upset. At least he wanted me back home.'

'Of course he does. And how was Nina? Did you have any joy?'

'None, she's not budging.'

'Well, I don't think either of us expected that she would.' She put her hand reassuringly on my arm. 'And what about this Frank person? Did you look for those clues?'

I forced a smile. 'Danny told me he's living there. And they were having a takeaway meal. Nina never did like to cook. Spent a fortune on ready-meals.'

'Frank the butcher might not like that.'

'It sounds like his company actually makes them.'

Jazz laughed lightly. 'Maybe that's why she fancied him.'

'They're planning to get married.'

She was surprised. 'Nina told you that?'

'No, Danny.'

'Ah, she won't be happy about that. Or that you know this Frank is living there, even as her unmarried partner.' Jazz's smile lit up her face. 'There's no way she'll get the settlement she's after now.'

In my seething anger, I'd forgotten that aspect. 'You reckon?'

'Just get a timed photograph of this Frank getting home from work and leaving the next morning. I'll do it if you like. In fact Zoë's been asking to have a sleepover at a friend's house soon. I could do it then.'

This was more like the old Jazz I once knew and fell deeply in love with. Bright, sparky and full of crazy ideas.

'You're one very special woman, you know that?'

'Of course. How about a drink to celebrate?'

As we'd chatted, I'd hardly been aware of the motor-cycle that had crawled past us, the rider and his pillion passenger looking left and right as though looking at house numbers. It pulled in outside my former home. The pillion, in leathers and a dark-visored helmet, dismounted and glanced furtively up and down the road before entering the gate and disappearing from my view.

'Fancy a drink?' Jazz repeated.

But I barely registered what she said. 'Something's not right,' I murmured, as I watched the rider turn his motor-cycle around to face the direction from which he had just come.

I don't really know what I thought. Maybe it was that

my years of experience of running surveillance ops had subliminally taught me about people's body language. Or was it possibly that curious sixth sense some have?

All I know is that I could feel tension in the air just like you do before a thunderstorm, and my son was in that house. I quickly opened the door of my van and stood up with my feet on the bottom edge so that I could see over the adjacent hedges to the front door. The pillion was standing in front of it, one hand tucked inside his leather tunic top. Suddenly the door opened and Frank Grint was standing there. Even from that distance I could see how deeply florid his face was, perhaps angry at the thought that I had returned.

Then I heard the thudding whistle of three silenced rounds, one after the other. Suddenly the pillion wasn't there any more. Grint had been thrown back against the doorjamb by the first round, his legs buckling beneath him as he slid down to the step. The second two bullets found their mark to form a cluster around the centre of his chest, blood pumping out of him, saturating his T-shirt.

'Bloody hell!'

'What's up?' Jazz asked.

Then I heard Nina's pitiful scream of terror as she found Frank's body.

The pillion was back out on the pavement, leaping astride the motorcycle as the rider revved for all he was worth.

'Man down!' I shouted to Jazz. 'Call an ambulance!'

With a twist of the throttle the motorcycle began rocketing towards my van. If I'd stopped to think about it, I'd never have done it. But I was in a perfect position, standing up, hanging outside my van, with one hand supporting myself on the open door. As the machine roared past, I launched myself at it. I was too late for the rider, but grabbed at the pillion passenger. I don't know exactly what happened next. My knees crashed painfully into the side of the motorcycle as my arms encircled the pillion, my fingers clawing at the slippery leather. I felt the machine slew as the wheels lost traction.

The next thing I knew the pillion and I were sliding at speed across the tarmac, joined together like a pair of bizarre Siamese twins. I felt the friction ripping through the material of my trousers and a burning sensation on my skin. We stopped with a jolt as his helmet cracked into the opposite kerb, my own head thumping into his chest.

I lay there stunned and winded for what must only have been seconds, but what felt like minutes. Further along the road I could see the rider rising groggily to his feet, the motorcycle on its side a few paces beyond him.

Then the body beneath me, which had cushioned my landing, began to move. I remembered he was armed, and with difficulty levered myself onto one arm, my other one trapped beneath his torso. His hand was scrabbling to find a way into his tunic and the silenced automatic he carried. I had no strength left to hit him, besides which he was wearing a helmet and the leathers were acting like body armour. So I did the only thing I could, I sunk my teeth into his wrist.

He screamed, but it didn't stop him. His hand disappeared inside the tunic. I sensed I might have only seconds to live. Then suddenly a shadow fell over the two of us. Oh, God, I thought, it's the motorcycle rider. I managed to turn round, just in time to see Jazz launch the most ferocious kick like a Wembley star, straight between the man's legs. He jerked and yelled like a soul possessed.

His movement allowed me to free my trapped hand and climb to my battered knees. I yanked his hand out of his tunic and found the gun myself, now looking around to find the other man.

The rider was regaining his orientation, limping around to inspect his motorcycle and glancing back and forth at the cars that had been forced to stop in both directions, blocking the road. Some of the drivers had left their vehicles and local residents were coming out of their front doors, others were already at their garden gates.

After hesitating for a second, the rider pulled out a weapon of his own and pointed it. Whether at me, or to silence his friend, I do not know. But I now had the pillion's silenced automatic in my hand, and raised it.

I think it was that and the gathering crowd and blocked road that persuaded the rider that discretion was the better part of valour. He turned and legged it, gawping pedestrians quickly stepping aside to let him through. There was no way I could risk trying to take him out with so many innocent civilians standing by.

I turned to Jazz who looked as shocked as I felt. 'Let's get this bastard in the van. I need to take a look at Frank.'

I grabbed the pillion by the shoulders and hauled him to his feet, before pulling off his helmet. I guessed him to be in his late twenties. He said nothing but I could see the real fear in his eyes. After forcing his right arm high up into the small of his back, I frogmarched him to the back of the van.

Jazz was talking rapidly on her mobile. A few moments later, she announced, 'An ambulance is on its way.'

'Are you okay with this?' I asked Jazz, handing her the automatic.

She smiled faintly. 'I think I can remember how to pull a trigger.'

I nodded, went to the cab of the van, pulled my new first-aid kit from under the driver's seat and ran towards my former home.

Nina was crouched on the front step, Frank Grint clutched in her arms, his blood drenching them both as it pumped from the three holes in his chest. But even more of the stuff was streaming out of the exit wounds in his back, dripping like a waterfall down the front steps into the garden.

It didn't look good.

Nina glanced up, her eyes full of horror and disbelief. 'Help me,' she pleaded in a small, frightened voice, and looked down at the ashen face with its eyes closed. Probably only ex-soldiers carry field-dressings in their first-aid kits, but I was glad I did and I did my best to staunch the flow, but it was a thankless task.

As I worked Danny emerged in the hallway. 'What's happened?' he asked, his voice quaking, not able to get a clear view of the wounded man.

Nina struggled to find her voice. 'There's been an accident. Uncle Frank's been hurt. He'll be okay. Daddy's helping us . . . Now be a good boy and go back upstairs. I'll explain later.'

Reluctantly Danny drew back and returned up the stairs to his room.

I turned to Nina. 'I'm sorry, this isn't looking good. There's no pulse.'

She shook her head, confused. 'I thought you had come back, ringing the bell. It looked like a motorcyclist . . . Why? Why Frank? . . . I know he'd made a few enemies, but this . . . You must save him, Phil!'

I heard the wailing siren of an approaching emergency vehicle just then, and prayed that it would be an ambulance. But it was a police car; paramedics would have further to come.

The two cops were young and looked totally out of their depth. Seeing me covered in blood, the older of the two men, maybe touching thirty years old, asked me, 'What happened?'

'I'd just visited my estranged wife. The injured man is her boyfriend. I'd just left when a motorcyclist came to the door and shot him. I've been trying to save his life.'

The constable looked at my blood-sodden shirt and

ripped trousers. He frowned deeply. 'Your estranged wife, sir?'

I suddenly realized what he was thinking. 'I didn't shoot him, officer,' I said firmly.

He didn't look convinced. 'Nevertheless, sir, I'm going to have to arrest you . . .'

Nina heard that and looked up, anger flashing in her eyes. 'Don't be such a bloody idiot, officer! Phil didn't do it!'

The policeman looked back at me. 'Are you Phil?'

'Phil Mason,' I confirmed, 'and I didn't shoot him. But I've caught the man who did.'

'What?'

'I managed to catch him as he made a getaway. Actually there were two, but the other one escaped.' I paused to let all this sink in as the policeman tried to think it through. Then I added, 'He's in my van now. C'mon, I'll show you.'

As I started to walk, he said, 'Wait a minute, are you armed?'

I smiled grimly. 'No, because I didn't shoot that man. Now for God's sake follow me and get your handcuffs out.' When we got to the open rear end of my van the officer, now completely overwhelmed, stared in at the pillion sitting meekly on the floor with Jazz standing over him with a pointed automatic.

'That's him and that's the murder weapon.' I was getting impatient now. 'He's a dangerous killer, so I suggest you get him cuffed, pronto.'

'And who are you?' he asked Jazz.

She smiled. 'Just a girl who likes to have fun.'

I took my temporary Security Service ID from my pocket. 'We're MI5. Now I suggest you get a senior detective down here.'

And that's what happened, but it didn't end there. Such was the total confusion and disbelief, that initially not only was the pillion arrested, but also Jazz and me. And even Nina, in case, through some bizarre love tryst, we'd set out to murder Frank Grint.

Poor Frank became irrelevant. In fact he became totally irrelevant, having been pronounced dead on arrival at hospital.

It took a further hour at the local police station before Nina was released and driven home. But it took yet another two hours and the personal intervention of Inspector Proctor of Special Branch before Jazz and I were freed. At least the police surgeon had cleaned up my knees and the coppers had magically produced a replacement pair of trousers from somewhere that were almost my size.

'You can't blame the local woodentops,' Proctor said, as we stood together on the pavement outside the station. 'They were confronted with a pretty bizarre scenario. A fairly professional hit-team, which would have no doubt got clean away had it not been for your timely – not to say foolhardy – intervention.'

'At least we've got the bastard,' I said. 'And the murder weapon. I know Frank wasn't the most pleasant of characters, but God knows who'd want to kill him. I've not heard of meat-pie turf wars in the area.'

Proctor smiled faintly. 'You think Frank Grint was the target?'

'He *was* the target,' I replied. 'Three holes in him to prove it.'

'All right then, the intended target?'

'Who else?' I asked. 'Certainly not Nina or Danny.'

Proctor said, 'The gunman claims to be a Somalian who came over here as an asylum seeker . . . I think you pouncing on him like that really shook him up . . . But to be honest with you, he appears to be afraid of his own people more than the police. Apparently he's pleading for protection against them.'

'His own people?' Jazz asked.

'He says he works with a criminal gang of Somalian and other Muslim asylum seekers. Reckons they'll try to kill him now he's been taken alive. He's being surprisingly co-operative.'

'Why should a gang of Somalians want to kill Frank Grint?' Jazz asked. 'Is this something to do with halal meat or something?'

Proctor turned to me. 'The man's been transferred to Paddington Green, Phil. That gang are common criminals, but also strongly jihadist with al-Qaeda connections. They carry out assassinations on request.' He paused. 'I don't think the target was Frank Grint. I think it very likely it was you.'

*

'God, Phil, I'm so sorry,' Jazz said. 'I had no idea.'

We'd finally got back to her home in Putney at ten o'clock that night. Her husband's parents, who had been looking after her daughter Zoë for the day, had earlier agreed it would be best for the child to stay over until the following morning.

Jazz invited me in for a coffee and I took the emergency bottle of whisky I kept in my van.

'Nor did I,' I said, pouring a generous portion into the tumbler she gave me, along with the mug of black, sweet coffee. 'Are you sure you wouldn't like a splash?'

She smiled across the kitchen table. 'Oh, to hell with it, why not?' Fetching a second tumbler from the cupboard, she added, 'But not too much, I've got out of the habit.'

As I poured her glass, I said, 'Of course, my name's still on the Electoral Register. So it could have been a case of mistaken identity. Frank answers the door, and they assume he's me.'

'He doesn't – sorry, didn't – look anything like you. It doesn't sound like their intelligence was very good.'

I nearly choked on the whisky. 'Damn well good enough, Jazz. If Proctor's right, how the hell do they even know who I am and what our team's working on? It's poor comfort to Frank and Nina that they don't know where I live now.'

In fact, Proctor had kindly and promptly provided police protection and a 'safe house' for Nina and Danny until interviews with the Somalian were complete and a full assessment made of any danger that they might still be in.

'I suppose this means our whole team could be at risk?' Jazz asked before taking a sip of her whisky. 'Ooh, yes, gosh, I'd forgotten just how good this stuff tastes.'

I smiled, but what she'd said worried me. 'We'll have to improve security.'

'We can't all move home,' she pointed out.

'I'll have to talk to Lassiter about it,' I said. 'Maybe it was just my name that they somehow got hold of.'

'Who from?'

'Who knows.'

Her eyes clouded. 'Popadom?'

I grimaced and shook my head. 'I don't really see it. Like the rest of you, he certainly knows where I actually live.'

'So poor and partial intelligence,' Jazz said thoughtfully. 'Somehow your name came on their radar and what you were about. They then hunted down the wrong current address.'

I drained my whisky and poured another. 'That makes me feel pretty damn uncomfortable.'

'Of course,' Jazz said, 'I feel desperately sorry for that man Frank. However awful he was, he didn't deserve that. But I'm so pleased it wasn't you.'

That gave me a nice warm feeling. 'So you do still care about me?'

Her eyes sparkled with mischief, and I was suddenly transported back over the years to our first days together in Bosnia. 'More than I should,' she said quietly.

Taking a chance, I placed my hand on hers. 'Is there really anything wrong with that? Fate brought us together again.'

'Actually, Phil, it was Joe Lassiter.'

'Ah, God really does move in mysterious ways, doesn't he? The point is, it happened and who are we to argue?'

'Philip Mason, are you flirting with me?'

'Undoubtedly. I've never felt happier since you came back on the scene.'

'That's nice.'

I wondered whether to risk asking her, then thought to hell with it, why not. 'And you?'

'When you first turned up here at my home, Phil, I wasn't sure. And I certainly wasn't sure it was a good idea working for you. I'm not one for believing in going back in life once you've moved on. And I wasn't at all sure how I'd feel about you.' She hesitated, then smiled shyly. 'But then how many men out there would have been crazy enough to launch themselves at an armed killer on a motorbike and make a citizen's arrest?'

'Crazy enough?' I asked. 'Or stupid enough?'

'My hero,' she said, teasingly. 'Yes, Phil, I'm very happy we've met up again. I think the magic we've always had is still there and I'm so pleased about that.'

'So am I.' I poured another whisky, then noticed the clock on the kitchen wall. 'I'd better make this my last. We've got an early start tomorrow.'

Jazz frowned. 'You've already had two large ones, Phil. And they weren't pub measures.'

I put down the tumbler, untouched. 'You're right. It's been a pretty exhausting day . . . needed to unwind. Perhaps I'd better leave the van outside and call a minicab.'

'Zoë's not here, Phil,' she said. 'I don't mind if you want to stay over. It would make more sense.'

I hesitated. 'No, maybe that's not a good idea.'

'No, really. There's a spare room.'

'You've talked me into it.'

When I'd finished my third whisky, Jazz led the way up the stairs to the first floor. She crossed the landing and opened the door to a small bedroom. 'I hope it's not too dusty, it doesn't get used. You'll find a sheet and duvet at the bottom of the wardrobe. There's also one of my husband's dressing gowns hanging in there.'

'Thanks, that's excellent.'

'Up at seven?'

'Fine.'

'I'm just taking a shower.' She smiled. 'See you tomorrow.'

I closed the door and stripped down to my boxers. It was then I realized I wasn't ready for sleep. My mind was racing, suddenly deciding it wanted to go over the events of the day and also to remember the times with Jazz in Bosnia that I'd almost forgotten. I opened the wardrobe and slipped on the dressing gown. It was a bit small for me but not too bad. I sat on the bed and made a roll-up, then went to the open window to light it. The night was quiet and peaceful, a sprinkling of stars between the drifting deep-purple clouds.

I was vaguely aware of the sound of the shower stopping and it triggered the mental image of Jazz changing in my bedroom at the office when Nina had turned up unannounced. The honeyed skin, the small taut breasts, the black thong.

I was so carried away with my thoughts that when Jazz knocked on the door, I jumped with surprise.

She stood framed in the doorway in a white, silk dressing gown. 'Phil, I've been thinking. Maybe this isn't such a good idea.'

That threw me. 'What? . . . Er, oh, fine. I understand. I'll get dressed and call a cab.'

Suddenly her eyes sparkled and she put a hand to her mouth to stop herself laughing. 'No, silly. I meant not a good idea you being in here. I've got a double bed in my room that hasn't been used in a long, long time.'

Thirteen

After a quick breakfast of cereal and coffee, Jazz loaded her large suitcase into my van and we drove across London to my place. Gerry Shaw was already waiting with his rather smart Land Rover Discovery, in which we'd decided to make the journey to Cambridgeshire.

'How many weeks you planning to stay?' he asked her as he transferred her luggage.

Jazz laughed. 'A girl has to be prepared for anything, Gerry. I might just get invited to the local hunt ball.'

He grinned. 'Never know.'

I left them to banter and went inside to check on the mail and any other developments with Kate. Apart from the usual bills, there were just a couple of letters. Nothing that couldn't wait until my return. We'd decided that a couple of days should be time enough to inspect RAF Larkheath and check out all the security arrangements for the president's visit.

I then went to the bedroom where I stored a holdall for emergencies; it was always kept filled with everything I might need for a few days away. Old army habits died hard. I just folded in a couple of extra summer shirts and made for the door.

It was an uneventful journey, picking up the south circular, then crossing the Thames at Woolwich before joining the M11, which would take us all the way to Cambridge. I was thankful that Gerry was in a particularly cheerful mood and hardly stopped regaling us with jokes and anecdotes. After Jazz's and my night of rekindled passion, I think there might have been some tense and awkward silences between us. I had little doubt that she was also wondering if it had really been a good idea, whether we'd both been expecting too much?

Her lovemaking had been as generous as I remembered, still uninhibited and adventurous. We had slipped into that easy rhythm of give and take that we'd always seemed to have, gentle but then slightly brutal, using both lips and teeth, kisses and gasps interspersed with fierce and challenging growls and unbridled lust. Yet it crossed my mind that maybe we were both trying a little too hard to make it the way it used to be? Perhaps only time would answer that.

Gerry's timing was spot on and we found ourselves approaching RAF Larkheath just prior to midday. The first thing I noticed was that there were no signposts on the main road when we turned off into a tree-lined B-road that ran between large cropfields. If it hadn't been for the car's TomTom navset we might easily have missed it. Carefully screened by trees and a low rise, the airfield still wasn't visible to us even when we turned left into the mouth of a narrow road that divided the air-force base into two parts.

And that was as far as we got. Apparently, although it was a public road, since 9/11 it had been closed except for access, military personnel and their families, and the few local residents who had special permits.

We obeyed the large red STOP sign at this outer checkpoint with its steel barrier and adjacent security hut. An armed MoD police officer in black trousers, peaked cap and white short-sleeve order approached the car as Gerry wound down his window.

'Can I help you, sir?'

'We're here to see Police Sergeant Ron Nash,' Gerry said. 'We are expected.'

The officer smiled. 'Just a minute, sir.'

He returned to the hut and spoke to his colleague who sat inside behind the glass screen. The man handed him a clipboard.

'Right, sir, may I ask your names and see your IDs, please.'

Gerry handed over the documents. 'Philip Mason, Jasmina Alagic and Gerald Shaw – attached to the Security Service.'

After a cursory glance the officer handed back the documents. 'That's fine, sir. I'll let Sarn't Nash know you've arrived.' He consulted the note on his clipboard. 'Now if you'd like to continue on down the main road, you'll see there's an hotel just over there on your right.

About seventy metres. You've got rooms booked there. By the time you get checked in and dump your luggage, I expect you'll find Sarn't Nash in reception.'

Gerry swung the car round the mouth of the road and continued in the direction we'd been travelling until he saw the car park outside a large old country house. At the roadside a swinging sign in gothic script read: *Welcome to The Larkheath Manor Hotel.*

The car park was surprisingly full with a lot of hire cars in evidence. After eventually finding a parking space, we made our way to the gloomy interior with its dark mahogany panelling, faint smell of must, and two obligatory suits of medieval armour guarding the sweeping grand staircase. The reception desk wasn't busy, but we could see there were plenty of people in the adjoining bar and restaurant. There was also no mistaking the babble of high-pitched American accents chattering away, many of them belonging to women and children.

Our rooms were all on the fourth floor which we reached by lift. Once in the corridor, I instinctively made my way to the end window to look out. It had a perfect view of the mouth of the narrow road and checkpoint through which any vehicle approaching or leaving the airfield would have to pass.

I was suddenly aware of Jazz standing beside me. 'Bang, bang,' she said quietly.

I nodded. 'Exactly. I hope they stick to their helicopter plan to get to Cambridge.'

From this height I could also see the airfield's perimeter

fence and large buildings beyond. Some of the apron and runways were visible, other parts obscured by the higher roofs.

Jazz gestured up to the ceiling. 'There's another floor at least.'

'We'll check it out later,' I agreed. 'Meanwhile let's drop this stuff in our rooms and get downstairs.'

An elfin grin flickered mischievously on her lips. 'I wonder if our rooms are adjoining.'

They weren't, and in a way I was pleased. I didn't want to be tempted to push things too fast, to ruin what might just be a wonderful future for the two of us.

We had only just gathered in the lobby when a tall, moustached MoD sergeant in his forties strode in, his uniform immaculate and black boots glistening.

I stepped forward. 'Sarn't Nash, I presume?'

The crow's feet around his deep-brown eyes crinkled as he gave an easy smile. 'Phil Mason, is it?'

We shook hands and I introduced Jazz and Gerry.

'Sarn't Nash, eh?' the officer said, repeating my military-style cropping of his rank. 'Ex-army, I presume.'

'Close. Royal Marines.'

He winked. 'Hell, someone has to be. Doesn't make you a bad person.'

'And you?'

'Grenadiers.'

I added, 'Jazz was in Army Intelligence and Gerry was with 321 EOD.'

'Thank God for that. I thought I might be lumbered

with some of those tossers from Five. D'you know a bloke called Lassiter?'

'Joe Lassiter? Has he been down here?'

'Briefly, a couple of days ago, to set things up. Lumbered me with the lunch bill, but managed to walk off with the receipt. Expect he'll claim for it on his own expenses . . . Don't tell me he's your best chum?' Nash read the meaning of my half-smile. 'Thought not. Anyway, enough about him. Welcome to little America . . . well, actually not so little, as you'll see. In fact, the Yanks announced they were going to close it down about the same time as Greenham Common. But they never got around to shutting Larkheath. Accident or design, I don't know. So unless you're an avid plane-spotter or military anorak – or a local – you'd assume it didn't exist any more.'

'Keeping it out of the media spotlight?' I suggested.

'Pretty much,' Nash confirmed. 'And from the rumours we hear, that must suit the Yanks down to the ground. Anyway, if you're ready, I'll take you down there. I gather there's some VIP visiting us shortly? And you're doing a sort of anti-terrorist assessment, is that right?'

I nodded. 'But you haven't been told who?'

Nash chuckled. 'Good Lord, no. Everyone treats us like mushrooms. In the dark and fed on bullshit. Anyway, I do gather he's pretty high up on the world stage, who-ever he is.'

Sergeant Nash's white Range Rover was waiting out-side and we set off back to the road-check. The same officer we'd seen earlier waved us through. High security fences topped with razor wire now ran along both sides of the road.

'Main airfield and admin to the north, on your right,' Nash explained. 'Living accommodation for servicemen and families on your left. Both areas within security fencing, but separated by this road.'

We'd reached a small crossroads, where Nash pulled into the kerb. Diagonally opposite was a busy little greasy-spoon café which looked as though it was doing brisk business.

'A bit incongruous that,' Nash admitted. 'Strictly speaking this is a public road although it leads to a dead end. But there are also a few privately-owned houses along it and, as you see, good old Freddie's Diner. Best burgers, fish 'n' chips and fry-ups for miles. The authorities tried to get it closed down, but lost their legal battle, thank God!'

'You sound like a fan,' I said.

'You bet. If it wasn't there, we'd have to use the USAFE canteen.' Nash jabbed a thumb towards the right-hand turn off the crossroads. 'That's the guarded entrance to the accommodation blocks in the southern compound. Passes required, of course. Now, we'll go left into the business side of the station, like stepping into another country.'

As Nash signalled, pulled out and turned towards the airfield's main entrance, Jazz asked, 'You mean like a foreign embassy?'

Nash nodded. 'Deemed to be US soil for diplomatic purposes. You even have to use American dollars to buy anything. And if any of your little terrorist friends are planning to try anything on, they'd better watch out. The US troops inside carry sidearms and deploy in armed vehicles. They tend to shoot first and ask questions later. Very gung-ho.'

'What about the MoD police?' I asked.

'We operate inside and outside the wire. Sort of inter-face with the military and civilian personnel. We're routinely tooled up with Heckler & Koch MP7 carbines.'

Nash drew the Range Rover to a halt before a security barrier that was lowered under the bricked-arch entrance. There, for the first time, I actually saw a sign for RAF Larkheath. Outside, beside a row of steel, spring-loaded anti-vehicle plates in the tarmac, stood a single-storey reception building.

'This is manned by locally employed civilians,' Nash said. 'They check, or issue and collect passes from con-tractors and visitors.'

Clearly that didn't apply to us today. An armed MoD policeman acknowledged Sergeant Nash, raised the bar-rier, and waved us through. On the far side we were greeted by two helmeted Americans in full combat smocks with holstered automatic pistols on their hips. In the containment area, beside a large brick guardhouse half a dozen more of them stood around. A couple car-ried clipboards, no doubt listing expected arrivals and deliveries. Another was handing out site maps of the station layout for visitors or newcomers. Still others carried hand-held metal detectors or long-handled mirrors for checking under vehicles.

It all looked efficient except that, on spotting the familiar face of Sergeant Nash, one of the guards leaned towards the driver's window and just said, 'Hi, Ron, how's it goin'? These the Brit security guys we're expecting?'

'Certainly are, Bill.'

The MP ticked us off his list. 'Mason, Shaw and a lady, Jasmina Alagic.'

'That's them.'

'I'm off duty this afternoon, Ron. You free for a poker game?'

Nash chuckled. 'Sorry, Bill, I'm baby-minding our guests for the next couple of days. So maybe next week.'

'Let's do that,' the American said with a grin and indicated to the gateman to raise the barrier.

As we drove slowly on, Nash said, 'Bastard cheats like a Mississippi showboat gambler – I just can't spot how he's doing it.'

Then Nash began a running commentary on the single and double-storey buildings set back beyond neatly cropped lawns on each side of the road. There were admin offices for the station, operations planning, command and control centres, more offices for their support staff, communications facilities, kitchens, various messes and canteens, off-duty bars, a ten-pin bowling alley, a small cinema, a bank, a library, crew restrooms, a medical centre complete with small ward, a separate terminal building where all transport aircraft disembarked their passengers . . . the list seemed extensive enough to support a small town which in a way, I suppose, it was.

At the end of the main drag there was a T-junction and we found ourselves facing a smarter three-storey building with some stone cladding and a flight of steps leading to a pair of open polished wood doors. Nash stopped in its small car park.

'This is the main reception building for more distinguished guests and visitors,' Nash explained. 'The RAF wing commander has his office here from which he runs the day-to-day administration of the station. Has his own secretarial unit and communications suite, plus a few posher meeting rooms for visiting senior officers, civil servants, VIPs etcetera. I've set one of these aside for you during your stay.'

We left the car and followed Nash up the steps and into what looked like an upmarket doctor's waiting room, with wood-panelled walls and a number of leather armchairs and coffee tables scattered with glossy magazines. I peered out of the far window at the vast expanse of mown grass which was intersected by strips of runway.

'Presumably that's the control tower at the edge of the apron?' I asked.

'Yes,' Nash confirmed. 'Virtually all RAF stations have their control towers at the southern edge of the field. Most runways run south-west to north-east with a second north-west to south-east so aircraft can take off into the prevailing winds. In the old days it was important that the controllers could have a visual on the aircraft without getting blinded by the sun.'

'Never knew that,' Gerry said cheerily. 'What a fascinating bit of useless information.'

Nash laughed. 'I'll just see if the wingco is free,' he said. 'Just for a courtesy hallo.'

He returned a few moments later in the company of a short, slim-shouldered man with a neat walrus moustache who was dapperly uniformed in air-force blue serge.

'Wing Commander Rex Page,' Nash announced before introducing the three of us.

'Gather you chaps reckon there's a good chance someone might take a pop at our VIP while he's here?' Page spoke quickly, his clipped words sounding like the staccato chatter of a machine gun. He pulled a terse smile. 'Can't have that at Larkheath. Just won't do. You've got the run of the place. I've oiled the way with the Americans, had a personal word with my opposite number.'

I nodded my appreciation. 'A USAFE colonel, I believe?'

'Quite. Colonel Coenen. Ralph's a good chap, but he is an American. Can be a bit volatile if you catch him on a bad day. Doesn't suffer fools gladly. This visit's already causing him a bit of stress. He'll be having both the American and our VIP protection wallahs swarming all over the place, so just make sure you don't get under his feet. Ralph may only be a colonel, but he's well-connected and respected.' Page paused for breath, picking his words carefully. 'You may have heard this station has been used for, let's say, special operations. I can't confirm or deny – I just administer the base. But Ralph is known to be expert in that sort of area.'

Nash said, 'He's quartered at Hollingdene Hall. That's a splendid former family pile on the south side of the road. It's situated within the accommodation compound.'

'Commandeered for operational planning during the Second World War,' Page added. 'Nowadays, military hierachy, dignitaries, world politicians and the like are often put up there when in transit to or from America. The less enviable part of Ralph's job is to entertain them. Full staff, butler and silver service. That sort of thing.'

Jazz said, 'And that's where the VIP will be staying?'

'As I understand,' Page confirmed. 'It's quite secure. Although it's within the sprawling accommodation compound, it has its own grounds and security fence.'

'And armed US personnel patrolling it,' Nash added. 'It would be a hard nut to crack. It's also nicely tucked away. Been used several times for sensitive or secret international negotiations. Palestinians and Israelis, Indians and Pakistanis, Bosnians and Serbs. Fly 'em in and out and no one's the wiser.'

'But we'll have access to it?' Gerry asked.

'If you need it', Page said, 'I'm sure that can be arranged. In fact, anything you want, Sarn't Nash here will oblige – or knock on my door any time if you need to . . . Now, if you'll forgive me, I need to grab some lunch before the start of what's going to be a very long and boring meeting.'

As soon as the wing commander had departed, Nash said, 'Talking of nosh, let's grab a bite in the American canteen. I've arranged for my opposite number in the USAFE police to join us. Then we'll give you the full guided tour.'

Ron Nash's opposite number turned out to be a youthful-looking, blond-haired sergeant in his late thirties. Gene Webb was the son of a cattle rancher from Wyoming. Apparently the utter boredom of his youth, in a small town surrounded by the empty plains, had driven him into the arms of the military in search of adventure at the tender age of seventeen. He was friendly, but in deadly earnest. It seemed that the visit of some obviously very distinguished international VIP to this particular patch of British turf, for which he felt he had personal responsibility, was the most exciting event that had ever happened to him. I think he'd have had apoplexy if he'd known it was his own beloved president.

It was actually quite a relief when we'd finished lunch and set off in Nash's Range Rover for a drive around the perimeter fence. It transpired that there were not actually any touch-sensors on the wire, although there were CCTV cameras at areas considered to be vulnerable. These were monitored from a state-of-the-art security centre at the far northern side of the airfield. This centre was situated next to the north gate, which was mainly used for access by aircraft maintenance staff, who worked in the row of huge hangars nearby.

As we drove Jazz and I studied the lay of the land beyond the wire. We chatted, discussing the various vantage points we saw that might be useful for sniper positions, while she recorded them and our deliberations on a digital camcorder. Being East Anglia, it was flat, but there were a few low hills and tall buildings in the area: water towers, barns and farm outbuildings, storage silos and some houses. Then there were the trees, many on the gentle slopes.

However, no professionally trained sniper would use such obvious firing positions unless he had a death wish – which, I suppose, a jihadist just might have. All that sort of stuff is normally pure action-movie hokum.

Depending on his firing position, a sniper didn't necessarily need a height advantage. In fact, it might be possible to fire directly from near the wire itself, given that a decent weapon, in the right weather conditions, can be deadly accurate up to several hundred metres. And there were a lot of wild shrubs amid the tall grass outside the wire that would offer excellent cover around most of the perimeter.

After some ninety minutes' slow drive we arrived back on the apron by the admin buildings.

'This is the position that the VIP's aircraft will taxi to,' Nash said, pulling on the handbrake.

I thought for a moment. 'Could you get the disembarking steps into the position where they'll be used?'

'I can arrange that,' Gene Webb said eagerly. 'When would you like to do that?'

'No time like the present.'

Twenty minutes later, after discussions with members of the control tower, the steps were wheeled into position. It was also agreed to mark the apron so that the exact same position would be used on the day of the VIP's arrival. Jazz and I scaled the steps to see which areas of the surrounding countryside could be viewed. She continued filming three hundred and sixty degrees at various stages as we descended the steps and made our way to the main reception centre where we had our temporary base. We gathered that this was where the president would be formally greeted by his old friend, USAFE Colonel Ralph Coenen.

When we entered the building, we found the American Secret Service man from the US Embassy in London waiting for us. Despite being indoors, Herbert J. Weatherspoon was still wearing his wraparound designer shades.

'Good afternoon,' he said. 'Thought I'd call in to see how everything was going.'

'Fine,' I replied. 'Everyone's been most helpful.'

Sergeant Nash said, 'I think we could all do with a coffee. Care to join us?'

And so Weatherspoon sat with us around the little conference table that we had been allocated. Nash phoned one of the canteens to organize the refreshments.

After they had been delivered by a pretty waitress in a

formal black dress and white apron, Gerry Shaw, who hadn't said much all afternoon, asked, 'The canteens and kitchens are manned by civilians, is that right? In fact, I've noticed a lot of civilians on the base.'

Gene Webb, the USAFE policeman, began pouring coffee into the white china cups. 'We sure do. Some seven hundred and fifty. All from roundabouts.'

'And they do what?' Shaw asked.

'Just about keep the place going,' Webb replied. 'From secretaries and admin staff to kitchen workers and wait-resses. Then there are maintenance men, including plumbers and electricians, gardeners . . . Quite a list.'

I could see where Gerry was coming from. He'd iden-tified a potentially major security weakness. I asked, 'And who's responsible for hiring these people?'

Nash said, 'Mostly that falls to us Brits. The Americans might interview a few clerical staff for non-classified work in their sector, but the MoD would actually hire them and hand USAFE the bill. But by far the majority of work is given by the MoD to outside contractors. Everything from maintenance to catering.'

'Any security or CRB checks on individuals?' Gerry asked.

Nash shook his head. 'Not generally. Just not practical or workable. In fact we've never had a problem with it. Well, that is nothing more than usual personnel stuff.'

Webb added, 'All outside contract staff have to have passes or photo ID.'

Jazz said, 'Can we see examples of these?'

'Sure,' the American replied. 'I'll bring some over for you.'

This whole line of thought was quite disturbing. 'And which other outside suppliers enter the base regularly?' I asked.

Nash pursed his lips. 'Oooh, now, let me see. This time of year, the gardening contractors bring in all their equipment. As you can see there's a lot of grass to be cut. Then there are groceries and stationery deliveries, and Securicor services the Bank of America branch . . . building materials, of course . . . In fact, quite a number.'

Gerry said, 'Could you provide us with a complete list? Both regular and intermittent suppliers.'

'Of course,' Nash said. 'I'll cross-reference our MoD police lists with the wingco's office. To make sure I haven't missed any.'

I added, 'Please be sure to include every company due to deliver anything between now and the VIP visit.'

Nash nodded, looking concerned. 'You think this could be a way of infiltration?'

I shrugged. 'It has to be a possibility. A potential terrorist operation only has to get one killer and one weapon into the base. And no security can ever be one hundred per cent.'

'If it's any consolation,' Nash said, 'we'll be having more armed MoD police during the visit.'

Herbert J. Weatherspoon spoke for the first time. 'We've put in a request for a further twenty-five officers,' he confirmed.

'That's a lot,' Nash said. 'They're being seconded in from all over the country – military bases, nuclear power stations, ammunition dumps – to make up the numbers. We've got a block booking at the Larkheath Manor Hotel for the duration. And, of course, all our leave is cancelled.' He didn't sound too happy about that.

I said, 'So from what I understand, during his visit the VIP will only travel by road from the north side of the camp to Hollingdene Hall in the south. Is that right?'

Weatherspoon nodded. 'I can confirm that. And the British government is going to supply three armoured limousines for the VIP and his entourage. He and his family will have armed US Secret Service bodyguards at all times. And the visit to Girton College will definitely be by helicopter given the increased state of alert following London's security warning.'

'What's the security set-up at Girton?' Jazz asked.

'Well, the college won't be open yet for the Michaelmas term,' Weatherspoon replied. 'So no students in residence, and only a small group of invited college dignitaries, who will be issued with special passes. Cambridgeshire police are providing officers, some armed, to cordon off the college. That's together with police marksmen positioned on rooftops. The distance between the helicopter landing site and the building will be no more than fifty yards.'

'We need to visit the place,' I said.

'No problem, Phil,' Weatherspoon said. 'If that's all for now, I'll get on to it straight away. Would tomorrow suit?'

With that agreed, Nash drove Jazz, Gerry and I back out of the north compound of RAF Larkheath, across the B-road, and into the vast accommodation compound. It was a typically functional and unimaginative estate of depressing military housing. Rows and rows of terraced buildings, thrown up in the fifties and sixties, with tiny gardens, most of which looked sadly neglected.

After a couple of minutes, the housing became more modern and smarter. There were even a couple of small apartment blocks with balconies.

'Officers' family-quarters,' Nash explained, as the double security gates of Hollingdene Hall appeared around a bend in the road.

The Hall was an impressive eighteenth-century building, somewhere the landed gentry of the time would have lived. Surrounded by lawns and spreading cedars, it was built in local stone. Complete with a fine entrance and large Georgian windows, it had two main storeys plus an attic floor for the servants.

Colonel Ralph Coenen wasn't at home, but he'd left instructions for us to be shown around, including all the areas that the VIP and his family were likely to utilize. Bedrooms, reception areas and dining room. It was furnished as magnificently as any stately home, the walls apparently hung with paintings from the government's collection. From each window Jazz made a point of filming the view for any potential sniper positions.

By the time we'd finished it was eight o'clock and the light was beginning to fade. Nash dropped us back at

Larkheath Manor Hotel and, after arranging for him to pick us up at nine the next morning, we headed straight for the bar.

'Security at Larkheath is about as solid as a sieve,' Gerry said once we'd found a table out of everyone's earshot.

'It was ever thus,' I said, after taking a sip of the local brew. 'If an enemy knows what it's doing and makes a detailed and professional recce, you will never make a place totally secure.'

'The layout doesn't help,' Gerry agreed. 'That public road dividing the two halves . . . old George W's going to have to cross over that junction between the airfield and Hollingdene Hall several times during his trip.'

Jazz said, 'That's exactly what I was thinking. We must look for sniper positions overlooking that junction.'

'He'll be in an armoured car,' I pointed out. 'Probably dark windows, certainly bullet-proof glass.'

'A bomb would be the best bet,' Gerry said. 'I'd use an old IRA trick. Grab the owners of that café on the cross-roads during the night, install some sort of directional IED in there, and blow up the whole bloody junction. Jihadists in this country have favoured gas cylinders for explosive. Just like the insurgents in Iraq. Old Georgie's armoured limo wouldn't count for diddly squat if one of those went off.'

'What about a simple car-bomb?' Jazz suggested. 'Just drive straight into the limo on the junction.'

Gerry wrinkled his nose. 'Mmm, he would have to get past the road-check on the main road.'

'Wouldn't be too much of an obstacle,' I said, considering the scenario. 'Two cars. First one with gunmen take out the armed police. Maybe ram that barrier, which is pretty flimsy. Second vehicle with the bomb goes through, gets close to the president's vehicle on the junction – and detonates.'

'Timing would be critical,' Gerry said. 'Maybe too critical.'

Jazz said, 'Timing's always going to be critical. It'll be just as critical for a sniper.'

'Or a straightforward assassination with a handgun,' I added. 'All those contractors and civilian staff worry me. Some seven hundred and fifty, aren't there? If al-Qaeda have infiltrated the system, it only needs one person to smuggle in a weapon. Then get to the target before he reaches his limo.'

'It's all going to depend on the strength of the enemy's intelligence,' Jazz said. 'I mean, how did al-Qaeda get to learn about this visit in the first place? According to Felicity Goodall, it's been a very tightly guarded secret in the UK.'

I said, 'Perhaps the leak came from somewhere in the States. If that is the case, the enemy intelligence could be extensive. Then we might be in big trouble.'

The next morning was spent in our makeshift office at the RAF Larkheath reception-centre, viewing Jazz's video footage on a laptop, then transferring a sequence of target positions in relation to angles of view and arcs of fire in chinagraph to Perspex overlays on an Ordnance Survey map. All buildings and stretches of terrain outside the wire that were of interest to us were duly noted and divided into zones. As the date of the president's visit approached, we would advise that the MoD paid particular attention to patrolling these potential sniper positions.

We then carried out a similar exercise on the high-risk areas inside the base, using large-scale site drawings. Of particular concern was that two low-rise apartment blocks in the officers' family quarters actually overlooked the otherwise highly secure grounds of Hollingdene Hall.

After lunch Herbert J. Weatherspoon joined us on a visit to Girton College. There we established the landing place for the presidential helicopter, the route of the short distance he would need to walk to reach the building. All parking would be banned. Only three top members of Cambridge University would meet the politician's daughter and her parents. Jazz took more footage and we were given copies of the college site drawings. Weatherspoon seemed confident that the senior university staff were not a security risk. From the outset he had made clear to them the importance of no one else knowing of the visit in advance.

The following day we took out the Girton site map and Jazz's new footage to identify all the potential sniper positions or opportunities for planting explosives.

By lunchtime we'd completed our work and, after a light meal in an American mess, we headed back to London.

*

It took several days to complete our risk assessment report for the US president's visit and make recommendations. It came with cross-referenced Ordnance Survey and site maps for areas inside RAF Larkheath and the immediate surrounding countryside that should be monitored and patrolled by the enlarged force of MoD police.

One thing puzzling me was the absence of Popadom since my return from the survey in Cambridge. Kate had assured me he'd said nothing when he'd left the office for the last time and he hadn't cleared his desk. I didn't have his home address or landline phone number, and his mobile was switched off. After the murder of Frank Grint, I was naturally concerned and had called Joe Lassiter.

'No worries, old son,' he'd assured me casually. 'Pops has just been redeployed for a while. The Service is a bit stretched just now on high priority work.'

'I understand, Joe. It just leaves me a bit short-staffed now I've got that new list of suspect names from you.'

'Pops was never going to be a permanent feature, Phil. But tell you what, why don't you ask Gerry Shaw if he'd like to stay on with your outfit for a time?'

'It's not his field,' I'd replied, feeling less than happy with Lassiter's high-handed action. 'He's never done intelligence work, although, I admit, he is useful to have around.'

'So why not ask him?'

And when I did ask, Gerry seemed to quite like the idea. 'Work with Smiley's People?' he'd chuckled. 'Always fancied being a spy.'

Just when I thought I'd sorted out my staffing problems, Jazz announced she needed a few days off because Zoë was unwell. It was clearly going to be a slow start to the investigation into our new list of suspects.

Then I learned that Lassiter had been less than forthcoming when Felicity Goodall turned up unannounced at the office just before lunch. She looked as stylish and well turned out as always, but her eyes looked tired and her face was noticeably drawn.

'Hallo, Phil,' she greeted. 'Good to see you again.'

I showed her into my living room which doubled for our operations centre. 'And you,' I said. 'To what do I owe this unexpected pleasure?'

She looked a little uncomfortable. 'It's about Popadom. I felt it only fair to tell you personally. We've decided to withdraw him from your service.'

I frowned. 'I know that. His absence has made a big difference. He's badly missed.'

'No, I mean, he's been put on paid leave-of-absence from the Service. In fact, he has been interviewed under caution by Special Branch. There are no charges pending – as yet. But he is being re-vetted. Several of us have had concerns about leaks and tip-offs on operations connected with your work.'

I nodded. 'I know, it got us all thinking . . . but that's just because he came from Pakistan as a boy. I mean, he's served in the British Army on intelligence work.'

She held up her hand. 'I know, I know. And he's worked for us for years with an exemplary record. And he has family connections with the Pakistani intelligence community that have proved very useful to us.'

'But?' I asked.

'That can be a double-edged sword.' Felicity gave a tight smile. 'We can't know if that information might not have become two-way traffic. Elements of Pakistani intelligence are well connected with the Taliban and al-Qaeda. If Popadom had a change of allegiance after various world events, then he would be in a position to cause a lot of damage to our security.'

'Is there any evidence to suggest this?' I asked.

Felicity shook her head. 'Thankfully not yet, and hopefully there won't be. But it was felt wiser to suspend him on full pay until internal investigations are complete. And definitely until after the US president's visit.'

At that moment, my mobile phone started its maddening jingle. I pulled it from my pocket and glanced at the screen. Leo Fryatt was calling. 'Forgive me,' I said, 'I'd better take this.'

As I pressed the button a look of mild irritation showed in Felicity's eyes. 'Hallo, Leo, how' you doing?'

'I'm doin' good, Mr Khan,' the youngster said cheerfully. 'I've managed to hook up with yer man, Akhtar Shahid – just like what you asked me to do.'

'Well done,' I said. 'And how is he?'

'He was fine, man. Like I was surprised, he was real pleased to see me again. 'Cos, you know, we didn't part on the best of terms when we got back from Pakistan.'

'And why was that, d'you think?' I asked.

'It's because I think he's involved in somethin' and now, like, he wants my help,' Fryatt replied. 'That's why I'm callin' you. Maybe we should meet. Shouldn't talk over the phone, right?'

Of course, he was right, but I wanted to make sure he wasn't just wasting my time. 'D'you think this is serious, Leo?'

'Sure, man, otherwise I wouldn't bother you. I don't know what, like, but he sure is planning somethin', that's for sure.'

I relented. 'Okay, Leo, how about where we met last time? By the river.'

'That's cool. But I gotta make it soon, 'cos I'm goin' up north with him tonight.'

'With Shahid?'

'Yeah.'

'Okay,' I said, glancing at my watch. 'Could you make it in an hour's time?'

'I can do that.'

I hung up and then reminded Felicity about Leo Fryatt and that Akhtar Shahid was a student at Imperial College under Dr Samir, the missing lecturer.

She nodded. 'Went to Pakistan for some training together, as I recall.'

'Leo thinks I'm connected to al-Qaeda in some way,' I said, feeling uncomfortable even saying the words. 'I persuaded him to make contact with Shahid again. Now Shahid wants to involve him in something. Leo wants to meet me urgently.'

'So you're going now? Shame, I was going to suggest we did lunch. But I do understand. Of course, the job must come first.' When she smiled then, it felt like being in a ray of sunshine.

Silently cursing Leo Fryatt, I made my way to the van and headed off towards Battersea Park. Once there I made my way to the Embankment walk.

I found Leo leaning with his elbows on the stone parapet, staring out across the sluggish green flow of the Thames, the hood of his jacket pulled up against the chill northerly breeze.

He didn't hear me approach. 'Touch of autumn in the air,' I said.

'Jeez, man!' he exclaimed, spinning round. 'You give me a fright, creeping up like that!'

I gave a half-smile. 'You'll learn, Leo. You were facing the wrong way,' I said. 'In this game, you always keep your back to a wall. Here, or in a pub, a café . . . wherever. So you're always aware who's approaching or entering a room.'

Leo couldn't decide whether to be impressed or angry with me. 'Thanks for the lecture, Iceman.'

'It might save your life one day,' I replied easily, playing it for all it was worth. 'It has mine. More than once.'

Then his big toothy smile broke out. 'You really are one cool dude, Mr Khan.'

'I'm an alive dude, Leo, and I'd like you to stay that way, too.'

He grunted and looked uncomfortable. 'Maybe not if

I get involved with Shahid . . . I told him already. Like I ain't goin' to be no suicide bomber.'

'Is that what he's got in mind? Some sort of bombing?'

Leo shrugged. 'I don't know. He's being real cagey, like it's all a big secret.'

'Can't be that secret, if you know about it.'

'Look, man, he was real surprised when I turned up at his pad. He greets me like his long-lost brother. We had a coffee later and he tells me he's putting an operation together. Like he can't tell me no details, but he's trying to form a cell. He's got a couple of mates from a study group at his mosque. But he doesn't know who else to trust.'

I wondered if all this was all just a young jihadist's fantasy. 'Is this all his idea?' I asked.

'He says there's some mysterious Mr Big behind the scenes.'

'D'you have a name?'

'Do I hell. He just refers to the Blackwidow when he talks about him. Like he's at the centre of the web.'

It was like being touched with a cattle prod. That codename Blackwidow; it had cropped up when I'd been listening in on the late Akmal Younis. That and the other codename, Dove. Could there be a connection?

'Shahid says he needs some people with more know-how in his cell,' Leo continued. Then he paused, and regarded me a little sheepishly. 'Like I don't know, but I wondered . . . it might be cool if you met him.'

That threw me. I'd been deep in thought and only half listening. 'Er, what?'

'Like if you approved. Join the cell.' Leo gabbled out the words as though he was afraid I'd deck him on the spot for suggesting it. 'You've got all the background. Fighting in Afghanistan and that. If you thought it helped the cause. Then if not, you could smash up his gang.'

In a moment of madness, I suddenly thought why not? Shahid had never met me, but with Leo's total hero-worship to back me up, he might just welcome my supposed experience and advice. I might even wangle my way closer to people behind the stunt Shahid reckoned he was planning.

I said in a measured tone: 'Yes, I could meet him if he wants. I have no problem with that. You said you're going up north tonight?'

Leo looked relieved. 'I'll be away for a couple of days. I'll tell Shahid about you. I'll contact you when I get back.'

'You do that,' I replied. 'By the way, whereabouts are you going up north?'

Leo shrugged. 'I don't know, man, I think it may be in Yorkshire, somewhere like that. It's called Cambridge.'

Fourteen

I decided I wasn't going to take the chance.

Young Akhtar Shahid may only have got himself involved with some firebrand Islamist cleric and a bunch of idiotic jihadist students who were more of a danger to themselves than the general public.

But not only had Shahid attended a military training camp on the Pakistani–Afghan borders with Leo, he had also studied under Dr Samir. The lecturer himself was possibly involved in a presidential assassination plot and could be anywhere in the country. Not only had Samir gone to ground, but the trail had frozen over. A potentially dangerous situation was developing fast. I was mindful that several people connected with our investigations had come to a premature and bloody end. Akmal Younis, Dave Mo Evans and Frank Grint, the victim of mistaken identity . . . for me.

'At least they don't have a photograph of you,' Inspector Proctor of Special Branch had confirmed to me a couple of days' earlier.

Apparently the Somalian gunman had been singing like a songbird in Paddington Green, more afraid of being murdered by his own gang for cocking up his mission than twenty years at Her Majesty's pleasure for murder. He'd confirmed that his gang had been given my name – he didn't know by whom – and they had traced my former address through the Electoral Register. After some inadequate surveillance, they'd decided that Frank Grint lived at the house and therefore must be me.

It was some consolation that apparently my mysterious and unknown enemy didn't know what I looked like, but not much. That situation, I supposed, could change at any time.

I went to my bedroom, then shifted the dressing table before lifting the carpet and prising up a floorboard. Leo's Smith & Wesson automatic pistol was still where I'd left it, neatly wrapped in bubble-wrap. I checked the breech and magazine, then stuffed it into the rear waistband of my trousers.

I'd just returned to the front office when Joe Lassiter arrived, dead on the dot of noon.

'Just came through in the nick of time,' he said, handing me a buff envelope, the contents of which I turned out on the desk. One British passport and one driving licence.

I thumbed open the passport. I hardly recognized the photograph. I looked distinctly Pakistani. Lassiter saw my expression. 'Had the lab boys touch it up a bit. Morphosis, I think they call it. Darkened the skin, neutralized the eye colour. Then added gloss to the hair, plus a moustache. Very handsome.'

'What's the point if it doesn't look like me,' I said, feeling irritated.

Lassiter looked pained. 'Imagine this, Phil. You meet this young Shahid and his mates. They're dubious about you. But you show them the passport. The photo is you, but they can see immediately your sub-continental back-ground — or they think they do. The boffins call it visual psychology.'

'I hope they know what they're doing.'

'They do.'

'Now you're sure you want me to go ahead with this?' I asked.

There'd been a fierce debate about the operation. Should I just meet up with Leo and tell him I'd changed my mind. Unbeknown to him, a surveillance 'box' of watchers from A4 would take up position around him and trail him back to Shahid and other cell members. Felicity Goodall thought that would be safer for me, but she was overruled by Medusa. Melissa Thornton was determined that we got as close as possible to any operation that might be targeting the US president. Lassiter, as always happy to place someone else's life on the line, backed her. The Ice Queen was out-voted.

To be honest, I wasn't unhappy. I was quite looking forward to it. Hopefully I wasn't underestimating the dangers of involvement with Shahid and his mates. In truth my impression was still that they were a bunch of useless callow youths who couldn't wait to get to heaven to get their legs over all those promised celestial virgins.

If I was wrong, Lassiter assured me, there would still be back-up.

'Jeff King's team's drawn the short straw,' Lassiter said. 'They'll have you and Fryatt "boxed" from the start. They'll have six other teams on standby. It'll be a big operation. If it goes to plan and you have your meeting, the other teams will latch on to anyone else present when they disperse.'

I nodded my understanding. 'And hopefully they'll lead us to everyone else involved in the cell.'

Lassiter gave one of those rare, sly smiles. 'If only things ever worked out that simple.' He dug his hand in his pocket and pulled out a mobile phone. 'This is yours. Don't take your usual one – can't have your contact numbers falling into enemy hands.'

I took it from him and glanced at it. 'Top of the range?'

'More than that. It's got a normal phone function, but conceals a radio transmitter with a range of about three miles. Best put it near the front of your trouser belt, try not to cover it up. We'll hear everything that's being said between you. It includes a GPS feature, so we should know where you are – in theory.'

'Very James Bond.'

'If it works,' Lassiter said. 'Oh, and memorize the number. If someone asks you for it, it'll look odd if you don't know it.'

I smiled at that. 'Took me months to remember mine, Joe.'

He looked irritable. 'Just do it. There's a short list of

numbers on it. Dial any one of them and you'll be talking to the same trained Security Service operator who's briefed on what's going on. Say anything you like, open code, they should cotton on to what you're saying. Again in—'

I finished the sentence for him. 'Theory.'

Just then the front doorbell rang. Kate glanced up at the security monitor. 'Looks like your taxi's arrived, Phil,' she said.

The black cab was one of MI5's large fleet. I fitted the new phone to my belt. 'I'll be off then.'

Lassiter pulled a tight smile. 'Good luck – or break a leg.'

'Good luck will be fine,' I replied and opened the front door. 'Thanks.'

I'd arranged to meet Leo Fryatt at the edge of the estate in Lewisham where he lived. He was waiting, leaning against the railings of the tower-block gardens, hands thrust deep inside the pockets of his 'hoody', which hid his face. As the cab pulled into the pavement beside him, he looked up suspiciously.

I flung open the door. 'Hi, Leo. Shall I pay the taxi off or will we need it?'

Leo had been secretive on the phone, refusing to give the location of the meeting he'd arranged with Shahid. Now he glanced nervously up and down the street before saying, 'Okay, man, we can use it.'

He crossed the pavement and climbed in to sit beside me. 'Where to, guv'nor?' the driver asked.

Leo leaned forward. 'Bexley Station.'

He slid the window shut, and turned to me. In a half whisper he said, 'Mr Khan, please don't call me by name in public.'

I frowned. 'What d'you mean?'

He looked tense. 'Like when you pulled up in this taxi. Bad security, see. Later the filth can make inquiries and this cabbie might remember. Cops can put together movements, CCTV, mobile calls and the like.'

'Someone been talking to you?'

'Only Shahid. Reminded me of all the security stuff like we learned in that camp. This is big. We gotta be like real careful.'

'So we're meeting him at the station? Or catching a train?'

Leo's white tombstone teeth showed in a nervous smile. 'No, man, we're going to change taxis. Throw off any spooks.'

'Why should there be any spooks?'

He shrugged. 'You never know, man.'

I said, 'You're being very professional. I'm impressed.' He looked pleased at that. 'So where are we going after Bexley?'

'I've been told not to tell you?'

'I'll know when we get there anyway,' I replied. 'You'd better lighten up, my friend, and decide if you're working for me or Shahid.'

He looked taken aback. 'Oh, yeah, of course. I just got taken up with things, you know. Got involved like.'

'And how was Cambridge?'

He chuckled. 'Well, man, like it ain't in Yorkshire. Big place, awesome.'

'You going to tell me about it?'

'I'm scared, man. Like if you let on – by accident like – I've told you. That Shahid's a mean mother, I tell you. Don't let them baby-face looks fool you.'

I smiled reassuringly. 'Okay, I'll wait and let him do the talking.'

We lapsed into silence. I was happy that the hidden microphones in the cab would have told control all they wanted to know. There'd be another MI5 cab waiting at Bexley, probably at the front of the rank. But if we didn't get in that one, we'd still be subject to a four-car box.

In the event, there were no taxis and no punters waiting outside the station when we stopped and I paid the driver. As he drove off, Leo looked around, agitated. 'Dammit, man, no fuckin' cabs.' He glanced anxiously at his watch.

On cue, a black cab came into view and pulled up alongside us. 'Where to?' I asked Leo.

'M25 services at Thurrock,' he replied tersely and scrambled in.

I smiled to myself. Leo was going through the motions, but his fieldcraft was pretty abysmal. If you change taxis like that, you should leave one, then pass through a pedestrian only area or through a large shop or department store with doors at both ends, before hailing the second cab. And now meeting at a service station was classic practice, to be one or two amongst many and so pass unnoticed.

After crossing north over the Thames into Essex, we were driven up to the entrance of a services complex. Paying off the driver, Leo, still with his hood up, led the way inside to the restaurant area.

He said, 'I'll get a couple of drinks. You want a Coke, tea or coffee or summat?'

I settled on a black coffee on the basis that it was harder to ruin than a decent cuppa. 'I'm a bit short,' Leo said. 'You can pay.'

Almost believing he'd been taking lessons from Joe Lassiter, I settled the bill and followed Leo as he led the way to a table in the far corner. Three young men sat there, all with dark complexions, each one wearing a baseball cap with a long peak that kept their faces partially in shadow. Hoods and baseball caps, it seemed, were becoming the trademark of aspiring terrorists in a country with more CCTV coverage than any other in the world.

Despite his youth, one had the distinct air of leadership about him. As I sat down, I recognized him from our surveillance photographs as Akhtar Shahid. 'First names only please,' he said in perfect, modulated English.

'This is my friend, Akhtar,' Leo said nervously.

Shahid regarded me closely. The first thing I noticed about him were the wire-rimmed swot's specs he wore, and behind those the eyes, dark and emotionless as those of a dead cod. He had the makings of an immature moustache on his upper lip. As he said something in Urdu I saw that his even teeth were white and bright enough to feature in a toothpaste commercial.

'I'm sorry', I said, 'I didn't understand that.' This was always going to be the tricky bit.

His frown barely made a crease in the smooth forehead. 'You are Pakistani and don't understand Urdu?'

'Pakistani descent,' I corrected. 'My parents left at the time of partition. I was born in the UK.'

'Pakistani mother and English father,' Leo added, eager to endorse my credentials.

'Other way round actually,' I said.

'I can't believe your father never taught you any words in Urdu,' Shahid said softly. 'At least hallo, I'm pleased to meet you.'

I smiled, what else could I do? I sipped at my coffee to give me a moment to compose my reply. 'It seems strange but my father was a great Anglophile. He'd worked all his life with the British in the colonial government. Sad, but I think he was rather ashamed of his origins, ashamed of the fighting between the people of India that led to the partition. There was a big family feud when he married my mother. My parents felt they had no option but to leave for Britain.'

'And now you are putting this shame right?' Shahid asked.

'I like to think so.'

'Leo says you fought in Afghanistan. Yet you spoke no Urdu with fellow fighters?'

'Afghanis mostly speak Persian Afghan or Dari, and many speak Pashto,' I said and rattled off a couple of phrases I'd learned when I'd served there.

Shahid couldn't hide his surprise. Somehow I don't think he knew that himself. 'I see.'

'And my contacts in Pakistani intelligence all spoke perfect English,' I added. 'They liked to practise on me.'

I thought it was starting to sound plausible and it seemed that Shahid was beginning to think so too. 'What did you do in Afghanistan?'

'Mostly training fighters in ways to combat the British,' I replied. 'I used to be in the Royal Marines, so I know their weaknesses as well as their strengths.'

For the first time I thought I detected a flicker of real interest in those expressionless eyes. He said, 'Forgive me, but I must ask you if you have some form of identification?'

I smiled. 'I'd be disappointed in you if you didn't.'

I handed over the passport and driving licence, which he took and scrutinized closely. 'I can see it is you in the photograph, but you somehow look a little different.'

'Passports always make people look like villains,' I returned glibly.

A half-smile flickered on his lips as he handed back the documents. 'Leo thinks you may be able to help us.'

'He told you how we met?' I asked.

'By chance.'

'I have not known him very long,' I continued, 'but he is very eager to help in the cause.'

'And you – if I may call you Ali?'

'Of course. I will help in any way I can. I have wide experience that may be of assistance to you, if I know the nature of the mission.'

'In due course. But I will assure you my operation is not directed at British citizens, if that makes you feel more comfortable?'

I shrugged. 'That no longer matters to me. I am used to killing people. I am a trained sniper.'

Shahid eyes widened. 'That is interesting. We must talk more, but not here. You will come with us by car, Mr Ali.'

'Of course,' I said.

We rose from the table in unison with Leo and I following behind the other three out into the car park. There was a chill in the air, a distinct sense that autumn was creeping up on us.

Shahid's car was a beaten-up old red Mondeo estate. He opened the driver's door and indicated for me to take the front passenger seat while the others squeezed together in the back. His driving was shaky and uncertain as he threaded his way through the car park and headed back to the M25. We joined the northbound carriageway and settled down at a steady fifty in the stream of traffic. At Junction 25 he turned off, south into the suburban neighbourhood of Enfield. Although I could spot no sign of them, I was confident that Jeff King and his team had us firmly in their sights.

Eventually we entered a shabby street of neglected

terraced houses. The presence of a number of pedestrians in traditional Muslim dress suggested that this was a small Islamic enclave. It was cheap housing, attractive to entrepreneurs for snapping up and renting out to fellow countrymen struggling to get an affordable place to live in the metropolis. Shahid found a gap in the lines of parked cars on either side and made a hash of reversing into it. Finally we all clambered out and followed him back a few metres to a house with a faded blue front door.

After putting a key in the lock, Shahid stepped aside to allow the others in. I followed as he closed the door behind me. We were in a dark passage with peeling wallpaper and a worn carpet that smelled of damp. The young man in the lead opened the door to a back room and disappeared inside. I and the others followed him in. Stepping back into the brightly-lit room I was momentarily dazzled, taking a second to register the straight-backed chair and length of rope coiled on the seat. Somehow I just knew what they had in mind . . .

And at that moment Shahid confirmed it. 'We need to talk, Mr Khan. That is, you need to talk.' I suddenly felt the muzzle of the gun pressing into the small of my back. 'Sit in that chair, or you get a bullet in your spine.'

A feeling of dread went down through my body like a lift cage in a shaft. With my stupid overconfidence I had walked straight into this.

One of his cell was standing by the chair and had picked up the rope. Leo stared aghast, his mouth dropping open. 'Hey, Akhtar, what you doin', man?'

If you're holding a man at gunpoint, there is a number one rule. Don't get too close. Shahid had either never been told the rule, or had forgotten it.

But you have to move fast and I had every incentive to do just that.

Swivelling on the balls of my feet, I swung my right arm round behind my back, following through with my whole body. In a split second, before he could react, my hand grabbed Shahid's wrist, pushing the gun away from me. I followed through with my left hand, snatching his elbow and pushing hard against the joint. A yelp of pain escaped his lips as his hand opened involuntarily and the revolver he'd been holding clattered to the floor at his feet. I kicked it back into the passage and threw him violently to the floor. Then I yanked out Leo's automatic from the rear waistband of my trousers.

The other two cell members were stunned and confused, but recovered fast from the shock of seeing their leader down and began reaching inside their jackets.

'FREEZE!' I yelled. 'Or you're dead men standing!' They stopped instantly, eyes wide with fear, like they were playing in some kid's game. I added, 'Now hands on heads, real slow.'

As they obeyed, I snapped, 'Leo, get any weapons off them.'

'Sure thing, Mr Khan!' Leo jumped to it and in a couple of seconds had located the revolvers and placed them on a table by the window.

I turned my attention to Shahid who was lying on the

floor. Nursing the torn ligament in his elbow, he glowered up at me. 'Now that wasn't a very nice Islamic gesture,' I snarled, 'to someone offering to help you, is it, Akhtar?'

'We had to be sure,' he murmured.

'By tying me to a chair and threatening me?'

'When a man is really afraid, he will tell the truth.'

'Is that what they taught you at training camp?' I knelt down beside him and he tried to back away, his shoulders pressing hard against the wall. 'When a man is really afraid, he will tell you anything he thinks you want him to tell you.'

I rose to my feet. 'Now get up, you're making the place look untidy. Stand over there with your friends.'

Shahid struggled to his feet and walked unsteadily across the room. While he did so, I picked up his gun from the passage and took it to the table with the others. I emptied out all the bullets.

I said to Leo, placing his automatic back in my waistband. 'Give them their guns back. We don't need threats to enable us to talk.'

Shahid drew himself up to his full height. 'Leave them on the table, Leo,' he countermanded, clearly trying to re-establish his authority. 'Mr Khan is right. We don't need guns.'

I said, 'You've got to decide, my friend, whether you want my offer of help or not. Whether you trust me or not. And I don't mean by interrogating me under threat. If you don't want my expertise, then I shall just walk away and you'll never hear from me again.' I paused, looking at their hangdog expressions. 'But from what I've seen, you clearly need it.'

Shahid stared at me and I could tell he was trying to hold his natural petulance in check. I think it was slowly dawning on him that he really could do with my help. He indicated the table. 'Let's sit down.' He turned to the others. 'Draw up some chairs.'

Finally the tension ebbed and we took our seats. I took out my pack of rolling tobacco. 'D'you mind?'

Shahid shook his head. It transpired he didn't smoke himself and I had the feeling he objected to it, but Leo and the other two were quick to fish packets of cigarettes from their pockets.

'You must understand, Mr Khan,' Shahid said slowly, 'that I do not know you. I must have some sort of reference that what you tell us of your involvement in Afghanistan – with al-Qaeda – is true.'

I smiled. 'Why didn't you just ask me nicely in the first place?' I'd rehearsed all this carefully with Joe Lassiter and Chas Houseman, the liaison officer from MI6. 'As you may know, Osama bin Laden remains the figurehead leader of al-Qaeda. Its meaning is "The Foundation" – as such it is a loose structure rather than a formal organization.'

Shahid listened carefully and nodded his understanding, while making notes on a sheet of paper.

I continued, 'Currently the de facto head of operations is the deputy chief, a man called Ayman-al-Zawahiri.

One of those immediately beneath him is Mustafa Abu al-Yazid, who is the senior Afghan commander and liaison officer to the Taliban. The senior field commander in the vital border region with Pakistan is Khalid Habib. It was with his men that I mostly worked. My immediate boss was a member of the Pakistani intelligence service, a senior liaison officer called Brigadier Patel.'

It was clear from his expression that Shahid himself wasn't familiar with these names. He looked up from his rapid scribbling. 'You can prove this?'

I said, 'You can. Phone the brigadier yourself. I can give you his personal satellite telephone number in Pakistan. Ask him about me.'

Shahid shifted awkwardly, as though he thought he was getting out of his depth. 'I don't know about that.'

'Look, Akhtar,' I said firmly. 'You're clearly not masterminding this operation, whatever it is. Right? But someone is, someone well-connected. Why not pass the request to speak to Brigadier Patel up the chain of command?'

Suddenly Shahid looked relieved. 'That's a good idea, Mr Khan. I will do that.'

Please, dear God, yes, I thought. And lead us to the missing Dr Samir or even the al-Qaeda facilitator, Naved Hussein. Of course, what no one else in the room knew was that Brigadier Patel was a double agent. Joe Lassiter had confided in me that, according to Chas Houseman, the brigadier had been 'turned' by an agent of the secret service of Sri Lanka. Historically the Sri Lankan government was on good terms with the British government, which had lent assistance in combating the Tamil Tiger rebels. It had returned the favour by using its security agents in the so-called 'War on Terror', who were well placed in looks, language and culture, to infiltrate al-Qaeda through its connections with Pakistan. It appeared that Brigadier Patel was thoroughly corrupt, and part of the large rogue element within the Pakistani military intelligence community who supported the Taliban and al-Qaeda. It had taken a combination of blackmail, money and a supply of pretty whores to persuade him to change sides. If he wanted to keep his money, his harem and his life, Brigadier Patel would have no trouble remembering me after a briefing by his Sri Lankan handler.

As Shahid wrote down Brigadier Patel's number, he said, 'I am sorry we got off to a bad start, Mr Khan. We will drive you and Leo back to the nearest tube station, if that is all right? Then we will call you when we have the necessary clearance.'

I breathed an inner sigh of relief. 'Akhtar, it will be a pleasure working with you, I'm sure. Allah akbar.'

Two days later I was having lunch with Jazz and Joe Lassiter at a pavement café in Covent Garden. He was in unusually high spirits. With a slight chill in the air, he was back to wearing his hat and grubby trenchcoat, while Jazz and I made the most of the fading sunshine in summer clothes.

'Bloody brilliant,' he said, slurping from a glass of Pinot Grigio. 'After Leo contacted you again and mentioned Cambridge, this case was upgraded from "non-affiliated" – that's acting on their own initiative – to "core" – a direct al-Qaeda op. After your meeting, the boys from A4 put tails on Shahid and his mates. Technical Branch bugged the house and their car. A detachment from 18 Signals Regiment had already been monitoring the calls on Leo Fryatt's mobile, so—'

'You didn't tell me that,' I interrupted.

Lassiter shrugged. 'Must have slipped my mind.' He took another mouthful of wine. 'Point is we already had Shahid's mobile number from when he called Leo, so we've been listening to him too. After your meet, as we'd hoped, Shahid called Dr Samir about Brigadier Patel.'

'Dr Samir?' Jazz echoed. 'Do you know where he is?'

'He had a pay-as-you-go mobile,' Lassiter said. 'So no address details, but we were able to locate him by GPS. He's holed up at a flat in Chigwell. Convenient for the M11 to Cambridge. The property's owned by a radical-ized cleric who's known to us.'

I frowned. 'So aren't you going to close the cell down now?'

'Are you kidding, Phil?' Now why hadn't I guessed it wouldn't be that simple? Lassiter put me right. 'Firstly we haven't caught the facilitator, what's his name?'

'Naved Hussein,' I reminded.

'Yeah, him. He's still on the loose. And we're certainly not going to close it down until El Presidente is virtually on his way here! Don't want the bastards coming up with a Plan B we don't know about. And we've got a man on the inside. You.'

'You hope,' I said.

'I know. Just heard, Dr Samir talked to Brigadier Patel in Pakistan by satellite phone. Seems he remembers you well. You were excellent apparently. He also remembered how odd it was that you couldn't understand Urdu.'

I shook my head at Lassiter's incorrigibility. 'Still can't believe we got away with that.'

Just then my own original mobile phone rang. I glanced at the screen before answering. 'Hallo, Leo?'

Lassiter frowned anxiously.

'Hi, Mr Khan. I just heard from our mutual friend. Like you're welcome to join the party, know what I mean?'

'Excellent,' I said calmly. 'But no nasty surprises next time, eh?'

'I didn't know that was goin' to happen. I think they's learned their lesson.'

'So what's next?'

'You gonna join us, man, and we're all goin' away for a few days. That okay by you?'

'Sure, when?'

'You free to leave tonight?'

'I can be.'

'Meet me same place as last time. I got wheels.'

'I didn't know you could drive.'

'Sure I can drive, like I just couldn't afford no car before. See you at eight tonight, okay?'

I confirmed and hung up. 'We're on,' I said.

*

Waiting by the railings outside the estate where Leo lived, I was aware of the deep bass thud of rap music several seconds before I saw the car itself, as it shrieked around the corner at high speed. It was a souped-up, middle-aged white Escort with dark windows, a huge chromium exhaust pipe and a ridiculous add-on spoiler.

The brakes squealed again as Leo hit the pedal and pulled up beside me. 'Hey, man, ain't she a beaut?' he called out through the open window. 'Jump in!'

I threw my small rucksack on the back seat and climbed in beside Leo. 'How'd you get this?' I asked, taking in the wooden steering wheel with its chrome spokes.

'This morning. Off some bloke on the estate. Not bad for three grand.'

I could barely hear what he was saying through the blasting decibels of white noise. 'Didn't know you had that sort of money.'

'From Shahid. He's not short of cash. Said we'd need some more transport.'

I shook my head. 'Did he say anything about not getting anything too conspicuous?'

Leo looked affronted. 'It's got smoked windows. Everyone drives cars like this round here.'

'Look, if you want me to go anywhere with you, you'll have to turn that racket off. I can't hear myself think.'

With reluctance, Leo obliged, before slipping the gear into first and screeching off down the road with a roar like a demented lion. 'And you'll also have to drive properly and safely,' I added.

He glanced at me with a wide grin. 'You soundin' just like me mum.'

'I want you to drive like you know *she* would. Don't want to be picked up by the cops because you're driving like an idiot – or you come off the road because you're not as good as you think you are.'

'Okay, man, like you've made your point.'

Indeed, I seemed to have done, because he became less excitable and his driving less manic as we proceeded to the M25 and joined the M11, heading towards Cambridge. On the way I began chatting about high-performance driving in a way that can make you fast but also safe. That seemed to fascinate him and at least I was able to relax a little more for the rest of the journey.

Our final destination turned out to be a rented former farmworker's cottage on a vast cereal farm not far from Ely. It was probably Victorian with a plain slate roof and rendered walls, and was approached by a half-mile drive along a cinder track. There were three nondescript cars parked outside, one of them the red Mondeo estate that Shahid had driven at our last meeting.

The door of the house opened as we pulled up and Shahid himself stood in the doorway to greet us. He shook my hand firmly. 'Mr Khan, I feel I must apologize for having doubted you.'

'Nonsense,' I replied. 'I'd not be here to help now if you hadn't been professional enough to check out my credentials. I've no desire to work with amateurs, however noble the cause. I don't want to spend the rest of my life in prison, or to die a martyr.'

Shahid was taken aback, his passionless eyes blinking behind the specs. 'A martyr's death is a glorious death.'

I smiled. 'If you say so.'

The front door opened straight into the living room where logs smouldered in a plain brick fireplace. The rooms in the cottage were nicely decorated in bland, inoffensive colours and prettily filled with cheap reproduction pub furniture. It seemed clear that it was the farmer's letting investment on the side.

This time I was introduced to Shahid's two sidekicks, both of whom appeared to be in their mid-twenties, dark-featured, quiet and introspective. Their names were given as Hussein, who was from Pakistan, and Nasar from Syria. Shahid ordered Hussein to go on sentry watch at an upstairs window, and directed Nasar to make us all coffee. When it was ready, the four of us gathered around the fire on the matching floral-covered sofa and armchairs.

I noticed the five mobile phones that had been placed on the low table beside the tray of coffee mugs. 'And these?' I asked.

'Clean pay-as-you-go telephones,' Shahid replied. 'I want you all to hand in all existing phones. Only these will be used until after the operation. They will not be used for anything except communication within the cell. No friends, families, or outsiders.'

That was a nuisance as I was, of course, using Lassiter's little gizmo.

Shahid continued, 'Here is a notebook for each of you with three-digit codes for various messages. For instance, three-one-seven means "I need to meet", and four-three-six means "abort meeting", etcetera . . . Text messages are more difficult for the authorities to intercept than calls.'

I said, 'Shahid, if I am to be of assistance to you then I must have some idea of the operation you are planning.'

The young man nodded solemnly, 'Of course, Mr Khan, my friend Leo was warned to say nothing to you until you could attend a personal briefing. The plan is to assassinate a world leader who is the sworn enemy of Allah and of Islam. He is one of the most heinous of infidels.'

'Who is this person exactly?' I pressed.

'I have told all members not to speculate. He is arriving at RAF Larkheath under great secrecy for a political meeting. If any one of you know who it is beforehand, there is a danger you will let it slip in public. And as the public will have been unaware of it until then, suspicion will immediately fall on you.'

I replied, 'If it's so secret, how do we know about it.'

'I understand there is a source within that leader's own government.'

'And how is the assassination to be achieved?' I asked.

'That is what we are planning and researching now.' Shahid took a large roll of paper and spread it out on the rug in front of the hearth. To my surprise, it was a large-scale site map of RAF Larkheath. They were far better organized than I'd imagined. 'Our target will be arriving here,' he said, pointing to the main runway. 'And staying at this big house on the other side of the camp, Hollingdene Hall. He will have close protection at all times. Additional British military police and police marksmen are being drafted in.'

I wondered just exactly how much Shahid's cell knew. 'Is the target staying here all the time?' I asked.

'Mostly. But he will travel by helicopter to Girton College in Cambridge on the afternoon of his arrival. This would be our preferred chance to strike. At low altitude when the helicopter takes off or comes in to land. It could be attacked from outside the base.'

'Awesome,' cooed Leo enthusiastically.

Shahid didn't smile. 'Unfortunately, because of the short notice, we do not have access to a surface-to-air missile or heavy machine gun to be sure of doing the job.'

Leo turned to me. 'You used to be a sniper, Mr Khan. Couldn't you just shoot the pilot between the eyes?'

Shahid looked at me and crooked one eyebrow in interest. I said slowly, 'Well, the helicopter would have to be at some height to ensure a fatal crash. Therefore the angle of elevation as it came into land – or took off – would present you with the underside of the fuselage. So you wouldn't see the pilot. Also we couldn't predict the pilot's approach method. If you did by chance get an angle of fire into the cockpit, you would still be faced with refracted light from the canopy and a moving target.'

'I thought snipers was like trained to hit moving targets,' Leo interrupted. 'Like the Kennedy assassination.'

'I agree with Mr Khan,' Shahid said. 'I did a sniper course in Afghanistan. The target may be moving, but it has to be moving towards you or away from you to allow you time to get a bead on it.'

I added, 'If it's moving, say, left to right it's much more difficult. Plus you have to allow for the wind velocity over long distances.'

Leo looked disappointed, but said nothing.

Shahid took a small case from the corner, unzipped a laptop computer and placed it on the coffee table. In a few moments one of a series of photographs came up on the screen. I recognized the scenes of RAF Larkheath and the surrounding area. They obviously looked similar to those my team had taken on our risk assessment visit.

'Where did you get these?' I asked.

'Another cell had already done reconnaissance on our behalf.'

'They're very good,' I said, and meant it. Shahid might look like a geeky student, but he'd had excellent, professional back-up from somewhere.

'I think that if the target is to be shot,' Shahid said thoughtfully, 'it has to be when he is outside of his armoured limousine with its bullet-proof windows. By sniper shot, or else close up with a handgun. That means when he disembarks from his aircraft, or is leaving. Or when he is in the grounds of the house where he is staying.'

Nasar the Syrian spoke for the first time. He had wide smiling eyes, snaggled teeth and a thin toothbrush moustache. 'If I can get into the base, I can just walk up to him with my explosive vest,' he offered. 'I won't have to get very close.'

The very thought of that made me feel sick. 'Are those our options?' I asked.

Shahid said, 'Mr Khan, come with me. Let me show you something.'

Intrigued, I rose from the sofa and followed him into the passage and up a flight of stairs to the next floor. Running off the landing was a bathroom and four separate bedrooms.

'By the way,' he said, 'I have allocated you a room of your own. A mark of respect.'

I nodded my appreciation.

He pushed open one of the doors. 'My room,' he explained.

Apart from the single bed, it was a veritable armoury. There were half a dozen handguns and ammunition laid out on a blanket box. Behind it, propped upright against the wall, was a Swiss-made Tanner SSG sniper rifle. In the corner of the room was a plastic container and some stubby camping gas cylinders. It didn't take a genius to work out that these were for making a car bomb.

'We use triacetone triperoxide for explosive,' he said, stumbling over the pronunciation. 'TATP from common household products. I think your IRA used a base of ammonium nitrate fertilizer.'

'Yeah,' I said thoughtfully, as I became distracted when suddenly noticing two human bomb-vests hanging from a hatstand in the far corner.

He saw my surprise and pulled a smug little smile. 'There are many seamstresses in the Muslim community. They have made the vests from instructions. The type has been used in Iraq. So, you see, these are our options.'

'Where did you get the weapons from?' I murmured.

'Mostly sourced from Lebanon and Syria, taken over the border to Turkey. I understand they are then smuggled in containers by various drug or people traffickers on our behalf. Given time, we can get almost anything we want.'

Although it was warm in the cottage, I felt a sudden unnerving shiver.

'So these are our options, Mr Khan. A sniper shot. Assassination at close quarters by a handgun or a suicide bombing. Or a car bomb.'

'I can't say you're not prepared for every eventuality.'

Shahid fixed me with a hypnotic stare, his eyes seeming to bulge behind the strong lenses of his glasses. 'It is a very important target. Very symbolic. As much as the Twin Towers were, but on a different scale.'

'At least this doesn't involve innocent people,' I said in an unguarded moment.

He looked at me curiously. 'Non-believers are not innocent, you should know that, Mr Khan, because they do not abide by strict Islamic law.'

'Sure,' I said, 'but more innocent than, say, soldiers or police protecting an infidel state.'

His curious stare remained. 'I am surprised at your view. A soldier is a soldier. He is paid and expected to die for his country if necessary. It is his job. Killing such people is worthless in the eyes of Allah. A harvest of ordinary, worthless infidels who turn away from him, is what is needed to truly appease Allah.'

I could have smacked him in the face right then, but instead I took a deep breath. At least his evil little cell would be stopped dead in its tracks before it could do any damage.

He must have seen the look in my eyes. 'Of course,' he said, 'I appreciate not all Muslims share that view.' His intonation suggested he thought that was wrong, but I don't think he wanted to fall out with me again. He added, 'So let us keep to business, Mr Khan.'

We returned downstairs where he produced several sheets of paper from his briefcase. 'This is a list of companies whose employees have regular access to RAF Larkheath, either working there or making deliveries. You will see there are maintenance and gardening contractors, fuel suppliers, brewers and catering suppliers. Both Hussein and Nasar have applied for jobs at several of the companies, but without success so far. This may change, but it is looking doubtful before the arrival of our target.'

As the evening wore on we discussed at length the role of each company and studied notes that the cell's observation team had made. I was anxious that we settled on a workable plan that would keep our cell busy right up to the moment that Special Branch pounced on them.

At last I thought I'd found a way. I turned to Shahid.

'You said you wanted my expertise. I think I have a way. It's a method used of old by the Provisional IRA in Northern Ireland. I don't think it ever failed.'

I think it was the only time I ever saw Akhtar Shahid really smile. And the sight of those even white teeth somehow made my skin crawl.

Fifteen

We'd had him under surveillance all day.

It had begun at five in the morning when the delivery van from the smartly named Doughboy Bakery left the premises. An enterprising small business, it combined a small bakery and retail shop in the nearby village of Larkheath itself. The only other commercial enterprises in the short, quaint high street were a combined post-office and general store, a hairdressers and a small pub. All the other shops had long ago been converted to residential use. Over the decades the neighbourhood had developed with upmarket detached houses and some small private and council estates.

Six years earlier the bakery had apparently been struggling. But a new owner had recognized the potential of sales to RAF Larkheath, changed the name of his shop, and specialized in some American favourites. His rye-bread, flapjacks, maplenut cookies, hamburger and torpedo buns marched off the shelves and soon he'd won a contract to supply the local US airbase. That included daily deliveries.

'I reckon that's our man,' I said to Shahid as we

watched the floodlit rear yard from his car. The white-coated delivery driver had emerged from the bakery to begin loading the van, which carried a jaunty cartoon graphic of a grinning First World War American soldier, in a wide-brimmed doughboy hat, striding along with a large loaf of bread under his arm.

Shahid clicked his camera.

When the driver left, we followed. With hardly anything on the roads we were able to settle down to a comfortable distance behind the van. I was driving and, as we reached Larkheath Manor Hotel, I pulled into its car park.

Shahid was on a mobile to Nasar. 'Delivery on its way.'

Nasar acknowledged. He had been pre-positioned, sent in ahead on foot, posing as an early morning jogger, to bypass the roadblock guarding the public road that ran through the centre of the American base. By now he was standing close to the main entrance of the airfield, taking gulps of Evian mineral water, as the Doughboy Bakery van swept in.

We later learned that Nasar had observed the MoD police and US guards give the van driver a cheerful welcome.

'Hey, Sam, any spare samples today?' one American had called out.

The driver laughed. 'Try today's special, Todd. Pecan slices,' he'd replied and had passed a package out of the window. 'Share it now, mind. Know you, yer greedy bastard.'

'Jeez, my favourite! Haven't had this since I left home.'

Sam'd replied, 'Might be a regular feature if it sells well.'

He was waved through. There was no security check, no search. There was no need. Clearly everyone on the checkpoint knew and liked Sam.

We picked up the van again when it left the airbase and followed it throughout the day's delivery round, some-times switching vehicles with Leo in his souped-up Escort. After stopping at countless grocery outlets, pubs and restaurants, the driver finally returned to the bakery just before two in the afternoon. He shortly emerged from the building without his white coat and hat, and climbed into a green Renault Clio.

We followed in our Mondeo estate north for a couple of miles until the Clio turned into the car park of a road-side pub. I drove past and pulled into a lay-by.

I said, 'Shahid, I'm going in there to try and talk to him.'

'Is that a good idea?'

'We need to know as much about him as we can and we're running out of time.'

'Okay, if you think so.'

I left the car and walked back to the car park. The main bar of the old thatched pub was gloomy with dark timber panelling on the walls. Apart from the driver known as Sam there was only one other customer who sat on a barstool in the corner. Elderly and wearing a tweed suit, tie and a flat cap, he looked like a regular. He regarded me with vague curiosity as I approached and addressed the plump, middle-aged woman behind the bar.

'A pint of best, please,' I said. 'And I suppose you couldn't tell me how I get to the Doughboy Bakery from here? Seem to have got myself lost.'

She chuckled as she pulled the pump. 'You're asking in the right place, sweetheart. Sam here works for them.'

I turned towards the driver. Close to I could see he was probably in his early forties with a chubby, clean-shaven face and pepper and salt hair. His considerable girth, stretching the bright-red jumper he wore, suggested he was more than a little partial to the bakery's delicacies himself.

'Yes, mate,' he said cheerily, 'you want the little village of Larkheath.'

'Ah, that's not the same as the airbase?'

'No, a lot of people don't realize there's also a village of the same name. Confusing that.' He glanced at his watch. 'But they'll possibly be out of today's bread by now. All right for cakes and stuff though.'

'That's okay,' I replied and sipped at my beer. 'I want to discuss placing a regular order. I'm thinking of setting up an American-style diner in Cambridge.'

Interest flickered in Sam's eyes. 'Oh yeah? Where-abouts?'

I shrugged. 'Not sure, yet. Estate agents are looking out for me.' I held out my hand. 'I'm Phil Masters.'

'Sam Goodwin,' he replied and shook my hand.

'Should do well with all the youngsters at Uni. Our products are good – and very popular with the Yanks at Larkheath.'

'You born locally?'

'Born and bred, man and boy.'

'Really? Whereabouts do you live? I'll have to be looking for a place.'

'I live in a little village called Fenwell, about two miles from here. D'you know it?'

'Afraid not.'

'Only downside is, it don't have a pub. I come in here for a couple when I've finished for the day. Got to be careful with the old drink-driving, you know?'

'Of course, specially if you've got a family to support.'

Sam chuckled. 'God, me missus would kill me if I lost me licence – and me job, of course. She'd have to find one herself. Not easy round here, but then she's got the youngsters to look after.'

'Really? My kid's eleven now. How old are yours?'

'Emily's seven and Adam is ten.'

'I guess the worst is yet to come,' I said. 'Adolescence.'

We chatted for a bit longer and, when Sam offered to buy me a pint, I politely declined and left, saying I had to get to the bakery and check out a property in Cambridge before the end of the afternoon.

I rejoined Shahid and brought him up to date as we headed for the village of Fenwell. We lay in wait on the edge of the village in the mouth of a farm lane.

Twenty minutes later Sam's green Clio passed by and

we followed at a discreet distance. Fenwell was just a quarter of a mile of mixed housing of differing vintage that lined each side of a high street. There was no post office, no shops, and, indeed, no pub. Like so many rural villages, it wasn't just dying on its feet, it was already dead. Sam turned right into the short drive of a small, modern three-bedroom infill house and I tucked into the kerb a little further back, so we could have sight of the front door as the man put his key in the lock.

We settled down to wait and observe. At just gone four-thirty in the afternoon, an ageing Jeep came along and parked beside the Clio. A rotund woman climbed out. She wore a long floral skirt, had flabby white arms and long greying hair. That she was Sam's wife was confirmed when a young boy and girl followed her from the car and into the house. Beside me, I heard the click of Shahid's camera.

After arranging for Leo and Nasar to take over the watch, we set off back to our base at the farmworker's cottage.

Later, after rustling up some sandwiches and lighting the log fire, Shahid, Hussein and I sat around the hearth.

'Do you still think your plan will work, Mr Khan?' Shahid asked.

I nodded. 'Couldn't be better. The fact that the delivery driver's got kids means he'll have an even stronger motivation to co-operate.'

'So how do you see it in practical terms?' Hussein

asked. He was a quiet and pensive young man who seemed to think a lot, but said very little.

I said, 'We strike while it's still dark. Black clothing and balaclavas. You and Nasar will wear suicide-vests. We jemmy a window at the back, then up the stairs and burst into the parents' bedroom. A bit of shock and awe. Yell and shout and smash some ornaments or mirrors. Basically scare them witless! Even fire a weapon if we've one with a silencer. Drag the kids into the bedroom.' I paused and nonchalantly took a sip of tea. 'Sam is told what to do – if he obeys in every way, his family will survive, if not . . . His wife and children are held by one of our suicide-bombers while he goes to work in the normal way. He will load his van in such a way as to allow access for the second suicide-bomber to be able to get to the rear of the cargo compartment where he'll be concealed from view.'

'You don't think the guards at the airbase will search the van?' Shahid asked.

'No, why should they?' I replied. 'They know the van and they know Sam. Why should they be in the least bit suspicious? At best they'll open the back and take a cursory look inside.'

Shahid said, 'So the driver leaves the bakery and makes a prearranged stop, where our second man with an explosive-vest – our glorious assassin – climbs in and conceals himself?'

'Correct,' I replied. 'He wears a set of workman's overalls and carries a toolbag. Then on and into the airbase.

The other beauty is, if any special passes are issued by the airbase beforehand, the bakery driver will already have one. As we have identified, there is an area, just before reaching the kitchen unloading bay, which is not over-looked by any windows or near to any doors. That's where our assassin slips out from the back of the van and just walks off. He might even have a hearty breakfast in the canteen at the infidels' expense.'

An uncertain smile flickered on Hussein's lips. 'What if he is stopped and needs to show an ID?'

For once there was a smouldering glow of passion in Shahid's eyes. 'Do not worry. Our support cell already has copies of the airbase ID cards, we just have to add the photographs.'

That took me a bit by surprise, but I tried not to let it show. 'Later, when the target arrives,' I said, 'our man just approaches as close as he can. What is more innocent than a maintenance worker in a fully secured military base? I assume our target may have bodyguards. Even so, when they feel they have to intervene to intercept this maintenance worker . . . it will all be too late. The blast will take out all of them.'

'Allah akbar,' Shahid murmured. 'Allah is, indeed, great.'

I said, 'All we have to decide is who is going to vol-unteer to be the glorious martyr.'

It was like experiencing the 'ground rush' in the last few seconds of a parachute jump as the last days before the US president's arrival flashed by. All the reconnaissance and planning work was complete. I cannot believe the others had not guessed the identity of their target, but they seemed generally surprised when Shahid finally shared his secret with us. Nasar and Hussein were almost swooning with joy, although Leo went very quiet.

However, when it came to it, Shahid didn't seem too keen to volunteer for an early arrival in paradise. Nevertheless, he put on a show of reluctant acceptance when both Nasar and Hussein pleaded, with tears in their eyes, to be the one to blow himself up. Shahid eventually decided on Nasar, as his skin was less dark and he spoke better English for passing himself off in the airbase.

Chillingly, Shahid returned to his mantra about killing civilians. To Hussein, he said, 'It may be a consolation prize, but after the president is dead, there is no need to release the family of the delivery driver. Wait until he returns at the end of the day, then destroy them all. Destroy the unbelieving infidel parents and all their evil spawn.'

Leo Fryatt had not volunteered to die and sat looking very unsure at this rant. He kept glancing at me as if for some sort of moral guidance.

I'd already established that I had to leave them before the date of the assassination, because my expertise was needed by other al-Qaeda cells. But I really wanted to get Leo out, too. He'd been duped into all this by me and it didn't seem fair for him to be with Shahid's cell when armed police closed it down sometime soon. But the logistics of the operation were such that they needed four people.

It was with a huge sense of relief on the Friday morning before the president's arrival that I walked out of the cottage with Shahid to be driven to Cambridge railway station.

He hardly spoke on the journey and my mind started wandering. Although I knew that all of us in his cell had been constantly followed and had been kept under surveillance by MI5 at all times, I had never once been aware of anything remotely suspicious. Despite knowing that, it was still unnerving to set up a perfectly feasible operation that could not only assassinate a world leader, but a perfectly innocent family of four, including two children. I think what nagged at the back of my mind was the fact that my gizmo mobile phone from Joe Lassiter had been taken from me on my arrival. Therefore the control centre of the Security Service would have been unable to listen in on it.

At last, when we pulled in at the station, Shahid turned to me: 'I should like to thank you for all your help, Mr Khan. It has been a privilege to work with you. I have learned a lot.'

'My pleasure,' I said, the words sticking in my throat.

He handed me back my confiscated mobile phone. 'Please don't use it until you are back in London. Should the infidels be monitoring your calls, they can locate you. For the same reason please do not call any of the phones of cell members.'

'Don't worry, Akhtar, I know all that.'

'Then good luck with your life, Mr Khan, and your war against the infidels,' he continued in that sickly, silky voice of his. 'One day you must go back again to Pakistan – this time to reunite with your father's family.'

'I'm sure I will.'

'Allah akbar.'

'Allah akbar,' I replied.

At last I was away from him and walking as fast as I could to the ticket office. I just wanted to be away from Shahid and his aura of evil; like the sweet smell of his cologne, it lingered and made me feel contaminated by my very association with him. By the time I reached the platform, the London-bound train was pulling in and I scrambled aboard.

Before I even looked for a seat, I was on my mobile to Lassiter.

He picked up immediately, so fast that I could almost believe he was sitting there awaiting my call. 'Hi, Joe,' I said quickly. 'I've just got on the London train from Cambridge. I'm afraid they took your phone off me as soon as I got here.'

'Don't fret, Phil,' Lassiter replied in the smug, oily tone he used when he thought he held all the cards. 'We heard what was going on. The boys bugged Leo's and Shahid's car overnight. They did the cottage the next day while you were all out.' He chuckled. 'Boy, do you know how you snore?'

I ignored that. 'So you know about Sam Goodwin and his family?'

'The bakery driver? Of course. All part of your cunning plan, eh? Very impressive.'

'Just make sure they don't come to any harm.'

'They'll be fine. We'll close Shahid and his chums down tomorrow morning before our VIP's flight takes off. Meanwhile we'll be watching round the clock.' He paused. 'Tell you what, Phil, I'll meet you at the station. Just give me your ETA?'

I told him, hung up and then punched in the office number to tell Kate I was on my way back. Feeling more relaxed now, I went in search of a seat, a sandwich and a newspaper. It looked like for me, at least, the ordeal was all over.

When the train arrived at Liverpool Street, Lassiter was as good as his word, waiting for me in an MI5 black cab. 'Well done, Phil, mission all but complete. If you hadn't already melted the Ice Queen's heart, you certainly will have done now. She might even be up for a promotion.'

On the drive back to my office, I ran over the events of the past few days, so that there was absolutely nothing Lassiter didn't know. As he dropped me off at my office, I asked if he was going to RAF Larkheath himself.

'Well, I've got to be there to supervise the round-up of Shahid's cell with Special Branch and SO19.' A self-satisfied smirk cracked his face. 'Never know, may also get to shake the hand of one grateful president.'

Shaking my head in disbelief, I trotted down the stairs to the basement and let myself in.

'Hiya, boss,' Kate greeted. I'd barely set eyes on her when I suddenly noticed Nina seated in one of the office chairs. She looked pale and drawn, still expensively and tartily turned out, but for once she didn't look if she'd just come out of Toni & Guy's and she was wearing little make-up.

She rose to her feet, a tight smile on her face. 'Sorry, Phil. Kate said I could wait. Hope that's all right?'

I threw a dagger look at Kate, but she deflected it with a shrug and a smile. I said, 'What do you want?'

'Can we talk?'

My heart sank. 'Sure.' I turned to Kate. 'Is there anyone in the dining room?'

'No, Gerry's out and Jazz is still off looking after Zoë.'

I indicated for Nina to follow me to our makeshift operations room. 'So what's the matter?' I asked as I closed the door.

She looked awkward. 'I wanted to thank you.'

That took me by surprise. 'For what?'

'For catching Frank's killer. It was some time before I learned what you did. It was very brave.'

'It was instinctive,' I said truthfully, 'and probably very stupid. If I'd stopped to think—'

'But you didn't,' Nina cut in. 'Despite what's happened between us.'

'No one deserved that. How's Danny taken it?'

'Not well. Truth is he didn't really get on too well with Frank despite what I told you.' The awkward smile was back. 'Frank always wanted Danny to treat him as if he was his real father and Danny resented that. Then Frank would get angry. He had quite a temper on him. Danny's become even more withdrawn than he was. But he misses you more than he'd ever miss Frank.'

'Perhaps I could drop round to see him. Maybe Sunday?'

'That would be nice. He'd like that.' She hesitated. 'The police advised us to leave the house for the time being. Something about the job you were on. We're staying with old Aunt Dot. I think she's glad of our company.'

I nodded and then I surprised myself by asking, 'And how are you coping?'

'A lot of tears. A lot of sleepless nights.' She focused closely on my eyes. 'And a lot of thinking. At first I blamed you for Frank's murder. And for us having to move out. Our GP arranged for some counselling. It was good to talk to someone. Slowly I began to realize that maybe this divorce is a mistake. Frank had taken an interest in me and I was flattered. But after his death I learned that his business was in trouble and he had high gambling debts. That's why he was always banging on about getting a high divorce settlement. Had me thinking the same way.'

'And now?'

'Can we at least be friends?' There were tears welling in her eyes. 'Maybe see more of each other, see how things go? Or at least try to have an amicable settlement?'

I forced a smile. 'You'll have to get rid of that dreadful solicitor of yours.'

'I already have.'

'Let me think about it,' I said, but I knew in truth there was no going back for me. 'Maybe we can chat on Sunday?'

She nodded. 'I'd better go. Come round for one of Dot's roasts, about one. I'm sure she'd like to see you again.'

'I will, thanks.'

Nina moved towards the door, then paused. 'The police said that man killed Frank, mistaking him for you. That he was acting for a terrorist group. Is that the sort of thing you do here?'

I said, 'Investigating possible suspects, that's all. More interesting than spying on errant husbands and wives.'

Her cheeks flushed slightly at that. 'And clearly more dangerous . . . That reminds me. That woman, the one from your army days. Are you . . . well . . . close?'

Ridiculously, I wanted to let Nina down gently. 'Getting closer.'

'I see,' she said stiffly, and continued into the hallway.

As we approached the front door, I heard the key in the latch as it swung open. Jazz was standing there. I don't know which of the three of us was the most surprised.

But Nina recovered first. 'See you Sunday,' she called back to me and, totally ignoring her, brushed past Jazz and up the steps to street level.

Jazz pulled a face. 'Oops, wrong time and wrong place.' She frowned at me. 'Are you two getting back together?'

I shook my head. 'No, I'm really only going to see

Danny. Seems he's got even more withdrawn since Frank was killed. I think I've rather let him down.'

She touched my sleeve. 'Not deliberately. You said what a fight it was with Nina to get to see him.'

I gave a harsh laugh. 'I take on a terrorist killer on the street, but I'm petrified of my own wife.'

Jazz shrugged. 'But she sounds like some awesome lady,' she said sympathetically.

Then I remembered. 'How's Zoë by the way?' I asked, following her into the front office.

'Lots better thanks, but she's been really poorly. The doc reckoned it was some mystery virus doing the rounds. But she'll be well enough now to leave with Ricardo's parents again, so I'm back in harness. Thought I'd pop in for the afternoon to pick up the threads. When I phoned in the other day, Kate said the Cambridge business was going well?'

I felt quite pleased with myself. 'Bit of a triumph really. Akhtar Shahid's little cell is sitting and waiting to hold the family of a local delivery driver hostage, while he takes his van into the airbase. A suicide bomber in the back.'

'Ouch, nasty!' she replied with a squeamish look on her face.

'The cell's all buttoned-up apparently. Lassiter's planning to pounce in the middle of the night.'

'Well done,' she said, a twinkle in those gorgeous brown eyes. She rose onto her toes and kissed me briefly on the lips. 'Calls for a celebration.'

Kate looked up from her laptop. 'Hey, you two,' She

said. 'Spare a young girl's blushes, won't you? Stop eating each other.'

Jazz laughed. 'That wasn't a meal, just a snack . . . Talking of which, Zoë's actually staying over at Ricardo's parents tonight. Come over for a meal after work. We can open a bottle of shampoo.'

'Champagne?' I asked. 'Will I have to drink the whole bottle myself?'

'You're a wicked man, Mr Mason. I think I'm getting my taste for booze back since I met you again.' She turned to Kate. 'Can we see the latest case files? We need to start planning for next week.'

'Sure, I'll fetch them,' Kate said cheerfully. 'Oh, and there's a pile of cheques for you to sign. Some very urgent.'

'Remind me before I go tonight,' I said.

I had a lot of catching up to do, and I hated office work. Meanwhile poor old Gerry had been struggling on his own through most of the week, doing everything from invoicing to some limited investigation work, even though this was officially his last day with us. Popadom's input was sorely missed, but then it was a question of better safe than sorry. Soon it would just be me and Jazz so I'd have to speak to Joe Lassiter for advice on how best to recruit more security-vetted staff.

After all the excitement of recent weeks, it really did feel boring to have to start on another shortlist of low-priority terror suspects. I thought there was no way we'd have the same luck again any time soon. It was just the law of averages.

I was quite relieved when we'd finished briefing ourselves on the list at five o'clock. I felt quite exhausted.

Jazz leaned across the table to me and placed her hand on mine. 'Hey, why don't we skive off early?'

I smiled. 'You've twisted my arm.'

'But you're the boss, boss.'

'Let's go.'

Minutes later we were ready. I stepped into the front office. 'Hey, Kate, any idea when Gerry's due back?'

'He phoned in to say he was stuck in traffic,' she replied. 'But he said don't wait to kiss him goodbye, because he can give us another week, if we'd like it.'

'Brilliant!' I said. 'That's because his wife's got a lot of DIY chores lined up for him. Anyway, Kate, have a good weekend and don't do anything I wouldn't?'

She beamed up at me. 'But you'd never go horse-jumping, would you?'

I nodded. 'That's true. My motto is never get on top of anything that's got more legs than you.'

Jazz thumped me playfully in the ribs. 'C'mon you.'

The ride across London in my old van wasn't the most romantic start to the evening I had in mind, but the laughter and banter between us held the promise of better things to come. Jazz seemed more relaxed and more like her old self, the pert and sassy soldier-girl I'd fallen head over heels for in Bosnia all those years before.

We discussed what she might cook and by the time we found a parking place near to her house in Putney, we'd settled on simple spag bol. I had no intention that we spend half the evening cooking and washing-up. We entered the house and I followed her into the kitchen.

Removing her jacket, she took a red-striped chef's apron from the cupboard. 'Phil, be an angel will you? There's a bottle of champagne down in the cellar in the wine-rack. The door to the cellar is under the stairs.'

'Sure thing,' I replied and wandered back into the hall-way.

I opened the door and peered down the steps that led into darkness.

'Light switch is just to the left,' she called out.

I ran my hand around the doorframe until I found it. Nothing happened. 'Damn, the bulb's gone,' I said.

'Oh, no,' she replied. 'And I know my torch battery's flat.'

'Don't worry. I'm not going to let a light bulb get between us and a bottle of champagne.' I pulled my cigarette lighter from my pocket and flicked it on to get a feeble flame that at least let me see down a couple of steps between the crumbling, white-painted brick walls.

Carefully I descended to the concrete floor, cobwebs brushing against my face as I went. It was hard to discern anything in the shadows. The place appeared to be empty apart from a single chair in the middle of the floor. I couldn't see any sign of a wine-rack. It was then that the thought occurred to me that Jazz had said she'd virtually given up alcohol and her errant husband Ricardo was a strict Muslim. I remember thinking why the hell should there be a wine-rack in their cellar . . . and at that moment I felt a nanosecond crack of excruciating pain at the back of my head before I was aware of myself falling into pitch-darkness.

I came to with a start, something icy and wet slapping on my face. Suddenly I was gasping for breath. A pain was thudding in my skull. It felt and almost sounded like a hammer against an anvil. My vision was blurred as if trying to see through a swirling red mist. There was a pool of light from a single, unshaded bulb. Beneath it were two dark figures. They were standing a few feet in front of me, but they refused to come forward into focus. I slowly recalled the steps down to Jazz's cellar, the light switch . . . where was I now?

Slowly the two men took shape. I squeezed my eyes closed and opened them again. Black overalls, black balaclavas. One of them held what I thought was a handgun, an automatic. The other held what seemed like a coil of electric cable. Now I could just make out the steps behind them. I was still in the cellar.

Then I realized I was sitting down. I must be on that chair I'd seen in the centre of the floor. I tried to move my arms, but I was paralysed. God, they've broken my fucking neck, I thought savagely! With a flood of relief, I discovered that my arms were bound behind the back of the chair. I looked down at my shirt and trousers. They were sodden wet and there was a bloodstain, like a vermilion glacier, seeping down from my right shoulder. Blood, my blood, dripping from a head wound. I'd been hit from behind.

One of the men said to the other. 'Get another bucket of water.' The accent was foreign, but I couldn't place it.

'That won't be necessary.' It was a female voice. It came from the shadow to the left of the pool of light.

The first man said, 'I want the infidel fully awake before we start. He must understand the questions, feel the pain.'

Jazz stepped forward. 'I said that won't be necessary.' There was a gun in her hand.

I barely saw what happened next. The silenced weapon spat out the flashes from two rapid double-taps, the first two rounds taking out the man with the automatic, sending him flying brutally backwards onto the floor like a puppet whose strings had just been cut. Jazz pivoted on her toes, fractionally adjusting her angle of fire to blast her second target before he had a chance to realize what had happened. The rounds slammed into his chest as he tried to turn and he began corkscrewing down to the floor as his legs gave way under him.

I was stunned, groggy, just couldn't think, the pain in my head clogging my brain function.

What I did feel was the huge relief at Jazz's timely arrival. I never thought to wonder from where she'd got a firearm. 'Jazz, thank God . . . They must have been waiting for us.'

She took a step forward. There was a rather odd expression on her face that I couldn't quite work out. She said slowly, 'They were waiting for you. Halim and Rafiq. Their plan was to torture you for information and then kill you. I couldn't let them do that. I've never wanted to hurt you.'

Was I hearing things? It didn't make any sense. 'What the hell are you talking about? Can you untie me?'

There was a look of anguish in her eyes as she shook her head. 'You don't understand, Phil. I'm part of a cell set-up by Naved Hussein.'

'Naved?' I echoed, half thinking the blow to my head really had damaged my brain. 'The al-Qaeda facilitator? The one we've been looking for?'

'Yes. Look, I'm not a supporter of terrorists or blowing up innocent people.' She glanced down at the two corpses in front of us. 'Men like Halim and Rafiq here mean nothing to me. Allah is welcome to them, but I doubt he'll let them through the gates of paradise now they're there. Let's just say their interests and mine coincided, for a time we needed each other.'

This still wasn't making any kind of sense. 'But the cell's finished, Jazz. Lassiter and MI5 have got them bottled up, you know that.'

Jazz allowed herself a slight smile. 'Poor old lecherous Joe Lassiter, always thinks he's so damn smart.'

I frowned, not even beginning to understand. 'So what's he got wrong?'

'That is indeed a cell. It's run by that lecturer, Dr Samir.'

Something suddenly occurred to me. 'Did you tip Samir off? Let him go on the run?'

'Yes, and I warned Younis that we were on to him when you followed him to his RV with Dr Samir.'

What was that codename? 'You are Dove?'

She nodded. It was all beginning to make some sort of sense now. When Kate had got our surveillance schedules mixed up and Jazz had surprised me outside Younis' house, wearing a hijab and pushing a pram, when I was listening in to Younis' phone calls. She must have got the surprise of her life. No wonder she left the scene and was straight on the phone to Dr Samir.

Jazz said, 'Look, I've sort of known Dr Samir and his wife for some years. He's not a friend, more an acquaintance who's helped me in the past.'

'Helped you?'

'Let me explain.' She sounded suddenly weary. 'When Lassiter and then later you approached me to work with you, I really wasn't interested. I had enough to do trying to earn a living and looking after Zoë. But I mentioned it to Dr Samir at a fund-raising event to raise awareness of the plight of untried prisoners in Guantánamo Bay. He persuaded me to take the job, as a way to penetrate MI5.'

I was still baffled, my mind working slowly, like it had been when I'd served with the Royal Marines in the Arctic cold. 'Did Dr Samir know he was a suspect?'

Jazz smiled momentarily. 'Well, I suppose he thought he might be, but it came as a bit of a surprise to him when I joined you and found out he was!'

'Did you know he was running a cell then?'

'Not at first, he didn't just open up.' She paused, thinking back. 'We met for coffee a few times. He told me he'd heard via an al-Qaeda intelligence cell in Washington that

President Bush was planning a private trip to the UK. They considered that their greatest prize would be to assassinate him. Later I learned Dr Samir had been a friend of Mullah Reda and their group were developing several embryonic cells over here. One of the cell leaders was one of Samir's students, Akhtar Shahid. Once there were more details about the president's visit, it was decided by their al-Qaeda facilitator, Naved Hussein, that they would try and use those cells for an assassination attempt. That's when I decided to help them.'

'By joining me?'

She nodded. 'As well I did, discovering you were look-ing at three people with connections to one of the clean cells that they thought weren't even on the Security Service radar.'

'And Dave Evans?' I asked. 'Did you tip them off about him?'

Now she looked distinctly uncomfortable. 'I had to, Phil. He'd got in deep and had already wreaked havoc with the cell networks they were trying to create. It was Evans who found out about Mullah Reda and the other organizers.'

'They murdered Evans, Jazz, blew his brains out,' I reminded darkly.

'I didn't know they'd do that, Phil, honestly!' she protested. 'Perhaps it was naive of me, but I just thought they'd cut him out of the loop or something.'

'Oh, come on . . .'

She was angry now. 'Like they knew about you, but

they never told me they were going to try and kill you. That was organized by someone way above even Dr Samir. He knew you and I had an emotional history. I'd never help on that. No one ever asked for your address, and I'd never have given it. My guess is it was Naved Hussein who decided you were doing too much damage. It was either revenge or his idea of self-preservation.'

The pain in my head had subsided a little and my thoughts became a little less woolly as I trawled my mind through recent events. 'Strikes me there are a lot of people dead because of you, Jazz. Yet you don't seem to think any of it is your responsibility.' That reminded me. 'And I suppose you had nothing to do with the murder of that elderly curry-house owner?'

'Akmal Younis?' She shrugged. 'Younis signed his own death-warrant when he told Dr Samir he wanted out. Younis knew too much and had threatened to go to the police. Dr Samir decided to use Younis' death for his own ends.'

'What the hell do you mean by that?'

'That laptop that was being stolen when we broke in . . .'

'When I got the killer's boot in my face as he escaped?' I recalled.

'That was a bit too close,' Jazz said. 'Bad timing. But you needn't have bothered having a go, because the laptop was going to be abandoned in the garden anyway.'

'Eh?'

'Dr Samir knew there was a message about President

Bush's visit to the UK on the computer. He knew full well MI5 would discover it in fairly short order. You were meant to find it. It was my idea, Phil. Dr Samir and I were desperate to draw out the details of the visit.' She hesitated. 'I couldn't guarantee it would work, but once MI5 knew the people we were investigating I thought there was a good chance you – our team – would be at least kept in the loop. Especially as Felicity Goodall would want to score points over her boss – and she had the hots for you.'

I ignored that. 'Well, your ploy certainly worked.'

'Better than I could have dreamed.'

'But it hasn't, has it? Lassiter's got the cell surrounded.'

Jazz shook her head. 'You still haven't got it, have you? Dr Samir and Shahid's cell has been hung out to dry. You, Gerry and I did their recce for them. But while everyone's been busy chasing them, the al-Qaeda facilitator – remember Naved Hussein? – has been quietly working on the real plan with me. Halim and Rafiq here were part of Naved's cell.'

'So who's going to assassinate Bush?'

Suddenly her smile was broad and genuine. 'With just a little luck, it'll be me?' She pointed to the far corner of the cellar. 'Remember those? I was given a choice of three sniper rifles to use. The trusty AI Super Magnum, the M76 I worked with in Bosnia, and the new Russian VSS. That is a beauty.'

This was all a weird sort of nightmare. 'This is no joking matter, Jazz. You've got a daughter to think of.

You'll get killed or jailed for life. You won't get away with this.'

Jazz turned on me. 'Don't worry about Zoë or me. She hasn't been sick, I took her to Bosnia. She's in safe hands. I called in some favours. I've got a new identity for both of us. And while I was there I took the opportunity to brush up on my old sniping skills with the VSS. I've still got it.' She stared wistfully at the three rifles resting against the wall. 'As soon as the job's done I'll be on a flight out of here. You're the only one who knows, Phil.'

My heart sank. I'd been saved from torture, but that was all. 'So I'm the next one to die?'

She laughed brightly. 'Poor Phil! No, of course not. I'll leave you here with water and enough food to get you by. When Zoë and I reach our final destination – no, not Bosnia, stupid – I'll do two things. Call your office to get you released. And I'll put details in the post to you about everything I know about the al-Qaeda operations over here, including the whereabouts of Naved Hussein. That should melt your Ice Queen's heart.'

'So if you want to destroy them, what's the point?'

'The point is the death of one of the most vile and evil men in history.' She almost spat out her words. 'How many innocent people have died needlessly and horribly maimed because of his ego, his stupidity, his reckless actions? Here in the UK, in Iraq, in Afghanistan. Innocent people held indefinitely without trial.'

'For God's sake, Jazz,' I said. 'I pretty much agree with you, but that doesn't give me the right to assassinate him.

Not to mention risking your life and Zoë's future. Are you mad?'

'You bet I'm mad,' she retorted. 'I'm damn furious!'

Had she really lost it? I said, 'There must be a reason. What the hell is it?'

She took a deep breath and relaxed her shoulders. 'My husband, Ricardo Alagic, one of the sweetest, loveliest men I've ever known. Very handsome, too. He's French-Algerian, a doctor. I met him when he worked for Médecins Sans Frontières in Sarajevo. He was working twenty hours a day, seven days a week, saving lives with very limited resources.'

'My loss, his gain,' I murmured.

She pulled a tight smile before continuing, 'When we were there we became friends with some of the Afghani fighters who came to help the Bosnian Muslims over-come the Serbs. Strange lot, but utterly dedicated. Totally different cultures, of course, but some were very fine, brave men. We remained in contact with some of those fighters over the years, even when they later joined the Taliban back in their homeland.'

I frowned at that. 'Did your husband support the Taliban?'

'Goodness, no. But Ricardo believed it was the Afghans' country and their right to run it. Ricardo was a devout Muslim, but no radical. He wouldn't hurt a fly.' She paused, remembering, and I saw that her eyes were moist. 'After 9/11 and the American and British responded with an invasion of Afghanistan, we learned what a hard time Taliban fighters had with virtually no medical back-up. Typically Ricardo thought he should help them, care for their injured. And that's what he did. All that he did.'

I shut my eyes, guessing what happened next. 'And he was killed in the fighting?'

'No, he was caught by the Americans.' Jazz glared at me. 'I've heard they grabbed him while he was tending a wounded prisoner. He was even wearing a white coat in a makeshift operating theatre in the caves. They took Ricardo away, and let the man die.'

Now it made sense. 'Guantánamo Bay?'

She nodded and sniffed hard to hold back her tears. 'He was travelling on false documents provided by someone in Pakistani intelligence. But no one I've met knows who that was or knows exactly what name Ricardo was using.' She ran her hand roughly across her eyes. 'The French government made some representations to the Americans, but they just didn't want to know. God knows if he'll ever be released.'

A deep silence fell between us for several moments. I felt a swelling in my throat that prevented me from talking, and guessed Jazz felt the same. At last I managed to find my voice. 'Don't do it, sweetheart. Bush isn't worth it and it certainly won't help Ricardo.'

She took a deep breath. 'But it'll help me. A change of leader, an election. A new policy. Don't think I haven't thought about it long and hard, Phil. My mind's made up, everything is in place.' Now her smile returned. 'I'm just sorry you had to be involved. I've no quarrel with you. I loved you once, very much. And I'm sorry you're going to have a very uncomfortable couple of days down here.' She glanced down at the two corpses. 'And I'm sorry about them. It's cool down here, they shouldn't smell too much.'

She moved away across the cellar and dragged over a small table I hadn't noticed before. She pushed it to one side of me and I saw she'd somehow managed to fix four large plastic bottles with straws to the top.

'Three of water and one of a vitamin drink,' she said. 'You won't die.'

'How thoughtful,' I sneered.

'Try, make sure you can reach them.'

I leaned to my left until my lips reached the furthest bottle. 'That's fine.'

She held out her palm with two capsules in it. 'Imodium. Might help clog you up, you know? Prevent an accident.'

That suddenly seemed a good idea. And I bent my head forward until my lips touched the skin of her warm hand, and my nostrils were aware of the smell of her. At least that hadn't changed.

I gulped them down and said again, 'Jazz, please don't do this.'

This time she didn't answer, but crossed the concrete floor to the three sniper rifles. She selected the silenced Russian VSS and placed it in a large holdall, then moved towards the bottom of the steps.

'I'm afraid I'm going to have to turn off the light. Goodbye, Phil, I doubt we'll meet again.'

It was my turn not to answer. As she climbed the steps, I pulled my hands hard behind my back. It felt that they were bound by professional PlastiCuffs and secured to the chairback itself. I frantically glanced around the cellar for something, anything I could use in some way to get free. The place had obviously been deliberately cleared and swept. There was nothing.

Then suddenly the light went out and I was plunged into total darkness.

Sixteen

I was wrong, it wasn't total darkness. There was a small crescent of light cast on the floor in front of me. As my eyes adjusted, it provided a barely discernible illumination of the cellar.

If I twisted awkwardly to look behind me, I could see a small, metal-barred fanlight window set some eight feet high in the wall. I reckoned it must be at pavement level outside. Even without the bars, it would be far too small to squeeze through. That was assuming I could even release the industrial ties behind my back or the ones that bound my ankles to the chair legs.

God, I was trussed like a chicken. I could see no way out of this. My shirt and trousers were still sodden from the bucket of water thrown over me earlier. I had become gradually colder as the minutes passed and now I was starting to shiver. I had to try to move somehow.

I leaned forward on my feet until the rear legs of the chair just cleared the floor. The only movement I could achieve at all was a sort of stiff-legged, side-to-side waddle which was exhausting. I managed barely half a metre, then fell back in the chair. I wasn't going anywhere fast.

Again I tried to move my wrists but the plastic ties held firm. I think I sat there for some twenty minutes, going through any possible options. I had a cigarette lighter in my shirt pocket. Even if I got to it, what could I do with it? Try to melt the plastic ties behind my back and burn the skin off my hands in the process?

Maybe there was something of use on one of the two corpses in front of me? But having to take the chair with me everywhere meant that, even if I managed to get down to them, I'd never be able to get up again.

All my options, or lack of them, just went round and round in circles in my mind, getting me absolutely nowhere.

Then a thought occurred to me. The ties holding my ankles were down at the bottom of the chair legs. In theory I should be able to slide the ties off the ends of the chair legs. But would I have to be a contortionist to do that? It was worth a try. After more consideration, I decided to wriggle-walk in the chair backwards until I was close to the wall. I began to sweat. If I got this wrong and I fell, I wasn't sure it would be possible to get up again.

At last I took a deep breath and leaned backwards, pivoting on the rear chair legs, as slowly as I could. Too hard and the chair would skid away forward under me, taking me with it. But I had to let go at some point . . . I had reached the moment.

The soles of my shoes lost contact with the floor and my shoulders thudded into the brick wall. My feet and the front chair legs were now some six inches clear of the concrete. Gingerly I began to push my feet towards the floor. The ties held firm.

I tried again and again and again. Finally, I was just about to give up, when suddenly the left-hand tie, still attached to my ankle, slipped free of the chair leg.

'YES!!' I yelled in triumph, the words echoing mockingly around the darkness.

I placed my freed foot firmly on the floor and began working on the other. With better leverage, I managed to free the right leg in much less time. I rocked forward until all four chair legs were back on the concrete and stretched out my calves to relieve my aching muscles.

It was small triumph, because I was still bound to the chair with my hands behind my back. Wherever I managed to walk at a stoop, the chair would still be clinging like the devil on my back. Nevertheless, I felt buoyed up with my success and suddenly had the ambitious idea of crossing the floor, still at an uncomfortable crouch, and mounting the cellar stairs. I had the idea that I might be able to shoulder open the door at the top.

Almost in an elated state, I did exactly that. But when I reached the top I realized the door opened inwards towards me and I'd be working against the hinges as well as the lock. I threw myself at it anyway. The door didn't budge a fraction and the pain in my shoulder was excruciating.

At that moment the front doorbell chimed. I blinked in disbelief. Was this God's answer to my unspoken prayers, a chance visit by the Jehovah's Witnesses? Or a cold-canvas double-glazing salesman? It didn't damn well matter – it was someone! I took a deep breath to fill my lungs and screamed. 'WHOEVER'S THERE – PLEASE HELP ME!'

There was a pause and I thought I heard the letterbox flap. 'Hallo? Is that you, Phil? Did I hear something?'

Good God, it was Kate.

Oh, sweetheart, I breathed, for once in your life, get something right. I yelled out again. 'KATE! CAN YOU HEAR ME!'

Her voice was faint. 'Yes, I can just about hear you. Can you speak up? What's wrong?'

'KATE, LISTEN!' I called back. 'I'M LOCKED IN THE CELLAR?'

There was a slight giggle, I think. 'Really?'

'I WANT YOU TO BREAK IN NOW! DO WHATEVER IT TAKES. DO YOU UNDER-STAND?'

'I'll try,' came the unconvincing reply.

Then there was silence and my heart sank. A couple of minutes passed and then suddenly there was an almighty explosion of breaking glass. It was followed by the sound of Kate fiddling with the lock.

'Kate! Are you there? It's the door under the stairs!'

I heard footsteps crackling on shards of glass, then the key turn in the lock. I shuffled back to allow the door to swing open towards me, then I virtually fell into the hall-way at Kate's feet.

Within a few minutes she'd located some heavy-duty scissors from the kitchen and had sliced through the ties behind my back.

I climbed unsteadily to my feet. 'Thank God you came round.'

She smiled sheepishly. 'I'm such a wooden head. I completely forgot to give you those cheques to sign. I knew you and Jazz were planning a romantic evening here, so I didn't want to disturb you. I told my mum when I got home and she said I ought to go back to the office and bring them round to you to catch tomorrow's post – otherwise they'll be cutting off the electricity.'

I reached out and held her head in both hands while I kissed the fringe of blonde hair. 'Kate, promise me you'll always be a wooden head.'

She looked taken aback. 'Oh, I'll try, Phil . . . But what happened? Were you burgled? Is Jazz all right?' Then she looked down at the glass. 'She won't mind that I've broken her front door?'

I regarded her carefully for a moment. 'Kate, you are not going to believe this. It was Jazz who did this to me. She's not what she seems. I can't stop and explain just now. She took my mobile – can I use yours?'

'Of course.' Not surprisingly she sounded puzzled as she began fishing in her shoulder bag. 'But the battery's nearly flat.'

In fact there was just enough power left for me to call Joe Lassiter. It was a miracle I could actually remember his number, but then I'd called it enough times recently. Only now I was to find that on tonight of all nights, his phone was on voicemail. As I started to leave a message, Kate's mobile went dead on me.

I glanced at my watch. It was nine o'clock. 'Look, Kate, no point you hanging around. Get off home.'

She frowned. 'Are you sure I can't help with anything?'

'Not that I can think of,' I said. 'You're already hero of the day.'

She smiled at that, not sure I really meant it. 'Okay. Have a nice weekend. See you Monday.'

I closed the door after her and locked it. There was nothing I could do about the broken glass. I wasn't sure there was much I could do about anything just now. I was getting colder and colder in my wet clothes and felt I needed to change them before I could even start to think clearly.

But first I went to the kitchen where I remembered seeing the landline wall-phone. I called Lassiter again. His voicemail was still on, and I left a message asking him to ring me urgently on Jazz's home number.

I could do with back-up and thought of Gerry Shaw. But for the life of me I couldn't recall his number and, anyway, I knew he was ex-directory. In fact, I didn't know the number of anyone who I felt I ought to contact – once again it made me realize how much we rely on modern technology. All the numbers I needed were in the book back at my office.

However, that would have to wait awhile. Remembering I'd seen some of Jazz's husband's clothes hanging in her bedroom wardrobe, I bounded up the stairs. I slid open the mirror doors. Her clothes had gone but, thank goodness, Ricardo's were still hanging there. I rummaged through them. He was obviously a little shorter than me and with a slighter build, but I found a size-small summer shirt which was generously cut so that it fitted me snugly. The trousers were more of a problem and I had to try on half a dozen before I found a pair I could actually zip up and still breathe.

It helped feeling dry and warm again, my brain beginning to function more rationally once more. As I started towards the bedroom door, I saw it on her bedside table. A mobile phone. No, not just any mobile phone, it was mine.

Jazz was heading to RAF Larkheath and had to be stopped. How was she getting there? Probably a hire car or one provided by her cell. The police could mount roadblocks on the approaches to the airfield in an attempt to stop her. So I had to speak to somebody – otherwise she might already be in the area.

I scrolled through my directory until I found Felicity Goodall's number and pressed the dial button.

Her voice was sharp and authoritative. 'Hallo, Phil.'

'Sorry to trouble you, Felicity.'

'Actually this isn't a good time, I'm at a dinner party. Can it wait?'

'I don't think so,' I replied. 'And Joe's not answering his phone.'

'That's because he's on an op. His communications will be by radio net. What's the problem?'

'Our assassin isn't Shahid and his cell. They're just the fall guys.' I took a deep breath. 'It's Jazz. Jasmina Alagic. She's been working for me.'

There was a brief pause. 'Yes, of course I know her . . . the sniper in Bosnia . . . But what d'you mean it's her?'

'Her husband's being held in Guantánamo Bay. She left London for RAF Larkheath just over two hours ago and she's taken a rifle with her. I'm afraid I don't know what car she's driving.'

'Shit!' I'd never heard Felicity swear before. There was a slight pause as she assimilated this sudden and unexpected news, then, 'She might already be there. Why did you leave it so long before calling someone?'

'It's a bit of a story.'

'Never mind, water under the bridge,' she said, but didn't sound like she meant it.

'All right, leave it to me. I'll get hold of Joe.'

I said, 'You'll maybe want more roadblocks, further out from the airfield. Try and stop her before she gets too close.'

'It may be too late for that. I'll alert Inspector Proctor, too. He's with Joe. They're at the Larkheath Manor Hotel.'

'Is there anything else I can do?'

She gave it a couple of seconds' thought. 'It might be an idea if you got yourself up to Larkheath. You did the recce with Miss Alagic — so if she does manage to get inside the sanitized area, your input could be valuable.'

'On my way,' I said. 'And also you might want to tell

Proctor that there are two dead terrorist suspects in the cellar of Jazz's house.'

'Oh, I really am not hearing this. What's the address?'

I told her and hung up before phoning Gerry.

'Hallo, Phil, old son,' he answered cheerily. 'What can I do you for?'

'I need you now, Gerry,' I said quickly. 'Up at RAF Larkheath asap. I'll explain when I see you.'

'I've just settled down in front of the telly with a take-away.'

'Kate said you're still working for me,' I replied. 'Is that right?'

'For another week, maybe more.'

'Then get up to Cambridge pronto. This is serious, Gerry.'

There was a second's hesitation, then, 'Yes, boss!'

I could just imagine the grin on his face. 'Suggest you head for the Larkheath Manor Hotel,' I said before switching off.

As I moved towards the front door, I had a sudden thought. I pushed open the cellar door, turned on the light and clambered down the stairs. I skirted round the two dead bodies to reach the far wall where the two sniper rifles remained. This might be a stupid thing to do, I wasn't sure. There would be police marksmen around RAF Larkheath, but then their training was markedly different from that of the military sniper. If someone as skilled as Jazz was on the loose with that deadly Russian VSS, then security for President Bush's arrival could be in big trouble. And it might not only be *his* life at risk.

I looked at the two models. I'd handled them both before, but decided on the AI Super Magnum. A derivative of the L96, it was so familiar, it felt like a natural extension of my own body. At least if I had it with me, I could offer my help to the authorities. I located the weapon's transit case and packed it hastily, adding a few four-round magazines of .338 ammunition.

Then I was out to my van and on my way north.

It was fifteen minutes past midnight when I finally pulled into the car park of the Larkheath Manor Hotel. I'd been delayed a few minutes at a checkpoint manned by armed civilian police some three miles down the road, so it was clear Jazz hadn't yet been stopped.

There was a small group of uniformed MoD police in the bar, still finishing off their drinks before turning in before the big deployment the next morning. I spotted Joe Lassiter in the corner. He was engaged in earnest conversation with Jeff King and some other members of the MI5 watcher team I'd been with in Leicester.

As I was persuading the barmaid to pour me a pint before the bar closed and ordered a much-needed sandwich, Lassiter spotted me and came scurrying over.

'There you are at last,' he said in a stage whisper. 'What kept you so long?'

'I take it that's a rhetorical question, Joe?' I replied, taking a deep swallow of beer. 'If not, the answer's miles.'

'What the hell's happened? The Ice Queen's having apoplexy. And I'm getting it in the neck for not re-vetting that bloody girl.'

'Why didn't you?' I answered.

'For the same frigging reason I didn't re-vet you. I bloody well knew her.' He glared at me. 'Besides, she worked for you, not the Service!'

I smiled politely at him. 'I don't detect some blame-shift going on here, do I? We both knew Jazz was Muslim.'

'You should have thought she might have been tainted,' he said, accusingly.

I frowned. 'You mean like poor old Popadom. Jazz was quick enough to suggest he could be a source of those leaks, when it was her all the time.' I drank some more beer. 'The truth is, it never occurred to either of us. You or me. Anyway, she's not exactly tainted. She's only after one man, our VIP. Then she told me she's going to send me details of everything she knows about al-Qaeda over here.'

That didn't seem to impress him very much. 'I want a full debriefing from you, Phil, now,' he demanded, scowling. 'Get that pint down your neck and we'll go to my room.'

Before I could reply, we both saw the tall American in the slick suit enter the room. Even at this time of night he was clean-shaven and crisply turned out.

Herbert J. Weatherspoon's eyes zoomed in on Lassiter and he made straight for us. 'I came as quick as I could,' he snapped. 'What's the problem?'

Lassiter forced a smile to his face, and indicated for us to move to an empty corner of the bar. 'The problem as such, Herbie, is that we've received intelligence that a professionally trained terrorist sniper may – I emphasize may – have penetrated our security cordon around Larkheath.'

Weatherspoon frowned. 'Is this an al-Qaeda threat?'

Looking distinctly uncomfortable, Lassiter answered, 'Indirectly, Herbie.' He clearly wasn't going to tell the American Secret Service officer that the would-be assassin was from within our own British security circles.

'You assured us – categorically – you have the cell "buttoned-up" as you call it.'

'Yes, we have. Everything's ready to close in for the arrest at two o'clock this morning. Before the president has even left Washington.' He took a deep breath. 'This is a new threat, part of another cell we've uncovered,' he said.

'I'm not happy about this,' Weatherspoon replied bluntly. 'And I don't think the president will be either.'

'At least we've found out about it, Herbie.'

'But what have you Brits *done* about it?'

'Not much that can be done about it until we find her.'

'Her?'

Lassiter waved his hand in a gesture of vagueness. 'Our intelligence is that it could be a female.'

'Do you have a description, a name?'

Lassiter put on his inscrutable poker face. 'Let's just say we know who we're looking for.'

'Doesn't sound like it.'

'Well, Herbie, we do. And that's why I called you in. Just as a precaution we'd like you consider bringing Airforce One down at an alternative airbase. Mildenhall or Lakenheath are in the same area.'

Weatherspoon blinked hard. 'You have to be joking, Joe? At this late stage. No specific security assessment has been done for those bases or the logistics of getting the president to Cambridge or to his meetings here at RAF Larkheath. Besides, you've got all our airforce police, your MoD reinforcements and police marksmen fully briefed and ready to position here. The base is like Fort Knox. No one's going to get a pop at the president here.'

I decided it was time to say something. 'Herbie, it could be possible for someone to try from outside the perimeter fence.'

The American seemed to notice me for the first time. 'Mason, isn't it? Your team did a security survey, right?'

I nodded. 'We did point out that fact. Unlikely but possible.'

He turned to Lassiter. 'Then I suggest you Brits get your act together, get your drunken policemen out of bed, and scour all the areas offering sniper cover according to Mason's survey. No sniper should be able move a finger without being spotted.' The American shook his head in despair. 'Now, if you'll excuse me, I need to brief my superiors. Keep me informed of any developments.'

'Of course,' Lassiter promised lamely.

As Weatherspoon strode back out of the door, I said,

'He doesn't know the first thing about sniping. Moving a finger is all a sniper has to do.'

'Very funny.'

'I wasn't joking,' I said. 'But I guess Herbie's right about checking out all the areas, arcs of fire and so on.'

'Yes, yes,' Lassiter said impatiently. 'I'll get on to Sergeant Nash now to get the MoD police organized. I'm going to be popular, interrupting their beauty sleep.'

He pulled a mobile phone from his pocket, switched it on, and wandered away into reception as he waited for Nash to answer his call. On his way out, he passed the night–porter bringing in my prawn mayo sandwiches, and helped himself to one of them.

The man looked perplexed. 'I'm sorry, sir, that man—'

I waved a dismissive hand. 'Don't worry, I'm afraid he is with me.'

I took the plate and wandered over to speak with Jeff King. 'Hallo, Phil, good to see you again. Still getting yourself into trouble?'

I smiled thinly. 'I do seem to be making a habit of it lately,' I said, taking a seat on the sofa beside him. 'You've been staking out Shahid's cell, I gather?'

King nodded. 'Ever since you arrived there with Leo Fryatt. The night shift's on now.'

'I was never aware of anything when I was there,' I admitted, 'and I knew a team was watching. That farm–worker's cottage is pretty exposed, too.'

'The only risky time for us was the first day you were there,' he explained. 'Once the techies got the microcamera and bug transmitters installed, it was all done remotely. After that the team and control vehicle just have to keep an eye on the entrance to the farm track for whenever they leave.'

'Anything interesting happen after I went?'

He shrugged. 'Nothing more than you'd expect. Oh, they bought another vehicle. A Land Rover.'

That didn't make sense. 'They weren't short on transport,' I said.

He shrugged. 'Maybe they thought a Land Rover more appropriate round here than Leo's flashy boy-racer job.'

The conversation lapsed as I tucked into my sandwiches. I'd just finished when Joe Lassiter came back into the room, looking a little happier. 'All done,' he said to me. 'Sergeant Nash is getting his team out of bed and organizing a dragnet of the possible firing zones around the airfield. Should be organized in about an hour.' He glanced at my empty plate. 'Could have saved me one, Phil, you selfish bugger.'

'Haven't you got work to do?' I replied.

'Don't worry, I'm leaving now. The SAS assault unit and the police firearms team are just about to get their final briefing before we go in at 0200.'

I looked at my watch. The hand was just nudging one o'clock.

Just then I heard the static crackle of a radio transceiver. Lassiter pulled the handset from the leather holster on his belt. 'Receiving, Control. Over.'

As he pressed the handset to his ear, the furrows slowly

deepened on his brow. 'Sweet Jesus,' he murmured after a few moments. 'Roger that, Control. Can you intercept? Over.' He paused again, then, 'Well do your best, I'll be with you as soon as I can. Out.'

'What's happened, Joe?'

Lassiter didn't answer, but turned to me. 'You told me the plan was for Shahid's cell to leave the cottage at three in the morning, right?'

I nodded. 'And hit the delivery-driver's house at three-thirty,' I confirmed.

'Well, there's clearly been a change of plan, dammit. They've already left.' Lassiter slipped the radio back into its holster. 'That was the control vehicle. The transmission bug in the living room went dead about fifteen minutes ago. Control thinks it may have been discovered. Then the remote CCTV camera outside picked them up leaving the house and into the Land Rover.'

King said, 'That shouldn't be a problem. Our vehicles are at the end of the farm track. We won't lose them.'

'They didn't use the farm track,' Lassiter explained irritably. 'They went across country. Most likely heading in the direction of Fenwell.'

'Oh, God,' I breathed. The delivery-driver's village.

'You may well "Oh God", Phil,' Lassiter snapped. 'We've got four terrorists on the loose with sidearms and explosive-suicide-vests and nothing in place that can stop them before they reach Fenwell.'

'Phone the house,' I said quickly. 'Tell Sam to get his wife and kids out, before they arrive!'

Lassiter glared at me. 'I haven't got their friggin' number, have I? This wasn't supposed to happen.'

King scrambled to his feet. 'I'll get a phone book from reception.'

I followed him out to find he had already found a directory by the telephone on the desk. 'What's the guy's name?'

'Goodwin,' I said. 'Sam Goodwin.'

He began leafing fast through the pages. 'Here we are . . . Gs. Goodwin. Bloody dozens of them . . . Ah, here's one in Fenwell. Not S though. W. Goodwin. Maybe it's in his wife's name for some reason. Meadow View Close.'

'That's not it,' I said. 'His house is in the High Street.'

'Are you sure?'

'Positive.'

'Then the poor sod must be ex-directory.'

In my mind's eye I could see Shahid and the three others, tense and nervous, bunched together in the Land Rover, the hot sweat of fear of what they were about to do helping to fug up the windows, the driver glancing up as they passed the road sign of Fenwell, and their point of no return.

I said, 'The worst mistake Sam Goodwin ever made.'

The journey to Fenwell took me twenty minutes. During that time it began to rain, a thin mist-like drizzle that had the appearance of floating in the air.

By the time I reached the village, the SAS assault team

and the police firearms unit, that had earlier been poised to raid the farmworker's cottage, had redeployed to prepare for an emergency assault on the home of Sam Goodwin and his family. I was waved down by a uniformed police officer on the edge of the village, where the street had been cordoned off. Just beyond the tape was a large van with full British Telecom livery which was, in fact, the MI5 control vehicle. Joe Lassiter was standing beside it, in earnest conversation with a couple of men in army combat fatigues.

There were other vans disembarking men in dark overalls from the SO19 'Blue Berets' unit with their rifles. I guessed that some of the plain-clothes people milling about were attached to TO7 Technical Support Branch and the SO7 'Dirty Tricks Department', which I knew had been on deployment to the farmworker's cottage.

I wound down the window of my van and flashed my security ID at the policeman. 'I wouldn't go any closer, sir,' he warned. He indicated a bus stop lay-by just behind me. 'Just back up and park there.'

I took his advice, locked the van and went to join Lassiter, who was now on his own, dragging nervously on a cigarette.

'What's the latest, Joe?'

'We're evacuating all the neighbours,' he answered irritably. 'Shouldn't be long. A few old people and disabled are slowing it up.'

'Has there been any contact with Shahid and others?'

Lassiter drew heavily on his cigarette and shook his head. 'No, but obviously they know the game's up.

There's been some curtain twitching at the front bedroom window. Our Technical Branch reckon the cell must have found one of the bugs and brought their operation forward. Suspicion might have fallen on you – as the only one not still with them – and you knew the planned time for their operation to start. And there's been no mobile phone contact between the members. Caught all of us on the hop. But at least everyone was already in place – even if it was the wrong place.'

'Are you going to try to talk to them?' I asked.

'Yes, as soon as the street is cleared. If they get excited and those explosive vests go off . . .' Lassiter winced at the thought. 'Of course we've got the landline number now and a couple of trained negotiators from the Cambridge Constabulary on their way . . . Meanwhile the SAS team are cobbling together an Immediate Action Plan in case things go tits up. Fire engines and ambulances are on their way.'

Lassiter stopped talking and turned his head as we both saw the flashing lights of a police car approaching at high speed. There was a squeal of brakes as the driver skidded to a halt just outside the cordon and a uniformed officer climbed out of a rear passenger door. His peaked cap was extravagantly adorned with gold braid.

'The chief constable,' Lassiter murmured from the side of his mouth.

Three other men, all in civilian clothes, exited the car and followed the senior officer. One of them was Inspector Ian Proctor from Special Branch.

'Hallo, Joe,' the chief constable called as he ducked under the tape. 'We seem to have a bit of a cock-up on our hands. I just hope we can retrieve the situation.'

'Yes, sir, if they'll listen to reason.' Lassiter turned to me. 'This is Phil Mason. He's one of our associates and has been heavily involved in all this.'

The police chief, a solidly built man in his fifties with a florid face and steady eyes, shook my hand firmly. 'Ah yes, infiltrated the cell and set this whole thing up, I gather. A bit too well, it seems.'

He'd hit a nerve. 'Of course, it wasn't supposed to actually happen, sir.'

The man placed a hand on my shoulder. 'Sorry, tactless of me. Courageous thing you did. Not your fault what's happened. But your input could be useful.' He turned to the three men behind him. 'These two men are our negotiators. Trained at Bramshill. Superintendents Holmes and Peters. And Inspector Proctor from SB.'

Proctor gave a crooked grin. 'We know each other, sir.' I wasn't sure he made it sound like a good thing.

At that point the uniformed police inspector in charge of the evacuation reported that all the houses had now been successfully cleared and everyone accounted for.

'Right,' the chief constable said, 'let's get inside the Control and see what stage we're at.'

I followed the others into the vehicle, which was fitted with banks of video monitors and complex radio communications equipment manned by MI5 Technical Branch officers. Behind them was a table at which two senior SAS soldiers were poring over a laptop showing an aerial image of Fenwell High Street.

The two soldiers looked up as we entered and one of them immediately addressed the chief constable. 'Sir, we've drawn up an Immediate Action Plan in case we have to go in prematurely.'

'Like, if there's a shooting?'

'Yessir.' The soldier drew himself up to his full height. 'I'm sure I don't need to tell you this is a tricky one. With suicide bombers involved and a cell of fanatics, it couldn't be more unpredictable. We must try and per-suade them to come out – even if it means offering to give them everything they want. Then your SO19 marks-men can take them out. It'll have to be clean head-shots, because it takes a split second to detonate a vest.

'Even then it could be risky. Some detonating devices work on a hand-grip relief principle. So if a bomber is killed his bomb goes off anyway when his grip relaxes.'

'God Almighty,' the chief constable murmured. 'And the SO19 marksmen, will they be at risk?'

'We've identified rooftop firing positions that should give them some hard cover in the event of an explosion – parapets, chimney stacks, that sort of thing. But we're limited by range and arcs of fire. So, yes, there has to be a degree of necessary risk.'

The other soldier spoke for the first time. 'The same applies to our assault squad, sir. They'll be on standby in neighbouring properties that have been evacuated. This will be very much a Plan B. To stand the best chance of success we'll have to get a team on the roof or into the family bedroom, where the Goodwins are being held – and in double-quick time. For that we need a properly fitted helicopter. Two Pumas are on their way from Hereford. And, of course, there'd be a simultaneous assault on the ground floor. Initially we'll have to rely on distraction and surprise, flash-bang grenades and gas, and a hell of a lot of luck.'

The other soldier added, 'The plan will be continually reviewed, amended and updated according to develop- ments and intelligence.'

'What intelligence do we have so far?' the chief con- stable asked.

Lassiter said, 'Our Technical Branch bods have just got a directional laser microphone in position, trained on the bedroom window.' He indicated the operators at the communications suite who were listening intently on headphones. 'The beam bounces off the glass and, when people are talking inside, the vibration differences it detects are translated into speech.'

'So what's being said?' Lassiter asked.

The TB supervisor looked up from his chair at the end of the suite. 'They're aware what's going on,' he said. 'Shahid's doing the talking. Telling them we'll be in touch to negotiate a hostage release. He's telling them no way. Doesn't sound good. Nasar and Hussein appear to be chanting. Passages from the Koran, I think. Leo's not got much to say for himself.'

'What about the Goodwins?' I asked.

'Not a peep,' replied the supervisor. 'I'm guessing, but they may be gagged. Parcel tape or something.'

One of the other TB officers removed his headphones. 'Leo's just announced he's going to take a dump. He doesn't exactly sound over the moon with joy.'

The negotiator called Holmes turned to the chief constable. 'I think the sooner we start talking to them the better.'

'I agree.'

The TB supervisor said, 'The house landline is patched into this phone here. We'll record everything and hear it on the headphones.'

A sudden thought occurred to me. 'I've got Leo's mobile number. I could try speaking to him while he's in the lavatory.'

'What's the point?' the negotiator asked.

'He's not running the show.' I said, 'But I don't think Leo wants to die. I might be able to persuade him to change Shahid's mind.'

'Worth a try,' murmured the chief constable carefully.

Holmes said, 'We're trying to locate a mullah in London to talk to them on the phone.'

Lassiter cut in. 'We might not have time for that.'

Holmes turned to me. 'If you phone Leo, the others will hear the ringtone.'

I shook my head. 'Shouldn't. Shahid's operational security rules were always that mobile phones be kept only on flash or vibrate.'

The negotiator relented. 'Go on then.'

'Use this green landline phone,' the TB supervisor said.

I pulled out my notebook and took the offered plastic swivel chair. Finding the page, I proceeded to tap in the number.

It seemed an eternity before I heard Leo's voice. He spoke in a whisper, his voice quavering slightly. 'Mr Khan?'

'You're in big trouble, Leo.'

'Hell, man, tell me about it.'

'I want you to tell Shahid that this is a bad thing. It would not be Allah's will to kill innocent civilians, especially women and children. If he surrenders to the police outside now, they will be treated more leniently by the courts.'

There was a shocked silence. 'How'd you know what's happened?'

'Because I'm working for the police. And so were you, although you didn't know it. You will just be a witness for the prosecution.' The chief constable pulled a face at that one. I continued, 'But don't tell Shahid that. Try to make him see sense.'

'He ain't goin' to like surrender, Mr Khan. No way.'

'Then try to persuade him to negotiate when we get in contact on the house phone. We'll promise him anything he wants. Safe passage, a helicopter away from here, anything . . . Just release the Goodwins and leave the house.' I paused. From the corner of my eye I saw Holmes nodding his approval. 'Otherwise you'll all end up dead.'

'I'll see, Mr Khan.'

'Do it, Leo. Do it for your mum. She loves you.'

He switched off. I looked up at the group of people looking at me and shrugged. 'He's terrified, but he might give it a try.'

'Right,' Holmes said, 'I'm going to try speaking to Shahid.'

He took the seat next to me and used the red telephone, as the TB supervisor handed me a pair of headphones so that I could listen in. The house phone seemed to ring for ever before it was snatched up.

'Hallo, Akhtar,' Holmes said quietly.

'How d'you know my name?' Shahid asked.

Holmes' voice was silky smooth. 'We know everything about you, Akhtar Shahid, and what you're doing. My name is John and I'm a police officer. I understand you are very angry about things and have reasons for what you are doing. I want to talk to you about your grievances, see what we can do to put them right.'

'Well, I don't want to talk to you! Infidel pig!' Shahid spat out his words. 'Our mission has failed to take out the Evil One! So we must make recompense to appease Allah. Nothing can stop us now!'

Suddenly I was aware of a commotion in the background, a voice I thought was either Nasar or Hussein. 'It's Leo! He's going downstairs. I think he's doing a runner.'

Shahid shouted, 'THEN WE DO IT NOW! ALLAH AKBAR!!'

I couldn't believe it. Leo was making a run for it. I

could visualize him racing for the front door and freedom. Would he make it? How would the others react? These thoughts raced through my brain so fast that I think I missed the significance of what Shahid had yelled. Ripping off my headphones, I stood and ran for the door of the van.

'Where the hell are you goin'?' Lassiter demanded as I brushed past him.

Outside the street was now deserted apart from our cluster of vehicles by the cordon. It was eerily like a film-set, pools of light cast from streetlamps and house windows reflecting on the damp tarmac and giving the houses the unreal look that you could believe were really just clapboard fascias. A black and white cat was stealthily beginning to cross from one pavement to the other, carefully skirting a puddle. It was a split-second image that registered in my brain as I struggled to make out the Goodwins' house in the distance, its lights off and curtains drawn, the Clio and the wife's Jeep parked neatly outside.

Then the front door flew open and I could just see a figure, hunched and running for his life.

'COME ON, LEO!' I yelled at the top of my voice. It was spontaneous, like urging a horse to the winning post.

Then the entire scene disintegrated in a blinding pulse of burning white light that seared into my retinas. The blast of the unseen hurricane blew me back onto the steps of the BT van at the same time as the earth-shaking roar of the explosion made the entire street tremble.

I tried to refocus my eyes, barely believing the carnage

before me. The Goodwins' home had simply vanished, along with the houses on either side of it. They were replaced by a pile of smouldering rubble and jagged remnants of brick walls protruding like rotten teeth. A geyser of water from a ruptured mains sprayed skyward to meet the heavenly shower of a million shards of broken glass that were falling with the drizzle to scatter on the surface of the street. Electrical shorts from power cables fizzed and spat amidst the demolished buildings. New sources of flickering orange light suggested fires were catching in nearby properties. There was no sign of the little Clio car, or the Jeep. And there was no sign of Leo Fryatt.

Somewhere in that devastation was the Goodwin family, the two young kids. I started to move forward, then felt a strong restraining hand on my shoulder.

Angrily I spun round, only to find myself staring into the face of Gerry Shaw. 'No, Phil, no one's survived that,' he said with quiet authority. 'And there could be a secondary – if both explosive vests didn't go off. Leave it to the experts.'

Lassiter appeared at Gerry's side. 'Sweet Jesus,' he murmured. 'There'll be hell to pay for this.'

I turned on him. 'I think, Joe, the price has already been paid.'

'Calm down, old son. Bomb disposal are on their way.'

'A bit late for that,' I snapped. 'Your people broke into the cell's cottage to place electronic bugs, right?'

'You know they did.'

'Then why the hell didn't they "jark" the weapons

and those fucking vests while they were in there. Disable the damn things or substitute dummy explosive?'

'There wasn't time.'

'There was plenty of time, Joe. Our people did it many times in Northern Ireland. Saved a lot of lives.'

Lassiter sighed as if he was a teacher explaining something to a particularly dumb pupil. 'Shahid was not stupid. He and the others were trained. If they'd tumbled a "jarking" I thought they'd pull the plug, abort that mission. And then try some other way to kill the president, something we didn't know about.'

'Well, we now know another cell was planning to do that all along,' I countered fiercely.

'All very well being wise after the event, Phil.' He glared at me, and tossed his head back to indicate the wrecked street. 'Sometimes shit happens. Now if you'll forgive me, I've got a busy time ahead.'

He walked back to join the chief constable, police officers and soldiers who had gathered in a state of shock to take in the extent of the catastrophe. An urgent singsong wail of approaching ambulances and fire-tenders began to fill the moist night air.

'Don't be too hard on Joe,' Gerry said.

I didn't answer. Inside I was seething with anger, emotion and not a little guilt of my own contribution to this disaster. It had been my idea to run young Leo Fryatt as an agent and my idea to take hostages for an assassination attempt I thought would never happen. Now Leo and an innocent family of four were all dead.

I said, 'I take it you went to the hotel?'

He nodded. 'One of the MI5 blokes, someone called Jeff, told me something was going on down here. Told me you had gone. Also said it was possible a terrorist sniper had got through the security cordon around Larkheath.'

'Did he say who?'

'No.'

'Let's get back to the hotel,' I suggested. 'I've a few things to tell you.'

Suddenly I noticed the black and white cat I had seen earlier. It was playing with something quite large and round on the pavement by a downpipe some thirty metres away.

'That one really must have nine lives . . .' I murmured. 'What's that it's playing with? Looks like a football.'

We both walked forward and it was only when we were quite close and the cat scurried away at our approach that I realized, with a sudden sick feeling in my stomach, what it was. The head had been neatly severed, so neatly that it might have been guillotined.

The black hair was unsinged, the expression on the perfect face serene. I was staring into the wide open, fathomless dark eyes of the suicide bomber Nasar.

'That'll be one of them,' Gerry said calmly. 'With those vests, the head goes off like a bloody champagne cork. Can land anywhere. Don't tell them that when they're recruiting. Problem screwing all those celestial virgins with your fucking head missing.'

Seventeen

It was the worst night of my life.

Leo Fryatt's body had soon been found, in five pieces, torn limb from limb and cast like a discarded kid's doll, in an alley opposite the wrecked house. The remaining body parts of the Goodwin family would doubtless take days to collect. It was even doubtful they'd find enough of them to place in coffins.

We got back to the hotel at just gone three in the morning. Gerry invited me to his room, suggesting we do some serious damage to the minibar. I felt I needed a drink, but was mindful we'd have an early start the next day.

He sat on his bed and I hunkered on the edge of an armchair, nursing a tumbler of whisky. And that was how I felt. On edge, unable to relax, unbidden images like photo-flashes in my vision. The explosion, Leo disappearing into the searing white heat of the blast. Then a split-second, almost subliminal, videoclip in vivid, high-definition colour – hot, eggshell sky; crusty, desiccated landscape; viewing through the crosshairs of the Schmitt and Bender sight, a human head between the calibration beads, and the little girl's head bursting like a ripe pumpkin.

Finally my mind began to clear and I felt able to bring Gerry up to speed about Jazz and my incarceration in her cellar. He listened in stunned silence while I talked and explained what she'd done and why she'd done it, and what she'd told me she intended to do today.

'D'you think she will?' he asked, clearly finding it hard to come to terms with what he'd just heard.

'I'm hoping she's had a last-minute change of mind,' I answered truthfully. 'But she killed two terrorists yesterday without blinking an eye, Gerry. And she didn't hate them like she hates George Bush. I just hope the cops manage to pick her up in the security cordon sometime tonight.'

Gerry sipped his whisky thoughtfully. 'If there's such a high risk, why don't the Yanks change their plans?'

I shrugged. 'I don't really know. Lassiter put it to them, quite forcibly, but they're not keen. Maybe they don't think the threat's convincing enough to disrupt carefully laid plans. Maybe they don't believe it's possible to get through their base security. And I'm sure they *don't* realize what a trained sniper as good as Jazz can do, even if they are guarding the base with police marksmen.'

'As you say, hopefully she'll get caught during the night.'

'Hopefully,' I echoed, but I know I didn't sound convinced. Draining my drink, I placed the tumbler on the coffee table. 'Sorry, Gerry, I need to crash.'

My friend looked at me knowingly, and nodded. 'I

understand, mate. I know it's difficult, but don't let it get to you. It was none of your doing.'

In his position, I'd have said the same. But they were just words to me then, words with no comfort, no redemption.

I made my way to my room, stripped off and climbed in between the crisp, clean sheets that smelled reassuringly of starch. I fell asleep instantly, but twenty minutes later I was wide awake again, my sheets sodden with cold sweat. For the rest of the night I just tossed and turned, blanking out images, trying to ignore the thoughts that crowded in on me, demanding my attention. I desperately tried to fall asleep again, but the harder I tried the more awake I became, aware of the agonizingly slow movement of the minute hand on the bedside clock.

Finally I must have drifted off, but it could only have been for half an hour or so before that same clock began shouting at me, drilling my head with its repeated, urgent buzz. As I threw off the covers and stood up, I felt like death, my eyes gluey through lack of sleep.

Even the ice-cold shower and a strong black coffee didn't help much. It was still dark outside as I made my way down to the restaurant.

Although it was only six o'clock every table was filled with the regular MoD police and many others drafted in from locations all over Britain. Clearly the hotel had made a special effort to cope with the huge influx of personnel needing an early breakfast. I guessed a lot of them had been out all night, combing the surrounding countryside in their search for Jazz. The air was filled with the sound of animated conversation in many regional accents.

I spotted Gerry Shaw and threaded my way between the tables to join him. He looked as though he'd had the best night's sleep of his life and was munching cheerfully through a huge pile of scrambled eggs and sausages. Sitting beside him, Lassiter looked a total wreck. As scruffy as always in his crumpled shirt and jacket, his eyes were unusually sunken and grey with fatigue behind his glasses, and his chin was blue with telltale stubble. Unusually for him when food was free, he was nursing just a slice of toast and marmalade with a disgruntled expression on his face. The third person at the table was Sergeant Ron Nash. Although the tall ex-Grenadier had no doubt also been up all night, he'd managed to shave and even wax his handlebar moustache.

Nash saw me first. 'Morning, Phil. Joining us for some scoff?'

I pulled out a chair and sat down. 'Any news about Jazz?' I asked.

Lassiter scowled at me. 'If there was, there'd be champagne and oysters on the table.'

'We've been running a dragnet around the surrounding countryside since the early hours,' Nash explained. 'We're just having this quick scoff break, then we'll start all over again. If she's there, we'll find her.'

'Why so confident,' I persisted, 'if you've found nothing?'

'I said we've found no *one* on the roadblocks or in the

dragnet,' he replied. 'But we have found something, a car parked in a lay-by, just outside the cordon area.'

Lassiter said, 'It could be hers, Phil. No paperwork in the glovebox, but the DVLA list the owner as a small car-hire company in London. Local plod have traced the director and are talking to him in his office as we speak.'

Gerry smiled and gave me an optimistic wink.

'Where is the lay-by?' I asked.

'About four miles north of the airfield,' Nash said. 'I'll show you on the map when I've finished this.'

At that moment a waitress appeared at my side. For many years I've had a soldier's appetite. Eat everything and anything whenever you can, because you never know when you'll get your next meal. But this morning that appetite had deserted me completely.

I just ordered a pot of black coffee and turned to Lassiter. 'Has Herbie Weatherspoon changed his mind?'

'No,' Lassiter growled. 'Spoke to him not five minutes ago. Says if the car is the sniper's and the ground is crawling with armed police, plus marksmen within the compound, there's no way an assassination is going to happen.'

Gerry said, 'Police marksmen are police marksmen, Joe, not military snipers. Different training, different animals.'

Lassiter looked irritable. 'So you say. But we haven't got any army snipers handy just now, if you hadn't noticed.'

I looked at my watch. It was six-fifteen and outside the

hotel window I could see the first fingers of light reaching up into the dull sky. 'The president's ETA isn't until eleven,' I said, 'so I'm certain you could get some. Fly them in by helicopter. I'm sure the Sniper School in the Brecons would be up for it. Get some instructors or even top students. The SAS have got helicopters on short-notice standby just over the border.'

Nash said, 'I don't think the boys in SO19 would be very pleased about that.'

'This isn't about the sensitivities of the Blue Berets, Ron,' I retorted. 'I want to see some army snipers out there on the ground.'

Nash raised an eyebrow. 'But you're not running this operation, Phil.'

'Now, now,' Lassiter said, raising his hand. 'Phil may have a point. I'd have to raise it with the chief constable – and my boss in London, of course. Get the necessary permission.'

Just then his mobile phone started bleating and he snatched it up from the table. He covered the mouthpiece with his hand. 'Local plod in London at the car-hire place.'

He listened intently for a few moments, then switched off. 'I think we've hit paydirt. The car was hired to a woman. A Mrs Erika Herenda.'

I said, 'I think that's a Bosnian Muslim name.'

Lassiter said, 'That would figure. Probably a false address, but the police are checking it out.'

'And a false identity,' I said.

'Then we'll get her in the end, one way or another,' Lassiter said smugly.

'She may have more than one identity,' I pointed out.

Just then everyone in the room, as if on an unspoken order, began rising from the tables and making their way towards the door. It was six-thirty and outside dawn was breaking. The hunt for Jazz was on again.

Ron Nash took an Ordnance Survey map from his pocket and spread it on the table, pointing out the location where the abandoned car had been found. As a sniper you train your brain to develop a near photographic memory for terrain and I immediately recalled the lay-by beside the entrance to a recently ploughed field.

'We've got a couple of tracker dogs now,' Nash said, refolding his map. 'I'm confident we'll find her. I'll be in touch later.' Then he joined the other uniformed MoD police in the steady exodus towards the waiting vans in the car park.

Lassiter followed him, intent on making some important phone calls from the privacy of his room, leaving Gerry and I to our coffees.

'I remember the field next to that lay-by,' Gerry said. 'It had been freshly ploughed when we were doing our assessment . . . now with last night's rain . . . Should leave a trail of footprints if Jazz went that way.'

I forced a smile. 'Do you really think she'd do that, Gerry? Jazz was in 14 Int and has done plenty of escape-and-evasion courses. I'm sure Nash thinks she'll be in

Zone B, the nearest one to the car, but I reckon that's the last place she'll be. After all, she's had all night to yomp across country.'

When Jazz, Gerry and I had done our risk assessment survey, we had divided the terrain surrounding the airfield into alphabetical zones from which it might be possible to fire a sniper round at the president as he left the aircraft and before he entered the safety of a building or climbed into his bullet-proof limousine. The zones radiated clockwise starting from the south-west – the south itself having any field of fire blocked by the airbase buildings. Zone A only offered one position, which was from the rooftop of the hotel we were in and that was anyway secured by SO19 police marksmen for their own use.

Zone B was in the north-west and was closest – and in that respect the best option – to the target area, but it also offered a narrow arc because of the airfield admin blocks. Zone C was to the north and on the far end of the base, the distance offering a poor chance of a one-shot kill. It was also behind the president's aircraft, which would shield him as he descended the steps. That meant any sniper would have a tight window of opportunity to get him when he was on the ground, before he was quickly obscured again by buildings. It would take luck and an extraordinary shot to get the target there. And I didn't think even Jazz was that good.

The final and by far the largest was Zone D which covered the entire eastern flank of the airfield. There were no residential buildings; it was mostly open and undulating country, offering plenty of dead ground as it rose away from the perimeter to a range of low hills, some thousand metres to the east. The area was scattered with occasional stands of broadleaf trees and a variety of bushes, interspersed with occasional derelict farm buildings, and remnants of cottages from a previous age.

Gerry said thoughtfully, 'So where do you think she'd go, Phil?'

'I'd put my money on Zone D,' I replied. 'It's the biggest and offers plenty of cover. It would be difficult to flush a trained sniper out of there in a short period of time. Especially with the limited number of armed MoD police available.'

'On reflection, I guess you're probably right.'

At that moment Joe Lassiter walked back into the restaurant. He didn't look pleased and was shaking his head as he sat down at our table. 'Chief constable isn't having any of it, Phil. He's still mighty vexed over the Fenwell incident last night. Up to his neck dealing with the media. Said last thing he wanted was a bunch of armed squaddies – improperly briefed – wandering around the countryside shooting at anything that moves.'

'Snipers aren't cowboys, Joe,' I replied. 'They are probably the calmest, most highly trained specialist professionals in the army.'

'Yeah, yeah,' he said irritably. 'It's just the perception, I guess. Anyway, he wouldn't budge. So I got on to the Ice Queen. Tried to get her to go over his head. Trouble was, she felt she had to refer it up to Medusa and Medusa turned it down. Said we had ample coverage with SO19 marksmen. Basically she agreed with the chief constable.'

I asked, 'And where are the SO19 boys positioned?'

'Roof of this hotel,' he answered, 'on the roof of the control tower, a church tower in Zone B, and the roof of Hollingdene Hall.'

'Look, Joe,' I said. 'Gerry and I have been chatting. We think she's most likely to be somewhere in Zone D.'

'That's not what Sergeant Nash thinks, or Weatherspoon.' Lassiter frowned. 'And the car was found near Zone B. Nash's men have got sniffer dogs down there now. That's the area they're concentrating on.'

'They're wrong,' I said. 'I know they are.'

I'd never seen Lassiter look so distraught, his usual cocky self-confidence shattered. 'My neck's on the line if this goes wrong. And there's nothing I can do about it.'

I said, 'I've got a sniper rifle in the van. I got it from Jazz's house. If you wanted, Gerry and I could cover Zone D as a precaution. Out there in the field.'

Gerry almost choked on his coffee. 'Hey, wait a minute, Phil, don't include me in this! It's twenty years since I did sniper training.'

'C'mon, Gerry, shooting's your hobby,' I replied. 'You've got medals for it. Besides, I'd just want you to be my spotter.'

Lassiter seemed cautiously interested. 'What do you have in mind exactly?'

'A good counter-sniper position. There's a rise to the

north of the zone that would give a pretty good view over its entire length. It's not perfect, there are trees and other obstructions, but it's the best there is. Hopefully we'll pick up her position before the president arrives. If it goes tits-up, we should be able to get her when she exfils.'

'What?'

'Exfiltrates,' I explained. 'Tries to get out of the location.'

'This is Jazz we're talking about, Phil,' Lassiter said, disbelieving. 'You two were shagging a few years back, maybe even still have been. You telling me you'd kill her?'

His blunt words took me aback. 'Look, Joe, I've no time for President Bush. His foreign policy has been a nightmare. But he is the elected leader of his country. If there's no one else to stop Jazz, I'll do it.'

'Are you sure about that?' Gerry pressed.

I said calmly, 'She's as misguided about this as any other member of an al-Qaeda cell. They've got their perceived justifications, too. Murder is murder, it's as simple as that.'

Lassiter pondered. 'Felicity won't give permission, Phil, I'm certain of that.'

'Why don't you make an executive decision, Joe,' I replied icily. 'If she's shot before or after any incident, Jazz will have been killed as a known assassin or an attempted assassin. Lot of brownie points for you either way.'

After a few moments thought, Lassiter said, 'No, you make your own decision. I won't stop you if you think it's the best thing to do. After all, it is just a precaution. But no mistakes like that one you made in Afghanistan. Don't want any local kids having their heads blown off because they were playing in the wrong place at the wrong time.'

Anger flashed in my head like a bright-red light. 'Shut the fuck up, Joe. A job's got to be done, that's all.' I turned to Gerry. 'Are you with me on this?'

He smiled awkwardly. 'I'm just the spotter.'

I looked back at Lassiter. 'I'll need somewhere safe to zero the rifle and get in some practice rounds.'

He scratched the stubble on his chin thoughtfully. 'What about an aircraft hangar?'

'Perfect,' I said.

Over the next fifteen minutes Gerry and I discussed a plan over an Ordnance Survey map borrowed from Lassiter, while he went off to organize our firing range with the wing commander and to find us two radios so that we'd be able to keep in the loop with the MoD police.

Later, the empty and near-derelict aircraft hangar proved to be an excellent and safe venue for putting the Super Magnum through its paces. It packed a terrific punch. Gerry and I were very impressed with it, and I think he quite enjoyed himself, especially when I let him try a couple of rounds himself.

After an hour's serious play-time, we left the airbase and returned to the hotel car park to prepare for our mission.

I opened the rear doors of my van and, before pulling on my ghillie suit, found Gerry a spare pair of my old army camo fatigues, which were a bit on the tight side for him, then handed him my trusty Leica Vecta binoculars with their built-in laser rangefinder. In a moment of criminal madness, I'd smuggled them out when I left the army. I was like a kid who just had to have his favourite toy.

I then took the Accuracy International .338 Super Magnum variant of the company's AW, or Arctic Warfare, weapon from its case, pocketed all its ancillary bits and two four-round magazines of ammunition, before starting to camouflage it with spare hessian and scrim lying around in the back of the van. Finally it was make-up time, smearing on the three-tone cam-cream facials.

Meanwhile the sky had formed a ceiling of high, bruised cloud which held a threat of more rain and there was still a haze of light mist in the air. I hoped it would persist and make it more difficult for Jazz to achieve her mission.

Once Gerry and I were ready, I started up the van and we set off north up the main road, through the three-mile roadblock, until we reached the lay-by where the rented car had been taped off. Regular and MoD police were milling around, seemingly not doing a lot. I drove on a short distance before pulling over beside a stile in the roadside fence.

Gerry jabbed a thumb towards his left. 'What's going on down there?'

When I looked I saw a group of MoD police and a couple of dog-handlers gathered at the edge of a stream that ran parallel with the road. One of the men was Sergeant Nash. 'Let's take a look,' I said.

Not wanting to cause any consternation or arguments, I left the weapon behind and climbed out to join Gerry. We scaled the stile and made our way down the slight incline. Nash saw us approach. 'Is that you Phil? Or Wurzel Gummidge on manoeuvres?'

I smiled. 'Can you believe it, in the sniper business, I heard every scarecrow joke going.' I glanced around at the small party of baffled-looking officers and two very excitable Rottweilers. 'Can I ask what's going on?'

Nash shrugged his shoulders. 'Started off well enough. Picked up a scent at the car. Over a couple of fields to the west, then turned north, then back eastward to here. Now the dogs have lost it.'

'Jazz used the stream to throw them off,' I said.

'Standard evasion training,' Nash agreed. 'So she could be anywhere.'

'So where are you off to in your fancy dress?'

'We're going to observe in Zone D.'

Nash frowned. 'On the east flank? I really don't think she'll be there. Not enough cover. Besides, we scoured that thoroughly last night.'

'Well, it's my hunch,' I replied.

'Haven't got enough men,' Nash complained. 'Nowhere near enough. Chief constable's trying urgently to get together a party of off-duty officers to help us, but it's a tall order at short notice. If you really think Zone D is likely, I'll try and divert some resources.'

'Good idea,' I said and pointed out our approximate intended viewing position on Lassiter's map. 'Please make sure the SO19 marksmen know where we are. I'd hate us to be mistaken for Jazz.'

'Sure,' he replied, scribbling down a note.

I added, 'Oh, and we're on your radio net. Callsign Tango Two.'

Nash smiled. 'Very funny. Well, I've got to get on. Good luck.'

Leaving him to puzzle how best to deploy his resources, Gerry and I returned to the road. I slipped the Magnum out of the van before we crossed the road east and entered Zone C. I was as certain as I could be that this was the least likely area Jazz would have selected. However, we had to keep to dead ground in case she was able to view us coming from the hide I suspected she had somewhere in Zone D. Gerry and I moved on slowly but steadily, keeping to depressions in the terrain so that we didn't expose ourselves. Sometimes this required us to leopard crawl from the cover of one position to another.

Finally we arrived at the northern sector of the eastern flank of the airbase that we had designated Zone D. Now we had to exercise even more extreme care as we manoeuvred our way, sliding slowly through the damp grass on our stomachs until we reached the slight rise in the ground. It was a landscape of rough scrub, the only visual cover it offered being the taller weed patches and a scattering of low bushes. We took our time to examine the area, eventually locating a slight dip just wide enough to allow us to lie side-by-side with our heads just able to see over the crest of the rise. It offered a view down into the full length of Zone D, stretching away to the south.

To our right was the eastern perimeter fence of the air-field with its vast expanses of shorn grass and concrete runways, blurred in the damp haze. In the far distance we could see the outline of the control tower and the spot where President George W. Bush would disembark from his plane. Annoyingly, however, the cloud cover was start-ing to break up and shafts of sunlight were filtering through, beginning to disperse the haze. Nevertheless, our observation location was ideal.

We both adopted the 'Hawkins' position because there was so little cover. By twisting my shoulders so that the firing line of my rifle was almost at right-angles to the rest of my body, I was offering a lower height profile than in the standard prone position.

The decision on our exact location made, we retreated back into dead ground and worked a buddy-buddy system to help each other perfect our camouflage, using dead grass and foliage from the location. It was easier for me with the ghillie suit and hood, but more challenging for Gerry as he only had a regular army camo smock and forage cap. But with the scraps of hessian and scrim scarf-ing material from my van, and a bit of initiative and imagination, he was soon successfully transformed into Wurzel Gummidge's twin brother.

I radioed in our confirmed position and map-reference to Zulu control before we crawled back into the location to begin our systematic mapping and numbering of the target area by landmarks. In this case these were mostly prominent shrubs or trees, an odd gate, the remains of a brick wall from a demolished cottage, hollows or rises – in bands of distance. The Leica made this much easier and more accurate, although I was still old-fashioned enough to somehow miss the primitive but effective methods of judging distance. Like estimating half-way to a feature, which is easier to judge, then doubling it. Or an experienced sniper's and observer's estimate added together and then divided by two.

Once the landmarks and distances were noted, Gerry wrote them down in map form at their approximate positions in his notebook – or range-card – then drew lines from them to the location of our position, resembling a sort of sunray effect, and actually known in my former job as the 'setting ray'. Gerry then added a reference grid for us to begin a detailed search of the area, both of us examining the same grid square together at the same time, working left to right. He used the Leica and I viewed through the sight on the Super Magnum.

As always we began in the sector closest to us. If Jazz was holed up there, this would be the greatest risk to us. However, we spotted nothing and moved on up to the next band of grid squares, further away from our position.

It was a long, slow process, but not worth rushing. Meanwhile we listened in to the MoD police net and did our best to follow other operations in the area. I was aware of the time ticking away yet was surprised to discover that my watch was telling me it was already ten o'clock.

Then I heard the ex-Grenadier Sergeant Nash calling us in my earpiece. 'Zulu to Tango Two. Finally got some men to put into Zone D. They'll be moving towards your position from the south. I've just been advised you're armed. Not happy about that. Just don't go using my men for target practice. Ex-bootnecks of your age should-n't be allowed to play with guns. Over.'

'Roger that,' I replied with a slight smile. 'Just make sure your woodentops don't shoot at *us*. Out.'

Moments later, barely visible to the naked eye, two white vans appeared at the far end of Zone D and, like minuscule figures on an N-gauge railway, armed MoD police began to appear, spreading out like beaters on a pheasant shoot. Beginning their second search of the area, they started moving slowly and steadily towards us. Somewhere in between us, I suspected, Jazz would be hiding. Hiding, watching, sweating with anticipation, adrenalin and — with the arrival of the armed police — fear. I could visualize her looking at her watch, urging the hands of her watch to move faster towards eleven o'clock. The hour when she could do the deed, and try to make good her escape. Jazz may have been running out of time, but then so were we.

'Okay, Gerry,' I said, 'let's start again — from the half-way point.'

Having done our utmost to ensure that Jazz wasn't anywhere near to us, we began, yet again, to examine each of the grids that offered the best firing positions. Each grid square covered approximately fifty metres and each was overlapped by some ten metres so that no patch of terrain was accidentally overlooked.

We prayed to see something, anything that was out of keeping. The reflection or dark shine of an undisguised optical lens or rifle sight; the glint of light on metal; the unnatural straight lines of a rifle barrel; any man-made items, or colours, even black, which is rare in foliage, usually only created by shadow. But I somehow doubted Jazz would make such an elementary mistake. In Sarajevo, it had been rumoured she'd created her own design of urban ghillie suit, made up by sewing brick-sized, straight-lined white, grey, rust and black pieces of material to it by hand. Just as no straight lines appear in nature, few soft edges exist in urban areas, even in bomb-damage rubble.

Far from dragging, the time flew as we again concentrated on each grid square, aware that all the time the line of MoD police were edging towards us. But it was slow work and they had probably only advanced into a fifth of Zone D when Sergeant Nash's voice came over the net.

'Zulu Control to all units, Bald Eagle in our airspace. A strong tail wind over the Atlantic means its ETA is brought forward to 1045 hours. I repeat 1045 hours. All units on maximum security alert. Over.'

Gerry glanced across at me. 'Five minutes.'

I nodded. Suddenly I wondered if we were searching

for someone who just simply wasn't out there. Maybe that abandoned car hadn't belonged to Jazz. Or it had, but when she'd seen the police presence, she'd decided to abort her mission. Again, even now, she could change her mind. Lie low until the president had landed, then slink away when the opportunity presented itself.

Faint music wafted through the air. A small brass band of RAF musicians, standing on the concrete apron by the control tower, was practising a quick run-through of 'The Star Spangled Banner' prior to the imminent touchdown.

Gerry glanced back over his shoulder, up into the sky. 'There's Bald Eagle, I guess. Over the horizon, coming in now.'

'Eyes front,' I scolded. 'Keep focused.'

'Sorry,' Gerry replied.

We lowered our optical sights to keep the whole of Zone D in eyeball view. The police line had advanced another fifty metres. On the airfield apron, a welcoming party of tiny figures had gathered along with two black limousines. Steps were wheeled into standby position.

The air was gradually filled with the deafening roar of jet engines as the aircraft approached and came in for touchdown. My eyes flickered sideways in time to catch its undercarriage tyres kiss the runway. Not Air Force One, that I'd somehow been expecting, but a Boeing 777 in American Airlines livery. I forced my eyes forward, just keeping the airliner in my peripheral vision as it reversed thrust to slow down. Then it began taxiing towards the apron. Minutes later it drew to a halt and the gantry steps were rolled into position. We knew the president was about to disembark because the RAF band burst exuberantly into action.

Then suddenly there was an unexpected swish of windrush over our position, whistling between us. A feeling of displaced air rather than an actual noise.

'EOW!' Gerry yelled abruptly, clutching at his ear.

'What the hell . . .?' I began. It flashed through my mind he'd been stung by a wasp; there'd been a lot around this autumn.

Then I saw the blackened hole in the earflap of his forage cap. Blood came away in his hand.

The penny dropped. When he'd looked up to the sky, he'd raised his head and for a split second had given our position away. Jazz was protecting her own position and had spotted him, and perhaps even had suspicions of our presence for some time.

There had been no sound apart from the air displacement of the passing round. Jazz must be using a suppressor, I decided, because I had heard no sound. Better for her security, but potentially less accurate. Although that shouldn't be too much consolation, because she'd told me she'd practised a lot in Bosnia just recently.

'Keep your fucking head down!' I hissed. 'She's out there.'

'I know that,' he replied irritably, overcoming his shock. 'Thanks for asking, but I'm not dead. Nice scar to show the grandkids though.'

I looked down over Zone D. The police line was continuing its slow advance, totally unaware of what had just happened. If Jazz's shot had come in right between us, but erred slightly – by accident or design – towards Gerry, then she must be almost straight in front of us, possibly a little to our right.

'Check linear vertical grids,' I snapped. 'Forty-five to one-oh-five.'

'Roger,' Gerry replied, recovering his composure.

Our eyes were back on the binoculars and rifle sight because now we had something specific to look for, running up in a straight line through Zone D. Rapidly first, then back again, slower this time. With minutes to go and knowing someone – us – was waiting to counter-snipe, Jazz had decided to disrupt our attention moments before the plane landed, forcing us to reposition at the vital phase of the president's arrival.

Well, I decided I wasn't going anywhere, we'd just have to stick it out.

I flicked on my radio. 'Tango Two to Zulu Control. Confirm Gatecrasher in Zone D. Repeat, Gatecrasher confirmed in Zone D. We've been engaged, no casualties. We are trying to locate. Suggest your police line advances with extreme caution. Over.'

I heard Sergeant Nash's expletive, before he said, 'Roger, and out.'

Suddenly Gerry said, 'I think I might have something.' We both glanced down at the range-card that lay between us. 'Grid seven-six,' he added.

Referring to the 'setting ray', I knew exactly where to look as I pressed my eye back onto the rifle sight.

'Go centre grid,' Gerry advised, 'then three o'clock some fifteen metres. I see a colour change and a straight horizontal line.'

'Gottit,' I breathed.

It was almost a straight line, mostly broken up by grass and foliage, but not quite. The line in its entirety ran for some seven or eight feet.

'A hide?' Gerry asked.

I was sure he was right. And I thought I knew what it was, the edge of a camouflaged bivvy sheet. If I was right, Jazz had used a small dip in the land or else dug herself a shell-scrape. Using chicken wire or some other light-weight material to form a top to her position, she'd added the bivvy-sheet and covered it with earth and rough turf. Then all she needed was an aperture the size of a rabbit hole in whatever direction she wanted to fire. There was not even the risk of an exposed rifle barrel. You'd actually have to stand on the damn position and collapse into it to know it was there.

Then I saw the dark shadow. Black. The firing aperture she must have used to engage us. I demanded quickly, 'Edict, Gerry.'

Before he could respond we heard the words in my earpiece. It was an American voice. 'The president is on the steps now, descending . . .' Then, suddenly, panic struck. 'Oh, my God!' A pause of incredulity, then, 'PRESIDENT DOWN! REPEAT! PRESIDENT DOWN!'

Like Gerry I'd been too wrapped up in our own work to pay any attention to the president's arrival. It seemed an irrelevant distraction.

'Edict!' I snapped again.

Gerry refocused his binoculars. 'Elevation, five-seven-zero metres. Deflection four clicks left.'

I made my adjustments to the rifle's aim, could see the firing aperture of Jazz's hide that pointed in our direction.

I was only vaguely aware of the American's commentary in my earpiece: 'He's taken a tumble. On the apron. Medic! Medic! Close protection in position. NOW!'

Gerry said, 'Indication, firing port in hide.'

At that moment I saw her face, or imagined I did. Actually, it must have been her eyes, big and white and bright, showing amid the dark mud and cam-cream covering her face in the dark interior of the hide. The eyes of the woman I had loved so, so much.

'Confirmation,' I murmured, 'Seen.' My finger curled gently around the trigger.

'Time to fire,' Gerry continued.

The eyes had disappeared. I said suddenly, 'I can't, Gerry. I can't do it.'

'What?'

Then we heard a yell from the still-advancing line of armed MoD police. I took my eye from the rifle sight just in time to see one of them collapse, his gun hanging uselessly by its strap as he clutched his face. A clean shot to the head. All the others dived for whatever sparse cover they could find, no one knowing where the shot had come from.

'Christ!' I hissed angrily beneath my breath.

I put my head down and refocused on the firing aperture of Jazz's hide. I tightened my finger on the trigger again. How many police might she take out to defend herself? I did not have an option any longer.

Suddenly in the false rabbit-hole, the eyes were back. Seeming to stare straight at me. For a second they were the eyes of a little Afghani girl, as if some remote computer hacker had managed to hijack my mind and brain. I squeezed my eyes tight shut for a fraction of a second, and the image cleared.

The eyes were still looking at me, searching into my soul.

'For God's sake, Phil,' Gerry screamed. 'She's pointing her fucking rifle at us!'

I steadied my breathing, a nice easy rhythm, my finger tightening gently around the trigger. My vision was becoming obscured with the sudden swell of moisture in my eyes. I fired.

There was an abrupt cry that never made it to a scream. The eyes had vanished from the rabbit-hole. I took my own eye away from the sight and took my hands from the rifle. They were trembling. Slowly I climbed to my feet, virtually unaware of the cramp in my legs.

Without looking at him, I said, 'Take over, Gerry. Give Zulu Control a sitrep.'

'Careful, mate,' he warned. 'She might still be alive.'

I left the Super Magnum resting on its bipod and started walking down the gentle slope towards the hide, tearing the hood off my ghillie suit as I walked. Somehow I didn't care if my shot had missed her or just wounded her so she could still shoot. If that was how it was to end, then so be it.

But I needn't have worried. When I got to the hide, its construction was much as I'd anticipated. I reached down and ripped away the turf, the bivvy sheet and chicken wire. And there she was, lying on her back, legs splayed where she had been thrown by the force of the shot. The Russian-made VSS was by her side. Her eyes were still open, staring at me from the pretty, cam-creamed face, a neat hole drilled just to the right of the centre of her forehead.

I leaned forward, pulled the scrim scarf from around her head and let her black hair fall free. Then I reached for her eyes and closed the lids. Blood was seeping into the hide from the exit wound that I knew would have taken out the back of her skull.

'Sorry, Jazz,' I breathed.

By this time Gerry had brought the MoD police up to speed, because they were advancing towards me at a gallop. The air seemed to be filled with the manic sound of ambulances all around, coming from down on the airfield and on the road where the police vans were parked.

The first officer arrived and stared down into the hide. 'Nice bloody shot,' he said tersely. 'Killed Andy. Fucking bitch.'

I didn't answer, just walked away.

Epilogue

When I returned to our firing position, I noticed that Gerry was watching me warily. It was pretty obvious he was struggling to think of the right thing to say.

I helped him out. 'Before you ask,' I said, 'yes, she's dead. It was a clean kill, she didn't suffer.'

He nodded. 'That's good. I guess the only good thing.'

I picked up the Super Magnum and broke down the bipod. 'Any news of the president?'

'I've just spoken to Nash on the radio and asked him,' Gerry replied. 'Gave me short shrift. Everyone on the net's been told not to discuss it. Security.'

'Doesn't sound good,' I replied.

'If he's survived,' Gerry said, 'I guess he'll get the best treatment money can buy.'

'He'll need it,' I said. 'Let's head back.'

We walked in silence, out of Zone D and all across Zone C to my van. The sky had cleared of all but a scattering of bubbling white cloud and it was turning into a very pleasant day. But I can't say it did much to lift my spirits. We changed out of our field clothes and into civvies in the back of the van, then washed off the worst of the cam cream with water from a container I kept for that purpose.

By the time we arrived back at the hotel, the drafted MoD police reinforcements were carting their luggage back into the white vans lined up in the car park. It didn't look promising. If the president was dead, clearly they wouldn't be needed any longer and would be returning to their duties at their regular bases. As we headed for the entrance I recognized the dark-blue Mercedes with the darkened windows parked by the doors. It was the Ice Queen's car.

After all the earlier hustle and bustle the hotel seemed remarkably quiet, the lobby almost devoid of customers. I'd just collected our room keys from the desk, when Gerry said, 'Take a look at this, Phil.'

There were half a dozen copies of the local daily newspaper spread out in a fan on an ornamental table. The front page headline screamed at me: FENWELL GAS EXPLOSION KILLS FAMILY.

'I don't believe this,' I said.

Gerry shook his head with disapproval. 'Looks like an official cover-up has started already.'

I said, 'I need a drink.'

'Couldn't agree more.'

As I turned towards the bar, I noticed Sergeant Nash standing by its entrance, wearing his uniform cap and with his arms folded across his chest. The panelled oak doors behind him were firmly shut.

'Hallo, Ron, can I buy you a drink?' I asked. 'Or are

you still on duty? I see all your reinforcements are going back.'

He shook his head. 'Not going back, Phil. They're redeploying to RAF Mildenhall.' He paused as he watched the puzzled expression on my face. 'And yes, I'm still on duty and the bar is closed at the moment. High-level meeting going on.'

'What's the latest, Ron? What's happened to President Bush?'

'Can't say. Security black-out.'

'For God's sake, Ron, everyone knows he was hit. Is he dead or injured? Just tell me that.'

As he went to speak, the doors behind Nash opened and I saw Joe Lassiter standing there. 'Ah, Mason, there you are. Thought I recognized your voice.' He didn't make it sound as though he was actually pleased to hear it. And I noticed the formal use of my surname. 'As you're here, you and Shaw had better come in.'

Nash seemed surprised, but stepped aside to let us through. Inside the bar was deserted except for two people seated on low armchairs next to a coffee table littered with empty china cups and saucers. One was Herbert J. Weatherspoon, the other Felicity Goodall. The American looked as sharp and slick as always, and the MI5 section chief was her usual smart business-like self. Neither stood as we approached and no one offered us seats while Lassiter rejoined them in another armchair. Why was it I felt like Gerry and I were like being treated like two naughty schoolboys summoned to a board of governors?

It was Weatherspoon who spoke first. He was poker-faced, but didn't seem particularly tense, I noticed. 'Well, well, gentlemen,' he began. 'Seems like you did the dirty deed. Nice to see someone on the British team knows how to take decisive action.' That earned him an icy scowl from Felicity. He added, 'Shame you were just too late.'

'For goodness' sake,' I said, 'will someone tell us how he is?'

'Fighting for his life. Being helicoptered to Westminster Hospital,' the American replied easily. Again I noticed he didn't sound particularly concerned. 'Bullet to the heart. Luckily he was wearing a bullet-proof vest. Unluckily our assassin used an incendiary round.'

Gerry asked, 'Do they think the president will survive?'

Weatherspoon gave a rather smug little smile and glanced at his gold wristwatch. 'I rather imagine he will. Unless he gets a brain haemorrhage with all that wisdom and knowledge. He's due to leave Girton College with his wife and daughter about now.'

'What?' I gasped.

Felicity said sharply, 'Herbie here is rather pleased with himself. Air Force One landed at RAF Mildenhall – one of the other nearby US Airforce bases – instead. The man who landed here was a stunt double. No one in the UK knew about the change of plan except the PM and our Director General. A highly classified operation was made to set up a new venue for the meetings a couple of days ago. The Americans decided to take care of all their own security arrangements.'

Now I realized why Weatherspoon hadn't taken Lassiter up on his earlier suggestion to switch the presidential arrival to another airbase – because that top-secret decision had already been made.

I was astounded. 'You knowingly let an innocent man become the target?'

Weatherspoon shrugged. 'I was assured by your people that the terror cell was under surveillance and about to be arrested. So we didn't really anticipate the threat would come to anything. But we didn't like the fact there was a threat at all and that our arrangements were clearly known to the enemy.' He smiled again and rose to his feet. 'In this game, it's always best not to let the right hand know what the left is doing. Now, if you'll excuse me, I've got to prepare for tonight's cocktail party with the president.'

As he walked past me, I stopped him with a hand on his shoulder. I said, 'That assassin only wanted to kill your precious president because her innocent husband is held without trial in Guantánamo Bay. Close the bloody place down – because it only makes every Muslim in the world start to think that, just maybe, al-Qaeda is right.'

Weatherspoon used his fingers to pluck my hand from his shoulder like it was something very unpleasant that had landed on him. 'Oh, Mr Mason, you should know these people can always come up with some reason or other to justify the unjustifiable.'

He walked on and left the room.

'Nasty piece of shit,' Lassiter growled.

'Enough, Joe!' Felicity admonished. She turned to Gerry and me. 'You two have left me with a nightmare to sort out. Although in truth, I blame Joe here more than you. We've got to explain what happened out there this morning. There's Alagic's body to be explained and that of the poor man she shot. The coroner will have a field day with us. We'll have to play the security card, of course. Keep as much as we can about what really happened out of the public domain. But we'll also have to admit your stupid actions were sanctioned by us as part of an anti-terrorist operation.'

'They were,' I said.

Felicity glared at me. 'One that went so badly wrong that it's given Melissa Thornton the opportunity she's always wanted – to get me transferred to the Northern Ireland Desk.' She jerked her thumb at Lassiter. 'And to make things worse, he's coming with me.'

Couldn't happen to a nicer couple, I muttered under my breath.

She continued, 'So I'm sure it'll come as no surprise to you that your company is no longer working for us. I want to put as much distance as I can between you and the Security Service. Especially as you saw fit to hire that Alagic woman. Someone will be coming round in the next day or two to remove all the specialist equipment we gave you.' She hesitated. 'Which reminds me, make sure you leave the sniper rifle you used with the police before you go. That's all.'

Gerry and I exchanged glances, as Lassiter rose to his feet. 'I'll show you out.'

When we were in the reception area, he said, 'Told you what she was like. And you were thinking you fancied her, didn't you?' He slapped me on the back. 'Anyway, nice shooting, Phil. And by the way, we did at least manage to pick up Dr Samir in his Chigwell digs. So a bit of a result, just a messy one. Anyway, to be honest, I wouldn't mind getting back to the Northern Ireland Desk. This one's been too much like hard work. See you sometime. Ciao.'

Gerry and I went to pack up our luggage and met back downstairs where we found that the bar was now open again. Lassiter and Felicity had vanished.

We had a quick pint before setting off in our separate vehicles.

'What are you going to do now?' Gerry asked.

'Back to matrimonial and commercial work, I suppose,' I replied thoughtfully. 'Might be a struggle though.'

'I was thinking, I've got pretty well-established in the international military lecturing and training circuit. Bloody well paid, too. And not many have your vast specialist surveillance and sniping knowledge. Perhaps we should form a partnership?'

That was an intriguing idea. 'I'll think on it.'

'One condition though?'

He winked. 'We retain the lovely Kate as our secretary.'

I laughed. 'Then we'll be doing each other's lectures on the wrong days.'

I turned the possibilities over in my mind on the drive back south, but I was so tired that I could barely think straight. When I finally arrived at the office, Kate had gone home. I couldn't be bothered to eat or shower, I just crashed out on the bed fully clothed.

When I finally went into the office on Monday morning, Kate was working at her laptop. She glanced up. 'Hallo, Phil, how'd you like my new blouse? It's a Stella McCartney and it was only eighty pounds. Last season's though.'

'Lovely,' I said, sipping from my mug of coffee. 'But has anything important happened while I've been away?'

'Popadom phoned a few minutes ago. He's back at work. Said he was sorry about everything, how he'd loved working with us, and was sorry to hear we're not contracted with MI5 any more.' She looked up at me and blinked. 'Is that right?'

I nodded. 'Anything else?'

'Your wife phoned earlier to give you a message. Would you like to have Danny next weekend?'

Things were looking up. 'I'll call her.'

'Oh, and this arrived.' She handed me the jiffy bag. Second-class post.

I opened it and pulled out the contents, a wad of typed paper and handwritten notes. It was Jazz's promised details on al-Qaeda. There was also a short letter: *Dear Phil, Sorry it had to end like this and hope you weren't too uncomfortable. Allah willing, I will make a new life with Zoë. If not, she is in safe hands anyway. And, with a new US president, maybe Ricardo will be released some day soon. Meanwhile this is the false identity Naved Hussein will be using when he is leaving from Heathrow. Love, Jazz.*

Naved, the key al-Qaeda facilitator who had eluded us for so long. I glanced at the attached note. He was getting out of the country this very afternoon.

'Kate,' I said, 'get me Lassiter on the phone. Now.'